The Darkness of Ragnarök: Shadows of Midgard

About the Author

Suzie Jay was born in the East Midlands, England. She has always loved getting lost in a good book. As an adult, understanding the paranormal and researching Norse mythology is an everyday occurrence. This passion has led her to present her debut novel.

Suzie Jay

The Darkness of Ragnarök: Shadows of Midgard

Olympia Publishers
London

www.olympiapublishers.com
OLYMPIA PAPERBACK EDITION

A CIP catalogue record for this title is
available from the British Library.

ISBN: 978-1-80439-591-2

First Published in 2024

Olympia Publishers
Tallis House
2 Tallis Street
London
EC4Y 0AB

Printed in Great Britain

Dedication

I dedicate this book to my husband, Simon.

Acknowledgements

Thank you, Roger, for your kindness. You helped make this happen.

CHAPTER ONE

Deena and Dan left the boathouse, scouring the darkness as they darted towards the pier. Deena knelt beside the boat while Dan untied it. Then, as the rowboat drifted on the calm surface, Dan took up the oars and rhythmically skimmed across the waters towards the first island. Deena watched as the shoreline faded with the backpack gripped between her feet. A gentle mist formed on the lake's surface. Deena looked behind her towards the island. The fog was getting denser the further they travelled across the water.

"Dan, I'm worried we won't be able to see to land the boat. The mist is thicker closer to the island," she whispered as she looked past Dan towards the shore. She was sure there was a silhouette of someone at the water's edge. She pointed over Dan's shoulder and whispered, "Is that Jack?"

Dan stopped rowing and looked behind him. There was someone, but it was impossible to determine who it was. They were too far out. "Try swinging the lantern. I'm sure he'll signal back if it's Jack," suggested Dan.

Deena stood and swung the lantern back and forth, but there was no response. She tried again, but still, there was no reaction. "Dan, I don't think that's Jack!" said Deena.

"If it's not Jack, I'm not sure who it could be. But whoever it is, they are either very brave or extremely foolish to be standing alone," said Dan.

Deena swung the lantern one last time to attract their attention, but the mysterious figure did not acknowledge it.

"Let's get going," said Dan.

As he reached for the oars, something struck the boat from below. Deena lunged forward, losing her balance, just managing to keep herself in the rowboat. As Deena toppled, the lantern went out.

"What the hell was that?" she said, panicking.

Dan searched the water on either side. Finally, he glanced at a flash of something silvery-white disappearing beneath the boat. "I just saw it. It's under the boat."

Deena clung to the side and leaned over, pointing to another streak of silver in the water.

"There's another one on this side as well!" exclaimed Dan. "They look like large fish, about four feet long."

"I don't like the fact that they are circling us. We need to get off this water quickly," said Deena, sitting down and reaching for Dan's lantern.

As she did, something pulled the rear of the boat down. Deena fell forward, and as she looked up, she caught sight of a small pair of hands letting go of the back of the vessel. "It's not fish!" screamed Deena as the boat rocked back and forth.

"What the fuck is it?" asked Dan, panicking.

"I don't know, but I saw hands letting go of the boat!" she said in disbelief.

"Fish don't have hands!" exclaimed Dan.

"Exactly! Get rowing, now!" screamed Deena.

Dan took up the oars, rowing as fast as possible towards the island. Deena struggled to get a sage bushel out of her rig. Every time she tried to light it, the boat was struck side to side.

"Keep going!" she shouted as she examined the blackness of the cold water. Deena suddenly recoiled as one of them surged out of the water in front of her.

"One, two, we found you!" exclaimed the voice.

"It's the Twins!" shouted Dan, as copious childish laughter echoed around them. Deena focused on trying to light another bushel. Then, one of the Twins grasped the edge of the boat. Slowly, a little white face appeared. Wet hair matted her porcelain features, and an intently evil grin was underneath.

"Three, four, Nanny's at the shore!" trilled the Twin.

Deena thrust the sage bushel at the Twin, dissipating the apparition. The mist was so thick now that they couldn't see what was coming from the water. She urged Dan to go faster. They had to get off the boat. Deena remembered what Megan had told them about their death. Ironically, they seemed very at home in the water now.

Dan cried a muffled scream as a Twin came up behind him, wrapping her icy, wet hands around his face. "Five, six, going to sink your ship!" she sang. Dan struggled against her, almost letting go of the oars. Deena leapt forward, waving the air with the sage.

"Keep rowing!" shouted Deena. "We're almost there."

Dan put all his energy into propelling themselves toward the island. The rising mist was filtering over the sides of the boat. Then, from behind her, the rowboat began to rock. Deena turned to see a Twin climbing in, giving a twisted glare with one bedraggled leg over the side. The black hairline cracks travelled up her face as she sang, "Seven, eight, your souls we'll take!"

"Like hell, goddamn freaks!" Deena screamed, plunging the bushel into the face of the demonic child.

Suddenly, they struck the island with force. Deena went flying, landing on hard ground. Scrambling to her feet, she helped Dan onto dry land. Then, hysterical with fear, they pulled the rowing boat out of the water. They stood at the water's edge, waiting for the Twin's next appearance. Instead, it was eerily quiet as the mist clung to the tranquil water.

"Do you think they've gone?" asked Dan.

"I hope so," whispered Deena, still clutching the burning sage.

Dan picked up the rope, securing the boat to a tree. "I don't fancy being left stranded," he muttered, "and I don't trust those bloody Twins have gone either."

It was a close call and one they hadn't expected.

Large raindrops spattered around them. Deena looked skyward and said, "We need to find shelter. A storm is coming in."

Dan retrieved the tarp, and they made a makeshift lean-to over the rowboat. Sat beneath, the raindrops got heavier, and the wind picked up. They held tight to their only shelter as a loud rumble rolled through the ether, accompanied by a deafening crack of lightning. Patiently, they waited as flash after flash lit up the island around them.

Finally, two hours later, the last of the storm petered out, and Dan and Deena emerged from under their canopy, ready to explore new territory. Deena's boots squelched as she stood on the thick layer of dead leaves that the surrounding trees had surrendered. Dan covered the rowboat with the tarp. Then, with the backpack in hand, he put his arm around Deena's shoulders, and wiggling his eyebrows at her, he grinned and said, "Are you ready for more adventure, Missy?"

"Do I have a choice?" she asked. Still grinning, Dan made his way through the gnarled trees. Twisted branches fanned out, intertwining with neighbouring trees. Finding a trail was impossible as they climbed over fallen trees and fought through brambles and gorse. "I don't know if it's because the trees are so dark and twisted or the low-lying mist, but this island is downright sinister," whispered Deena.

"Do you think we'll run into anything, you know, bad?" asked Dan reservedly.

"I wouldn't like to say. I wasn't expecting the Twins on the lake, but they appeared," replied Deena.

"Yeah, Nanny went walkabout! How about that! But I don't get that she stood watching us, no light source, by herself, as if she knew she had nothing to fear from anyone or anything," Dan muttered. "I reckon she must have known where we were."

"You can see down to the boathouse from the manor. Maybe Megan's been watching for a chance to set the Twins on us," suggested Deena.

It took over an hour to get to the other side of the island. Woodlands nestled at the edge of the lake to their right. Then, to their left, a break in the tree line gave rise to the intimidating manor in the distance. They followed the water's edge, watching for another appearance of Megan. It seemed to Deena, too, that the nanny was hiding something. Was she still watching them, waiting for the next opportunity to try and kill them? She certainly had power over Emily and Charlotte. But as Dan said, Megan wasn't fearful for her own life as she stood at the edge of the lake, and she wasn't going to volunteer any answers either. Finally, exhausted, Deena stopped to rest.

"We can't cover every inch of these islands. It's going to take too long," said Dan.

"I agree. How about we zigzag the centre and then walk the perimeter?" suggested Deena.

"Even better if we split and work parallel. We could cover more ground that way," proposed Dan.

"I don't like splitting up," she said, concerned. "What if one of us gets into trouble?" she cautioned.

"We both have lanterns. So, how about we walk far enough to keep our lanterns in sight of each other? Then, we'll be close enough to holler if we come across anything," suggested Dan.

"I suppose," she said. "Please promise me you won't go wandering off. I know what you're like!" she lightly teased. Dan grinned at her and promised to stay in sight.

As planned, they zigzagged parallel, left to right. Dead leaves immersed the ground, and branches looked stark against the moonlight. Deena couldn't help but feel unwittingly cast in an unscripted horror movie.

"Dee!" shouted Dan. "I've found a huge mound. I don't know if it's artificial or what. I'm going to take it down using my boot to check that nothing is in it." Deena took the opportunity to sit on a fallen tree, letting him get on with it. She could hear the dull thud of his boot as he repeatedly kicked at the heap of soil and leaves, taking it down, layer by layer. Then, Dan started yelling. Deena strained her eyes into the darkness to see his silhouette dancing around.

"Dan, are you okay? I'm coming over! What in hell's name is wrong with you?" she asked, watching his strange twitching, itching, and slapping dance routine.

"It's a fucking ant's nest! They've gone up inside my trouser legs, and ouch, aghh, they're biting the crap out of me! Stop laughing and help me! There are thousands of them, Dee!" he begged.

"I'm not going anywhere near that ant's nest. Sorry, but you're on your own with this one. There's only one thing for it!" she giggled. "You'll have to strip and dunk yourself underwater to get them off you."

"What? Dee, I'm not doing that!" he said between yelps.

"Oh, okay, I guess you'll be bitten to death," she muttered. "I'm very impressed with your war dance. How long do you reckon you can keep that up?" she reasoned.

"Fine! Help me get this rig off!" he grunted, writhing and scratching. The woodland ants were relentless in their attack on Dan for destroying their nest. Deena grabbed a branch from the forest floor, and at arm's length, she picked up his clothes while he awkwardly made his way to the lake. Finally, he stood at the water's edge, scratching like a flea-ridden dog, frantically pulling off his socks and boxer shorts. Deena turned away from him in hysterical laughter as she heard the sharp breath intake accompanied by a pitiful yelp as he entered the icy water. Deena turned to see only his head above the water.

"Please… could you… shit, it's so cold in here… get the ants off my clothes?" he asked before dunking himself entirely underwater. Deena tried to keep a straight face as Dan gave her a sorrowful look, muttering,

"They've bitten me in places you don't want to know about."

"Oh, wow. That's more information than I needed. But it would help if you warmed up, so how about we try and get a campfire going, and you can dab some of Dot's elixir on the bites," she suggested.

Dan feebly nodded, whinging, "The bites are burning. It's really, really bad!"

The campfire had almost burnt out. Dan had warmed up from his dip in the lake, so they decided to move on and finish exploring the islands. He stamped out the remaining embers and watched the last smoulders filtering through the handfuls of dirt he threw on top. They split to their respective places before Dan's incident, zigzagging down the island's centre. Then, at the far end, Deena said, "We may as well walk the perimeter towards the boat and row to the other island. We've found nothing so far. I think we are wasting our time," said Deena.

Dan reminded her, "Anywhere we search won't be a waste of time. We have no idea where the skull is."

Much mist had lifted off the lake, making the crossing visually better. If anything should come at them, they could see it. Thankfully, the boat was still where they had left it. They kept a close eye on the water's depths to the lake's far side as Dan kept a steady pace. It was a tense crossing.

"Do you think the Ground Crawlers can swim?" Dan asked out of the blue.

"What? No, I wouldn't have thought so. They're too big and heavy," said Deena.

"Yeah, well, so are hippos, and they swim," said Dan sarcastically.

Deena narrowed her eyes and said, "I've had the displeasure of getting too close to one or two of them; there are no gills or webbed feet, and they smelt of rotting flesh and dirt, so I don't think it's something we need to worry about."

"But they could learn though," he muttered. "The Twins could give them lessons."

"Seriously, Dan! Are you trying to wind me up?" she retorted.

"Yep," he chuckled, "and you bite every time."

He was right; she did bite easily. He was always catching her out. Deena smiled, knowing that it was one of the things about him that she

16

liked.

Having secured and covered the boat with the tarp, they chose to explore as they had the first island. Together, they began their trek through the complexity of interwoven trees. An owl shrieking in the distance stopped them in their tracks. Deena looked skyward, searching for a glimpse of the graceful glider. Another ear-piercing screech sounded closer than the last.

"I can't see it," said Deena.

"It could be in a tree somewhere. There are lots of woodlands on the estate," said Dan reassuringly. So, they walked until stumbling upon another ant's nest. This one was much bigger, with smaller mounds around it.

"Do you think it's one colony or several?" asked Deena, wondering how such tiny creatures could build formidable fortresses. "Look," she said, pointing at the central column, "there's something in that one. It looks like glass."

"No, no way! I'm not going anywhere near it. Thanks, but I've been bitten enough," said Dan, wincing.

"It could be important," she said persuasively with her big green eyes.

Dan groaned, "No, It's just a bit of glass, Dee!"

Deena gave him the eyes again and said, "It might not be just a piece of glass, please? Use a long stick to dig it out, and then you won't disturb the ants too much."

Resigned to her pleas, he looked about for the longest stick he could find. Then, carefully, he stabbed at the mound around the glass. It took a little doing, but he persevered until it tumbled. Dan worked it across the ground when Deena pounced on it, brushing off the dirt. "Not just a piece of old glass!" she exclaimed, thrusting it under Dan's nose.

Dan took it from her and held it up to his lantern. As the candlelight passed through it, every light spectrum colour shimmered. "It's the purest clear quartz I have ever laid eyes on!" he said. "Look how clean the cuts are on the faceting."

He balanced the crystal on the palm of his hand and stared into it. It was cleanly faceted up the column of eight inches, topped off with a perfect conical. Deena took the crystal from him. Then, taking a closer look, she counted the facets. "Thirteen perfectly faceted panels. Thirteen crystal skulls, do you think this has something to do with how we use them

17

together?" she asked.

"It could be. Crystal quartz is known to amplify energy, but we have no idea how old it is as quartz can't be carbon-dated," he said thoughtfully.

"When we did the tests back in the lab, George said something about quartz having a memory capacity," said Deena.

"Yes, and when we ran those tests, we also determined that clear quartz has a positive and negative polarity, which means they can also generate electricity," said Dan.

"It's mind-blowing that the skulls and this crystal can produce so much power. Do you think that perhaps each of these facets relates to a specific skull?" she asked.

"Possibly; I'm hoping that's something George or Trevor will know more about than us," said Dan taking the crystal and carefully placing it in the backpack. "Let's get moving, Dee."

They continued with renewed hope for their progress. Deena took the crystal and washed off the remaining dirt as they reached the water's edge. They held their lanterns on either side of it, mesmerised by the colours that swirled and danced inside. There was so much more to figure out. Finally, Deena picked up a stick, scattering the woodland's blanket of leaves as she went.

From a distance, they could still hear the owl's screeches. Deena looked but couldn't see enough through the density of the tree branches. The screeches got shriller, and the high pitch left a ringing in her ears. It was all around them, circling, getting louder and louder. The piercing was so intense that Deena reached for the cotton wool she'd taken from the boathouse. She parted a couple of pieces to put in her ears. Then, she ditched her walking stick in favour of putting her hands over her ears, decreasing it further. Suddenly, without warning, a white mass passed by her. Deena screamed out, and Dan raced over. "What's wrong?" he asked urgently.

"I'm not sure. It was so fast. I couldn't see what it was, and then it disappeared," said Deena. She was shaken but composed herself, apologising for being silly. Then, shuddering, she placed a determined foot forward. She wasn't going to be scared by a stupid owl. But then, the screeches gave way to a series of wailing and moaning. Deena froze, 'That does not sound like an owl!' she thought.

"Dan! I've got a terrible feeling. Get over here!" she shouted.

Dan cocked his ear to the piercing screeches. It was so intense that the pain in his ears was unbearable. He collapsed to his knees, hunching himself forward, covering his ears. The sound penetrated his very core, resonating through his bones. Deena knelt beside him, urging him to take the cottonwool, gesturing to put it in his ears. Dan looked up at her. His eyes were bloodshot. Whatever this was, it was after them. Frantically, Deena looked around, trying to find who or what was creating the shrieks. Then she saw it. It was coming right at them.

Deena rose to her feet, disorientated, weakened by the force of the inward-bound entity, and thinking straight was tricky. 'Salt, where's the salt?' she thought desperately. With that, the entity was right in front of her. "Don't look at her! It's a Banshee!" she screamed out. The Wailing Banshee aimed its shrieks at Deena. She watched in horror as the air distorted around her. The powerful sound waves hit, propelling her backwards, landing in a crumpled heap. Then, the Banshee turned, redirecting its attack on Dan. It was him she was after. Deena could only hope he remained curled up and didn't look at her. The Banshee hung in the air, circling his still body. She was a withered older woman, barefoot and wearing torn rags that hung from her emaciated bony corpse. Her breasts hung from her skeletal rib cage like empty shrivelled sacks. Her grey hair was wild and wiry, and her gnarled hands with long fingers cupped her mouth, directing the devastating sound waves. Her eyes bled with the strain of her wailing.

Deena had no salt in her rig, it was in the backpack, but that was under Dan. She tried to focus on lighting the half-burnt sage from her jacket pocket as she looked on in terror at the relentless, ear-shattering sound wave attacks she was imposing on Dan. Deena had to act quickly before the Banshee killed him. She crawled along the ground with the sage lit, waving it in Dan's direction. She reached for the strap to the backpack. The smell of sage wafted towards the Banshee, making her back off, but it didn't stop her. Deena's only hope of warding this thing off was throwing salt at it. So, she opened the bag and took out four pouches. Carefully, she opened the first one and hesitantly glanced to see where the Banshee was. She couldn't look directly at her for fear of making what would be fatal eye contact. She would have to chance she had enough salt to make at least one direct hit. With her target located, she flung the first pouch into the air. The Banshee screamed and quickly flew higher. Had she missed it? Deena watched her periphery until she descended, waiting until the Banshee concentrated her audacious wails at Dan. Dan didn't move; Deena knew he had to be alive for the Banshee's attacks to continue. She hadn't taken his soul yet, but Deena didn't know how long he could hold on. She threw the salt in an arc as high as she could over Dan.

The shrieks that followed were excruciating. As fast as Deena could, she untwisted the third pouch. Glancing again, Deena saw her opportunity, hurling salt directly at her. The Banshee's shrieks turned bloodcurdling, becoming distorted, and as seconds passed, the shrillness dissipated, as did she. Deena crawled to Dan, trying to wake him. He lay unconscious, so she remained by his side, keeping watch, hoping the Banshee wouldn't return. When he finally stirred, he had little recollection of what had happened.

"I need to get you back to the boat," said Deena. Dan tried to get to his feet. He was unsteady and disorientated. He stood limp, barely clinging to a tree, while Deena got the boat in the water. Finally, as Dan got into the boat, he curled up on the tarp and passed out. Deena took up the oars and kept an assiduous eye on their surroundings. She held a slow, steady pace as she rowed towards the pier.

Something ran along the edge of the lake and disappeared behind the boathouse. At first, Deena wasn't sure what she had seen. Deena stopped rowing, sitting still, observing. Thoughts of Megan and the Twins came to mind. However, she quickly dismissed that theory because whatever it was, was four-legged, but it wasn't a Ground Crawler. Their bluish-white skin made sure they stood out in the darkness.

Nevertheless, she was convinced she had seen a creature unknown to her. Then, she heard low guttural growls. Flashes of vicious teeth gnashed together as they excitedly patrolled the water's edge in anticipation. Menacingly, they paced up and down, baying and fighting amongst themselves. They weren't going to go away; she and Dan were captive on the water. Deena counted six. Their orange eyes reflected in the darkness like hairless wolves, but more significantly, they were muscular and were more than ready to tear them apart. Terrified, she slowly backed the boat away from the pier. She shrank beside Dan, hoping they would give up if they couldn't see her. But their macabre, hostile growls didn't stop.

Deena lay at the bottom of the boat. It was cramped, but she didn't dare to be seen by what was waiting at the shore. Dan's breathing was shallow in his unconscious state. She tried to wake him but couldn't get a response, not even a murmur. The Wailing Banshee had almost killed him. The sounds of howling calmed over the hours she'd laid beside him. Finally, Deena found the courage to peek over the boat's edge. She was horrified when she saw that they had slowly drifted back towards the pier, and there, waiting, was an enormous wolf-like creature, watching in anticipation of the boat getting that little bit closer. It had seen her. It growled and jarred its teeth together, slavering and licking its muzzle. The creature strained forward to get to the boat. Its paws were more significant than a lion's. Its body was not only hairless but skinless too. Its muscles flexed as it paced the pier, highlighting tendons and gristle. Its ears stood upright like a guard dog, only flattening them back to howl, calling its pack.

Deena desperately rowed to deeper water. The group swarmed together, chasing up and down the pier in frustration. She didn't stop until she was almost back at the island and swinging the oars into the boat, she broke down in hysterical sobs. Deena was petrified, and Dan was still out cold. She lay beside him, fighting back her tears. Staring at the moon above her, Deena cast her mind back to the facility where this nightmare had begun two weeks earlier.

CHAPTER TWO

Deena remembered the tiled floors and white walls being blinding under the fluorescent light as she ran down the slope to the metal detector. She slung her bag and keys on the tray for inspection, mumbling an apology to the security clerk. Then hurriedly, she pushed the button on the lift. She knew George would have a sarcastic comment waiting for her. The elevator reached its lowest level, and as the doors pinged, Deena shot through them and followed the endless corridors toward Zone A. She swiped her passkey and entered her code to enter the laboratory.

Almost falling through the door in haste, George curtly greeted her, "Ah, good morning. How nice of you to grace us with your presence."

'And there it is,' thought Deena, rolling her eyes at him. "Never mind being an expert in mathematics and physics, George. Perhaps you should add sarcasm to your résumé?" retorted Deena.

George is a short, rotund man in his late fifties with a thick white beard and black-rimmed glasses, which he repeatedly pushes back against the bridge of his nose. Four of them, including Deena, make up the team. Although not anyone was in charge, George took it upon himself to organise everyone whether they liked it or not. Deena readied herself for the day's objectives, taking her white coat from the peg. She stood by the reinforced glass chamber, looking at the crystal skull in the centre of the podium.

"Is the preparation complete to start the tests?" she asked.

"Almost," replied George, "doing the final checks, now. Where the hell are Dan and Trevor?"

Dan strolled out of the backroom carrying another crystal skull, followed closely by Trevor. Dan carefully placed it on the stainless-steel table.

Dan came to the team highly recommended in archaeology and anthropology. He's in his early thirties and the most handsome of the three with his rugged good looks. Trevor's specialist field is in electrical and nuclear energy resources. Maybe he was a little shy and on the quiet side, but he was considered a bit of an 'oddball' by the others. Perhaps his thin, six-foot-six stooped stature added to this consensus. Finally, Deena had a master's degree in parapsychology and metaphysics and was world-renowned for her research and experience.

Over centuries, twelve crystal skulls have been found by archaeologists all over the world, from Peru to Mexico, Yucatan, and Africa, to name a few. There is a rumour of a thirteenth skull. Its discovery is yet to be determined. The speculation attached to this thirteenth skull is that it combines and represents the collective consciousness of all the worlds. What worlds? No one knows. However, the energy and power these skulls possess are more critical to the United States Government.

Further testing will now begin as they have acquired all twelve in one location. Preliminary tests have already concluded that each has unique energy properties. Photographing them individually using Kirlian photography shows an internal and external energy field. When two skulls are placed side by side and photographed, they interact, directing energies back and forth. The team hopes to determine the type of energy housed in each skull, electrical impulse levels, electrical discharge, and power fluctuations. Why do they interact the way they do when placed close to each other? Could this energy be stored and used in some way? There are so many questions about the mysterious nature of these artefacts, and the team's objective is to quantify all results collated regarding the skulls.

Deena picked up the skull on the table, scrutinising it. "Do you think we'll get the results we need?" she asked.

"Well, we are about to find out. Dan, Dan! I wish he'd pay attention. Bloody archaeologist, more like a bloody dreamer! Dan!" shouted George. Dan was right behind him as he turned to look for him.

"You called, sir?" Dan said mockingly.

George gave an indignant look and said, "Make yourself useful. Check the other skulls for weaknesses or stress cracks before testing. I don't want them blowing out under the lasers!"

"Why? They're fine," said Dan, shrugging his shoulders.

"Please, could you just do it?" sighed George.

Dan turned on his heel towards the back room. Deena, with arms folded, sidled over to George, and with a slightly accusing look, asked him, "Are you trying to keep him busy and out of your way?"

George turned his head to Deena and blatantly replied, "Yes, am I that obvious? I don't even know why he's here."

She leaned towards George and, tapping his shoulder, whispered, "Now, George, play nice. He's part of the team. Company policy says he must be present when handling artefacts."

A disgruntled mumbled "Humph" was barely audible as George turned to look at the printout screen. Trevor sniggered behind his clipboard, which annoyed George even more.

"Right, can we start now?" asked George.

As the team performed tests, the day passed slowly. Dan leaned against the table, looking incredibly bored as print readouts spat from different digital machines. The scientific nature of the tests held no interest to him. George, it seemed, was right when he said he wasn't of much use to them. After all, his experience and knowledge were out in the field, not in a laboratory. But the job pays very well, and when the government requests your presence on a project, they make it hard for you to refuse. Deena stood by the glass chamber, writing notes whilst observing.

Meanwhile, George was resetting the laser output at the computer. "Dan, can you get the last skull, please? Time's getting on," asked George.

Dan retreated to the back room. On his return, he placed the skull on the cold steel of the table. Trevor rifled through copious pages of test results. His confusion was evident when he threw his hands up in defeat, slumping back in the chair. "They don't make sense! These results shouldn't even be possible!" he exclaimed.

"Calm down, Trev. Let's finish the tests first. Then we can analyse everything, okay?" said George.

"Nearly done, guys. I suggest we finish up and save the analysis for tomorrow. It's nearly eight p.m. I don't know about you, but I have a family to go home to," said Deena.

Without warning, the ground shook violently beneath them, dislodging shelving and cabinets, causing everything to crash to the floor. Flung off her feet, Deena screamed. Then, the chamber exploded, showering her with glass. "Shut it down… the lasers… shut it all down, for Christ's sake!" shouted Trevor, desperately hanging on to the desk to stop his chair from rolling across the room.

But his effort was to no avail as the chair spun, flinging him into filing cabinets. Dan grabbed the skull, hugging it between his chest and knees; he crouched behind the table. A piercing siren sounded. The power went out, the emergency generators kicked in, and the orange hazard lights flashed behind their metal mesh casings. They looked desperately at each other, waiting for an answer as to what had happened.

Finally, George regained his feet and began shutting down the computer system, shouting, "Is everyone okay?"

Deena groaned and lifted her head from the floor, brushing off the shattered glass and wiping blood from her face. She crawled to the chamber's base and sat against it. Deena regained her senses and saw Trevor lying unconscious, his head bleeding profusely.

"Trevor, answer me!" she shouted. There was no response, and Deena feared the worst. So, she called out to Dan, "Dan? Where are you?"

"Over here, Deena. What the hell just happened?" he shouted over the siren.

Dust filled Deena's throat as she struggled to speak. "It's Trevor," she coughed, "he needs help."

Dan took off his jacket and wrapped it around the skull. Pushing the steel table against the wall on its side, he placed the artefact inside. Another tremor juddered as Dan tried to get to Trevor. George was still desperately trying to shut down the computer systems when a data machine burst into flames. George pulled the fire extinguisher from the wall and quelled the fire. Clouds of smoke filled the room, making visibility difficult. The acrid smell of burning wire and plastic hung heavy in the air. They could hear the pristine, white porcelain wall tiles cracking and falling. Deena could make out Dan sitting with Trevor through the thick smoke. Trevor made a groaning noise. Deena was relieved he was okay. She pulled herself to her feet, and as she looked around, she saw the other crystal skull amongst the glass. Scooping it up, Deena gingerly made her way through the debris to Dan and Trevor.

"How's he doing?" she asked.

"I think he will be okay," said Dan. "I need to stop the bleeding."

He took the skull from Deena, placed it on the floor and asked for her lab coat. Without hesitation, she slipped it off. Dan tore a sleeve, making a makeshift bandage around Trevor's head, leading to painful moans and groans. Dan laughed, "That's a good sign. I think you'll be fine, Trev. Sit and keep pressure on it until the bleeding stops."

"Quite the hero, aren't you," said Deena.

"Not really," muttered Dan, embarrassed. He picked up the skull, carefully wrapped it in the remnants of Deena's jacket, and then placed it with the other one.

"Dan, what do you think happened?" asked Deena. "Is it an earthquake?" she speculated.

George stood against a desk. Then, out of breath and grimy from putting out the fire, he said, "Maybe, we get them frequently here, although I've not known one of these strengths. They're usually between 1.9 to 2.6 magnitudes, Northeast or Northwest. We don't usually feel them down here, so it must be huge to do this damage."

The colour drained from Deena's face as realisation set in at the enormity of their situation. "I need to get out of here," she exclaimed. "I have to get to Martin and the kids."

"Lockdown is set at a minimum of twenty-four hours; it's pointless trying to get out of the facility," said George flatly.

Being empathic was not George's nature, and his short, concise reply did little to comfort Deena in her panic-stricken moment. So instead, Dan tried to offer a solution. "You could try the phones," he suggested. George looked at Dan and, pushing his glasses back to the bridge of his nose, raised a thin but well-meant smile at Deena.

Deena picked her way across the room where Trevor was initially sitting. The phone should have been on the desk. But unfortunately, nothing was where it should have been. Eventually, she found the phone cord under scattered papers and pulled it gently. It seemed to be in one piece, giving Deena a fleeting moment of hope. Then, the team watched with bated breath as she lifted the receiver to her ear with a shaky hand.

"The line's dead," she said in a hollow voice as a tear rolled down her cheek.

Dan gently took the phone, placing it back on the floor as she sobbed uncontrollably. Each of the men looked to the floor in silence, knowing from the force of the tremors that it would be chaos on the surface. The reinforced underground facility should withstand these events and worse. They knew they were relatively safe but sustaining damage to this extent left them questioning how bad it was on the surface. The tremors continued with no way to tell when the next would happen. The team sat, bracing themselves for the next seismic wave to jolt the facility. The siren continued its screeching wail, accompanied by the intermittent orange hue of the emergency lights.

Deena took a deep breath, wiped away her tears and tried to pull herself together. The laboratory was devastated. So, Deena attempted to open the door to get out. "Dan, help me. It's jammed!" she said.

"It's no good. It won't budge. Wait, let me get something to lever it open," said Dan, going towards the chamber and pulling a metal strut away. "George, go and check on Trevor. He's gone quiet," said Dan as he passed him. Eventually, he managed to force the handle off entirely. "Good," he said, "now I can dismantle the locking mechanism."

George shouted to Dan and Deena across the room, "We don't know if the rest of the facility is holding up, and I, for one, do not relish the thought of being buried alive. So, hurry up and get that bloody door open!"

"Will you shut up? Just shut up, George!" shouted Dan angrily. Then, with a hint of childish sarcasm, he added, "Bloody pessimistic arsehole. Mr I'm a bloody scientist. I know everything!" Tempers were fraying with fear and uncertainty.

Finally, with an unmistakable tone of frustration, Deena said, "Dan, you're not helping matters. Quit arguing, please? Let's focus on getting out of here."

Dan went quiet and endeavoured to dismantle the door lock. It took much effort, but the door finally burst open. Exhausted, Dan threw the metal bar across the room. George got to his feet and encouraged Trevor to do the same at the prospect of a way out. Limping and holding his head, Trevor leaned on George's shoulder for support. If it weren't for the gravity of their situation, their height and build differences would undoubtedly have had an undeniable comedy factor.

Deena and Dan peered down the corridor. There was noticeable damage to the plaster on the walls, and they could see doors further down the hall that had twisted away from their hinges, but other than that, it looked reasonably sound. Dan went first, with Deena close behind him. Trevor and George slowly followed. They checked for personnel as they passed the doors to various offices.

Then, suddenly, Dan stopped. "Shush! I think I can hear someone," said Dan stepping into the room. Carson, their head of department, hurriedly greeted him.

"Thank God you are all okay. Quick, help me with this," said Carson.

He spun around to lift a heavy filing cabinet off the floor. As Dan waded through the disarray, he saw someone trapped beneath it. He recognised the uniform to be that of a General. His breathing was shallow, with the weight of the cabinet crushing his chest. Dan turned and shouted to George for help. Grasping either side of the cabinet, Carson and Dan lifted it enough for George to help the General from underneath. Carson picked up a chair for the General to sit down. They were all silent as he clutched his chest, catching his breath.

The office was in shambles. Desks, which housed high-tech computer systems, were scattered across the floor. Expensive monitors lay smashed amongst an array of office equipment and papers. Finally, the General regained his breath. George stared at Carson, waiting for an explanation. He wanted answers to what was going on. For George, surmising was not an option. He only had time for cold, hard facts. But another tremor hit the facility before he could ask for answers. Everyone braced themselves as the ground shook ferociously. Office furniture shifted across the room, and more filing cabinets toppled, crashing to the floor, narrowly missing Deena.

When the tremor ceased, all in the room could feel sighs of relief. Carson called Dan, "Help me move these cabinets out of the way." Dan went to help, giving Deena a reassuring smile as he passed. The unknown quality of what was happening above the facility played on everyone's minds. Dan felt Deena's grief through the sadness in her eyes. Suddenly, George abruptly halted the moving of the cabinets.

"Who the hell is he anyway? He's not personnel," he demanded.

Carson stood upright and curtly replied, "If you are referring to 'him,'" he said, pointing to the General, "He is General Montgomery. He is here to brief you. I'll explain later. But first, help lift these cabinets out of the way before someone is badly hurt."

They fell silent, and Carson could see the team exchanging

questionable looks. It was evident that something serious was going on. Generals do not attend official briefings unless they are significant to the military and the Government. Carson stepped over the shambolic mess that now adorned the office floor. He shuffled papers with his foot, ardently staring at every file. Deena watched curiously. Whatever he was looking for, it had to be something to do with the General. Determined to find out, she gathered various files and papers as she worked toward Carson. Deena recognised most of the paperwork. But what she didn't identify was an old brown file beneath a chair.

Deena picked it up, casually placing it with the bundle of papers in her hand. Then, with her back to Carson, she observed the front of the file. It was an old card file with a string tie fastening it. The front cover is stamped in red ink, 'Top Secret.' 'Dwight Eisenhower / WW2 prep mission, 1943.' Deena wondered if this was what Carson was looking for; it certainly wasn't a file belonging to their test processing office. "Is this what you are looking for?" she directed Carson, waving it at him.

"Give the file to me. You haven't got a security clearance for it. Give it to me!" demanded Carson. His tone took Deena aback. She had never seen Carson so defensive.

Her hesitation towards handing over the file initiated the General to intervene. "Hand it over, Kross. I will explain everything once the siren stops."

Deena reluctantly handed the file to General Montgomery. While they waited for silence to prevail, thoughts and anxiety were interrupted by the appearance of a young soldier in the office doorway. He looked as terrified as they felt. His uniform was dirty and unkempt. His eyes darted around the room until he saw the General. "Sir!" he shouted, accompanied by a hand gesture resembling a salute.

"Private Barker?" queried the General.

"P-permission to… speak, sir?" he stuttered.

"Yes, permission granted," said the General.

Barker is a Private in accompaniment to the General as security. Barker took a moment and several deep breaths, focusing on what he needed to say. As he did, the siren ceased its repetitive wailing. So, Barker took the opportunity to speak without shouting over it. "Sir, all external communications are down. As a result, we can't contact perimeter security.

We have also lost visuals on CCTV. There is a partial collapse in Zone B on the south side, sir," said Barker, fighting to hide his tears. A grave expression came over the General's face.

"What's in Zone B?" asked the General with dread, hearing everyone exclaiming deep concern.

Barker's voice wavered with emotion as he explained. "Sir, that's where the in-house living quarters are for facility personnel. It… it's unlikely anyone's survived. The collapse is from the internal entry hall back."

From across the office, George spoke quietly, quoting the facilities policy. "In the event of the siren, all in-house personnel are to report to their specified assembly point: Zone B, south side."

No one spoke; they let the devastating news sink in. Then finally, the General asked if there were any survivors. If there were, it would be of some comfort. They needed a little solace amongst this tragic and senseless loss of life. "Yes, sir, survivors from Zones C and D," replied Barker.

"That's good," said the General, taking a slow breath. Then he asked, "How many?"

"Including ourselves, twenty-one," he answered wistfully. "Sir, most are twilight staff. Most of the personnel travelling into the facility had signed out."

The General lowered his head into his hands; he knew what was happening. He could have saved lives if he had prepared the briefing twenty-four hours ago. He wasn't the only one that didn't believe it would occur. Higher up the chain of command, some scoffed at the idea as preposterous. The General was relieved they had seen fit to put a fail-safe in place. But the team didn't know that they were the official fail-safe plan. He sat upright and, putting his hands together as if in prayer, muttered, "It's as he feared. It has happened."

Deena quickly responded, "Um, who feared? And what the hell has happened? We have a right to know," she voiced in frustration.

Deena was cut short by the siren as another influx of tremors began. Despite holding onto the doorframe, Barker could not stay on his feet. As Dan unsteadily moved across the room, he was knocked to the floor by a lighting unit, striking him across his shoulders. Dan crawled to Deena as she sat against the wall until the quakes lessened.

Deena turned to him tearfully and said, "Oh god, how much longer? I need to get to Martin and my children. I must know if they are okay." Dan didn't say anything. Instead, he put his arm around her shoulders, comforting her in the wake of the General's cold-hearted comment to sort herself out, and no one was going anywhere until this was over. Waiting for the tremors to subside was unbearable so the siren would cease its irrefutable warning. The General knew their immediate future was changing dramatically.

The General clutched the brown file in deep thought at the pending explanation he owed the team. Then, finally, the General asked Carson, "Carson, you've already been through this briefing, so could you accompany Barker?"

Carson agreed, understanding that the young soldier needed support.

"Barker, continue your duties with the survivors. Carson will stay with you. Report back at 03.00 hours," commanded the General.

"Yes, sir," replied Barker.

As they turned to leave for Zone D, the General placed a chair in the middle of the office and sat down, the brown file still in his hands. "I'm not sure exactly where to begin, but first, I need to ensure the security of the crystal skulls. They are critical to what is going on." The General then addressed Dan directly. "Are they undamaged?" he asked.

"Ten are in the artefacts safe. The other two are still in the lab. We are, or should I say, 'were' in the middle of doing tests," Dan replied. "I don't understand what…?" he began.

"First things first," the General cut in. "I need you and Kross to go and secure the skulls. Check them over and put them in the safe with the others."

"But what has…" Dan began to ask.

The General stopped him in his tracks. "I will explain everything when you get back, but right now, the skulls are far more important."

Dan and Deena looked at each other, resigned. The General wasn't going to give any information until they had done what he'd requested.

Dan got to his feet and offered Deena a hand up. Unfortunately, the damage had gotten worse as the tremors persisted. The flooring was uneven, with raised broken tiling and light fittings that had come down, reminding Deena of the injury Dan sustained earlier. "Are you okay? One of those came down on you," she asked.

"A bit sore, but I'll live," said Dan.

When they entered the laboratory, Deena's heart sank at the devastation before her. Then, making light of the situation, she casually said, "I don't think we'll be doing any testing for a while."

"That's for sure. But be careful. There's glass everywhere. The skulls are inside the steel table down there." Dan picked up the first skull, giving it to Deena. He then retrieved the second, inspecting it for damage. "Let me see that one, Dee," requested Dan.

Handing him the skull, she asked, "I don't understand any of this. I know the skulls have significance. Otherwise, we wouldn't be running tests, but how can they be tied into what's happening now?"

"I have no idea. I'm as confused as you are. Well, the skulls seem fine," said Dan. "Let's get them in the safe. The sooner we get back, the sooner we can get answers."

The backroom was messy, but Dan was relieved the safe was unscathed. He turned the wheel, punched in the code and the deadbolts unlocked. Dan placed the skulls carefully in their compartments and checked the other ten for peace of mind. Then, closing the door, he paused, listening to the deadbolts engaging. When they returned to the office, Deena noticed Trevor had removed the makeshift bandage. "Has the bleeding stopped?" she asked him.

"Yeah, I still feel dizzy, and I've got a headache, but I'll be fine," responded Trevor.

Dan went to inspect his head wound, to which Trevor pushed his hand away, exclaiming he was okay and to stop fussing. "Sounds like you're almost back to normal, Trevor," laughed Dan.

The General stepped forward and asked, "Are the skulls undamaged?"

"Yes, the skulls are fine. They are in the safe like you asked," replied Dan.

"Thank god," he said, relieved. "We need them for the mission."

Deena looked at the General through narrowed, perplexed eyes, as did the rest of the team. "What mission?" she asked.

"The one I'm sending you on, Kross," he said.

Deena stood, her mouth open in disbelief that the General had volunteered her for a mission. "I don't do missions, General. I work in a laboratory, or has that escaped your notice?" Deena said defensively.

Angrily, he pointed, stabbing the air with his finger whilst shouting, "You don't have a choice, Kross! So, I strongly suggest you sit down and listen up!"

The General's attitude subdued her. To Dan, there was no excuse for speaking that way to her, who, like him, couldn't grasp what was happening. None of them could have possibly understood why the General was so belligerent.

The General sat down, held up the brown file and said, "Firstly, I'll explain this, and then you will better understand what is going on now. During the Second World War, Hitler was ardently bombing Great Britain. He was relentless in his quest to invade the country. He was heavily into the paranormal and, most crucially, Norse mythology and had learned of an artefact that could've given him unimaginable power. Dwight Eisenhower's mission was to ensure that this object was well hidden and that Hitler nor his army could ever find it. The Government decided that a secret location off the coast of South Wales would be the best place to conceal it. The coastline there was already heavily guarded by both British and American troops. Over time it became obvious that Hitler had somehow learnt that the object could be, or was, in the designated area due to the repeated bombing of that coastline. Fortunately, the Germans missed the target and were not successful in breaching the coast's defences either." The General paused, which Deena took as an opportunity to interrupt.

"With all due respect General, I don't understand what that has to do with now," she said.

"Never mind that. I want to know what the artefact is," said Dan.

The General raised an eyebrow at Dan and replied, "It's the thirteenth crystal skull."

Dan could barely contain himself as he tried to look at the file in the General's hand. "No way," he exclaimed, "there has always been speculation of a thirteenth skull!"

The General swiped the file from Dan's prying eyes and, glaring at him curtly, said, "For Christ's sake, man, will you sit down!"

Then, at the risk of the General losing it with him, he hesitantly asked, "Is it still there?"

Dan met with a wall of silence from the General. Then, as he was about to carry on the briefing, Deena interrupted again, "Why won't you answer my question? What has this got to do with now?"

Exasperated, the General snapped back at the team. "If you give me a chance, I will explain. Especially you, Kross. You will need all the facts for your mission as every piece of information I give you will be vital to your success."

Deena closed her eyes momentarily and asked, "Why me?"

The General firmly said, "It must be you, Kross. You are the only person remotely qualified to deal with what is happening outside this facility. Whether you want to or not is irrelevant; you are doing this mission."

Then, Barker turned up at the door before the General could say anything more, looking distressed. "Sir, reporting at 03.00 hours as requested," said Barker.

The General glanced at his watch and told Barker, "Gather the survivors and secure a safe area for them. Then, get supplies and bunk down until further notice."

"Sir, yes sir, but… something…" began Barker.

Tired of interruptions, the General cut Barker dead, shouting, "Go, will you! I'm busy!"

Barker knew better than to answer back, and whatever he had to say, it would have to wait until the General was more receptive.

"Right, now, can we do the second phase of the briefing?" requested the General.

The General put the file down. He did not need it regarding what he was about to reveal. "We are not experiencing earthquakes," he began. "NASA has been tracking a comet storm for weeks. It was supposed to pass Earth, but it changed course at the last minute. We don't know how or why this happened, but this is what we do know. The destruction is going to be vast and on a global scale." He glanced at their horrified faces and quickly said, "We can expect the comet storm to last seventy-two hours. Nothing must happen to any of you. So, do not put yourselves at risk. Kross, I'm sorry this mission is on you; your understanding of the paranormal and metaphysics makes you the most qualified person to carry it out. This mission will be the most important thing you will ever do. Right, does anyone know anything about Norse mythology?" he asked. George and Trevor avoided eye contact with the General as the gravity of their situation began to sink in.

Dan lifted his hand in acknowledgement and said, "I do." But the General already knew this. The Government had ensured it in case of this event. When choosing the team, the highest officials scrutinised them for their knowledge and abilities.

Deena gave Dan a surprised look and asked, "You do?"

"Yeah," Dan replied, "history was a big part of my archaeological studies. Norse mythology was my dissertation paper for my university degree."

"Excellent!" said the General. "You can spend the next seventy-two hours teaching the rest of the team what you know." Dan groaned loudly at having to take on a teaching role.

George pointed at Dan laughing, "Hey, Mr Archaeologist may have a use after all."

Dan shot back at him, "Shut up, George!"

The General scowled at them in disapproval and carried on with his brief. "We believe this comet storm is what they predicted in Norse mythology as Ragnarök. Dan can explain the intricacies, but it will end the world as we know it. The thirteenth skull will complete the set when placed with the other twelve. We are not sure exactly how, but collectively, they are capable of a massive energy force that will regain light to our world but can destroy it if used negatively. So, no guesses why Hitler wanted it." The General looked at the team, waiting for an onslaught of questions.

Trevor frowned and remarked, "Ragnarök? Where do you get this shit from?"

George joined in as he remarked, "This has got to be a wind-up!"

"You had better believe it because your lives and everyone else's depend on it!" shouted the General. He drew breath, and the siren sounded another wave of tremors as he did. They braced themselves with renewed dread. Trevor curled up in a ball with his arms around his head, crying into the office floor carpet tiles. No one else heard or cared. There was no way of knowing how far away the impacts were except for the ferocity of the tremors. Then, as the quakes lessened, Barker and Carson turned up carrying blankets and a large box.

"Sir, we have supplies for you. There is bottled water and pre-packed foods," said Barker.

"Thank you," said the General. "Leave them here. You'd better get back to the others and maybe get some rest."

Carson nudged Barker, accompanied by a look of encouragement. "Sir, permission to speak with you privately?" asked Barker tentatively.

"Whatever it is, it will have to wait. I will come and see you when I am ready," the General said abruptly.

Carson rolled his eyes at Barker's pathetic attempt to get the General's attention. "Yes, sir," replied Barker, sighing in resignation at his feeble authority.

Upon leaving the office, Carson said to Barker, "We must tell him what we've seen! Yes, he needs to brief the team first, but this is, well, it's not, they're not normal and what if they..." Their voices trailed away as they headed towards Zone D.

Ten hours into the comet storm, the sirens continued to cut in and out, warning of the tremors. Each time it sounded, unfeigned terror gripped their already fragile existence.

It was twenty minutes since the last impact, and the siren had fallen silent. The General picked up the World War II file, and as he did, George asked, "So, what exactly is this Ragnarök, General?"

The General answered, "Ragnarök means the doom of the gods. Theoretically, it is the destruction and re-order of the cosmos, which, in turn, throws our sun out of orbit, plunging our world into darkness. In Norse mythology, Ragnarök will also destroy the gods' worlds. For Earth, it means widespread devastation, and life, for the most part, will be destroyed with it."

"And how do the crystal skulls fit into this?" asked George.

The General paused and stated, "History foretells the skulls were placed on Earth by the Norse gods for us to regenerate light and, in turn, the rebirth of our planet by drawing our sun back into orbit."

"What are we supposed to do with the skulls for this regeneration?" asked George.

"I don't know. I wish I had a better answer, but we'll figure it out once the last skull is retrieved. Kross, that is your mission."

"Whoa, you expect me to find this skull. It's not even in this country!" Deena said defiantly.

The General handed her the file and calmly said, "Familiarise yourself with Eisenhower's mission. There are handwritten notes in the back by the man himself. It should give you some indications of the location and what you need to do."

Deena took the file with a look of disdain. Dan gave blankets to Trevor and George, placed one around Deena's shoulders, and sat beside her. She smiled, pointing at Trevor. They suppressed a grin as they watched him roll himself up in his blanket so tightly that he resembled a butterfly in its chrysalis. Finally, exhaustion got the better of them all.

Sleep was short-lived. The sirens' sudden piercing whines jolted them out of their oblivious, unconscious state and back into a reality of sheer terror. Dan shook Deena's arm, getting her attention. "Dee!" he shouted, pointing to the file beside her. "I've been thinking."

"And?" she asked, hoping he had a plan or something that meant she wouldn't have to go on this mission.

"I need to go through that with you," said Dan. "Then I can tell you what you need to know about the Norse predictions."

Deena's heart sank. There was no light-bulb moment, no bright idea offered, and no get-out clause. As they rode out the tremors, Deena's mind was racing. She had no idea what dangers she would face. She thought about Martin, Lily, and Ben. Were they safe? Images of little Lily with her cute pigtails and Ben's cheeky smiles haunted her mind.

The siren's silence was a liberation, albeit for the ringing left in their ears. Then, without knowing how long the respite would last, the General gave out water and food to the team. Dan took an extra bottle and gave it to Deena. Then, thanking him, he sat beside her and said, "No trouble, considering you're gonna save the world, or at least what's left of it."

Frowning, she picked up the file, offered it to him and replied, "Yeah, how about that. Here, knock yourself out." Dan flicked through the file, scanning it with enthusiasm. Deena watched curiously; he was like a little boy on a big adventure. "Dan, I don't think I can do this," she exclaimed.

He looked at her; her big green eyes were brimming with tears. Dan put the file down and said, "Look, none of us has a choice in what is happening. I'm sure you will be fine once you get there. You'll be back in no time."

"I still don't understand why it must be me. Why not you? Or Trevor? Or even Carson, for that matter?" she said between tearful breaths.

"Or George?" offered Dan, chuckling.

Deena couldn't help but smile. "George, really?" she said, giggling and wiping away tears. "He'd be out of puff before getting to the end of the corridor!" she joked.

Dan re-opened the file, still chuckling to himself and continued reading. Deena hugged the blanket and catnapped while Dan read the file, cross-referencing pages back and forth. Then, he tapped her shoulder to wake her and asked, "Do you want to know why it must be you?" Deena sat in anticipation as he explained what Ragnarök would bring about for her. "Norse mythology is a huge subject, so I'll give you the basics and how I think it will affect your mission. Is that okay?" Dan paused, organising his thoughts. "Okay, so Ragnarök is the destruction of the gods' worlds. As the General said, it's the re-order of the cosmos, hence the comet storm. I can't say these gods' worlds exist for sure, but the Norse people certainly believed and worshipped them. The belief structure goes back at least five thousand years. More important is the situation now. Norse mythology foretold that during Ragnarök, a comet storm would destroy the Earth and most of humanity. Darkness will descend, and all things unseen will exist and rule. The darkness empowers them; they will wipe out what is left of any life to keep that power, and they will do whatever it takes to prevent anyone from restoring light for the regeneration of our planet."

Deena sighed, "Now it makes sense why it has to be me."

"Yes, the General is right. You are the best-qualified person for the mission. I'm sorry, but everything is riding on you getting the thirteenth skull back here."

"No pressure then," she said with a heavy heart. Armed with the new information Dan shared, any chance Martin and her children could have survived was fading rapidly in her mind.

The General walked to the office door and turned to the team. "Stay put, all of you! I need to find Barker while it's relatively safe to move about."

The General was barely through the door when George took to his feet, rummaging through the food box. Trevor was right behind him, trying to get a look-in. Angry at not getting past George, he curtly spat at him, "Hey! We've got to eat that when you've finished rifling through it!"

"Yeah, well, are you going to stop me?" George snapped back.

"Well, your waistline says differently!" said Trevor spitefully.

Dan had heard enough and took the food box from George and said, "Look, George, we don't know how long we will be stuck here, so we must make the food last! Consider yourself on a diet."

"Who put you in bloody charge?" demanded George.

Deena couldn't take any more arguing, "Please stop! Just stop arguing. George, Dan is right; we need to pace the food and water."

Disgruntled, George threw the Twinkie bar he was clutching back into the box and went to sit down, humphing as he went.

Meanwhile, the General picked his way through the rubble towards Zone D. He thought it odd that Barker hadn't reported to him that morning. A sense of dread overcame him as he recalled Barker telling him of the partial collapse on the south side. The General's head swam with thoughts of returning to the team with more devastating news. Pushing the horrors of what could be to the back of his mind, he continued searching for them. As he approached the facilities centre, the smell of death was more potent. The General began to retch. Searching his pockets, he pulled out a handkerchief and cupped it over his nose and mouth to quell the stench.

The facility was unrecognisable, and the damage was extensive. The General approached the collapse and scanned the descent, and as his eyes lowered, he saw a woman's shoe protruding from the debris. He knelt to pick it up, and suddenly realising it was still on the person's foot, he quickly pushed it back on, muttering, "Oh god, I'm so sorry." George's words of company policy rang in his head. His eyes rose, and other body parts became visible in the orange lighting. He was sickened by such a terrible loss of life and understood why Barker was such a mess when he reported to him. Barker was right. No one could have survived this collapse. So, he went back to the facility's centre. Zone C, on his left, was the kitchens and food courts for the staff. He made a mental note for more supplies on his way back. For now, it was more important to find Barker's group. Turning right, he went to Zone D. Unsure where Barker and Carson were situated, he checked every room and office on his way through.

Nearing the end of the zone, he could see filing cabinets and desks piled up in the corridor. The General could only surmise that Barker and Carson were responsible. 'But why?' he thought as he stood in front of the giant Tetris puzzle. Carefully, he took chairs and cabinets down and climbed over. Jumping down the other side, it was the end of the zone, and there was only one office. Placing his ear to the door, he listened, his hand resting on the door handle.

Finally, the General called out, "Barker?" There was no response. He called out again, louder, "Barker! Are you in there? Carson?" The General tried to open the door but couldn't. Perplexed about what was going on, he shouted again, "Barker! Carson! Let me in!"

A shaky voice whispered on the other side of the door. It was Barker. "Sir? Shush! You will get us killed!" he whispered.

"What the hell are you going on about, man? Open this door now!" demanded the General.

"Please, sir, they'll come; I've seen them eating dead bodies," whimpered Barker.

"Have you lost your mind? You're not making sense. Open the door!" said the General firmly as he rattled the handle, trying to push it open.

"Sir, we need to move things out of the way first," whispered Carson. From behind the door, they began the task of moving their makeshift barricade. Carson whispered to Barker, "He's not going to believe you, you know that, don't you? So, you must show him."

Barker shot a terrified look at Carson. "No fucking way. I'm not going back there! You show him." Not surprised by Barker's reaction, Carson carried on clearing the doorway. The General stepped into the room. Survivors huddled in the far corner, and on the other side lay two bodies with blankets draped over them. The General lifted the corner of a blanket and stood looking somberly at the face of the dead man.

"How many of us left?" he asked.

"Nineteen now. These two died in the night, sir," replied Barker.

The General put the blanket back over the dead man and faced Barker and Carson. His gaze rested on Barker. "Who are 'they?'" he asked.

Barker gulped a deep breath and frantically said, "Creatures, sir… big… weird creatures… eating dead bodies… tearing them apart, sir…"

CHAPTER THREE

The General fell silent. Either Barker had lost his marbles, or there was more to what he was saying, and judging by the terrified look on his face, something had scared him witless. Carson gave Barker an empathic look and began to explain. "While looking for survivors near the collapse, we noticed small debris coming through a gap right at the top. So, we climbed up to have a look. There is a breach directly to the surface, sir. That's when we saw them."

"We… we blocked it up though, sir… the best we could," rambled Barker.

"I, well, we have never seen anything like them, sir," said Carson. Then, before the General could absorb the information, the ground beneath them began to shake again. The siren resounded, and the screams from the survivors faded to a whisper by comparison. A calm came an hour later when the siren stopped. After that, the only sounds were feeble cries of discontent filling the room.

"I need you to show me what you've seen," the General said hastily to Carson and Barker.

Barker begged the General, "Please, sir, don't make me go back there, please."

Barker's nervous disposition showed in the emotional quiver of his voice. "It's okay, Barker," said Carson. "I'll show him."

The General looked hard at Barker, taking stock of the young soldier before him. Tears from his bloodshot eyes formed streaks down his dirty face. The terror he was experiencing was more than existent with the knowledge of an unknown enemy that wouldn't only kill them but tear them apart and devour them. Finally, the General agreed, saying, "Stay here with the others and take care of them, soldier. Barricade the door after we leave, okay?"

"Yes, sir, th-thank you, sir," said Barker, relieved at the prospect of not having to face these creatures again.

The General turned to Carson and asked him to help move the bodies out of the room. "It's not going to help anyone having them in here as a constant reminder," he remarked.

They removed the bodies into a small room off the south side. The stench of rotting flesh had a sickly smell that increased as time passed. Then, laying them out with as much dignity as possible, they returned to let Barker know they were off to investigate the creatures above the breach. "We won't be long, Barker. Barricade yourselves in and wait for us," the General said lowly.

"Wh-what if you don't come back, sir?" stammered Barker. "They… they are flesh eaters. What if, oh god, what if they…"

"We'll be back, don't worry," reassured the General. As Carson and the General left the room, Barker was already moving things to secure himself and the survivors. Beads of sweat mingled with tear-stained streaks found their way down to his shirt collar in his effort to keep them safe. Finally, Carson and the General left him to it. They stood and examined the mountain of rubble. The stench of death was getting worse. Finally, the General asked through his handkerchief, "Where's the breach?"

"See the door right at the top, sir? Barker and I jammed it in to block it. We couldn't think of any other way of stopping those things from getting in," explained Carson.

"Do you know the depth between the top of the facility and the surface?" asked the General.

"It's the shallowest part, hence the breach. It's approximately fifteen to twenty feet," replied Carson.

"Right, let's get up there and look then, shall we? I want to see these creatures for myself!" said the General.

The General had seen much during his service but felt sickened at the prospect of climbing the rubble with body parts protruding. So, they ascended quietly, and Carson held one end of the door and signalled the General to slide it across. Then, Carson pulled a small penlight out of his pocket, giving it to the General. He shone it up the shaft and turned to Carson as he said, "Fifteen to twenty feet, you say?"

"Yes, sir," said Carson nervously, "but… but be very quiet, or these things will know you are there."

"I'll be careful. Now, give me a leg up," stated the General.

Carson cradled his fingers together and boosted the General into the shaft. He went slowly, desperately trying not to make much disturbance. If Carson and Barker's information is accurate, having a lunch date with them was not on his agenda. As he neared the surface, he stopped and turned out the penlight. Before raising his head above ground, the General took slow, deliberate deep breaths. The south base hanger was directly in front of him, about four hundred metres away. He could see a couple of the creatures beyond the hanger, but they weren't close enough for him to get a good look. He turned his head to the right and froze.

'Oh hell no!' he screamed in his mind. Only twenty feet away was another of the creatures. It was humanoid, with long sinewy limbs, and wasn't a standard flesh colour but white with a bluish-purple hue, as if the skin was a translucent membrane. The jaw protruded below the nostril pits, but what struck the General most frightening was the six-inch, razor-sharp, scissored teeth on which human entrails hung like meat on a butcher's hook.

He believed everything Carson and Barker said. The General waited for an attack, but nothing happened. It hadn't seen him. Then, as the creature turned its head, sniffing into the air, he realised why. They had eye sockets, but the translucent skin covered them. They were utterly blind. The other intriguing thing was that they had no ears or orifice for hearing. The General decided to put it to the test. He slowly lowered himself, looking for a palm-sized rock in the shaft. Carefully, he dug one out of the soil.

Again, the General raised his head; it was now to his left. He poised his arm in readiness and threw the rock past the creature. As the rock hit the ground, the creature leapt towards it. 'Damn, that thing can move fast!' he thought. The speed and agility as it followed the rock's path were astounding. It sniffed it and made its way towards the hanger to join the rest of its kind, realising it wasn't a food source. Satisfied he'd learnt as much as possible about them given the conditions, he inched his way back down the tunnel to rejoin Carson. "Did you see them, sir?" whispered Carson.

"You don't need to whisper, Carson. Those things are deaf and blind. From what I can tell, they hunt by detecting vibrations and tracking scents. Now, help me put this door back, and whatever you do, don't bang or drop anything," said the General.

"Was there many, sir?" queried Carson.

"I saw three," said the General, "but there could be more." They took prodigious care climbing back down the collapse. Falling debris could cause enough vibration to alert the creatures to their presence below. If those things wanted to get into the facility, there would be no way of stopping them, and neither would they be able to defend themselves against a ferocious attack by something that size and strength.

These creatures would become known as Ground Crawlers. They emerged from depths far below the Earth's crust. The deep fissures created by the comets pounding the Earth have opened a new world for them. They hunt in packs known as hordes and have gained a taste for human flesh. For now, the Ground Crawler's appetite is satiated with the reek of decaying bodies. They can climb vertically with suckers on their fingers, toes, and vicious talons to grip. However, it will not be long before they start to track fresh meat. After that, it will be a battle of nerve and wits against them to stay alive.

As they walked back, the General and Carson decided to play it down for Barker's sanity. Moreover, the threat to their lives from these Ground Crawlers was massive. So, outside the door where Barker and the survivors were, the General firmly called out, "Barker, it's us. Move the barricade and let us in, but don't bang or scrape things across the floor or walls."

They waited patiently, and as they stepped into the room, Barker's eyes danced with relief to see them back safely. "Are... are they still out there?" asked Barker.

"Yes," said the General, "but they are blind and deaf and respond to vibration and scent. So, we should be fine if no one makes loud noises like dropping things or stomping around. They won't come looking if they don't know we are down here."

Barker's shoulders relaxed in response, but he still raised his eyes to the ceiling at the thought of those hideous creatures roaming above their heads. The strain of holding himself together was starting to tell in the creases of his constantly furrowed brow. Finally, he managed a tight-lipped smile to the General and whispered, "As quiet as a mouse, sir."

Then, the General turned to Carson and suggested he remain with Barker for the duration of the comet storm. The last thing they needed was for him to lose the plot, putting them all in danger. The General had seen it happen before. When a young soldier with a fragile mental state faces a dangerous, unpredictable situation, common sense and training do not figure in their thought processing.

"I'm going back to tell the team. They need to know what we've seen," said the General. Before leaving the room, he stopped and said, "Oh, and Carson, ration the food and water; we need to make it last as long as possible." With that, he left for the kitchens.

Three kitchens serve the food courts. First, the General needed to know how much food and water there was. Calculating how long they could survive below ground was imperative to the time he could give Deena on her mission. Each kitchen had chillers and freezers, stocked at about seventy per cent. Utensils and steel pots and pans scattered the floor. Next, he found the dry goods. It wasn't as well-stocked as he hoped. 'Nineteen survivors less two,' he thought. If they rationed everyone, they could survive for about ten, maybe twelve weeks. Next to the dry goods was an area for bottled water. He was thankful there was good stock. It was going to be a stretch, but it was possible. He filled a box with supplies and then returned to the team.

The General hadn't realised how long he'd been gone. George and Trevor were both wrapped in their blankets, getting some rest. He stopped by Dan and Deena, puzzled at the food box between them. Without looking up at the General, Dan casually said, "George, need I say more?"

"Ah, right," muttered the General. "Well, I need to speak with you all on a couple of factors, supplies being one." George began to stir, giving Trevor a shake to wake him. "Everyone, we need to ration food and water. So, with nineteen of us, supplies will last two to three months if we are careful." George took it personally and rolled his eyes at Dan accusingly.

"Nineteen, is that all?" gasped Deena.

"I'm afraid so," said the General. "Two died from their injuries during the night, and there are no other survivors."

"Are Barker and Carson bringing them here?" asked Dan.

"No, I have asked them to remain where they are for two reasons. Firstly, it's better to spread out into two groups. Barker is hanging in there, but his mental state is not at its best. So, Carson will oversee that group. Second, I do not want them to know about the mission yet. I will deal with that once you are on your way, Kross," said the General. "The collapse in Zone B has breached the surface. Carson and Barker noticed it when they were looking for survivors. So, they investigated and saw large, flesh-eating creatures roaming the surface that no one has ever seen or encountered."

The General went on to explain what he had witnessed. He did not spare any details with the team. He needed them to fully understand the horrific nature of these Ground Crawlers and what it meant for them and their continued existence. Mind-numbing disbelief encompassed the team. Their options were diminishing, as were their prospects for staying alive. The supplies would only last for a short time. Being buried underground with Ground Crawlers above them was nothing short of a prolonged, painful death from starvation. And facing indiscriminate, flesh-eating creatures was not on anyone's agenda either.

"I can't see how I can do this mission, General," said Deena. "Especially with those Ground Crawler things out there. And, what's more, how am I supposed to get to the United Kingdom? From what I know, it's not next door!" she protested.

The General said, "Getting you there isn't a problem. There is a plane specifically stored in case of this event."

The General didn't have the heart to tell her they would have to cross overground to the south side hanger to board it. Deena realised there was no getting out of this mission. It had been thought out and planned by high-ranking officials, but she felt angry that they had not given herself or the team the relevant information about the skulls, let alone what was happening. 'Dan was right,' she thought, 'it's all politics. Joe Public was dispensable and used to an end.'

"It doesn't look like anyone will get a choice in this," she murmured to Dan.

Dan slowly shook his head as he idly tapped a water bottle against his boot and said, "Nope."

The General spoke up. "We should stay in one place as much as possible. Considering what is above ground, we don't want to draw attention to ourselves. Trevor, how are you feeling now?" he asked.

"My head is sore, but I'm okay," he replied.

"Go with Dan and fetch supplies to last us the next forty-eight hours," he commanded.

"Shit, for a moment there, I thought you cared!" said Trevor, struggling to his feet.

"We need to ride out this comet storm. So, I can't engage this mission until the impacts have completely stopped," said the General, ignoring Trevor's sarcasm.

It took Dan and Trevor a few trips back and forth to get enough supplies. Finally, they found blankets in a storeroom, so they took them too. "We found where Barker got the blankets from, so we may as well be comfortable while we wait," said Dan, handing them out and giving Deena an extra one with a mischievous grin. "For our heroine," he said as he did a swift bow.

"Idiot, thank you," Deena said, smiling. As the team got comfortable, Dan continued to teach them about Norse mythology. The waves of tremors continued sporadically. Each time, the siren blared its warning. Minutes felt like hours as each focused on their survival.

Day and night blurred into one, and there had been no impacts for the last twelve hours. Nevertheless, the General had to ensure the comet storm was over before readying for the mission. He was concerned about why the lockdown hadn't automatically lifted if the storm was over. He needed to go to administration in Zone D to override the system manually.

As the team slept, the General lightly put a hand on Dan's arm to rouse him. Opening one eye, Dan looked up at the General. "Keep everyone here. First, I'll look in on Carson and Barker. Then, I'm going to the administration office to check out the override system," said the General.

Barker and Carson were taking no chances judging by the length of time it took to clear the doorway. "How is everyone, Carson?" the General asked, looking around the room.

"Not too bad," he replied. "Barker is a little fragile, but he's holding it together for the sake of the survivors."

"Best to make him feel useful," the General suggested. "That way, he won't have too much time to think. You have it well organised. I have some things to attend to, but I will come back in the next twenty-four hours to speak with you regarding our situation. In the meantime, carry on as you are."

The General headed towards the offices housing the visual and audio security. The control panel for the steel doors should be in one of them. All

Government underground facilities have a manual override. First, he went to the CCTV monitoring room. He cast his eyes; some surveillance monitors had fallen and smashed. Nothing was live. A part of him was hoping that if a couple were still working, he could at least see what state the area was in before venturing out.

Then, the General went to the communications office. He looked around at the broken panels. Phones, headsets, and walkie-talkies were littered everywhere. Finally, he came upon an office at the rear. The plaque read, Authorised personnel only. A large control panel in a crescent shape was in the centre of the room. The filing cabinets had crashed to the floor, spilling their content, creating a paper carpet. Intent on the issue at hand, he studied the digital board. It was dead. Under the top control board were cabinets. Kneeling, he found a locked unit. On the front, it said MAN. O.R. 'Great,' he thought, 'where is the key?' It had to be in the office as the facility policy stipulates the key must be on hand for emergencies. He eventually found bunches of keys at the bottom of an overturned filing cabinet.

Half a dozen manual switches were inside the unit with LED lights beside them. The General had never authorised using one of these systems, let alone done it himself. The override was a mechanical lever. 'Right, the electrical switches for the exits should also be fed by the generators. Only one way to find out,' he thought as he flicked the first switch down. The LED came on, so he lit up all six and gripped the lever.

Then, a sudden dread overcame him, and he instantly let go. He thought about the implications. Once he opened them, there was no way to shut them again if they needed to secure the facility. Only the lockdown procedure could do that via the control panel. Opening the steel doors to the outside would compromise their safety. He wasn't going to make it easier for the Ground Crawlers to get in. He switched them off, closed the cabinet, and locked it. It could be their end if anyone got it into their heads to open the facility. He placed the key firmly in his trouser pocket. He decided that putting the idea of opening the exits out of everyone's mind was the best approach. 'If they think the system for the override is too badly damaged to open the exits, perhaps they wouldn't be tempted to try and find it, let alone use it,' he thought.

The team's attention turned to the General as he walked into the room. He pulled up a chair and sat down before he spoke. "Listen up, everyone, please. I've been to see Carson and Barker, and they are fine. But Dan has probably told you I also went to find the override system," said the General. "The system is not intact. So, there is no way of opening any exits." The General didn't like lying to the team, but he didn't want to take any chances. "But that's probably a good thing. We don't want to make it easier for the Ground Crawlers to get in. The steel doors are an effective way of keeping them out."

"General, we must leave at some point. How will Deena get to the plane?" asked Dan.

"The only possible way is the breach in Zone B," replied the General. "Kross, I need you to start preparing for your mission. Find your backpack and take any equipment you think will be useful. Don't overload yourself."

"Anything I can do, General?" asked Dan.

"Give Kross a hand. I will need your help to get to the south side hangar. I'll speak to you about it before we leave," the General replied.

"What about the Ground Crawlers? You said yourself that they are incredibly fast. We can't outrun them," said Dan, concerned.

"No, we can't outrun them, but we can outwit them. I've got a way we can do it," said the General.

"Glad you've got a plan. You have got a plan, haven't you?" asked Dan with an edge of excitement. He loved adventure. Little did he know, this would be an adventure of a lifetime.

"My research gear is in the laboratory. Are you coming?" asked Deena.

"Right behind you," he said, pirouetting around her.

She raised an eyebrow and said, "Chill, will you? Your enthusiasm is a little overwhelming. But you can do the mission if you're that keen."

"No can do. That job is all yours. What kind of gear will you take?" asked Dan inquisitively. "I don't know anything about what you use for— what do you call it? Ghost hunting?"

'Here we go,' thought Deena. "I am not a ghost hunter! I am a fully qualified paranormal researcher and investigator. There's a big difference."

"Sorry," said Dan. "I don't know much about it. But I want to learn."

Deena smirked at his attempted recovery from insulting her. "Really?" she asked.

"Yes. Considering the situation, I think I should, don't you?" said Dan.

Deena smiled and said, "Fine, I will run through some equipment."

They entered the laboratory, and Deena grabbed her backpack. Next, she opened the store cupboard to find its contents were in an entangled heap on the floor. "Help me move this stuff out," she said. "My equipment is at the bottom of it."

"I hope it still works after this stuff landed on it," remarked Dan.

Deena smiled, pulled out two large, ridged, black high-impact cases, and gave one to Dan. She said, "Sensitive equipment needs proper protection." Moving to a clear area, Deena knelt and set the cases down. She undid the airtight seal and opened it, revealing a range of research paraphernalia sunk into dense protective foam.

"Wow, that's impressive!" exclaimed Dan. "And you use all this in your research?" he wondered.

"Yes," she said. "This is a small selection of my equipment. I have more at home."

"Have you an idea of what you'll take?" asked Dan.

"I'm not sure," she said. "I don't know what I'm up against until I get there. I need to take equipment to detect them. Some of this won't help me, and I'm limited on what I can carry."

"It's dark out there, and daylight is a thing of the past, so maybe a flashlight would be a good start?" offered Dan.

"Good thinking. I only have one battery pack, but it's better than nothing," said Deena. "These should be a help too."

"Binoculars?" he questioned.

"They are night-vision goggles. But you can switch them to infrared as well," said Deena.

"Oh cool," he said, surprised, "so you can see them with these? Definitely take them," said Dan.

"This will help," she said, handing him a handheld thermal imaging camera, "and these," she said, placing rectangular units with gauges on the floor.

"What are they for?" he asked.

"These three different meters measure electromagnetic energy fields," she said. Then, she showed him a particular one. "This does a bit more. It's a tri-field meter. It indicates different energy fields and the direction of an approach, which will be a big help," she said as she put them into her backpack along with spare battery packs. "Basically," she stated, "it's all about different types of electrical energy and various sound waves."

"So, we really are dealing with everything unseen?" asked Dan.

"Yes, you got it," she replied. "That's as much as I can fit in. Let's get back."

Dan took the backpack from her. There was much more to Deena than he had given credit. She had caught his curiosity and imagination. He wanted to understand more. So, on their return, he asked her what he perceived as well-thought-out questions. He didn't want her to believe he was ignorant. The truth be told, he was. He knew nothing of this kind of thing.

The General waited for them to return, pacing back and forth, deep in thought at the pending mission. "Did you get what you need, Kross?" he asked as they walked in.

"Yes. As much as I can feasibly carry that is of most use," replied Deena.

"Excellent, we should make our way to the breach. George, Trevor, stay here and please, stay out of the food supplies while I'm gone," he said abruptly.

Dan and Deena gasped at the rubble, laced with bodies of personnel they had once worked alongside. Distraught and sickened by the scene, Deena cried and turned away from it. She tried to wipe away her tears as she sobbed, "I'm sorry. I didn't expect it to be like this."

"I should have warned you, but I'm afraid this is the reality of what we are dealing with," said the General. Deena nodded, desperately holding in the grief already embedded in her heart. Thoughts of Martin, Lily and Ben flooded back to the forefront of her mind. Finally, the General turned to Dan and said, "I need you to go to the kitchens. Find whatever herbs and spices you can and bring them back here."

Dan looked at the General, bewildered, shrugged his shoulders, and went to the kitchens.

Dan returned twenty minutes later with his trouser pockets bulging with sachets of spices, sauces, and an assortment of dried herbs.

"No fresh ones. These spices are all I could carry," Dan said. "There are more if you want me to go back?" he queried.

51

"This should be enough to stretch between us," said the General, picking up the dried herbs and sniffing them. "It should work."

First, the General began stuffing herbs in his pockets and rubbing his clothing down. Then, he opened a sachet of spices, rubbing them on his face, wincing at the strong odour and stinging sensation it was causing on his skin. Dan and Deena looked at him bizarrely.

"What are you doing?" asked Deena.

The General stopped only momentarily to say, "Do the same. We need to mask the smell of our bodies." Dan and Deena shrugged shoulders at each other and followed suit. "The Ground Crawlers hunt by scent. Hopefully, this will disguise ours enough so they can't track us," the General explained.

"What about our movements overground? We will be dead meat walking if they detect our footsteps," said Dan.

"I've thought about that, and the only way to distract them is by diversionary tactics," said the General, swooping down and picking up a golf ball-sized piece of concrete debris. "This should be heavy enough to divert them from us if they get too close. Up there, we go one at a time. Move slowly and light-footed. Use the stones to throw away from you, sending them in the opposite direction. You both clear?" he asked.

Dan picked up some stones of similar size, then looked at the General, unsure of his master plan, asking, "Are you sure this will work?"

He could see the fear in their faces, and there was no pretending that there was every chance it could go wrong. "No, but it's all I've got," said the General. "Whatever you do, do not run!" With that, he pointed to the door blocking the breach. "Dan, come up with me first to move that door. Then, Deena, once Dan is in the shaft, climb up as you go next. I'll follow behind. Clear?" asked the General. "When you are on the surface, don't walk around. Wait until we are all above ground before moving out."

Deena stood at the base of the rubble, watching them climb. Her hands hurt from gripping the stones so tightly. Her legs felt like jelly with the dread of facing these hideous creatures. The Ground Crawlers are what make fantastic nightmares. But there was no way of waking; she had to live it in reality. Her mind was racing with a deep-seated fear of what she was about to embark on. She watched Dan disappear into the earthen tunnel. Then the General beckoned her. Deena grimaced at the bodies intertwined with the debris and desperately avoided contact. Finally, the General offered his hand as she neared the top. Deena looked towards the bottom of the collapse. Then, understanding what was going through her mind, the General said, "There is nothing we can do for them. I know it's devastating, but you are alive, and we must keep you that way. You must focus, Kross. Remember, when you get up there, tread softly. No matter what, you do not run. Now, are you ready?"

Deena struggled with a subdued, "Yes." Her petite build meant the General had no problem hitching her up into the shaft. She braced herself against the walls of the earth surrounding her. Then, nearing the mouth of the surface, she whispered to Dan, "Help me up!"

Dan stood with his feet firmly set apart over the shaft. He reached in, took the backpack first, and then took hold of her forearm; she gripped his in turn, and with one swift pull, she was out. Dan pulled her abruptly towards him and grabbed her around the waist, slowly sliding her down onto her feet to minimise any vibration to the ground. As awkward as Deena felt, she accepted he was merely being careful. With her feet firmly on the floor, Dan couldn't help but give a mischievous grin, to which Deena muttered, "Was that necessary?"

Dan ignored her comment and pointed toward the hanger. "Do you see them?" he said in a low voice. "I've counted five. Three over by the hanger and two to your right about six hundred feet away."

Deena strained her eyes in the darkness at the bluish-white creatures. "What the hell..." she said in disbelief, "they are monstrous!"

The General appeared behind them and said, "I'll go first. You follow, Kross. Dan, you're at the rear. One at a time. Wait until I signal you before making your way over."

The General glanced back at them and nodded as if to say, 'Wish me luck.' Deena turned away. If his plan didn't work, she did not want to watch him being torn apart by the grotesque creatures. It took the General twenty minutes to reach the hanger. Dan could make out his silhouette against the wall of the building. They waited patiently for the General to signal them. "You'll be fine. Follow the General's path," said Dan reassuringly.

She strapped her backpack tightly across her shoulders and gripped the rocks. Each time she took a few softly trodden steps, she glanced around, noting the movements of the Ground Crawlers. One of the creatures to her right was getting too close for comfort. Deena's stomach knotted. She felt sick with fear. A moment's loss of focus was all it took for her to stumble. She wavered on one leg, desperately trying to regain her balance. Finally, the backpack's weight shifted enough to take her down.

"Oh, fuck no!" exclaimed Dan. He wanted to run to help her, but he knew he would be signing their death warrants by being impetuous. The heels of Deena's hands hit the ground hard, and the rocks grasped in her hands dug into her palms. Her knees jarred on the compacted earth. She froze, her eyes wide with terror. Within seconds, a waft of hot, putrid breath was on her neck. She could hear it salivating, sniffing her backpack. It made a low, gruff sound as it licked at her.

CHAPTER FOUR

Deena prayed that the herbs and spices would work. But then, its scissored teeth brushed against her cheek as it blew out its vile breath on her face, spattering her with mucus. She gritted her teeth, holding her breath, not wanting to give herself away to the creature. Dan watched in horror and began throwing well-aimed rocks ten feet away from Deena and the Ground Crawler. He threw them as hard as he could, bouncing them off the ground, frantically trying to distract them away from her. The General likewise threw rocks from the hangar until it was far from Deena. "Stay there, Dee. I'm on my way. Don't move," called Dan.

Deena watched him slowly walk to her. She choked back tears of mixed emotions: anger for being so careless and sheer relief that she was still alive and breathing. Dan stooped down and lightly brushed her hair to the side with his fingertips. "Yuck, what's that on your face?" he asked.

Deena wiped her face with the back of her hand and mumbled with disgust, "I think it sneezed on me."

Dan put his hand over his mouth. Laughing seemed inappropriate, considering what she had endured. He stifled it with a cough and asked her, "What the hell did you rub on your face?"

"I don't know. I used the white spice sachets. I didn't look to see what it was," Deena said disparagingly.

"We need to get moving. Can you get to your feet?" asked Dan.

"Yes, but my knees hurt," she replied, wincing as she struggled to stand.

"You can lean on me if you need to," offered Dan.

Deena linked her arms with Dan. The last thing she needed was a repeat performance if her knees gave way.

The two Ground Crawlers joined the three on the other side of the hangar. "Are you okay, Kross?" asked the General. "That was a close call."

Deena was embarrassed she had endangered them with her lapse of concentration. "I'm so sorry. I'll be more careful," she apologised.

"We need to get inside this hangar," said the General. "There is a side door at the bottom. Again, one at a time, in the same order. Be vigilant."

The General went first. As he got to the door, he signalled Deena. Her knees ached as she picked her way with one hand against the building for support. "Signal Dan while I unlock this door," said the General.

Running his hand down the edge of the frame, he felt for the keypad. Then, punching in a six-digit code, he pressed the entry button, opening the door. "How do you know the code to get in here?" asked Deena.

"I may not know the main underground facility, but this hanger, with the other four, is my business," he replied. "How far is Dan?" he pressed.

"Nearly halfway," she said.

"Go in and wait for us," the General said, ushering her inside. Then, he signalled Dan to hurry up. The longer they were outside, the more chance something could get to them.

Inside the hangar, the same orange lights ran along the base of the wall and ceiling. Dan turned to the General and asked, "Where is the plane?" His voice echoed, and he threw his arms up in question to the space and stated, "I don't see a plane, General."

"It's not here, that's why," the General said, striding across the hangar towards a workstation at the rear. The General walked into a small office and then disappeared down a flight of steps. "Be careful. They are steep," said the General.

It was evident that the General was very familiar with where he was going. They followed him through a tunnel to an adjoining section; the General turned sharply into it without faltering his stride. They walked for half a mile with nothing but concrete walls and sporadic lighting. Dan noticed that Deena's backpack weighed heavy on her shoulders. "Here, let me take that for a bit. How much further, General?" asked Dan, slinging the backpack over his shoulder.

"Not far, a quarter of a mile. We could've driven it in a service vehicle if it wasn't for those Ground Crawlers. Of course, this way is a long way around, but it is the safest route considering our circumstances," responded the General.

"I'm happy to be going 'the long way,'" exclaimed Deena as she remembered her up-close and personal encounter with the creatures. The tunnel ended abruptly with a thick steel door with similar security features as the primary facility entry. The General punched in a series of codes. Then, he stared into the screen.

"Security clearance granted," said Dan mimicking the electronic voice he and Deena were used to hearing on arrival for their workday. The General ignored Dan's idiocy as he leaned into the heavy door, pushing it open to reveal a sizable underground hanger. The sight of a Beechcraft Model 18 aircraft made Dan press past the General. He stood in wonderment for several minutes.

"Is this the plane for the mission?" asked Dan curiously. "I've only ever seen these in collections and museums. It's a Beechcraft M18 C-45."

"Yes, it's Eisenhower's plane that he used during World War Two," replied the General.

"No disrespect, General, but this plane isn't going to get us to the United Kingdom," Dan said, confused.

"Why not?" asked Deena. She knew nothing of aeroplanes other than the boarding procedure at the airport.

"Okay, as beautiful as this plane is, with its wonderful forty-seven-foot wingspan with Pratt & Whitney Wasp Junior radial engines, with four hundred and fifty horsepower each, perhaps the General has forgotten it will only take us one thousand, five hundred and twenty-eight miles with total fuel capacity! So, if my calculations are correct, Wales is at least four and a half thousand miles away!" The General stood grinning wildly at Dan in his 'I know-it-all' rant.

"You're right, or you would be ordinarily. This C-45 was modified specifically for this mission. It is a six-seat staff transporter, but there are no longer six seats. Take a look," offered the General. Dan didn't need a second invitation. No sooner had the General suggested it than he was at the plane's rear, hauling himself inside. He stood in awe at the extensive modifications.

Dan exited the plane to speak with the General, leaving Deena sitting against the wall. Planes had never been on her agenda, but the thought of running out of fuel over the Atlantic was not something she relished. So, Deena watched on as Dan and the General spoke. Finally, tiredness and the cold got the better of her. So, she pulled her knees up, folded her arms, and rested her head. Although unsure how long she had slept, she awoke to Dan and the General's voices next to her. "… and I'll start the fuel pump. Get Kross sorted out with what she needs on board first."

"No problem, General, and thanks," said Dan.

"What have I missed?" asked Deena groggily.

"Hello, wakey wakey, we've got stuff to do," said Dan grinning like a Cheshire cat.

"What are you so happy about?" she asked.

"Nothing," he replied, desperately trying to curb his enthusiasm. "Come on; we need to get you some supplies for your trip."

Dan marched towards the hangar's storerooms with Deena. She wasn't looking forward to the mission and summoning any enthusiasm was getting more difficult as time went on. Dan swung the door open to the first storeroom and began rummaging in a box.

"What are you looking for?" asked Deena.

He looked back over his shoulder at her and grinned. "Army food sachets," he replied. Dan continued rummaging and put aside tan-coloured boxes with pouches inside them. Curious, she picked up a couple and read the labels.

"MRE Beef Stew with potatoes and vegetables, Vegetarian Chilli with beans, Cheese Tortellini? How the hell do they work?" she asked.

"Open the box up, and there is a waterproof sachet. You put it in the plastic bag, add a little water, reseal it, and it heats up. Soldiers use them in military operations. I don't know if they taste nice, but I suppose you'll eat anything if you're hungry enough," Dan said. "Here, put some in this duffle bag."

"I'm glad I smuggled cookies in my backpack now," said Deena.

"Better take these as well," he said, handing her emergency water sachets. "Right, next storeroom. Okay, it would help if you had a jacket, it's cold, and it will get colder without daylight," Dan said. "Try that on. What shoe size?" Dan asked as he handed her a thermal jacket.

"An eight," she said. Dan handed her a pair of hiking boots.

"The General said there are thermal blankets in here," he muttered, shifting boxes. "Go through that pile of stuff," he said, pointing to a stock of camouflage clothing. "They may be amongst that lot. Vest tops... ah, thermal socks? Good idea," he said, throwing a couple of one-size-fits-all over his shoulder. "Here we go, 'Emergency thermal blankets,' put a couple in," he said. "Okay, that's it, you can't take anything more. The plane is on maximum load with the fuel modifications. So, this and your backpack are as much as you can take."

"I'm a bit warmer now," she said, hugging herself in her new thermal jacket. "I hate being cold."

Dan laughed, picked up the duffle bag and said, "Let's get this stuff on board. I'll give you a plane tour while the General finishes fuelling up."

Dan pulled himself into the plane and offered his hand. As he helped her into the aircraft, she did a double take at the interior. "What the hell is that in the middle of the gangway?" she asked.

"That is the extra fuel tank to get us over the Atlantic. The plane's strengthened to carry the extra weight of the tank, which feeds fuel to both wings via lift-check valves," he said. "They give a constant fuel feed. Oh, and the engines have been changed. They are still Wasp Junior, but the SC-G gives more horsepower and a quicker take-off."

Deena's mind had gone completely blank by this point. "Tell me, will it get us there?" she asked.

Dan laughed. "Yes, it will," he reassured her.

"Good. Then that is all I need to know," said Deena.

Dan went to the front of the aircraft, placing the duffle bag on one of the two remaining seats in the plane. Deena sat and stretched her legs as far as space would allow.

"The General and I still have a few checks before you leave, but you can stay in here," he said, leaving for the rear exit. "We shouldn't take long."

Deena sat, lost in her thoughts. She missed Martin, Lily, and Ben so much. Not knowing if they were safe was killing her inside. But there was no time for feeling sorry for herself. Realising this, she jolted herself to the mission at hand. But then, the thought arose at the prospect of being stuck on this long flight with the General, and it was not an enthralling one. She wondered if he had a sense of humour; otherwise, this flight would be very laborious.

The General discussed the coordinates with Dan on the location map. "According to this, the coordinates for the Welsh coast are 51° 33′ 18.3" N 3° 46′ 20.7" W. The location target is 4.4 miles inland. The landing strip is outside the main walls. It may be a tricky landing as the only lighting will be from the plane," stated the General. "The flight will take around thirteen hours."

"Great, nothing like flying blind," Dan remarked. "Are you sure the runway is still there?" he checked.

"I liaised with the location three months ago. They confirmed the runway is still there but inactive for years," answered the General. "The refuelling tanks are topped up and located near the runway. What concerns me is if it's afflicted due to the comet storm. If so, it may have to be either a beach or field landing, which means hiking into the location. That said, refuelling will be impossible. Let's hope it is still okay."

"I wouldn't tell Deena. She has enough to deal with," suggested Dan.

"It's going to be challenging and dangerous. We don't know what Deena will encounter there. But, I agree, there is no point in causing undue stress. Is that her backpack over there?" queried the General. "Can you put it on board? She must have her equipment on this mission. Also, I need you to go through the final preflight checklist."

"Sure, no problem," said Dan.

Dan grabbed Deena's backpack and boarded the plane, squeezing himself past the fuel tank. Deena got up and gladly took it from him. "Thanks, I'd be in real trouble without that," she said. "I don't fancy my chances without it."

"You're going to be fine," he said. "You know what you're doing, but I understand why you're so nervous about fighting the unknown."

"Thanks for your vote of confidence. This trip will be a real blast with the General in tow," she said with a pinch of sarcasm. "Any idea on how long the flight is?" she quizzed.

"Thirteen hours," said Dan, grinning.

"How long!" exclaimed Deena. "No way! The General doesn't even have a sense of humour."

Dan laughed, "I need to do the preflight checks with the General. So, sit tight. I'll come and see you before takeoff."

Dan found the General at the plane's rear with a checklist. "I've done the exterior checks, is the interior in order?" the General asked Dan.

"Seems to be," Dan replied.

"Do a proper check," he said, handing him the checklist. "We need to be sure. We don't want anything going wrong mid-flight, do we?" he drilled.

Dan held his tongue and boarded the plane. Then, with preflight checks completed, the General beckoned Dan to follow him. "We must ready the bay. The hanger door works on a manual wheel," said the General, elevating the gigantic doors with ease using the geared wheel. "This is the internal door. There is another above ground, opening onto the runway. The airway tunnel between is on a steady incline to the surface."

"What speed do you taxi at?" asked Dan.

"A steady fifteen knots. The external door needs to be open for the plane to keep its speed, but we don't want to open it too early because of the Ground Crawlers. So, we must be ready to do it quickly. The plane needs to anticipate its speed with the elevation rate of the outer door," said the General. He pulled a ratchet handle beside the wheel to lock the hangar door open. "Are you okay with everything, Dan?" asked the General. "Once we embark on this, you know there is no going back, don't you?" he queried.

"Yes, General, I know," said Dan stretching out his hand. The General smiled, shaking his hand firmly.

Deena watched Dan and the General shake hands through the plane's windscreen from the cockpit doorway. Then, like old friends, they casually walked across the hangar. As they disappeared under the nose, she sat and waited. As annoying as she found Dan, she had developed a soft spot for his silly sense of humour and boyish attitude. It wouldn't be proper not to say goodbye. Also, there was an element that perhaps they would never see each other again. They had all been through so much already, and the success of this mission was entirely on her head. "Kross, are you ready?" asked the General.

"Hi, General," she said, surprised. "Sorry, I expected to see Dan before leaving."

"I wanted to say I understand how much pressure is on you," he said earnestly. "And I fully appreciate you're on the front line with this mission. Do you need anything further before taking off?" he asked.

"I think I'm as ready as I can be, and thanks for saving my hide with that Ground Crawler. Do you think they are specific to here?" she asked.

"There is no way of telling. They could be anywhere. So, keep your guard up," he advised.

"Where is Dan? I was hoping to see him before we leave," she asked.

"He won't be long," he said, giving her a casual salute as he left the plane.

Dan boarded the aircraft and stood in front of Deena with a big grin. "Are you ready to go?" he asked her.

"Yes, I will miss you, you idiot," she said, smiling at him.

"Aw, really?" he said, giving her a wink. He turned towards the cockpit without another word and sat in the pilot's seat.

"Where's the General?" asked Deena.

"This is your Captain speaking; please buckle up. We are ready for take-off," said Dan.

"Quit messing around! The General won't find it funny," giggled Deena.

"Who's messing around? Come on, get yourself up here. I need a co-pilot," he said.

Deena stood in the doorway, looking at Dan, confused. He pointed through the windscreen at the General waving across the hangar, then turned to walk into the airway tunnel. "Wait, where's he going?" she asked Dan.

"We need to give him ten minutes to get to the outer door before taxiing," he said.

"You mean you're flying me?" said Deena in disbelief. "Since when? Can you fly this thing?" she quizzed.

"Yes, I am flying you to the United Kingdom, and yes, I can fly this plane," said Dan, laughing at her incredulous face. "Come on now. We're a team, aren't we? There's no way you are leaving me behind," he added.

"This is bloody awesome!" she exclaimed as she sat in the co-pilot's seat, grinning from ear to ear.

"Are you sure you're not going to miss the General? He can fly you if you like," said Dan.

Deena shook her head fervently. "Nope, I'm cool flying with you," she replied.

"Right, let's get these engines fired up. We have a big adventure ahead of us," said Dan, flicking switches and checking dials.

"What do I do?" asked Deena, panicking.

"Don't worry. I'll give you clear, step-by-step instructions. Treat the controls gently. Slow controlled manoeuvers, okay? Don't worry; you'll soon get the hang of it," he reassured her.

Dan gently increased the speed to fifteen knots. The plane approached the airway tunnel as they began to taxi. When Dan saw the General opening the access door, he eased back, allowing him time to raise it high enough. Then, Dan increased his speed until they were on the runway. Opening the throttle to one hundred per cent, he dropped the flaps, ready to climb. When the tail wheel began to lift, Dan eased up the nose of the plane, maintained a steady pitch and retracted the landing gear. Deena watched in amazement. "It all looks so complicated," she said.

"Once you know what the instruments do, it's easy. Think of it like driving a car, but a little more complex. We'll have you flying this thing before we get to the Welsh coast. I'll teach you."

Deena wasn't so sure, but then she never thought she would be saving the world either. She gave Dan a nervous smile. "If you say so," she said.

"How about you figure out those MRE sachets," suggested Dan. "I don't know about you, but I'm hungry. You eat first, and then you can take over while I have mine. Don't worry; you won't have to do much. I'll be right here if you need me."

Dan couldn't help but think about how she had taken everything in her stride. 'She is a woman any man would be proud to have by their side,' thought Dan as a waft of food drifted into the cockpit. "Something smells nice," he said. "What you got?" he asked.

"Garlic and herb chicken breast," she replied between mouthfuls. "Yours is heating. Do you want to show me what to do with this plane?" she said. She sat in the pilot's seat as Dan explained how to maintain airspeed and altitude and keep the wings level with the altitude indicator.

"If the plane tilts, or the nose dips or rises, shout me. Just keep her steady 'as is,'" said Dan.

Dan unbuckled himself and followed his nose to the food. He watched her for a few minutes before eating. He laughed inwardly at the petrified but focused expression on her face.

CHAPTER FIVE

Dan and Deena spoke of what they may encounter and what they had been through at the facility. Also, Deena taught him about the spirit world and her experiences, and they prepared for what may lay ahead. Neither wanted to be exhausted from the offset, so they took turns to catnap during the flight. It was an arduous thirteen and a half hours before hitting the Welsh coastline. "I'm dropping our altitude to look for the runway," said Dan.

Deena watched below through the window as Dan banked the plane. "There's a landing strip between a walled estate and woodlands," said Deena.

"I see it," said Dan. "This place is huge. It will be like looking for a needle in a haystack." Dan aligned the plane and dropped the landing gear. "Buckle up. It's going to be a rough landing," he said.

As they descended, Deena glimpsed the manor house and its immediate grounds. "It's an ancient Gothic-style Victorian manor. Very creepy!" she shuddered.

The plane hit the runway, and the airstrip was uncomfortably close to the estate's wall. Deena braced herself as Dan slowed the aircraft. "Well, we're here," said Dan. "Let's have a quick look before refuelling."

Deena grabbed her backpack. Hugging themselves against the fifteen-foot stone wall, they crept alongside until they reached a pair of impressive wrought iron gates. Dan rattled the padlock and chain. Then, their eyes followed the long driveway to the dark silhouette of the foreboding manor house on the horizon, dominating the grounds.

They could hear undiscerning noises beyond the gates, and an ear-piercing scream resonated through the air. Dan gripped Deena's arm, terrified. Then, without taking his eyes off the grand manor, Dan exclaimed, "What in hell's name was that?"

"I've no idea. First, we need to find a key for this gate," replied Deena, yanking the padlock and chain. "Any ideas where we might find it?" With no response, she whispered firmly, "Dan!"

"What?" he asked, fervently glancing at the tree lines on both sides of the driveway.

"The key? Any ideas?" she asked him again.

"They should be expecting us, so it must be here somewhere. Let's get back to the plane first and refuel. If we need to make a fast getaway, we must ensure the plane is ready," said Dan.

"I don't fancy staying here any longer than we must either," said Deena. "Once we enter the grounds, the entities will know who we are and why we are here if they don't already."

Back at the plane, they looked for the fuel tank. When Dan had refuelled, he said, "The plane is ready for when we leave, which I hope is sooner rather than later, judging by the unearthly screeching we heard earlier. Do you want to eat before looking for the key?"

"Good idea," she said quietly. "It's not the most inviting place, and once we are within the grounds, we won't be able to return to the plane until we've got the crystal skull."

"Why not?" asked Dan.

"Entities can manipulate electrical systems and drain batteries to gain energy. So, we don't want them following us and messing with our only way out of here," said Deena.

"You're kidding me, right?" exclaimed Dan. "Shit, we don't stand a chance," he said, disheartened by this new revelation.

As Deena heated food in the back of the plane, she taught him how they could keep safe within the manor's walls. "We will have to find food within the grounds. There must be kitchens, but that's not what I'm most concerned about," said Deena, handing Dan his meal. "The General said Ground Crawlers may be here too. So, we must be careful. Perhaps we can find herbs as we did before."

"So, if we find useful stuff, we pick it up as we go?" asked Dan.

"I think that's the best way to do it. I don't know what's on the other side of the gates any more than you do. Speaking of which, any ideas where the key is?" she asked.

"Well, I know one thing. It's not under the welcome mat," he said, laughing.

"Can you try and be serious?" giggled Deena.

Dan grinned and said, "No, sorry, it's what gets me through this kind of shit. Seriously though, where would you hide it?"

"The most obvious place is where the fuel pump is, but it's not there. The only other place is in the walling itself," Deena puzzled, "but the wall is huge, not to mention miles long around the estate. It would take forever to search it," she said.

"Okay, how about the wall areas, such as the gate posts or finials?" asked Dan.

"Wait, that's it!" exclaimed Deena. "The key to any building is the foundation stone!" She eagerly grabbed her backpack and called to Dan, "Are you coming?"

Deena steadily crept alongside the wall towards the first corner. It seemed solid. "It's not here," she said, disappointed. "Let's work our way around." Deena searched for possible hiding places at the base of the gate pillars, but there was nothing, so they skirted to the far corner. As her hands felt the stonework, she found a crevice in the mortar. As Deena gripped the edge, it moved. "I think I've found it!" she said. "Give me a hand." Dan knelt and inched the stone until it finally surrendered, revealing a key behind it. Dan gave the key to Deena, and she waved it at him with a glint in her eye that held an edge of fear and excitement. Finally, they stood in front of the gates. Deena paused before turning the key. "Are you sure you want to go in with me? I understand if you want to wait in the plane," she said.

"Are you kidding me?" he said, surprised. "There is no way I'm letting you go by yourself. We do this together."

Deena was relieved to hear him say that. She turned the lock and unravelled the chain around the wrought iron gates. Dan pulled one open wide enough to slip through. The gate grated and squealed with the enormous weight on its hinges. "Well, if they didn't know we were already here, they do now," said Deena, cringing at metal scraping against metal as Dan closed the gates. Dan threaded the chain and snapped the padlock shut. "There's a small zip compartment on the front of my backpack. Put the key in there so it's accessible if we need to leave quickly," she suggested.

Deena and Dan walked the long driveway towards the manor. The fine gravel crunched beneath their feet. The dark trees on either side were terrifying. Dan suddenly stopped. "Something is following us through the trees. I heard twigs breaking," Dan said, unsettled. "It feels like there are eyes on us. As if something is watching us."

"Keep moving," urged Deena. Dan's eyes darted left to right, figuring out what was following them. Each time he searched the darkness, he glimpsed movement or shadows but could determine very little. Deena kept her eyes forward and walked with steady determination.

"Aren't you even scared?" he asked, mystified at her unwavering advancement.

"I'm petrified," she said with a steely look. "But you can't let them sense that. They see it as a weakness and will attack before we get to the manor. So, please, keep moving."

The tree line broke as they approached the drive a third of the way. The ground now lay open. Dan felt more comfortable as whatever was following them seemed to stop in the confines of the trees.

"Over there," said Dan pointing right. "They look like old cottages. Do you want to go and have a look?" he suggested.

"No, let's get to the manor house and work our way around methodically. That way, we know where we have and haven't been," she said.

Dan felt deflated as his sense of adventure kicked in. Fallen statues and shrubs sporadically decorated either side of the drive until they came to a path leading to a long building. It was adorned at the front by two large ornate fountains on either side, with stone balustrades that housed flower beds. But, unfortunately, at the far end, some stonework had collapsed.

"This is amazing," Dan remarked. "Do you know what this is?" he questioned.

"You're the archaeologist, you tell me," she said sarcastically.

"It's an orangery, the biggest I've ever seen," he said.

"Fascinating," Deena sighed. "Come on. We need to go."

The closer they got, the more colossal the building looked as it loomed over them. The moonlight behind cast shadows from the many turrets and towers down the driveway. They stared at it from the bottom of the steep steps before them. "It's like something out of a horror movie," Dan said as he climbed the steps. Beautiful railings ran up each flight, and every plateau boasted grand rockeries and flower beds. They were glad to leave the steps behind them as they walked towards the main house.

"There's a maze over there," he said, pointing east of the manor, "with a pagoda in the centre."

"Dan, this place is massive; it will take weeks to search," said Deena.

"Well, apparently, neither of us has anything better to do," he said casually, standing at the manor's main doors. They were arched, solid wood double doors studded with heavy metal fastenings. Dan turned to Deena and said, "Hey, if I knock, do you think Lurch will answer?"

"You're not funny," she giggled. Deena playfully pushed him aside and twisted the hooped iron door handle. She heard a bolt latch lift on the other side. She looked at Dan and said, "It's open, come on."

Deena asked Dan for the flashlight. Dan closed the door behind them as he passed it to her. She swung the beam of light around. An elaborate marble fireplace was seated on the wall to her right, with wood-panelled walls. The ceiling was beautiful with embellished plasterwork. In front of her was a set of identical wooden doors. It was a grand foyer for an exquisite manor. The slate flooring was smooth from footsteps coming and going over centuries. Dan looked in astonishment. "The British certainly did it with style," he said.

"Right now, I'm more intrigued at who or what we will find behind these doors," she replied, pushing them open.

Nothing could have prepared them for the vast reception room. In the centre was a stately staircase. The two-tiered stairway built in carved stone was met at the top by a doorway. The steps continued to the left and right onto a circular balcony on either side. Deena shone the flashlight above them, revealing a hexagonal domed glass ceiling. Thick, stone pillars met in arches supporting the balconies above. Rooms were accessible all around them. The enormity was overwhelming. "Where do we start?" asked Dan.

"I need to find the basics. So, let's start left," said Deena, pointing through an archway at the door nestled under the balcony. Deena opened it, peering in and panned the flashlight down the room's length. "It's a library," she said.

A writing desk at the far end had books piled on it untidily. Shelves ran from floor to ceiling, some had collapsed, and books littered the floor. Dan gasped, catching Deena's attention. They stood motionless in fear as a white lady in a Victorian dress appeared from nowhere. A hazy, blue hue surrounded her ghostly aura. She appeared for a few seconds, pointing at the writing desk before vanishing through the far wall. Dan slowly turned to Deena and said, "Please tell me you saw that."

"Incredible, a full-bodied apparition!" she said in disbelief. "I've never seen one that clearly before."

"Perhaps it's the darkness," Dan said. "Remember, I told you how the darkness shall empower the unseen."

"That makes sense. It takes enormous energy for an entity to manifest, but if the darkness feeds them power, we should expect they can do more too."

"What do you mean, more?" asked Dan, worried.

"Like throw or move objects, inflict injuries, affect our emotions and so on," she said.

Dan's stomach somersaulted. He exclaimed slightly higher than usual, "You are joking! Are you messing with me?"

"No," said Deena. "I wish I were. What was she pointing at anyway?" she implored.

"The writing desk," answered Dan, shuddering. He picked up a couple of books and read the titles. "Some of these are old but not significant," muttered Dan.

"Maybe," she said, "there's something in it we need to find." There were four drawers on each side of the desk. Deena searched one side and Dan the other. "Found anything?" she asked.

"No," he replied. "I'll search the top again."

He took books from the top and stacked them on the floor, and as he lifted the third pile of literature, there was a small wooden box. He picked it up and opened it, revealing three candles. "That's handy," said Deena smiling. "I haven't replacement batteries for the flashlight."

"No matches," he said. Then, he paused and asked, "Do you think the white lady is trying to help us?"

"Seems that way," said Deena.

As they left the library, Dan wondered who the white lady was. She was well dressed and stately in manner. 'Perhaps,' he thought, 'a former Lady to the manor.' She was beautiful and moved with grace and elegance, encompassing an aristocratic air of authority and dignity. They walked under the balcony to the far corner. Deena placed her ear to the door. She knew sooner or later that they would encounter something unpleasant on the other side.

"Dan, pass me the tri-field meter. It would be safer to have an inkling before entering any more rooms," she said. Unsure, Dan picked out two meters. Deena took one and switched the unit on, placing her thumb on the small metal disc to earth herself. She adjusted the two dials until the LEDs showed green. Slowly, she opened the door, sweeping the meter from side to side. The walls were wood-panelled halfway, above which huge paintings hung. Finally, Dan got the torch and shone it on each picture. "Look!" exclaimed Deena. "There's an aerial picture of the grounds."

"That lake is huge, and there are islands. There are lots of outbuildings, too," he remarked.

"This gives us an idea of what we are up against," said Deena, trying to memorise it.

"That's her!" said Dan, pointing the flashlight at a portrait. He read the brass inscription, "Lady Amelia. 1872–1910."

"She must love this place to be here still. She must have seen everything over the years, perhaps even where Eisenhower hid the crystal skull!" exclaimed Deena.

"The date she died would suggest it," said Dan.

As they walked back through the gallery, the tri-field meter flickered orange, indicating energy to their right. Deena stopped. "Wait," she said. The LEDs turned red as she swung to face the wall. "There could be something on the other side. But the walls are too thick for the meter to detect through them."

Deena ran her hands down the wood panelling. Then, startled, she snatched her hand back. "Something touched my hand!" cried Deena. Nervously, she put her palm back against the panel. An ice-cold hand grabbed hers, pulling her forward, jarring her wrist. Deena was amazed to see a hidden door swing open. "What the hell?" she exclaimed, opening the door. She turned to Dan, "It leads back into the library."

"So, the white lady is trying to help us," said Dan.

Deena wasn't happy about being grabbed by an entity, but at least she wasn't a threat. They stepped back into the gallery, closing the secret door. Deena reset the tri-field meter before continuing under the balcony, leading to the rear of the main staircase. "Shush, can you hear singing?" whispered Deena.

"Is it coming from upstairs?" whispered Dan.

"I'm not sure; it's echoing all around us," said Deena.

Deena stood beside the staircase, trying to pinpoint the sound. She could see the balconies above. "It sounds like a little girl singing a nursery rhyme. It's eerie." Suddenly it stopped. "The singing; I can't hear it now," she said, retracing her steps.

Slightly unnerved, they carried on as planned. A couple of arches took them to a corridor at the rear of the house. Directly in front of them was a big heavy door with two doors on either side. Dan opened the one now in front, then quickly closed it. "What's wrong?" asked Deena, laughing. "You look like you've seen a ghost."

Dan shook his head, "Ground Crawlers!" he muttered through gritted teeth.

Deena froze on the spot. "The General said they may be here." She slowly opened the door to her left. Peering in, they could see Ground Crawlers through the window. "I think we've found the kitchen, though," said Deena, whispering.

Dan put his finger to his lips and whispered, "Be very quiet and look for what you need. I'll keep watch."

The kitchen had wood-burning stoves running along the outer wall. Deena searched for matches. Finally, she found a box and shook it. There were only five, but it was a start. She systematically searched every cupboard, shelf, and pantry. Working her way to the rear, she came upon another door. She opened it, but with no windows for moonlight, it was pitch black. Not wanting to waste the few matches she had found, Deena asked Dan for the flashlight. Dan glanced out of the window, double-checking on the Ground Crawlers before taking it to her. "I found matches, sea salt, and this," said Deena, handing him a small glass vial. "It looks weird."

Dan took the vial and held it at eye level, tilting it back and forth. "They used these vials to keep medicines in years ago, but I have no idea what the liquid is. It's thicker than water, with a strange pearlescent glow," said Dan. He pulled the tiny cork stopper out of the bottleneck and sniffed the curious fluid. Immediately Dan's nose wrinkled, recoiling at the strong odour. "It stinks!" he exclaimed. "It smells like aniseed and antiseptic. Here, you smell it."

"No thanks," said Deena distastefully. "We'll take it with us; perhaps we could use it if it has antiseptic properties." Dan went back to check on the Ground Crawlers while Deena panned the torch in the next room. It was another kitchen. At the far end was a small laundry room to one side, and at the back were two doors. She opened the one to her left and was surprised

71

to find a servant's stairs that went up to the first floor to an arched doorway and then turned up to the second floor in a spiral fashion. Deena resisted the temptation to see where it led. Instead, she opened the other door; steep, cold stone steps carved their way into the darkness of the cellars. "I hate cellars; they're creepy places," she muttered as Dan appeared by her side.

"The Ground Crawlers have moved into the woodlands. So, what's down there?" he asked.

"Cellars, and that one," she said, pointing to her left, "is the servant's stairs to the upper floors."

"Handy to know if we need another way other than the main staircase," he remarked. "Did you find any herbs?" he asked.

"No, but they may store them in the cellar. Also, there is food in some of the cupboards. So, people must have lived here before Ragnarök," said Deena.

"Maybe they left before the comet storm as we haven't exactly had a welcome party," said Dan.

"Let's go. I'm not wasting time searching for people," said Deena.

Walking back through the kitchens, Deena paused at the window. Much to her relief, there was no sign of the Ground Crawlers. They crossed the corridor to the room opposite the kitchens with the tri-field meter and flashlight in hand. The door opened into an elaborate hall where luxurious drapes dressed the tall windows. A polished mahogany dining table was in the centre with twenty-eight Georgian high-backed banqueting chairs. Silver candelabras decorated the centre line of the table. Dan ran his fingers across the smooth, lustrous surface, briefly stopping to pick up one of the candelabras, testing its weight in his hand. "This is worth a small fortune," he said with a whistle of admiration. A chaise longue sat between two double doors halfway down. Dan's eyes swept upwards of the flock wallpaper and velvet drapes, resting on the stunning crystal chandeliers dominating the ceiling. At either end, in each corner, there were matching seventeenth-century cabinets intricately inlaid with mother of pearl in a petite flower design. Dan asked Deena if she wanted to go through them.

"Let me know if you find anything. I'll search this one," replied Deena. Opening one of three drawers across the top, Deena sifted through what was probably the most refined silver cutlery she had ever seen. Then, kneeling, she opened both cabinet doors stacked with dinner service plates. Dan went to help her, handing her a box of matches. Having emptied the cabinet of its contents, Deena shone the flashlight inside; there was nothing more to find. She grasped the edge of the cabinet's frame to steady herself, and as she pulled herself up, her fingertips felt the top plinth inside the cabinet move. "That's odd," remarked Deena, kneeling again. She stuck her head back inside the cabinet. Then, she placed her palms on the plinth, pushing it outwards.

"It's a secret drawer. Don't struggle. I can pull it out," said Dan. Deena wriggled out of the cabinet. "I'm not sure what this is. It's burnt on one end," said Dan, handing her two candles, a third that was half burnt, and a whole box of matches.

"It's a sage bushel! You use it to combat spirits! Entities can't stand the smell of dried sage when it's burning. It repels them."

"So, that's good, right?" he said.

"It's more than good. It will be a massive help if we can find more," said Deena.

Deena examined the other three cabinets to see if they also had a secret drawer, but they yielded no more hidden compartments. Dan caught up with Deena at the other end of the hall. "So, if the sage smells that bad, can we use it against the Ground Crawlers?" he asked.

Deena nodded. "It's not that it smells horrible. On the contrary, it's a powerful smell. I don't know why it repels spirits. All I know is that it works and has for centuries. Of course, it won't work the same way with the Ground Crawlers because they aren't entities, but we could use it to disguise our body scent as we did before with the herbs. If someone has gone to the trouble to bind one sage bushel, it stands to reason there will be more," she said.

Deena paused in the doorway to get her bearings. It was identical to the corridor they crossed between the kitchen and the banqueting hall. The heavy door to her left would no doubt lead outside. She shone the flashlight right and saw the arches continue under the balcony towards the manor's front. Deena stepped across the passageway, motioning for Dan to follow. Cautiously, she twisted the doorknob, and as she was about to open it, she heard children giggling. Dan's eyes widened with fear, accompanied by a visual plea for an explanation from Deena. She had no answer.

CHAPTER SIX

Deena grabbed Dan's arm, pulling him into the room and shutting the door quietly behind them. "Do you think they are survivors?" asked Dan, reservedly.

"I doubt it. If they were living, they would have shouted hello or something. But, instead, it sounded etheric; it was everywhere, but nowhere," whispered Deena.

"Yes, but we are talking about kids. We should check if they are okay. The acoustics would make anyone sound echoic in this place," whispered Dan.

"Don't be fooled," she said, shaking her head with gravity.

"They're just kids. Even if they're not living, how much of a threat could they be?" he said. "I think we should check, that's all."

"And maybe that's what they or it wants. Are you aware that demons are known for disguising themselves as children to lure you into a false sense of security? So, go if you feel you must, but count me out," said Deena.

"Put like that, maybe not," muttered Dan.

"If you want to stay alive, let me give you some advice. When dealing with the unseen, nothing is as it seems. Demons and malevolent spirits are masters of deception," she said firmly.

Deena took stock of the room they had entered. Tall, neatly spaced windows were swagged in silk and cascaded onto the highly polished floor, giving an impressive appearance. To the left was a beverage bar, which met a stage encompassed by theatre drapes. Chaise longues and luxury chairs sat amongst ornate tables across the room. Deena began searching behind the bar. Shattered glassware crunched beneath her feet. The location had not taken any direct hits, but the comet storm had shaken its walls. Nevertheless, this manor had stood the test for hundreds of years before Ragnarök.

"Dee, come here," said Dan, peeping outside between the window drapes.

"What's wrong?" she asked. "Are the Ground Crawlers back?" she continued.

"They don't have eyes," he said, concerned. "Watch the tree line to the far left of the lawn."

Deena watched for a few minutes and spotted several pairs of orange eyes glinting in the moonlight. "They could be a herd of deer," she said.

"They look a lot bigger than deer," muttered Dan.

"We can't worry about that right now," she said.

Dan began searching the nearest cabinet to him while Deena returned to the bar, working her way towards the stage. She pulled the theatre drapes aside to find cubbyholes. Deena ran her hands across the shelving. Besides much dust, each cubby proved empty until she knelt to check the bottom shelf. Her fingers fumbled for a small disc-shaped object in the far corner. Deena placed it in the palm of her hand. It felt strange to touch. A tingling sensation prickled her fingertips as she traced the peculiar symbol. Finally, she called to Dan, "Hey, Dan, I need your expertise, any idea what this is?"

"It's a rune, the Algiz." His eyes lit up, explaining that, in Norse mythology, runes were not only an ancient alphabet, but each symbol had a meaning and a deity. "The art of rune casting is still practised in some circles of paganism to tell the past, present and future."

"I've heard of it, but I've never delved into it, to be honest. So, do you know what this rune means?" asked Deena.

"It's the rune of protection and defence. We certainly could do with some of that," stated Dan.

"How do we use it?" she asked, not understanding how such a small object could offer them protection.

"The runes have an energy of their own," he told her.

"Is that why I could feel a tingling when I touched the symbol?" she asked him.

"Yes, the deity attached to this rune is Heimdall. He is, or should I say was, 'The Watcher' at the Bifröst Bridge in the gods' worlds.

"What's the Bifröst Bridge?" asked Deena.

"The Bifröst Bridge connects the gods' worlds to ours. Heimdall's duty was to sound the horn to warn the Norse gods of Ragnarök's impending arrival. All you need to do is focus on the rune's energy, call upon Heimdall and ask him to grant you protection," he told her.

"Do you want it?" she asked Dan.

Dan placed the rune in her palm and closed her hand over it. Immediately, she felt the energy spreading through her fingers and tracing up her arm. Deena quickly put it in her pocket. "Have you finished in here?" she asked.

"Not quite. There are a couple of cabinets on the other end," replied Dan.

"You do one, and I'll do the other?" suggested Deena.

They searched the cabinets, but there was nothing more to find. However, before they left, Dan felt urged to look for the eyes in the woods. But from this end of the ballroom, he could only see an open courtyard with stable blocks on one side and coach houses on the other. An elaborate archway spanned the carriage driveway into the yard from the far end. He headed back to Deena, who was already poised to leave.

The door to the next room was already ajar. Dan gently pushed it open. The room was L-shaped with ornate leaded windows swathed in blue and gold velvet drapes. They were beautiful but not as sumptuous as those in the ballroom. There was an oak stand with a large globe. So, Dan separated it at its hinged equator, revealing a whiskey decanter and glasses. The dual functionality amused him. Deena sighed, "They certainly liked their creature comforts. It's going to take ages to search this room."

Deena searched the section to the front of the manor, and Dan started at the fireplace. It was a slow process of elimination, one piece of furniture at a time. Finally, Deena came upon a bureau. Inside the roll-top were tiny letter drawers. She pulled them out one by one, examining the contents. "Hey, Dan, what do you make of this?" she asked, handing him an old rolled-up parchment neatly secured with a white ribbon.

"It says 'Spirit' on it," he said.

Deena pointed to the pictograph and said, "That's the symbol for spirit. It's one of the elements. In Wiccan belief, there are five elements, each with a symbol. The other four are earth, air, fire, and water. I have a gut feeling that this scroll could be important. I'm not sure why, but we should take it," she said.

"Was there anything in the drawer to explain what it's for?" he asked.

"Only a couple of paperweights," she answered.

Dan picked up one, rolled it around in his hand, and said, "I don't think

76

they are paperweights. They are usually flat on the bottom. The smooth side is a deeper oval shape than the diamond-cut side."

"Do you know what they are cut from?" she asked.

"If my geology studies serve me right, they look like black onyx. But I confess," said Dan, pondering their structure, "I have no idea what they are for or if they are just decorative. I've seen a lot of crystals and ornate stones archaeologically, but not of this shape." Dan put it back in the drawer with the other and closed the bureau, not realising their significance and the part they would play in their mission to restore light to the world. Having searched the drawing room, they had come full circle and were back at the manor's entrance. Cautiously, they stood at the bottom of the imposing staircase. Remembering the childish giggling they heard earlier echoing from above, they looked at each other and then up the impending steps. They shared a combination of uncertainty and dread about who or what was up there.

As Dan climbed the first step, Deena held him back. "Wait a minute," she said, grabbing his backpack. She pulled out the Gaussmeter, switched it on, offered it to Dan and said, "I think it would be better if we both had one. I've got a bad feeling about what's up there, so put this salt pouch in your pocket." Then, she took out the sage bushel and the matches, stuffing them into her jacket pocket. "We need to be prepared to deal with whatever may be."

"How do I use this?" he whispered.

"Push the button and point it around, and if it reads any electromagnetic energy, it will sound an alarm. The stronger the energy, the higher the pitch. No rocket science involved," said Deena. She took the initiative and began climbing the staircase. Every step was a concerted effort for Dan. His legs felt like lead, weighing heavy with fear. Finally, halfway up, they reached the plateau. Deena shone the torch around the balustrade, skirting the balcony above. It was eerily quiet. The stillness in the air breathed wariness into the core of their souls.

Deena cautiously walked the plateau, flicking the flashlight around them. Then, she pointed to the left of the stairs, indicating to start that side and work around. Dan opened the iron-hinged wooden door at the top of the staircase, revealing the servant's stairs running down to the kitchens and up to the floor above. He closed it and quickened his pace to catch up with

Deena. "There are so many bedrooms. Do you want to do alternate rooms each?" asked Dan.

"No chance. I don't think splitting up is a good idea," she whispered as her eyes scanned the balcony.

"Thank God. That's what I was hoping you'd say," said Dan, sighing with relief.

Deena readied herself to open the first bedroom door. She glanced at the tri-field meter, not a flicker. Finally, she asked Dan, "Could you watch my back, please? Use the Gaussmeter." Deena's request gave away how nervous she was. Dan gave a reassuring smile. But there was no fooling each other. They felt an overpowering sense of trepidation far more reaching than anything they had experienced thus far. The room they entered was huge. There was a queen-size four-poster bed complete with a canopy, walnut wardrobes, chests of drawers, and a vanity table housing personal effects. Dan picked up a full-length mirror that had fallen. He stood before the swivel stand and slotted it back onto its hinges. As he did, he glimpsed his disfigured reflection in the broken shards. But that was not all. He spun around, aiming the Gaussmeter in front of him. Deena rushed over. "What's wrong? Did you see something?" she asked urgently.

Dan tried to speak, but the words didn't come. His expression was gaunt, and with a fixed stare, he raised a trembling hand, pointing to the corner of the room. Hurriedly, Deena delved into the backpack for the night vision binoculars. Switching between infrared and night vision, she scrutinised the area where Dan was pointing, but there was nothing. Confused, she asked Dan again what he had seen. "It was a kid, a little girl with pigtails and ringlets, standing behind me, staring at me!" he exclaimed. "I only saw her for a split second in the mirror's reflection, but when I turned around, she'd disappeared." Dan shuddered; nothing was freakier to him than the prospect of being haunted by a ghost child.

"Well, there's nothing here now. How old do you reckon the child is?" asked Deena.

"About eight or nine years old, wearing a long white dress and Victorian boots. It must have been her we heard singing and giggling earlier," replied Dan.

"Expect trouble then," said Deena. "Girls of that age are a bloody handful. Everything naughty is funny. They spend their time seeing how far they can push adults before they lose their temper. Then, they turn on the waterworks to get their way," stated Deena.

"Oh, wow. It sounds like your parents had their hands full," chuckled Dan.

Deena chose to ignore Dan's cheeky remark. Instead, she kept her poise and continued the search. Deena came upon a washroom with an elegant, free-standing bath in the centre, with his and her porcelain sinks to one side. She opened the wash cabinets, searching through the odds and ends on the shelving. Deena sighed; exhaustion set in as she opened the cupboards below the sinks, pulling out towels and flannels. In keeping with his promise, Dan watched her back. As he aimlessly stared at the bundle of towels on the floor, he saw something sticking through one. It looked like the tip of a blade. So, he squatted down, unwrapping the towel to expose what looked like a broken ornate knife. He held the six-inch knife blade to the moonlight at the window. It was a double-edged blade; through its centre were three runic markings, and a fourth was partially visible at the jagged end. He turned it over, showing more runes. It seemed to be forged from neither metal nor stone.

Deena hadn't found anything of use and began putting the towels back. "Dee, can I have the flashlight?" asked Dan.

Deena passed it to him while cramming towels into the cupboard with the other hand. Dan held the flashlight to the blade, trying to determine its physical matter. Finally, Deena asked, "What have you found?"

"I'm not sure. It looks like hard granite, but there are silver metal threads through it," Dan pondered.

"Is it possible to combine the two?" she asked.

"There are runes inscribed on it," he said without taking his eyes off the blade.

Deena re-opened the cupboard, took out a face flannel, and handed it to him. "Here," she said, "wrap it up. We can figure it out later. We need to get moving. I don't want to stay in one place too long," she said hurriedly.

They left the washroom, and Dan walked to a door at the far end. "Have you looked in here yet?" he asked.

Deena shook her head. "Not yet."

Dan was about to open it when a little girl's laughter filled the room. They both turned to see the apparition Dan saw in the mirror's reflection earlier. She stood innocently with her hands clasped behind her back, smiling. "Hello, I'm Charlotte," she said, giggling.

"What the… actual fuck!" exclaimed Dan in a hoarse whisper.

Deena backed up slowly towards Dan and shook his arm hard, muttering, "Get out… get… out!"

Before they could enter the adjoining bedroom, Charlotte giggled, teleporting towards them, singing as she got closer, "One, two, we see you!"

Together they stumbled through the door in their haste. Dan kicked the door shut as he fell to the floor. As he rolled onto his knees, he saw Deena suddenly stop. In the far corner of the bedroom, the little girl stood staring. Her eyes bore into them. "Dan! Give me the salt!" screamed Deena.

Dan frantically fumbled in his pocket for the salt pouch, throwing it to Deena. Without taking her eyes off the child, she opened it, grabbed a handful of salt crystals, and threw it towards the apparition. The little girl laughed, glaring at them with cold, dark eyes as she shot her arms up, launching the salt back at them using telekinesis. Their faces stung from the force of the salt pelting their skin. "I'm Emily," she giggled, "we're having fun."

Deena and Dan panicked. There are two of them? They frantically looked about; there was no way out except to return the same way they came in. Deena pulled out the sage and matches from her pocket. The terror flowing through her body caused her hands to shake uncontrollably. She struck it too hard, and it snapped. Emily's giggles resonated around them. Dan helped Deena light the sage; she gently blew on it, encouraging it to smoulder. Thick smoke began to billow, and Deena wafted it in Emily's direction.

As it wisped around her, she disappeared. With the sage still burning, they ran back into the first bedroom. Charlotte was waiting for them. She was sitting innocently on the edge of the four-poster bed, swinging her legs as she sang with a haunting laugh, "Three, four, don't open the door!" Deena kept a smokescreen between them and Charlotte.

Stepping back onto the balcony, Deena and Dan desperately smothered the door behind them with the smoke, praying it would be enough to stop the Twins from following them. They listened to the silence. Perhaps it was over for now. The sage was burning low. Deena knew they needed to find more, and quickly. So, she tapped the burning end against the stone wall, stubbing it out. Dan headed towards the main staircase, stopping by the servant's stairs. He put his ear to the door.

"What now?" asked Deena, her shoulders slumped with weariness.

"I can hear a kitten mewing," he whispered, and without thinking, he pulled the door open. Firstly, he looked down the steps. He couldn't see anything moving that was kitten-sized. Then, his eyes rose to the stairs above. He listened again. There it was—faint —but it was a kitten's cry. He stepped through the doorway onto the stairs, glaring into the dark, searching for the little furry critter. Finally, his eyes rested at the top of the steps. Suddenly, there was a familiar giggle, and one of the Twins jumped down a step at him from out of the darkness.

Dan jumped back, pushing Deena out of his way. "Five, six, we play tricks!" sang Emily, cocking her head disjointedly. Dan grabbed Deena's arm, slamming the door shut, and they frantically ran down the stairs. Deena tripped, and Dan tried to grab her, but she was too far in front, and she tumbled down the steps to the plateau. She cried out in pain as she clutched her ankle. Dan helped Deena to her feet and tried to support her. He dared to look back; Emily and Charlotte stood at the top of the stairs, holding hands and watching with delight. Amusement and hilarity laced their laughter. To stop now would be suicidal. As Deena took the last step, Dan turned to look up the stairs once more.

In unison, Charlotte and Emily sang, "Seven, eight, there's no escape."

Dan watched, horrified as hairline cracks began to travel up their necks, splintering as they formed. Their childlike faces started to disintegrate. A thick dark mist seeped from within them, causing chunks of their ghostly complexion to fall away. Their eyes turned the deepest black. Dan had seen enough; this was the most disturbing experience he had ever witnessed. Terror filled his mind, and he wasn't waiting to find out what followed 'nine, ten.' He quickly pulled Deena around the base pillar of the staircase; she was in so much pain. Balancing on one leg, she reached down to rub her ankle. The disc in her pocket pressed against her thigh as she bent over. A tingling sensation prickled her skin. She thrust her hand into her jeans pocket and grasped the rune. Then, realising what she had in her hand, Dan frantically urged her to use it. Above them, he could hear the Twin's distant voices.

"We tried, Nanny," one said.

"Nanny, Nanny, he got it," said the other, followed by a loud door slam.

"Hurry," said Dan panicking. Deena pressed the rune tightly between her palms. An emotional wave came over her as energy charged through her being. Her veins felt like a hot web of electrical wires, pulsing through every fibre of her body. Finally, Deena closed her eyes and screamed out in her mind, 'Heimdall, Heimdall, we need your protection, I beg you. Please, please grant us protection. Heimdall...' Each time she pleaded, the pressure in her head intensified. Then, on the verge of passing out, her leg gave way, and she fell back against the staircase wall. Dan tried to support her, but he fell forward, putting his hand against the panel inset behind her to keep her on her feet. It swung inwards, and together they fell into a hidden room under the stairs.

Stunned by what seemed to be an aided discovery, both sat silently for a moment. Dan spoke first. "It seems Heimdall heard you," he said, shocked.

"We would never have found this," said Deena shakily. "It was weird. I wasn't here when I called on Heimdall."

"You're not making sense. I was standing beside you," said Dan.

"I wasn't... I don't know," Deena gestured to herself. "I wasn't in my physical body. I was nowhere. Then, the next thing, I'm spiralling out of control, and I'm in here. Do you think I had an out-of-body experience?" asked Deena.

"I don't know, maybe," he replied. "I'm beginning to believe in things I never thought were possible or even existed."

"Well, whatever, it seems to have worked," said Deena, smiling.

Dan switched the flashlight on and pushed the panel back, enclosing them under the stairs. "Find a candle, save the flashlight for emergencies," proposed Deena. The flame flickered, giving a gentle light to the room. Deena realised they were under the plateau of the main staircase. "Do you think we'll be safe in here? I need to rest my ankle and perhaps get some sleep," she suggested.

"Sounds good to me," he replied. "I think we'll be fine. No one knows we are in here." Dan took the candle and began methodically pushing on the walls, looking for other hidden doors. Such was his focus, he wasn't expecting the ground to disappear under him. As his hands flailed to save himself, he dropped the candle putting them in complete darkness, which he accompanied with a string of profanities.

"Dan, are you okay?" whispered Deena, fumbling for the flashlight.

"For fuck's sake! There's a fucking hole in the floor!" whispered Dan irately.

Deena pointed the flashlight toward the endless spiel of foul language. Deena couldn't help but laugh as only his left leg, head, and shoulders were visible.

"Yeah, yeah, very funny. Could you give me a hand, please?" asked Dan, painfully self-conscious of his predicament.

Deena rested the flashlight on the floor and offered him a hand. Dan eased himself out and rolled across the floor, nursing his crotch. Then, Deena flashed the torch down the hole and said, "Not just a hole. There are steps leading to cellars." Then, with the candle re-lit, she melted a few drops of wax at the edge of the steps, set the candle in it and turned off the flashlight. "Are you okay now?" she asked.

"Yes, thank you," muttered Dan.

"Could you pass me the backpack?" asked Deena. Dan slid the bag across with his foot. Deena pulled the contents out and set the items they had found to one side. "We can't carry everything," she said. "The backpack is full as it is. Perhaps we could leave stuff here to return to."

"That would work, as it has two access points. So, you mean to use it as a base room? It's a good idea," said Dan, yawning.

Deena picked up the knife tip wrapped in the flannel and held it to the candlelight. "Have you given this more thought?" she whispered. There was no response. Deena looked at him, 'Great!' she thought. 'It looks like I'm on the first watch then.' So, she quietly made herself comfortable.

Deena managed to stay awake for an hour before dozing off. She woke up to Dan murmuring loudly in his sleep. In his dream state, he was desperately trying to cry out. As he lay on his back, his cries became more beseeching. Concerned, Deena attempted to wake him. "Dan, wake up; you're having a nightmare. Wake up!" she urged. There was no response, and his cries got louder. So, Deena knelt by his side, and as she reached to touch him, a demonic growl filled the room.

"He is mine!" snarled the presence.

Deena scrabbled backwards across the floor as bronze, snake-like eyes flashed in front of her. A female, winged, skeletal horned entity was hovering over him. "Get away from him!" screamed Deena. As Dan's chest rose from the floor, his arms and head hung limp as he let out a deathly moan. Deena shot back across the room to him. "You can't have him!" she screamed, grabbing Dan's shoulders and pushing him to the floor. Deena shook him violently. "Wake up!" she sobbed hysterically. Tears streamed down her face as she desperately tried to wake him. "Please, wake up, Dan. Wake up! Please, you can't leave me! Wake. Up!" she pleaded.

Dan abruptly drew a deep breath, and his eyes opened wide. A sudden wind rushed around the room, extinguishing the candle. The sound of beating wings and the deep hostile growls of the demon occupied every corner of the room. Then, stillness reigned. Deena pulled him close to her.

"I thought we'd be safe here," he said weakly.

"It's okay. We couldn't have foreseen her," said Deena.

"Who was she?" Dan asked. "I thought it was a dream at first."

"What you experienced was a succubus. In your dream state, you are vulnerable. It's what they do," explained Deena, fumbling for the matches to relight the candle.

"She was so beautiful and alluring," he muttered. "Her hair was flowing all around her and so seductive. Talk about a perfect body…" he trailed off.

"Sounds like you were enjoying yourself a little too much," she interrupted. "She only wanted your soul, Dan, nothing else. A succubus will do whatever it takes to get it."

"I realised that when she put her hand on my chest. I couldn't move. I was paralysed and at her mercy. I tried to shout, but it was impossible. What happened next was grotesque. Her flesh stretched and peeled away from her, leaving a grey, leathery skin. She had horns and the wings of a giant raven," he said, rubbing his hands over his eyes, trying to erase her image from his mind.

"If it's any consolation, a male demonic form preys on women. It's called an incubus. I don't think either of us is safe to sleep until I find more supplies," said Deena.

"So, why didn't you get attacked?" asked Dan.

"I wasn't asleep long enough. I had just started to doze off when I heard you crying out. Good job," said Deena, "otherwise, we could've been in real trouble."

"Where do you want to go next for supplies?" he asked her. "Do you want to go back to the kitchens?" he proposed.

"I was thorough. I don't think we'll find anything more there," said Deena.

"I'm not going upstairs with those bloody Twins. Did you hear what they said before we found this room?" he asked. "They were talking to someone called Nanny. They told her, 'He found it.' Do you think they were on about that knife tip?" he wondered.

"Why would the knife tip be so important?" asked Deena.

"Because I reckon it's forged from what they call in mythology, Uru metal. It combines metal and stone forged in the gods' world, Asgard. It's supposed to be extremely resilient," he told her.

"So, what's it doing here?" she asked.

"There are rune markings on it, which makes me think we are supposed to find it," he replied.

"But, if it's unbreakable, why is it in pieces?" she asked.

"I said resilient, not unbreakable. But, think about it, if it came from the gods' worlds during Ragnarök, perhaps it shattered on impact," implied Dan.

"Do you believe that?" asked Deena with a hint of disbelief.

"I think we should keep an open mind with everything that's happened since we got here, don't you?" replied Dan.

"You're right. But I have a problem getting my head around this Norse mythology stuff. The concept of its existence is beyond me. So, you're asking me to believe in something I've never heard of and know nothing about," she said.

"Um, says the paranormal expert to the rookie!" said Dan, laughing.

"Okay, you got me there," she said, grinning. "So, what do we do with it?"

"If we can find all the pieces, perhaps we can figure it out," suggested Dan.

"About the supplies," began Deena, "the only place we can go is down. We've been around the ground floor, and the upper floors aren't an option for the moment, and we are not prepared enough to go outside yet."

"Cellars it is then," said Dan.

"If I can find enough salt, I can protect us while we get some proper rest before continuing upstairs," she said as she lit a new candle.

At the bottom of the steps, they turned into a small cavern that opened into the main cellars. The pillars and passageways were reminiscent of a rabbit warren, a complex system of arched support pillars that housed storage within its catacombs. "You wouldn't believe this was down here looking from outside. These cellars are so cool," whispered Dan. The adventurer kicked back in as he wandered off towards the catacombs. Deena grabbed him and pulled him the other way.

"We can explore later," said Deena as they went under a massive archway, leaving the catacombs behind. They stood together in a large room. To their right was a corridor to a further storeroom. Before them was another room parallel to their one, and beyond that was the kitchen store cellar. Deena found cellar steps leading to the back kitchen upstairs. Having gotten her bearings, she and Dan searched for salt amongst oak barrels below thick timber shelves. Wooden cupboards stood between worn Welsh dressers. The candlelight cast shadows on the walls, playing tricks on their eyes. Deena's heart began beating hard in her chest as fear escalated. Cellars on this scale made her feel worse than a claustrophobe in a closet. She turned to look for Dan, only to find that he had wandered off again. "We're supposed to be looking for supplies," she said.

"I found another passage," said Dan, pleased with himself. "It runs the length of the back of the house, and there are more rooms on either end."

Deena, in frustration, turned on her heel and returned to her search, followed by Dan. A sudden clattering noise from across the cellar stopped them both. It came from an area that had old furniture against the far wall. "Probably a rat," said Dan. Deena wasn't buying it. She summoned courage and went to investigate. There were a couple of large wardrobes amongst broken chairs, tables, and even an iron bedstead. Deena gestured to Dan to be still while she listened. "There's nothing here. As I said, rats," reiterated Dan.

Again, Deena shushed Dan. She pointed to a wardrobe and whispered, "I swear something is moving in there."

"Fine," he muttered, resigned that Deena wouldn't leave it be. "I'll have a look."

Dan flicked the flashlight on before moving a broken chair to the side to get to the wardrobe unhindered. He paused before swinging open one of the doors. At first glance, it looked empty. Then, as the other door slowly swung open, Deena and Dan were astounded to see a plump older woman hiding in the corner as far as feasibly possible. "Whoa, who the hell are you!" asked Dan, surprised.

The woman cowered, covering her eyes from the beam of Dan's

flashlight. Deena lowered Dan's arm, "Turn it off, Dan. She's scared." She offered her hand to the woman and said, "It's okay; we're not going to hurt you. What's your name?"

"D-Dorothy," she stuttered. "Everyone calls me Dot," she said in a strong Welsh accent.

"Dan, can you find something for her to sit on, please?" asked Deena.

"Is there a war? I don't know what's going on, I... I haven't seen daylight in over a week. Oh, they haven't dropped the bomb, have they? They have, they must have..." said Dot in her confused state.

Deena ushered her to sit on a stool Dan put beside her. Dot continued rambling as she perched herself on the edge of the seat. "Why is it dark all the time? I saw mutants through the windows. Are they mutants? They are, aren't they, mutants. That's what happens, isn't it?" she said, perplexed.

Deena knelt and held Dot's hand and tried to reassure her. "They haven't dropped the bomb, Dot. But I suppose it's a war of sorts out there."

Dot looked at them both thoughtfully, and out of the blue, she said, "You sound American. Are you American?"

"Yes, Dot, we are," said Dan.

Dot's eyes widened as if she had an epiphany, and with a strained smile, she said, "Just like Eisenhower! Apparently, he came here. Oh, but that was way back; I think it was during World War II. But, yes, I remember the family talking about it once during dinner. 'Of historical importance,' they said. Typical upper class."

Deena smiled at Dot and said, "Yes, just like Eisenhower."

Dan interrupted, "Dot, is anyone else here with you?"

"This place is run on skeleton staff. The family doesn't live here all the time. A couple of months ago, they left to stay in their other place in England," Dot replied. "We keep things ticking over for them."

"We?" questioned Deena.

"Myself and three or four others. A few come in part-time but don't live in the house. I'm the cook," she said proudly. "I do a bit of cleaning as well, you know, to help out."

"Do you know where the other staff are?" asked Deena.

"No, my dear, I don't know. I heard the bombs dropping, and I came down here. I went up for water, but those mutant things were outside," said Dot.

Deena and Dan looked at each other. Dot's age and fragility could be heard in the crackle of her voice when she mentioned the 'mutant' Ground Crawlers.

"What were you looking for, dear?" asked Dot.

"We need salt and sage," said Deena hesitantly. She wasn't sure how to explain to Dot why they needed it. But thankfully, she didn't question her bizarre request.

"I can give you some, dear, come with me," she said, walking towards a storage room. Dan and Deena watched as Dot picked up five squares of brown paper. She laid them out, spooned sea salt onto the centre of each one and twisted the corners together to form pouches. She handed them to Dan smiling and asked, "And sage, you said?"

"Yes, if some are dried, that'd be great," said Deena.

Dot nodded, making her way to the other end of the storeroom. She opened the door to a pantry cupboard. Inside, different types of herbs were hanging up to dry. Dot picked out a couple of bunches of sage, smelling them as she passed them to Deena. "These came from the herb garden. Jack is very good at growing things," said Dot.

"Jack?" asked Deena.

"He's the gardener here. He grows all sorts for the kitchen. He's got green fingers," Dot said with fondness.

"Thank you," said Deena. "This is a huge help."

"No problem. You be careful whatever you need to do," said Dot as she kindly pointed to the door at the other end of the room. "That way will be quicker for you." Deena turned and walked towards the door. "You're limping, dear. Are you all right?" asked Dot.

"I sprained my ankle," said Deena.

"Wait there," said Dot rummaging in her apron pocket. She took Deena's hand and gave her a small glass vial identical to the one they previously found in the kitchen. "My secret recipe," she said, tapping her nose and winking. "Rub a little on the sprain. It's a little miracle cure in a bottle."

"Thank you, I will," said Deena gratefully. "Oh, and Dot, please, stay here where it's safer. It's dangerous outside."

"I'll be fine," she said bravely. "You mind those shadows, my dear? They come alive, you know."

CHAPTER SEVEN

Deena and Dan were walking toward the catacombs when suddenly, Dan stopped and faced a pile of timbers stacked against the wall under the stone steps. He switched off the flashlight, staring at it in the dark.

"Dan, what are you doing?" asked Deena.

Dan didn't answer. Instead, his eyes remained transfixed, so Deena walked over to him. "Cover the flame, Dee," he asked quietly. "I swear I saw a flicker of light between the timbers. It was only for a second. Perhaps I'm wrong. It hasn't happened again."

"Tiredness, perhaps?" suggested Deena. Dan agreed, and they wearily made their way back to the hidden room.

"Did Dot give you enough sage to make some bushels?" asked Dan.

"I can make at least three from what she gave me. Let's get some sleep first," she said. Dan gave the salt pouches to Deena. He watched as she made a salt line around the cellar steps. Then, a line in front of the panel door and a pinch in each corner. "Right, that's the entry points protected. Now, to protect us," said Deena. "We'll have to huddle in the centre of the room." Deena picked up the backpack and told Dan to sit in the middle with it. She then created a large salt circle. "We need to keep within the circle's confines to stay protected. I know it's cramped, but we will be safe," said Deena, sitting beside him.

"As long as I don't have to face that succubus. I'd rather be in a pit filled with vipers than go through that again," said Dan.

Deena laughed, "Be careful what you wish for," as she rubbed a little of Dot's potion on her ankle. She curled up on her side and closed her eyes. Exhaustion took over as they welcomed sleep.

Dan was the first to stir. He felt stiff and ached from lying on the hard floor. Dan remained beside Deena, unsure whether to step out of the protective circle when he realised he couldn't establish any perception of time. He could not fathom how long they had been there or if it was daytime or night. With no sunrise or sunset, the continual darkness marred time itself. Finally,

Deena awoke, switching on the flashlight to find the matches. She noticed a brown paper parcel and a water jug at the cellar steps as she lit the candle. In the spreading light of the flame, Deena sat with Dan and opened the package. "I think Dot has left us breakfast," she said, handing him a ham and cheese sandwich. Although a little stale, Dan's stomach appreciated Dot's effort.

"I would say today is a new day but is it? I don't know what day it is or if it's morning, afternoon, or night," said Dan.

Deena popped the last morsel into her mouth and pressed the side of her watch, lighting it up. "Four a.m., May the ninth," she said. "We flew out on the sixth, which was Friday."

"I can't help thinking about the General," Dan said. "I hope he got back to the team all right."

"He's a highly skilled military man. I'm sure he got back okay," replied Deena. "But we must keep track of time. Even though time does not seem to exist, it is still an enemy in many ways, especially for the team."

"Waiting for us to return must be excruciating," Dan said. "They don't know if we are dead or alive."

"Dan," said Deena firmly, "now is not the time to worry about that. It's too much of a distraction." Tears filled Deena's eyes as thoughts of Martin and her children flooded her mind. She choked them back as she reached for the sage. "We need to make the sage bushels. Here, I'll show you how to do it," Deena said, trying to take her mind away from home. She took the string around each bunch of sage, taught Dan how to lay it out, and then bind it. "Not too tight," she said. "The air must be able to draw to make it burn and smoulder." They made four bushels from what Dot gave them. Deena knew they would need to find more. But this would at least ensure some safety.

"I don't understand why the Twins didn't follow us downstairs," Dan said. "We need to find out more about this nanny. Perhaps she could give us some answers."

"No time like the present," she said, getting to her feet. As Deena put her weight on her ankle, there was no pain. She smiled and said, "As good as new. Dot's remedy works. Oh, can you put two bushels in the backpack, please?" Deena lit a new candle and extinguished the one by the cellar steps. "Ready?" she asked.

"As ready as anyone could be, I think," he replied unconvincingly.

At the foot of the stairs, Deena lit the used bushel and said, "At least we know what we are running into with the Twins. But this nanny could be a different matter." Dread ran through their bodies, making each step arduous. Finally, Deena chose to bare right at the top of the stairs. "I think we should use the Gaussmeter. I've got my hands full. Can you manage it?" asked Deena. Dan nodded, switching it on. Every bit of protection possible was welcome. Deena stood ready at the first door, exhaled a long breath, and turned the doorknob. Deena looked at Dan, confused. It was locked. "So, do we knock?" she asked.

"I guess so," said Dan, giving a couple of sharp raps.

They could hear movement behind the door. Then, a woman quietly but firmly asked, "Who's there?"

"Hello," said Deena. "Could we speak to you?"

The bolt slid across, and the door opened slightly. A woman peered through the gap, asking, "What do you want?"

"Could we talk to you, please? We need your help," asked Deena.

The woman shook her head as she glanced at the two of them. "I can't help you," she said as she went to shut the door.

Dan quickly jammed his foot in the doorway. "Are you the nanny?" he asked.

The woman scowled as Dan pushed his way into the room. Deena stood in the doorway in disbelief at his rude behaviour. "Get out!" the nanny shouted.

"You must be the nanny judging by how bossy you are," said Dan curtly. "What do you know about the Twins?"

The woman completely ignored Dan's question. Instead, she glared at Deena and said abruptly, "You can put that out. It stinks!"

"It's okay, Dee, stay there. I've got this one," said Dan sauntering around the room. As he picked things up and put them down again, the tall, overweight woman followed him around the room, fussing as she rearranged her things.

"Will you stop!" she said, frustrated with his meddling. "Yes! I am the nanny and housekeeper, all right! Just stop touching my things."

Deena couldn't help but find the scene amusing. Dan knew exactly how to get her attention. Now that he had, he asked her again. "What do you know about the Twins? Why are they in contact with you?" he reiterated.

"I only keep house and take care of the owner's grandchildren when they visit," the nanny replied.

"Well, I heard the Twins talking to you. You know whom I'm talking about, so why would they come to you?" Dan quizzed her.

The nanny sat on the bed, shoulders back, and her head held high. This is a woman who runs a tight ship. Her stern expression gave the impression of a strict, no-nonsense dictator not to be messed with on any level.

"They died over a hundred years ago before Lady Amelia was born. Emily and Charlotte were naughty children. They were always up to no good, and it got them killed," the nanny said to Dan.

"How did they die?" asked Deena.

"They drowned. The children weren't allowed downstairs or outside without their nanny. But they would slip down the servant's stairs and go out to play. One day, they took the rowboat out on the lake. The boat needed repairs, and it sank halfway to the islands. The Twins couldn't swim, and by the time the groundsman realised the boat was missing, it was too late," explained the nanny. "After the Twins died, the family needed an heir to the estate, and a year later, Lady Amelia was born. She died in childbirth. Her son survived her and is the father to the current owners."

"Seems like they still enjoy playing games," said Dan.

"Yes, well, it wouldn't have happened on my watch!" said the nanny. "Now, leave. I can't help you with anything more!" she said, ushering Dan out of the room.

As Dan turned around, the door slammed in their faces, accompanied by the sound of the bolt sliding back into its latch. Surprised at the deft nature of their exit, Deena raised an eyebrow as to what had just happened. "She's hiding something," said Dan.

"Why do you say that? She told us about the Twins, and we know how they are descendants," said Deena.

"Yes, but the information was nothing more than a ploy to side-track us from why the Twins are in contact with her," remarked Dan.

"You're right," said Deena. "Do you want to try to ask her again?" she suggested.

"No, she won't open the door to us now. She wouldn't let you in because of the sage. Surely, she would want that protection as she is on the same floor as the Twins. So why haven't they harmed her? Unless she doesn't need protection from them," said Dan.

"Perhaps we should be careful around her," said Deena.

Dan looked down the long balcony and the rooms they needed to search. The following two bedrooms proved to be void of furniture. The third door opened into a corridor leading to two smaller bedrooms. Again, there was nothing to find besides storage cupboards with old clothing. "Seems like most of the rooms this side are unused," Dan said, disappointed.

"We still need to search them. Storage means possible supplies," she said.

The next couple of rooms yielded nothing. Finally, as they rounded the end of the balcony, Dan's eyes flitted around the building. Deena knew he was watching for the Twins, and it was only a matter of time before they showed up again.

The first bedroom in this row was a guest room. Neatly placed towels sat on a plush, four-poster bed. Bedside cabinets and wardrobes sat along the back wall with an elegant lady's dressing table with a buttoned stool. "This looks promising," Dan remarked, opening a bedside cabinet, and finding two candles and a box of matches. He made his way to Deena in the washroom, smiling at her as he waved his finds before putting them in the backpack. Deena handed him a glass pot half filled with pink crystals.

"What's that?" he asked.

"I know it's perfumed, but it's still sea salts," said Deena. Dan went over to the bed, stripping its four plump pillows and feather quilt. He bundled it together and took it to the balcony. Then, hastily, he threw them over to the floor below. Deena looked over at the pile of bedding at the foot of the stairs. "Not planning to jump, are you?" she asked, amused.

"Nope. I woke up today very cold and aching. I felt like I had done ten rounds in a boxing ring," Dan said. "We can sort it out later."

"I like your style," said Deena, peering over the balcony.

The next bedroom was opposite the top of the main staircase. Deena went down a narrow corridor with candle and sage in hand until meeting a long passage running the width of the building. The far left had stairs leading to the next floor. A window looked over the front of the estate to the right, and more rooms lay on each side. "Which way do you want to go?" she asked Dan.

He pointed left, suggesting they work clockwise. "Then, we can go back onto the balcony and search the bedrooms at the front of the house.

We know we've covered this floor before going up to the next," he said.

There was only one room on that side of the passage. Dan opened the door to find odd ends of furniture dotted around. After finding nothing, they crossed the hallway at the bottom of the stairs and entered the next. Open shelving was full of folded linen. Dan remembered the knife tip he found hidden in towels. It was time-consuming, but he didn't want to overlook anything, running his hands between every sheet. Behind the door were bedding chests. Deena pushed the lids up and found antique lace-edged linen and three sage bushels. She showed Dan, excited at her finds. "Shush!" he said, pointing at the ceiling. "I can hear someone walking around up there."

Deena stopped and listened. She, too, could hear scuffles and footsteps. "Do you want to go up?" whispered Deena.

"Not yet," he whispered back. "Let's get this floor done first." They made good time through the next four bedrooms as they were sparsely furnished. Then, finding nothing more, they crossed the passageway into a long room. Intricate tapestries hung on the walls. Comfortable chairs with a mahogany coffee table were in the centre of the room. To brighten the space, Deena lit a paraffin lamp on a bookcase. Dan picked up a book, reading the title. "Charles Dickens, Great Expectations," he muttered with a smile of approval. "Someone likes a bedtime read with their cocoa."

Double doors on either end of the room led to the passage at the back. Opposite, two double doors led back onto the balcony. Deena began looking for anything of interest as Dan checked that all was good. As he swung the door open, Emily stood there waiting with an innocuous, wide-eyed expression. "One, two, we're gonna get you!" she sang.

Dan cried out in horror, fleeing across the room, and falling, hitting his head on the table's edge. Deena hurriedly blew on the sage to increase the smoke while trying to help him. Blood trickled down his face from a gash on his head. He wiped it away with his hand. Then, looking at the smears of claret, he cursed the reappearance of the Twins. "We need to get the hell off this floor!" he muttered between gritted teeth.

They dashed to the door leading to the rear corridor, and Deena gave Dan the bushel. Then, she grasped the doorknob. "Make for the stairs to the next floor up. We're too far from the main staircase to get to the ground floor," said Deena.

She took a deep breath and opened it a fraction. She caught sight of

Emily, or was it, Charlotte? What did it matter? "Three, four, there's blood on the floor!" came the voice. Deena quickly slammed it shut. The twins had them trapped. Had they deliberately waited for them to get to this room to play their games?

"What do we do?" asked Dan desperately. "We can't stay holed up in here."

"Pass me the backpack," she said. She lit another bushel, gave it to Dan, and then urged, "We must get out of here, now!" She beckoned Dan to follow her to the door leading to the passage closest to the back stairs. "The likelihood is that one or both Twins will be behind this door," she whispered. "I'll go first; you follow. We need to run, so we'll use the flashlight," she said, blowing out the candle. Standing behind her, Dan was ready as she opened the door to one of the Twins.

"Five, six, the clock tick ticks!" the Twin piped up. Deena didn't hesitate. She thrust the sage, swiping at the apparition, dissipating its energy as the smoke cut the air.

"Run, Dan!" she shouted, bolting up the hallway.

As they passed the short corridor to the balcony, there was the other Twin, giggling at their antics. "Seven, eight, it's too late!" she sang menacingly. Deena and Dan sprinted to the next floor.

As Dan sat at the top of the steps nursing his head, he muttered, "Damned kids!" Deena took out the vial and dabbed it on his wound. Dan winced out loud, "Ow, it stings!"

"Try and keep it clean until it heals," she said, wedging the cork in the vial. Then, taking the bushel from Dan, she stubbed it out.

"It will be tough to finish searching the middle floor," Dan said. "I still think the nanny is hiding something. Do you think she sent the Twins after us?" he pondered.

"Surely no one is that callous, not even her. Okay, she is a very bossy, stoic person, but to cause us harm, deliberately?" questioned Deena.

"She couldn't wait to get us out of her room, and I'm sure there's another room off hers. There is always a nursery next to a nanny's room," said Dan.

"I don't think we'll get any answers from her. So, we'll have to leave that floor for now. But maybe, at some point, we can trick the nanny out of there so we can search her room properly," said Deena.

"The cogs are already whirring," said Dan. "Leave it to me."

Deena did not doubt he would come up with some hare-brained scheme. She got up to survey the area behind them. Moonlight beamed down through the magnificent glass-domed roof, supported by thick wooden trusses on top of stone arches indicative of the rest of the manor. Over the decorative railings, they could see the main staircase on the ground floor. There was an expanse of open floor space directly in front of them. "I think this floor must be for the staff," said Deena. "Do you think someone is up here?" she quizzed.

"If there is, I hope they are living. Those fucking kids have put me on edge," muttered Dan.

"It seems they are only running about on the middle floor. The Twins didn't follow us to the ground floor, and they haven't followed us up here either," said Deena.

"Good!" exclaimed Dan. Then a thought came to him. "Unless Nanny goes walkabout. She said, 'They were not allowed to go anywhere without their nanny.' So, if the Twins have connected with her, she may not be their nanny, but she's a nanny all the same," he said diplomatically.

"Shit, I hadn't thought of that. Let's hope the nanny stays in her room!" said Deena. "I've had enough of their sick nursery rhymes for one day."

Deena gave a sage bushel to Dan and opened the first room on the far left. The candle gave a gentle yellow glow to a bedroom as she stepped in. The walls were unpainted, and cracks ran through the plasterwork. The floorboards creaked as they walked to a single metal bed made up, but not with the type of luxurious bedding they found on the middle floor. Instead, a scratchy blanket covered a stiff cotton sheet. Dan picked up the single pillow that was devoid of a slip. It was lumpy and hard. It was a stark difference from the way the family lived.

"I expected this room to be bigger," said Dan. He walked out, and after a minute, he came back in. "There must be a room behind this. The wall in this room ends at the top of the stairs. So, where is the access to the space behind it?" he reasoned.

Deena stuck her head around the door, looked at the distance to the stairs, and then checked the depth of their room. "You're right. There should be a room behind it," said Deena.

"Keep an eye out for possible ways in," said Dan.

The next couple of rooms were much the same. So, Dan crossed the hall at the end and stood before a large arched door. With stiff iron hinges, Dan grunted as he pulled it open. It was apparent that no one had ventured in there for many years. Inside was a stone-cased tower with steps to another level. Dan switched the flashlight on and went up. Small alcoves in the stonework were within the walls at arm's reach, so Dan searched them. Finally, he stood in front of the lead window on the upper platform, looking out. The view was fantastic. He could make out the coastline by the moonlight bouncing off the surf. On the windowsill was an old paraffin lamp. He picked it up and gave it a shake; it was empty. Judging by the undisturbed cobwebs hanging heavy with dust, he guessed he was probably the first to enter the tower in years. At the bottom of the steps, he wondered if the space behind the first bedroom was also a tower. "What's in there?" asked Deena as Dan shut the door.

"It's a disused tower. I didn't find anything, but it did make me think perhaps that's what's in the space we haven't figured out," Dan said.

"Maybe we missed it," she suggested. "We flew up those stairs so fast."

"Good point. Come on," said Dan, bounding across the communal space.

He hesitated and groaned at the top of the stairs, "I just realised I left your meter in the Tapestry Room."

"We can get it later. Let's do this floor, and we can nip back," suggested Deena.

Cautiously, Dan checked the stairs, pointing out a door similar to the other tower. He opened it, and Deena followed him in. Standing in the centre, Dan got the flashlight out. There was a staircase, but not as one would expect. Dan followed the walls around, picking out built-in stone plinths intermittently jutting out of the walls. As in the other tower, small recesses dotted the walls above. "What's your balance like?" Dan asked her.

"Are you suggesting I go up?" asked Deena, grimacing.

"Yep, I would definitely fall off. Those plinths aren't very wide, and you have smaller feet than me," said Dan.

"What kind of an excuse is that?" Deena asked. "Fine, I'll do it. But make sure you keep the flashlight steady."

She put the candle and bushel down and looked up at the steps.

Climbing them would be dangerous. Each plinth was more than a stride apart which meant leaping from one to the next. She could only keep herself steady if she could get a grip on the wall's stonework as she jumped. "Please don't get distracted with the flashlight," Deena pleaded. "If I miss a step, you will finish this mission by yourself."

"You'll be fine. Take your time and be sure of your balance before jumping," said Dan.

If Deena had said she wasn't scared, she would be lying. The tower's height was about twenty feet, and with no window, it was pitch black other than the candle and flashlight. "If I find anything, I'll drop it down," she said, surveying the platform.

Deena pulled herself onto the first stone slab and closed her eyes, gaining her sense of balance. When she felt ready, she focused on the next plinth. Dan stood behind her with the flashlight, highlighting the next slab's edge. She fumbled for a firm grip on the wall and launched herself, landing squarely. Deena's concentration didn't waver as she conquered the following two plinths. Above her head was a recess. So, she hugged herself against the wall and ran her fingertips across the space. She couldn't feel anything; six plinths, three cavities later, and still nothing. "I think someone has already been here. I'm wasting my time," she said.

"There are only three more plinths," he called to her. "Even if someone has been up there, they may have missed something. There are four more alcoves above you." It wasn't until the last of the recesses that she found anything. In one, she found a scroll. In the other, a pair of crystals. Deena dropped them one by one. Dan waited until she was down before examining them. Then, at the third from the last plinth, she swung to the ground with the elegance of a cat. "I'm impressed," said Dan.

Deena smiled coyly, sat on the floor, and picked up the scroll. She plucked the white ribbon undone and held it to the candlelight. "The symbol is different on this one," she said. "Take a look."

"Fire," he muttered. "Is that the right symbol?" he questioned.

"Yes, this is the second scroll with an element on it," said Deena. "There are five elements, so there should be another three scrolls. But I still don't know what to do with them," she said, picking up one of the crystals. Dan put the scroll in the backpack and peered at the crystal Deena was frowning at intently.

"These crystals are the same shape as the black onyx with the other scroll. So, don't you think it's strange we are finding them in pairs?" said Dan.

"These are amber," said Deena.

Dan smiled and said, "You're right. I don't think it's a coincidence that we're finding them, either. We need to return to the drawing room and get the others."

Deena quickly brushed herself down to get the cobwebs off, and as she ran her fingers through her hair to ensure no unwanted spiders, she suddenly stopped. Their eyes met in question to the sound of restrained sobbing. "Where's that coming from?" whispered Deena. Dan had no idea. He walked around, listening, trying to figure it out.

"Come over here, Dee," he whispered, putting his ear against the inside wall.

Deena went over and listened. She could hear crying, too, so she checked the stairwell. But there was no one. Back in the tower, she shrugged her shoulders at Dan in confusion. "I thought someone may have been on the stairs, but..." began Deena.

Dan put his finger up to his lips. "Shush."

CHAPTER EIGHT

Dan meticulously inspected the wall from the ground to about five feet high with the flashlight. Then, halfway across, he called Deena over and pointed to an area about waist height. There was a space in the mortar to put in his fingers. He could feel a small metal flat bar. "I've found a latch," he whispered. He lifted it with his fingertips and pulled it towards himself, and the wall opened, revealing a small room lit with candles. "Hello? We can hear you crying," Dan called out.

There was no response. Deena scanned the room with the tri-field meter. Whoever was in there was flesh and blood. "Where are you? It's okay, I'm Deena, and this is Dan," she said.

A shuffle under the old single bed and a pitiful sob gave her away. Deena knelt and pulled back the bedsheet that draped to the floor. The girl scrunched herself as far back as possible. She lay on her side, knees hugged to her chest, staring at Deena like a rabbit caught in headlights. Finally, Deena reached under the bed, offering her hand.

Slowly, the girl gave a trembling hand and squirmed her way out. Deena sat her on the bed, putting a comforting arm around her. Dan stood back, feeling awkward. Deena brushed the woman's long dark hair away from her face, and as she began to calm down, they discovered she was a local girl named Bronwyn. At the tender age of seventeen, she had started her new job at the manor as a live-in housemaid only weeks before Ragnarök hit. "How come you're hiding in here?" asked Deena.

"I barricaded myself in the tower at first. I only found this room by chance. But I feel safer in here. Things are happening in this place and, and…" sobbed Bronwyn.

"We've come across things too, and it's terrifying. When did you last eat?" asked Deena.

"A few days ago. I had some junk food, but there's nothing left," Bronwyn stammered between sobs.

"We'll let Dot know you're up here and arrange food for you," said Deena.

"Is Dot all right?" asked Bronwyn.

"Yes, a little confused but doing well," said Deena.

"There are stairs at the far end connecting to the kitchens, and thanks. I'm sorry I'm a mess," said Bronwyn, wiping her tears.

"Sit tight. We won't take long," said Deena, reassuring her.

Deena and Dan left Bronwyn in her room. As they looked across the balcony towards the servant's stairs, Deena said, "We'll get Bronwyn food before anything else." So, Dan switched on the flashlight, and Deena fanned the sage, increasing its smoulder. "Don't stop for anything," she said. Deena went first, and Dan raced after her as she went as swiftly as her legs would allow down the four flights of stairs. She flung the cellar door open, gasping for breath. "Made it!" said Deena breathlessly.

"Hello, you two," said a smiling Dot poking her head around the door. She beckoned them into the room. Dot had made herself very comfortable in her chosen hideout. "Here, sit yourselves down. What brings you back here?" asked Dot in her Welsh singsong accent.

"Bronwyn," Dan said, still out of puff.

"Such a lovely girl. Where is she?" asked Dot.

"Stuck on the top floor. She's too frightened to come down and get food," replied Dan.

"Well, we can't have that now, can we? Please leave it to me. You rest there a while," said Dot disappearing through the door. Within twenty minutes, Dot returned with a hot sweet cup of tea and a sandwich.

"Thanks, Dot," said Dan, "and it was kind of you to leave food for us this morning."

"I can't have you going hungry. It's so cold now. I've lit a wood burner to cook pasta; it won't take long. The two of you and young Bronwyn could use a hot meal," Dot said, striding off.

Dan finished his sandwich and took a sip of his tea. It was piping hot. "While that cools, I'll nip the things we've found to the base room. The backpack is cramped," said Dan. He returned ten minutes later and asked Deena where Dot was.

"She's still in the kitchens but has been gone ages. Do you think we should check she's okay?" asked Deena.

They were about to leave when Dot walked through the door with a hessian bag bulging with food. "That will keep her going for a while. The

101

pasta is almost ready," she said as she returned to the kitchens.

Dan was getting bored and began poking around. Then, he opened the cupboard, which had the herbs. "Dee, look. Dot's the one making the sage bushels we've been finding," said Dan, surprised. He took out four, all neatly bound. Deena got up, giving them a closer look. "How did she know to make them?" asked Dan.

"I think she's worked here long enough to know this place was haunted a long time before we got here," said Deena.

Above them, the sound of glass shattering and screams filled the air. "Dot!" Deena cried out as she flew towards the cellar steps.

"Dee!" Dan called after her. "You don't know what you're running into!" he exclaimed.

At the top of the steps, Deena turned to Dan, tears streaming down her face. Dan took her by the shoulders and moved her away from the kitchen door. "Please, please, stay here," he said firmly.

The screams dissipated to the sounds of pots and pans bouncing off the stone floor. Dan opened the door to the back kitchen; to his relief, the door opposite was still closed. He crept over and listened. His heart sank. Intuition had already prepared him for what was behind it. Summoning courage, he peeped through a crack in the door. He felt sick as he watched the Ground Crawlers tearing her body apart, dismembering, mutilating, and stripping the flesh from her bones with razor-sharp teeth. Entrails unravelled from her torso as one of the creatures jumped out the window with a mouthful. At least six Ground Crawlers had infiltrated the manor, putting them all in danger. He sank to his knees and put his hands to his head, slowly rocking back and forth. Deena watched on, horrified. She sat at the top of the cellar steps, emotionally numb as tears flowed. There were no uttered words amongst the heartbreak. Instinctively, she knew what had happened to dear, sweet Dot.

Dan gathered his senses. They needed to secure the area to prevent them from getting further into the house. Questions muddled around Dan's head. Did Dot open the window? Was it the smell of cooking that attracted them? Was she making too much noise? He didn't have the answers, and no amount of surmising would change what happened. He couldn't help but blame himself. He had failed to tell Dot what the mutants were. If he had explained they could viciously attack, perhaps Dot would still be alive. He whispered to Deena, "Are you okay?"

Deena's tears encapsulated deep sadness. She whispered a croaky "Yes," while wiping her face with the heels of her hands.

"Can you help me secure the kitchen?" he whispered. Deena nodded and got to her feet. Once again, there was no time for grief.

In the cellar, Dan took the bushels Dot had made, put them in the backpack, and looked for anything else they could use. He found the sea salt, remembering how Dot made pouches with the squares of brown paper. There was enough to make another six. Then, he took two boxes of matches from the herb cupboard drawer. Finally, Deena relit the sage that had burned out in their absence and said, "Bronwyn needs that food. But first, we must secure the kitchen, and I think we should tell her about the Ground Crawlers."

"We should've told Dot," Dan said with regret. Deena placed the bag of food at the bottom of the cellar steps. She returned as Dan took the dried herbs out of the cupboard. He handed half to Deena, using the other half for himself. When they finished dousing themselves, they went to the main cellars to find something to barricade the kitchen. Dan found a length of blue nylon rope which he put to one side.

"Could we use this metal bedstead?" asked Deena.

"Yes, we could jam it under the door handle. I have got an idea. See if you can find hollow metal rods," suggested Dan. Deena took apart an old clothing rack for the poles. "That should be enough," said Dan. "We need to wait out the Ground Crawlers before securing the doors. Let's get this upstairs."

Deena stayed by the cellar steps as Dan didn't want her to see the carnage on the other side of the kitchen door. Spying through a crack, he could see two Ground Crawlers still picking at Dot's remains. He waited until they had filled their bellies. Watching them lick bloody remains from each other's mouths was a grotesque scene. Finally, they grunted and snuffled in mutual, ritualistic grooming of contentment before jumping out of the smashed window. The coast was clear.

They managed to secure the back kitchen door using the old bedstead as planned. Dan put three hollow poles and the rope to one side. "I've thought about the kitchen door opposite the banqueting hall. We need to secure that too," he said. "It will be safer going via the cellars." Deena felt reassured that Dan was taking charge. Planning and tactics seemed to be an inbuilt trait in his persona. She thought about the option she gave him at the gates to return to the plane, but instead, he chose to stick by her side. Deep down, she knew they had a real chance of getting through this with him.

Moreover, she had a newfound respect for him for all his boyish charm and joking around. "Shush, we don't know if the Ground Crawlers have returned," he whispered as they rounded the rear of the staircase. Deena watched, perplexed, as Dan laid out the poles on the floor in a triangular shape. He tied the rope to the doorknob leading outside. Then, he threaded it through the corresponding bar on the floor. Next, jamming the pole between the back door and the kitchen handle, he knotted it tightly around the doorknob. He repeated the same process from the kitchen to the banqueting door and back to the outside door. "It means we can't use these doors either because one opens inward and the next outward. So, now it's impossible to open any of them. The bars will give it extra strength," whispered Dan.

"Genius," uttered Deena at his elaborate contraption.

Satisfied with their security measures, they returned to the cellars. Dan retrieved the backpack, picked up the hessian food bag for Bronwyn, and carried it up the steps. They slipped through the cellar door to the servant's stairs. Dan switched the flashlight on and said, "You take one handle, and I'll take the other. It will be quicker if we share the weight."

Deena and Dan got to the top floor as quickly and as agile as possible. They took a moment to relight the candle and sage. Bronwyn was surprised to see them, gasping at the giant bag of food they put by her bed. She grabbed a bread roll and began eating. Then, delving back in, Bronwyn broke off a chunk of cheese, and between mouthfuls, she sighed with gratitude, "Thank Dot for me."

"We need to talk to you about things since we went to get you food," said Dan.

"Why? What's happened?" asked Bronwyn.

Dan and Deena told her about the Ground Crawlers and what happened

104

to Dot. Bronwyn broke down in tears and sobbed, "It's my fault. It would never have happened if I hadn't been up here."

"You can't blame yourself, Bronwyn," said Deena. "Dan and I should've warned Dot about the Ground Crawlers when we first met her. She thought they were mutants. She had no idea how dangerous they were. So, please stay up here. Don't be tempted to go wandering about the building. We'll make sure that you have a steady supply of food."

"Will I be safe?" asked Bronwyn. Deena nodded and hugged her. "Oh, before you go, I have something for you." Bronwyn dug about in a bedside cupboard. "I took them from the tower next door. I have loads," she said, handing Deena candles and matches. "It's what you were looking for, isn't it? You need to light the shadows."

"Thanks, that's a huge help," said Deena.

"We'll be back in a few days," said Dan.

At the top of the staircase to the servant's floor, Dan asked Deena, "Where do you want to start?"

"We may as well start with these rooms and work clockwise," she replied. There were five rooms the length of the communal area. Dan opened the door to the first. Unfortunately, there was only an old, dilapidated bed stripped bare. The following rooms were unfruitful, so Dan stood facing the other side of the balcony. Opposite him, a small corridor with a window looked out over the front of the manor. He strolled over as Deena crossed the top of the servant's stairs to discover the adjacent rooms were bathrooms. Dan went to help and remarked, "There's another tower at the other end, which makes three, so there must be a fourth."

"Have you checked the stairs? Here, take the sage and flashlight and look," she said, searching under the wash sinks. Then, leaving the backpack with Deena, he examined the first flight of the servant's stairs. Ten minutes later, he was back.

"Nope! There's no door," he said.

"Maybe there isn't a fourth tower," replied Deena.

"Yes, there is. I'm sure of it. The same space that confused us is also at this end," Dan articulated.

"I'll help you look when I've finished here," offered Deena.

"I'll look for an entrance in the bedrooms. I might have missed something," said Dan.

Dan returned to the bedrooms spanning the back wall and pondered them. The first two were easy. The third had the most furniture in it. Deena was still busy, so he moved the lighter furniture away from the walls. The bed and cabinets revealed nothing. Dan didn't want to risk moving the wardrobes without help. They were solid oak and exceptionally heavy. He left the flashlight and sage in the room and leaned over the balcony with his arms folded; he idly waited for Deena as he stood in the shadows, watching the floors below. Dan suddenly turned to look behind him. He was sure he saw something in the corner of his eye. Something moved. He scanned the area around him. Then, satisfied it was nothing, he resumed his stance at the balcony rail.

Dan was starting to get impatient, and as he turned towards the bathrooms, he felt something grip his ankle. Dan looked down, puzzled as to why he couldn't move his foot. A shadowy black hand had a vice-like grip on him. He desperately tried to pull away, but the grip got tighter each time. Slowly the shadow took form. It rose from the floor, and red demonic eyes glinted at him in the darkness. Then, as he tried to call for Deena, another shadow formed, taking hold of his thigh. Dan panicked as more shadows emerged out of the darkness. Four more wrapped around his torso. Their wispy, shadowy appearance was deceiving. The strength they possessed made it impossible for Dan to move.

"Dee… Deeena! Deeeena!" he screamed.

The Shadow Men curled themselves around his chest; breathing was getting hard. As a constrictor snake kills its prey, the squeeze gets tighter with every breath he takes. The pressure was building in his head, and his eyes watered with the strain. Finally, Dan gave one last concerted effort to cry out as they ferociously wound around his shoulders.

Dan screamed out, "Deee… nnnna!" as a Shadow Man drew up to his face, and its eyes met with his.

Alarmed, Deena sprinted around the balcony to him. The red glints of eyes surrounding Dan were ominous. Pushing her hand through the demonic forms, she tried to grab Dan and pull him away from them. Instead, the Shadow Men took hold of her, and the sound of rushing hollow breaths engulfed them. Deena panicked as they held her captive, no matter how hard she tried to pull away. Finally, she cried out as shadowy hands wrapped around her waist.

CHAPTER NINE

Deena caught sight of Bronwyn, walking towards them, clutching four lit candles. Dan began to choke on the dark evil invading his lungs. "Hurry, Bronwyn!" pleaded Deena.

"I'm coming. Hold on!" Bronwyn shouted over the intensifying rushing breaths. First, she thrust a candle amidst the dark forms into Deena's hand, and as the light of the flame spread, the Shadow Men began dissipating. Then, she plunged one into Dan's hand, and the Shadow Men's grasp weakened again. Finally, Bronwyn placed the third candle at their feet, releasing the anchors of the dark force that welded them to the floor. She walked around both with the fourth flame, driving the Shadow Men and their malevolent intent back into the darkness. Calm eventually prevailed, and Dan and Deena collapsed on hands and knees to the floor.

"What happened, Dan?" exclaimed Deena.

"I don't know. I was standing at the railings, and the next thing..." Dan began.

"The Shadow Men," said Bronwyn. "I thought you knew about them. That's why I gave you the candles."

"To light the shadows," reiterated Dan.

"I remember Dot said something about the shadows coming alive, too," said Deena. "It did seem odd at the time."

"I'm sorry," said Bronwyn. "I should have been specific. I've seen them a few times up here."

"But we can at least defend ourselves as long as we have a light source," said Dan, coughing and spluttering.

"None of us knows what's hiding within the darkness. So, we must learn to keep ourselves guarded," said Deena. She sat next to Dan, placing the candle between her feet and asking if he was okay. Dan rolled up his trouser leg and rubbed his ankle. Deena took a closer look. "Have you seen the bruising?" she exclaimed. She lifted his clothing to reveal more in the shape of handprints on his back and chest.

"Oh, Dan, that's bad. They've left marks all over you," said Bronwyn, upset.

"Stay with him. I'm going to get our stuff. Then, we'll go to your room to help Dan properly," said Deena as she cautiously watched the shadows. The first thing she had learnt was never to be without light. The other was, don't stand in one place too long, for they will see you. So, finally, Deena returned and said, "I think I've got everything."

Dan winced with every step. "You wouldn't think something with no physical substance could do so much damage," he said, hobbling to Bronwyn's room.

Deena opened the backpack and sifted for the small glass vial. "Found it! Right, Dan, strip off," she said, trying to hide her smirk.

"What? No way, I am not stripping off in front of you two!" he hollered.

"Now is not the time to be bashful. How else am I supposed to put this stuff on you?" said Deena, winking at Bronwyn.

"Oh, you two think this is hilarious, don't you? Okay, fine! But I'm keeping my underwear on!" he said. So first, Dan stripped to his waist. Then, with his hands on the waistband of his trousers, he gave a disgruntled look and turned his back. His actions were met with unrestrained giggles from Bronwyn and Deena.

"Quit it!" said Dan, embarrassed. "You're not funny. Turn around, and stop staring at me, please?" he begged.

Deena and Bronwyn turned their backs in fits of giggles. "Are you done yet?" spluttered Deena.

Slowly they turned around. Deena bit her lip to stifle an outburst of uncontrollable laughter. The vision of Dan standing in his underwear, eyes raised, with hands cupped over his delicates was too much to bear. Neither could help themselves; a barrage of hilarity erupted. Finally, Dan looked to the floor, not wanting to make eye contact with either for fear of perpetuating their heightened state of amusement. "Are you done?" he muttered.

"Ahem, I think so…" said Deena through tears of laughter. "Sorry, Dan. Ahem, okay, yep, I'm done." Then, having treated the deep purple and black handprints on his back and legs, she dabbed the elixir on the bruised finger trails marking his chest, arms, and abdomen. "Could you move your hands, please? I can't get to all the bruising," she asked.

Dan cringed and said, "Nope, not happening. Workaround it." Deena pursed her lips together, trying not to laugh, and Bronwyn wasn't helping with her intermittent fits of giggles.

"You can get dressed now," said Deena. "Do you want to rest rather than struggle to finish up here?" Dan lay on Bronwyn's bed, rolled onto his side, and insisted he was fine as he wasn't ready to give up his search for the fourth tower. "They will know you are weak and target you," stated Deena.

"Deena's right. You can't fight them like this. What would happen if you needed to run?" asked Bronwyn.

"You're not giving me any choices, are you?" said Dan, groaning in pain.

So, Deena thanked Bronwyn for her help. "It was a pleasure," she said, still giggling.

Back in the base room, Dan sat against the wall. "I'm going to get the bedding you threw over the balcony so you'll be more comfortable," said Deena.

"Thanks," he said appreciably.

The pain was in his voice, and to be hampered in their mission with injuries worried her. They hadn't ventured outside yet, and other than the Twins, Ground Crawlers and the Shadow Men, they had no idea what else lay waiting for them. Deena retrieved the bedding and repeated the salt protection. Curled up in the foetal position, Dan was already asleep. Deena lay by his side, listening to the rhythmic sound of his breathing. She curled behind him, desperately needing the comfort of knowing she wasn't alone.

When Deena awoke, she checked the time and date. They had been there for five days and were no closer to finding the skull. Deena's stomach was cramping. She debated whether to wait for Dan to wake up or find food alone. Deena didn't have the heart to wake him. So, she quietly slipped out, vowing not to venture far. At the bottom of the steps, she panned the flashlight around. Its beam was dimming. She quickly walked the catacombs to Dot's storage room, thinking about where the main food supply was. There had to be a fridge or freezer, but she didn't remember seeing such appliances. Deena wasn't about to embark into unfamiliar areas, so she searched the cupboards for whatever she could find. The growling hunger of her belly would graciously accept anything edible.

When Dan awoke, Deena was back and munching on cookies. "Hey, how are you feeling?" she asked.

"Like a baseball bat was served upon me. Breakfast in bed, nice," said Dan, reaching for the cookies in Deena's clutches.

"Here, these are for you," she said, giving him the other packet. "When I was looking for food, I realised there must be storage for cold foods because Dot had ham and cheese," said Deena. "We can't keep going on cookies and stale bread."

"I still want to go and find the fourth tower," said Dan.

"Ensuring a food supply first is essential. Also, the batteries aren't too clever in the flashlight, so we need to use candles more," said Deena. "But, before we go anywhere, I want to look at the bruising." The marks had faded considerably. So, Deena smeared more of the elixir on the remnants of the Shadow Men's brutal attack before gathering what they needed to return to the cellars.

They paused at the central archway, facing the catacombs. "We haven't been down this end," said Dan. On either side, pillars led into domed rooms. Tentatively, Deena and Dan walked as shadows bounced off the stonework from the flicker of their candles. A corridor at the end led to the passage running the length of the manor's back. Another route sloping even deeper was to their right.

"There are so many ways around this place," said Deena, exasperated. "It's confusing."

"I know, but we need to learn how they connect. For example, there are buildings at the back we couldn't access from the main house. Perhaps we can get to them from the cellars," said Dan walking to the far end. Stopping at the door to his right, he held the candle close. The flame flickered and danced as a draught whistled through, and Dan said, "This must go outside." He opened it a fraction to reveal steps leading to the rear of the house. Closing the door, they continued under the arches until they reached an entry on their left. It backed onto Dot's storage area, opening into a large room with old wooden brackets with trusses bolted to the stonework at the far end. "This may be where they stored ammunition during the war," said Dan, lifting the top of a wooden barrel.

"Do you think there are any guns left here?" she asked Dan.

"I doubt it. The military wouldn't leave guns behind," Dan said. "It would be great if they had. The Ground Crawlers would make great target practice." Deena knew revenge for what they did to Dot would be high on his agenda, and visions of blowing them away with a high-powered rifle did give a sense of satisfaction.

Dan looked through the doorway into an adjoining room and said, "This is so cool. Look at this, Dee." Dan pulled a dust sheet off an old motorbike. A Norton 16H. Sitting astride it, he shook it side to side. A sloshing sound came from the tank. "It's got petrol in it," he said. "It looks like it's had some maintenance over the years." Dan took hold of the handlebars and pushed the bike off its kickstand. "I wonder…" he began.

"Don't!" said Deena abruptly. "The Ground Crawlers may sense the vibration. We are directly beneath where they came into the kitchen."

Dan gave a disappointed look and jolted the bike back onto its stand. Then, he walked across the room, motioning for Deena to join him. He handed her the candle and opened a door far enough to see steps leading to the manor's front. "There are a few doors leading outside. We could use any of them if we could get the bike started," said Dan.

"We would have to plan it carefully. We don't want to be pounced on as soon as we get through the door. Is there much petrol in it?" asked Deena.

"About half a tank, giving us about seventy to eighty miles at the most," said Dan pulling the dust cover back over it.

Deena found ammunition chests stacked in the corner of the room. She lifted a couple of lighter ones from the pile and opened them. The old, green metal chests had heavily sprung clips securing their hinged lids. Rust had corroded the metal in the deep scores of the flaked paint. Dan felt like a ten-year-old child who had walked into a candy store. First the motorbike, and now a treasure trove of crates to rummage through. The empty ones, Dan stacked aside. He sifted through old ropes, empty shell boxes and broken straps for goodness knows what. "Found anything yet?" asked Deena.

"Yes, lots of stuff," he said.

"Nothing useful then?" stated Deena, amused.

"No, but I'm not giving up," he said, putting aside another chest. "Twelve down, nine to go," he said, picking up another.

"What's this for?" she asked, pulling out a bundle of webbing straps with pockets attached.

"Now, this is useful! It's a chest rig," he said excitedly. He took it from her and placed the straps over his shoulders, ensuring they crossed at the back. The camouflaged pouches lined up under his chest. "Dee, could you buckle this up?" he asked. Deena tightened the belt around his torso. Then, he spun around, striking a modelling pose, making her laugh. "This is awesome! We could use this to carry extra stuff when we're out and about. Is there any more?" he asked.

Deena delved into the contents of the chest. "Hang on. Yes," said Deena, pulling out another rig. Dan examined it, making sure the straps were good.

Dan quickly looked through what was left, and with renewed optimism, he eagerly said, "Next!" They had been in the cellars for some time, so Deena lit more candles as the memory of the Shadow Men sprung to mind.

"Four more to go," said Dan, setting down another crate. He lifted the lid, and old coiled ropes filled it halfway. He moved them aside, taking out a small chest. "I have a good feeling about this one," said Dan, pointing to the padlocks on the hasps. "You haven't found any keys, have you?" he asked.

"No, can you force it open?" asked Deena.

Dan found a metal bar, braced the padlock, and gave it an almighty kick. Bits of padlock and latch went flying across the cellar. Then, he did the same to the other lock, scattering it. "Now, for the moment of truth. I hope this is worth it now," he said. "Damn it, is that it?" he muttered, pulling out a small camouflage net.

But Dan removed the net no sooner than Deena grabbed a cloth bound around something. She carefully opened it. "Look what we've got," she squealed with delight.

"Whoa, don't point it at me! You don't know if it's loaded," said Dan, ducking out of her sight.

"Oh yeah. Sorry, Dan," she said, sheepishly handing it to him.

Dan took the gun, and with a closer look, he said, "It's a Smith and Wesson. Those Ground Crawlers are going to get it now. This gun dates to 1940. It's a square butt, thirty-eight calibre special. A fairly accurate target revolver for its time. It has an adjustable sight on it too."

"That's all very well," said Deena, "but it's no good without ammunition; unless you're planning on clubbing them over the head with it?"

"Oh, you're funny," he said, laughing. Dan opened the cylindrical chamber. "Dee, there are two shots in the chamber. Perhaps, if we can find more thirty-eight calibre cartridges, we'll be able to hold our own against the Ground Crawlers," he said excitedly.

"There's always a horde of them. The Ground Crawlers will have a bite out of us before we've even got a shot in," said Deena.

"I'm not suggesting we don't still use the sage and herbs, but we don't want to rely solely on the gun either. But it gives us extra protection if we get in a tight situation with them," said Dan.

"I must admit, I would feel safer out there with a loaded gun," said Deena. They sifted through the remaining crates. But unfortunately, they didn't find anything else of use.

"There are still rooms above to explore. I'm hoping they are also gunnery rooms," said Dan.

"Any idea how to get to them? There are no cellar steps other than that one, which goes out to the front of the house," said Deena, pointing to the only door in the room.

"Which means the only access will be from the ground floor. Thanks to the Ground Crawlers, the back door by the kitchens is out of the question," said Dan.

"There are only two routes I can think of, and that's the ground floor between the banqueting hall and ballroom or the long corridor at the rear of the manor," said Deena.

"Either way means we have to go overground," said Dan wistfully. "Let's finish up. Then, we can drop this stuff in our base and find food."

"Good! I'm starving," said Deena, jumping to her feet.

Dan picked up the rigs, slung the backpack over his shoulder and brandished the revolver. "I'll keep this," he said. Deena didn't mind; guns weren't her thing.

In the base room, Dan said, "After food, I want to return to the servant's quarters. The fourth tower is bugging me."

"Perhaps we can check in with Bronwyn while we're up there. Then, if we find food, we can take her some on our way up," suggested Deena.

"Great, we'll do the outside buildings after that," Dan said. "Can you help me put this rig on? I can't keep the gun in my hand all the time, and I'm not leaving it here," he asked her.

113

Dan chose the rig with the most pockets. He cut the corner of a pouch using the rune blade and slid the revolver into the compartment. The barrel protruded through, allowing the chamber to nestle in far enough so Dan could secure the pocket flap. Then, slipping the webbing straps over his shoulders, he asked Deena for some equipment and suggested the most needed items for the day's excursion.

"Awesome!" he said, and with a wicked glint in his eye, he leaned forward, looked over his shoulder at her and asked, "Does my butt look big in this?" Deena couldn't help but laugh. He spun around, bowed, and picked up the candle. "Are you ready to dine, madam?" he jested as Deena emptied the backpack.

"We should drop food up here also, then we can carry more for Bronwyn," said Deena. If ensuring Bronwyn's safety meant keeping her in one place and bringing supplies, she would do that. So, with an empty backpack, she followed Dan to the cellars.

They went through the catacombs to the far end and into the short corridor. The passage sloped dramatically, making it the furthest cellar and deepest underground. Then, Dan paused at the first door to their left. He opened it and looked in amazement. "Which wine does one require with one's dinner?" he chirped in his best English accent. The room was floor-to-ceiling with wine racks. Dan's eyes popped out of their sockets at the sight of so much alcohol. "I'm going to visit here before we go home," he said, spying a bottle of whiskey.

They skirted the room and found a case of still mineral water and one sparkling. Deena suggested taking some for themselves and Bronwyn. Although Bronwyn had access to water, she could refill bottles. The less Bronwyn was out and about, the safer she was. They left the wine cellar, crossing the corridor to a modern laundry room. There were washers, driers and deep ceramic sinks with bedsheets soaking in stagnant soapy water. Free-standing cupboards at the far end had shelves above. A small step ladder leaned against the last washing machine, so Deena erected it. To Dan's frustration, the first cupboard was full of cleaning agents. Above were cluttered drawers. Dan sifted through it.

"It's a man drawer!" said Deena, looking at the disorganised mess.

"A what?" asked Dan.

"A man drawer. Every house has one, usually in the kitchen. Martin has... had one. Filled with screwdrivers, screws, nails, and other crap women would sensibly chuck in the garage, but no, you guys decide you must hoard it all in one bloody drawer," said Deena.

"Wow, it annoys you then. Yeah, but look what the man drawer has in it!" said Dan triumphantly, waving a pocket flashlight.

"Does it work?" she asked.

"Ah, no batteries. There must be some here somewhere. No one has a flashlight and no batteries," Dan said fervently, searching the drawer. Finally, he held up two twin packs of disposable batteries while embarking on a victory dance.

"Brilliant, but we should still save the flashlights for emergencies," said Deena.

Dan opened the other cupboard as Deena worked her way across the shelves. "I've found more candles," said Deena, handing them to Dan.

"I'll tell you what we are short on, and that's matches, and we need a lantern for outside. Otherwise, we will spend all our time and matches relighting them," said Dan. The first drawer had old tools. But he found a Swiss army knife amongst the next drawer's contents, which Dan put in his rig. "I'm hungry. Are you done?" he asked.

"Yeah, I've finished," she said, climbing down.

The passage sloped sharply into the furthest cellar. Deena could see Dan's cold white breath as he walked in the candlelight. "There's food down here, and lots of it," he said.

Deena didn't need a second invitation. In the blink of an eye, she was right behind him. "This must be where Dot was getting the chilled foods," gasped Deena. Pulling a chunk out of a cheese wheel, she began eating while looking for the next thing to satiate her hunger. Above them, salted meats and cooked hams hung from the thick wooden beams, glistening in the cold air. They satisfied their bellies before filling the backpack with food.

"There's a basket of bread rolls," said Deena, picking one up and tapping it. "They're frozen. Do you think they'll be okay if we defrost them?"

"I don't see why not," said Dan. "Just a sec. I want to check where this door opens before leaving."

Dan opened the heavy door to steep steps leading outside. He motioned

Deena to stay where she was. Crouched, Dan climbed the stairway. Slowly, he stuck his head above ground level. Dan couldn't see much to his left. 'That building is above the wine cellar,' he thought. 'So, the door to that must be around the corner.' He looked to his right at the building above the cold room. "We can get into the building above. This room is the furthest to the rear of the house. We'd be too exposed to get across to the gunnery, but we can get upstairs," he said, pointing to the ceiling. "Do you want to have a quick look?" he proposed.

"May as well," she said. "But I'll light a bushel first." Dan handed her one from his rig. Deena lit it, nurturing the smouldering smoke. Then, holding it close to herself and Dan so their clothing absorbed the smell, Deena whispered, "Just in case." Dan knew the Ground Crawlers had become her biggest fear. Leaving the backpack at the bottom of the steps, she followed Dan. Again, Dan scrutinised their surroundings. A gravelled path and a small lawn separated them from another route. But, what worried Dan, was the woodland beyond.

He whispered to Deena, "It's not far." So, with their backs to the wall, they sidled towards the door. Dan tried the latch. As restrained as he was, it still gave a loud clunk as it left the fitting on the other side. Then, ear-piercing screeches filled their ears, accompanied by twigs breaking in the trees, making Deena grab Dan's arm.

"Open the door!" she urged. As Dan pushed the door open, something white flew at them from the woods. Wings and talons tangled in Deena's hair. She flailed her arms to fend off the creature. Finally, she cried out as Dan pulled her into the building, quickly shutting the door. They stood in the dark, trying to compose themselves. Dan began to laugh. "What's so funny?" asked Deena. "I'm attacked, and you're laughing?" she reproached.

"It was only an owl," he said, striking a match to relight his candle.

"Well, it bloody attacked me!" she said resentfully.

"It's probably hungry. You can't blame the owl for that," said Dan, grinning broadly. But, of course, Dan couldn't help it. When Deena got in a huff, he found her highly amusing.

Deena lit her candle, enhancing the light in the room. Hessian sacks lined the inside wall, so Dan opened one. It was full of flour. Deena placed her hand inside another before refolding the corners to close them. Food was scarce enough without wilfully exposing it to deterioration. Deena stuck her hand into another and squealed, yanking her hand out quickly. "Something bit me!" she said, waving a bloody finger.

Dan opened the offending sack, and there, looking up at him with big eyes and twitchy whiskers were a couple of plump rats feasting on rice grains. "That explains why the owl is lying in wait," he said. He grabbed a piece of lumber, swiping at the rats. The critters shrunk back, baring long sharp teeth. Dan took another swing, the sack split open, and rice grains scattered on the floor. Deena danced as one of the rats leapt towards her. The other launched itself at Dan in a vicious attack. The rice slid under his feet, and he lost his balance. "Dee, open the door!" he shouted as he pried the rat's teeth from his jacket. Deena opened the door, and Dan flung the rat as far as possible. A flurry of brown fur followed its buddy outside. "Dinner's ready, Mr Owl!" he muttered.

Deena shut the door quickly, preventing them from scampering back in. Dan retrieved his candle, scowling at the mess. "I'll sweep up," he said, grabbing a broom in the corner. As Dan swept the rice into a pile, the broom head shifted, so he upended the brush to solve the problem. The long handle had carvings and four grooves towards the broom head. He pulled the brush head off to find a deep slot cut into an elaborately carved end. Dan checked the other end, and it, too, had a deep aperture. But this end splayed outwards.

"Is it broken?" asked Deena.

"Yes, well, it is now, but this isn't the proper handle, look," said Dan.

"Are they rune markings like on the blade you found?" she asked.

Dan nodded as he held the shaft close to the light, tracing his fingers over the markings, deciphering them. What stood out to him were four runes. "Odin," muttered Dan in awe.

"Who is Odin?" asked Deena.

"Odin is the Norse god I told you about back in the facility. Remember, I told you the story of how he came upon the knowledge of the runes? First, he impaled himself upon his spear and hung in the tree of Yggdrasil for nine days and nine nights. Then, Odin spied the runes below on the ninth night and gained the knowledge of the runes."

"Oh, right. So, what's the tree, Ygg… What you call it, got to do with it all?" she pressed.

"Yggdrasil is the Tree of Life. It's a giant evergreen ash tree. It connects and branches out, embracing the nine worlds in Norse cosmology," explained Dan.

"Ah, okay, I've heard of the Tree of Life. So, Odin has a connection to the Tree of Life, the runes and whatever that is?" stated Deena, pointing at the wooden shaft.

"Yes, and if I'm right, this shaft is ash. With Odin's name carved in rune symbols, I think this could be the shaft to his spear, Gungnir," he said.

"Gungnir?" sighed Deena. "If it's okay with you, I will leave you to figure out this Norse stuff. I'm still struggling to get my head around it."

"I know it sounds complicated, but you'll pick it up. Hold it while I finish cleaning this rice out of the way," he said, handing her the shaft. Dan stooped, picked up the broom head and hastily brushed the grain against the wall. "Let's get back to our base, and then we'll go straight up to Bronwyn."

In the base room, Deena sorted food for themselves with two water bottles and put the rest in the bag for Bronwyn. "I'm ready when you are," chirped Deena.

Dan sat on the bedding, studying his new find in one hand and the knife tip in the other, muttering, "I'm sure these belong together. I feel intoxicated when I hold them. I know they are important. I must find all the pieces."

"Hey, Mr Archaeologist, we need to find the crystal skull too, remember? Don't you think that is more important?" she reminded him.

"Sorry, but I think this is as important. I can't explain why, but I feel strange empowerment when I hold it," said Dan.

"To be honest, a lot doesn't make sense, but if you or I have a strong gut feeling about something, perhaps we shouldn't ignore it. So, if you feel that, that…" she said, pointing to the shaft, "is important, then I promise I'll help you find the other parts." Deena had become resigned that perhaps they wouldn't fully understand the implications of everything they may encounter during their mission.

"Thanks. I suppose it's the same with the scrolls and crystals. You know they are important, but we don't yet understand why. I guess we'll figure it out, somehow," said Dan. "Oh, speaking of crystals, I want to get the black onyx ones from the drawing room."

Dan grabbed the backpack and chose to use the servant's stairs behind the main staircase as he needed to check if the barricade was still holding between the two kitchens. Then, they set off to see Bronwyn with a lit sage bushel and candles. Bronwyn was excited to see them when they whispered her name. "Hi, we've got you more food," said Deena. "There are some water bottles as well."

"I still have food from before," she said, opening the bag to see what goodies were inside.

"We don't know how long it will be before we can come back. It could be days, so go easy on it," said Dan.

"Dan's right. After we have finished up here, the next stage is outside, which will take time. This estate is huge," said Deena.

"But I will see you again, won't I?" exclaimed Bronwyn, upset. "The Shadow Men are still around. They watch me as I walk to the bathrooms."

"Refill the water bottles so you don't have to go back and forth as much. But you know, they will leave you alone if you have light," said Deena.

"I know, but I'm scared up here by myself. Can't I come with you?" asked Bronwyn.

"I'm sorry, what we have to do is too dangerous. You'll be safer here," said Dan firmly.

Bronwyn swallowed hard, trying not to burst into tears. The loneliness was getting to her. It crossed Deena's mind that Bronwyn could have stayed with Dot if she was still alive. But unfortunately, there was only one survivor they knew of, and that was the nanny, prompting Deena to ask Bronwyn, "What do you know about the nanny?"

"Do you mean Megan?" she questioned.

"Is that her name? We met her a couple of days ago," said Dan.

"Fussy, bossy old cow!" grumbled Bronwyn under her breath.

Dan laughed, "Yeah, that's her. What's with her anyway? She wouldn't help us at all."

Bronwyn went on a rant about how 'she' had one of the best double bedrooms in the house on the middle floor, and she had to stay right up the top of the house out of the way, and the fact 'she' lorded it over her that 'she' was in charge and could sack her anytime she wanted. By the time Bronwyn had finished, a picture had emerged of a relentless, power-crazed dictator running the household.

"So, staying with her then isn't an option?" said Dan, smirking.

"Like hell," stated Bronwyn, huffily folding her arms.

119

Deena couldn't help but giggle and said, "It's okay. Neither of us likes her much, and I don't think she's someone we can trust."

"I know I wouldn't. Megan's more likely to stab you in the back than help you," said Bronwyn.

"Dan, before we look for your fourth tower, I must get the Gaussmeter from the tapestry room. Are you coming?" asked Deena.

Dan wasn't happy about revisiting the middle floor, but, roaming the estate, he knew they would need all the equipment they had to hand.

"Stand guard with the sage in the hallway. I'll run in quick and get it," suggested Deena.

"Do you want this?" he asked, giving her the flashlight.

"With any luck, I'll be in and out before they've fathomed what we are doing. We won't be long, Bronwyn," said Deena as they left.

Dan waited beyond the steps where the hallway met the corridor to the balcony. Deena ran around the first door into the tapestry room and grabbed the meter. Dan was relieved to see her running back toward him without incident. He turned, and they ran up the stairs and into Bronwyn's room. Deena gave Dan the flashlight and the meter to put in his chest rig.

"Right, now can we go and find this tower?" asked Dan.

"We'll pop back later, Bronwyn. If we don't find this damned tower, I think Dan will burst a blood vessel," said Deena.

"No worries," replied Bronwyn, giving a wave goodbye.

Anxiously, they stood at the door where the Shadow Men attacked Dan. "I've already looked in the two rooms towards the back stairs. So, if there is a way in, it must be in either this one or the other three further down this section," said Dan.

"Right, so what furniture have you moved in here?" whispered Deena.

"Only the lighter stuff," he said. "I pulled the bed out, but nothing is behind it."

"So, the two wardrobes and the chest of drawers," she said, stepping towards the chest.

She tested the weight. It was heavier than she thought. So, Dan pulled out the top drawer to get a good grip. "We only need to move it out far enough to see behind it. Ready? One, two, three, lift!" grunted Dan as they moved it forward. He ran his hand behind it, but the wall was flush. So, he sized up the wardrobe. "We'll have to walk it out. Don't worry if you can't lift it. I'll do it," said Dan.

Deena and Dan stood on either side of the wardrobe. It took a while to get it far enough from the wall to see behind it. "It looks like there is a built-in cupboard on the wall. I need to get the wardrobe out more," he said. Finally, they could see a small hatch, measuring two feet square, sitting above the floor. Dan knelt in front of it. There was no fancy handle, only a hole big enough to put your finger through to pull it open.

"Well, open it," said Deena curiously. Dan hooked his finger through, pulled it open, and lit the recess with his candle, revealing a crawl space in the eaves. He couldn't see where it would lead or if it went anywhere. But, to him, it must go somewhere if there was a door, and hopefully, it would lead to the tower he so badly wanted to find.

"Follow me," he said to Deena as he wriggled through the tiny door.

Deena grabbed her candle and the sage bushel and disappeared after him. It hurt their knees as they crawled from one beam to the next. Cobwebs draped across their faces like a veil as they progressed. But, as uncomfortable as it was, Dan's gut feeling was strong, and he knew it would be worth the trouble. It paid off as he came to the end of the eaves and there, in front of him, was an identical miniature door set in a stone wall. Dan sat on his heels, turned to Deena behind him, and chuckled, "I feel like Alice in Wonderland." He pushed the door open and entered headfirst. He bent down and grinned inanely at Deena through the door. Then, feeling pleased with himself, he said, "Guess what we found?"

"A giant white rabbit with a pocket watch? Or maybe the mad hatter?" said Deena sarcastically.

"Be careful. The roof has caved into the tower," said Dan.

Deena looked skywards at the roof and walling that had collapsed. It was cold and draughty, and the smell of rotting timbers was pungent. The stairs up the sides of the tower were stone plinths jutting out of the wall, as in Bronwyn's. Deena held her candle to the lower ledge covered with thick, damp moss. Above her, ivy had taken a grip and covered most walls. "Why isn't anything easy," she muttered, knowing it would be her to go up. Deena idly flicked bits of moss off the stone plinth and said, "This tower has been collapsing for a long time, judging by its state."

Dust and stone chips fell away from the wall above Dan. Instinctively, he ducked, brushing whatever it was out of his hair. "Shush, standstill," he said, examining the area of the wall above him. A series of tiny squeaks and clicking sounds were audible. A little more stone and mortar cascaded. Dan held his candle up, and a frenzied black mass of leathery wings emerged from the dilapidated stonework as a colony of bats spiralled towards the dark sky. Deena squealed in fright, shying away from them. Their candles blew out, so Dan switched the flashlight on while Deena re-lit them and fanned the sage to boost it. "I'm guessing, but I reckon there are recesses in the walls behind the ivy, as in the other tower," said Dan.

"I know, your feet are too big!" she said, giving him her candle and the sage.

Deena brushed the moss off the first plinth and then searched amongst the rubble for a length of wood. Finally, she picked up a piece that was about three feet long. "What's that for?" asked Dan.

"So that I don't break my neck slipping on the wet moss. I can scrape it off the next plinth before jumping onto it. Can you use the flashlight as before?" asked Deena, climbing onto the first plinth.

Dan wedged Deena's candle on the floor between stones in the tower's centre. Every bit of light he could source was essential for Deena to see each plinth. Using the length of wood, she took her stance and repeatedly dragged it across the next stone until she'd scraped enough of the moss away. Grabbing the ivy, Deena gave it a quick tug making sure it would hold her before launching onto the next buttress. She diligently searched behind the ivy for the tiny cubbyholes as she ascended each. Ivy root trails crept in and out of the stonework, and bits of mortar broke away as she moved it aside. Creepy crawlies seemed to be abundant amongst its growth. Deena spent more time spluttering on bits landing in her face and squishing bugs than searching.

"Are you okay up there, Dee?" whispered Dan urgently.

Deena looked down at him, nodded and replied, "Yes, but I'd do anything for a nice long soak in a hot bubble bath."

Six plinths up, and she had found nothing. She grasped the ivy, leaned forward with the wooden baton, and began scraping moss off the next ledge. Her motions did not match the sounds of what she was hearing. She stopped and listened. Still, there was the sound of scraping on the stonework, and it wasn't her. She looked down at Dan standing in the tower's centre, looking back at her. "Dan?" questioned Deena, her voice wavering with fear.

"Shush, stay there," he said as he picked his way quietly across the debris. Then, finally, he stood below her and placed his ear against the wall. "Shit! Something is coming up the wall. Dee! Catch!" he whispered as he urgently threw the sage bushel to her.

Deena braced her back against the wall and clumsily caught the burning sage. Instinctively, she knew what was coming. The fear Deena felt at this moment was much higher than it was on her first encounter with them. She knew what these flesh-eating, indiscriminate killers were capable of doing. Deena was far too high to even consider trying to get down to Dan. Holding onto the ivy, she carefully reached the end of the plinth and picked up a handful of moss, smearing it over her face and scrunching it into her hair. Deena shrunk back against the wall and pulled ivy trails over her. Holding the sage bushel close, she hoped the smouldering smoke would linger within the leaves long enough to fool them. Dan backed into the far corner of the tower. The thirty-eight-calibre special was poised, ready with the hammer cocked in his hand. His finger traced the trigger. Dan trained the gun's sight on the visible area of the sky. The candle in the centre of the floor flickered erratically in the draughty tower. Dan prayed it would stay alight. It seemed like an eternity as they waited, but in essence, it was only minutes. Like waxwork dummies, they remained motionless in their positions.

CHAPTER TEN

The ascending sounds of scratching on the stonework got closer. Finally, sharp talons appeared over the edge of the fractured wall. Collapsing inwards, the Ground Crawler leapt into the tower amongst an avalanche of stone. The weight of the beast thudded to the floor. It growled and snuffed at the dust in the air, shaking itself off. Deena didn't dare move. The smoke from the sage was making her eyes water and burning the back of her throat. She closed her eyes, desperately swallowing hard. Dan's finger curled around the trigger. He was more than ready to blow the creature's brains out. Nothing would give him greater pleasure than to watch its brain matter spattering the walls. The only thing stopping him was not knowing if more were scaling the building, as he only had two shots. Dan remained transfixed on the Ground Crawler.

It growled from deep in its throat, stretching its neck forward, making its rib cage rattle. Methodically, it moved its head from side to side. Dan wondered if it had an echolocation system like the bats. Was it the bats that bought it up here? It was undoubtedly the weirdest, most badass creature he had ever had the misfortune of being this close to. The rattling growls suddenly stopped, and in one swift movement, it twisted itself around and lurched towards the wall near Deena. Dan felt the pressure in his trigger finger increase. He eased off when he saw it clawing at the stones six feet to her side; Deena was terrified. The fear racing through her body kept her rooted to the spot. Dan was struggling to stay calm; it was so close to her. The Ground Crawler's talon emerged from a crevice with an impaled squealing bat, its wings beating wildly in a futile attempt to escape certain death. The clash of sharp scissor teeth silenced the tiny mammal, a mere morsel to such a large predator. From behind the ivy leaves, Deena watched with disgust as it licked the remnants of the bat from its teeth. Clinging to the wall, once again, it emitted its guttural sound. Its chest again rattled in unison as it searched for its next mouthful.

The sound stopped, and Deena held her breath, anticipating an attack. Dan gripped the gun firmly in both hands, keeping it focused on the back of its head. The Ground Crawler climbed up and across a few feet. It was directly above her head. Ivy rustled around her, and the smoke from the sage filtered upwards. Quietly, she slowly exhaled and drew another breath. The claws of its hind feet gouged grooves as its body weight shifted, probing for another tasty bat. Stone chips, mortar, and ivy trails fell as the Ground Crawler foraged. Finally, it turned course above her and began descending the vertical face.

Terror struck when she opened one eye, and its chest was over her, only inches away. She held her breath as the guttural growl started up once again. It was a resonant death rattle. A twitch, the clench of a muscle or a single breath could define her end. Dan held the gun steady. His unwavering effort caused beads of sweat to form on his brow. He didn't dare wipe it away. Slowly, the beads rolled down his cheek, dripping onto his jacket. The Ground Crawler's head swivelled in Dan's direction, and the density of its growl increased as it stretched out its neck. Deena desperately resisted the urge to scream at the top of her lungs. It was there at the back of her throat, ready to escape. Another globule of sweat dripped onto Dan's jacket.

The guttural sound ceased, and the Ground Crawler leapt to the floor in a split second. It raised its head, sniffing the air. Dan knew he was in trouble. The only thing between him and it was the flicker of the candle in the middle of the tower. Dan slowly raised his hand to wipe his brow; another drip would bring more trouble his way than he wanted. No other Ground Crawlers seemed to have followed it up, but it remained in his mind that maybe the rest of the horde was not far away. Death stared blindly at Dan. The Ground Crawler knew he was there. The creature raised its head again and took in a deep breath through its nose, its nostrils quivering in anticipation as it drew in Dan's scent. He watched its body tense as it opened its mouth, salivating at the prospect of human flesh. It was enjoying instilling fear, relishing the hunt for its favourite meat. If that rattle is echolocation, they will also be able to detect moving objects and track them by vibration, making them an extremely dangerous predator, more so than they first envisaged.

Dan kept the gun pointed at the Ground Crawler, slowly moving towards him. A sense of satisfaction filled him with the knowledge that its so-called prey would inevitably stop it in its tracks with a squeeze of a fingertip. He raised the revolver, staring down the barrel. With only two shots, he couldn't afford to miss. The Ground Crawler let out a blood-curdling screech as it leapt towards him. Dan's hand trembled as it loomed in the air. "Take the shot! Kill it!" Deena screamed hysterically. It was as if it was happening in slow motion. Dan's focus was so intense that Deena's hysteria faded into the background. The Ground Crawler was in the air, launching itself towards him. Its vicious teeth glinted as it soared high above the candle. Dan raised the revolver, aiming at its chest, his finger snug against the trigger.

As the Ground Crawler began to bear down on him, he squeezed firmly, and a deafening shot rang out, echoing around the tower and into the ether. Dan rolled out of the way of the impending weight of the creature as it hurtled towards the floor. Scrambling to his feet, he stood ready, cocking the gun again, aiming it at its head. If he had to use their last shot, he would. The beast writhed on the floor, shrieking in pain. It was a blood-curdling sound that would make the hairs stand up on anyone's neck.

"Just fucking die!" yelled Dan, as he watched it vomiting blood. Then, twitching and convulsing in its death throes, the Ground Crawler fell silent. Dan didn't move, nor did he take the gun away from its head until he was sure it wouldn't get back up again. A few minutes passed before he heard Deena call out to him.

"Dan? Is… is it dead?" she asked. Her voice trembled as she balanced on the plinth, looking down at him and the Ground Crawler. She was still clutching the ivy growing from the wall that she had so desperately clung to throughout the ordeal. Dan took a couple of tentative steps toward the creature.

"Looks like it," he said, still aiming the revolver at its head. An uncontrollable rage bubbled inside him as he stood over its lifeless body. Killing the ruthless flesh-eating creature wasn't enough. Dan looked down at it, and without thinking, he lifted his boot and kicked it as hard as he could. The sound of its jawbone splintering was so satisfying that he continued his physical attack on the already dead beast.

Deena climbed down the plinths. Dan's raging assault continued as she jumped to the ground. She reached out, taking hold of his arm, distracting him from the Ground Crawler. Dan turned and looked at her. He pulled her close and held her tight, taking deep breaths to bring himself back under control. "That was for Dot," he whispered as he glanced at the remnants of the disfigured, bloodied features of the already hideous creature.

Deena didn't need to say anything. She understood why he felt the need to go that far. "Can we get out of this tower now?" she murmured. Dan relaxed, put his hands on her shoulders, nodded and made his way to the tiny door leading to the crawl space. Placing the revolver back in its makeshift holster, he looked at the carnage he had inflicted upon the bloody, lifeless creature. Dan put the flashlight on; he had neither the energy nor inclination to struggle with keeping a candle upright.

Deena spilt through the wall onto the bedroom floor, exhausted. Dan followed suit, closing the tiny doorway behind him. Deena sat on the bed and burst into tears as he struggled to push the wardrobe back against the wall. Dan sat beside her, not knowing quite what to do. Deena put her head in her hands and tried to stop her sobbing. Finally, Dan put an arm around her and held her tight. She was so beautiful. Her perfectly shaped cupid lips quivered as she choked back her tears. He lifted her chin, gently wiped the flow of sorrow away with his thumb and leaned in to kiss her. Horrified, Deena abruptly stopped him. "What the fuck do you think you're doing!" she shouted, throwing her arms up in the air at him.

"Sorry, Dee. I just thought…" said Dan, embarrassed.

"Well, don't!" she shouted at him. "How dare you! You know I'm married to Martin!" she snapped.

Dan remained silent. There were no excuses for what he had done, but knowing he was falling for her, he found it incredibly difficult not to express it. She was unique, beautiful, funny, and so very brave. He deeply regretted his actions but couldn't change how he felt about her. "I really am sorry," said Dan, apologising again.

Dan and Deena's attention was suddenly diverted to Bronwyn, standing in the doorway. "Is everything all right? I heard shouting," she said, looking at them in turn. "Shit, what on earth happened to you two?" she asked.

"We're fine. It's nothing to worry about," said Dan quickly.

"Didn't sound like nothing," muttered Bronwyn.

Neither Dan nor Deena cared to explain the outburst she had overheard. So instead, Bronwyn gave Dan a cheeky smirk and a wink. Then, trying to save face, Dan asked Bronwyn, "Do you mind if I sit in your room for a while? I think Deena could use some girl time and clean up, if that's okay?"

Bronwyn giggled, "Sure," and moved out of the way to let him through the door.

"Are you okay?" she asked Deena. "You sounded very cross at him. It can't be that bad whatever he did, can it?" she wondered.

Deena sighed, "He tried to kiss me."

"Seriously? Is that all?" giggled Bronwyn. "You lucky thing. I wouldn't have said no. He's like... lush and well fit." Deena's jaw dropped at Bronwyn's revelation. "I'm just saying, that's all," she remarked.

"It's complicated," sighed Deena.

"I've got some shampoo. I'll help you wash your hair if you want. The water's freezing, though," offered Bronwyn.

Deena grimaced, lifted a section of moss-riddled hair, and said, "Thanks, I'd like that. I do smell a bit, don't I?"

Dan watched from the far end before going down the steps to Bronwyn's tower as Bronwyn and Deena walked towards the bathrooms. He lay on the bed, crossed his ankles, knitted his fingers together behind his head and thought about the situation he had caused. 'You are a stupid, stupid man,' he thought. His only saving grace was the possibility that Bronwyn may smooth it over and Deena would forgive him for being such a goddamn idiot.

Dan swung his legs off the bed and quickly sat up when he heard the girls talking as they neared Bronwyn's tower. A hollow dread somersaulted in the pit of his stomach. As they came through the door, Dan stood up. Deena made eye contact with him which made him feel even more awkward. He looked to the floor as Deena sat on the bed, drying her hair with a hand towel. He wasn't sure which was worse, her not saying a word or ranting at him.

"I left the shampoo and a towel by the sink if you want to use it," said Bronwyn casually. Dan muttered thanks, grabbed a candle, and scuttled off.

"How long will you give him the silent treatment?" she asked Deena.

"Long enough to let him know this isn't the time or place for stuff like that. I do like Dan, but I must consider Martin. I'm still coming to terms with the possibility that he isn't, you know, but I must know for sure, and even then, it wouldn't be right," explained Deena. Bronwyn thought better of interfering between them and offered Deena her hairbrush. "Thanks, it feels good to be clean again," said Deena.

"Well, you did smell a little ripe!" giggled Bronwyn. Deena laughed at her cheeky remark. But it was as Dan said, she needed some girl time.

Dan managed to shave to some degree using the rune blade. Then, with his ego still on the floor, he looked at himself in the mirror. 'You're not such a bad-looking guy,' he thought, smiling at himself. A couple of nicks were still bleeding, but it was worth it. The facial fur was gone. He finished getting brushed up and returned to Bronwyn and Deena. He stuck his head around the door, and with a sheepish grin, he asked, "I haven't got a white flag. Is it safe for me to come in?"

"No white flag needed. It's fine," said Deena.

Dan stepped through the door, hoping his embarrassment didn't show. "There are some rooms we haven't gone through up here. I'll do them if you want to spend more time with Bronwyn," he suggested.

"After the performance with the Shadow Men, I think I'll come with you," said Deena curtly.

"I thought that maybe you needed some time out," he said awkwardly.

"It's fine, Dan. You and me, we are fine! It's only you that is making a big deal out of it. The only thing I am interested in is getting this mission done. So there, is that clear enough?" said Deena, exasperated.

Dan's eyes widened, and raising his hands to chest level, he defensively said, "I get it. I'm over it. Awkwardness over, and mission on!"

"Good, then I suggest we get on with it," she said. They lit a couple of candles, leaving Bronwyn in her room. As they walked the balcony below the glass dome, a plethora of shadows and flashes of red eyes followed them. It took nearly two hours to finish searching the servant's floor, and they both felt exhausted. Finally, Dan suggested they say goodbye to Bronwyn and get some well-earned rest.

As they returned to the base room, Dan said to Deena, "We should sort out what we need to go outside safely," muttered Dan, opening pockets on his chest rig. "I think you should prepare a chest rig, too. We can use the backpack to store food, water, and anything we may come across that we can use."

"I'm dreading going out there, especially knowing the Ground Crawlers seem to roam the back of the house," she admitted.

"The horde is one less now," he said quietly. "We have to make sure we keep our wits about us, that's all." Their encounter in the tower was too close for comfort, and what happened had taken its toll on them. "There's something I need to do before we turn in. Keep watch for me," said Dan, grabbing a candle and the remnants of a sage bushel. He pushed the panel open, and before stepping through it, he whispered, "I won't take long."

Dan crept past the main staircase to the other side of the manor. Finally, Deena realised he must be going to retrieve the black onyx crystals from the bureau. Silently, he slipped under the balcony and into the drawing room. Fifteen minutes later, Deena was getting worried. Then, she glimpsed his silhouette, standing motionless against the doorframe, but there was no glow of his candle. Then, Deena heard footsteps above her and a door closing. Dread filled her as she thought of the nanny on the prowl. Finally, Dan hurriedly returned to Deena when the coast was clear.

"What took you so long?" she asked.

"You'll never guess whom I saw," he said eagerly.

"Megan?" she asked.

"Yes, but I'm not on about her. I saw Lady Amelia! She appeared by the window," he replied, giving Deena the black onyx crystals.

"And you didn't freak out?" she said, surprised.

"No, I didn't. I was searching in the bureau and saw a bluish-white glow in the corner of the room. When I looked at Lady Amelia, she looked directly at me and pointed out the window at something. Then she vanished," rambled Dan excitedly.

"And?" said Deena expectantly.

"And I went to see what she was pointing at, and I could only see the maze over the far side of the gardens," said Dan.

"Do you think there is something we need to find there?" asked Deena.

"I reckon there must be," he said. "But we will be vulnerable, and finding our way to the centre will be a nightmare."

"What was Megan doing up there?" she asked.

"I don't know. She was at the top of the stairs sniffing the air like a bloodhound. I think she must have smelt the sage," said Dan.

"I wouldn't worry too much about her. What's the worst she can do?" remarked Deena.

"Set the Twins on us again?" he said with a shudder. "I'd rather avoid her. I don't want her to know we are hiding in here."

"You're right. It's better not to invite trouble. Are you ready to turn in?" asked Deena. Dan waited for her to perform the protection ritual so they could sleep without fear. Deena stepped into the salt circle with Dan, and they made themselves comfortable; it wasn't long before they fell asleep.

Deena lay quietly, enjoying the warmth and comfort of the bed. It was the best night's sleep she'd had since they had landed in Wales. Then, Dan began to stir, so Deena sat herself up, had a stretch, and reached for the food. He looked at her through bleary eyes. "Are you feeding your face already?" he asked sarcastically. Cocking an eyebrow at her, he asked, "Can I have a ham roll?"

Deena split the roll in two and placed a chunk of the ham. "When you've finished 'feeding your face,' we can sort everything ready to go to the gunnery," said Deena. She reached for the spare chest rig, examining the size of the pockets and deciding what she could fit into them.

Amid their discussions, they decided to split the equipment. Dan kept the gun, and Deena gave him the Gaussmeter as he was familiar with it. "This way, if we get split up, we've each got what we need," said Dan.

"Let's hope that doesn't happen. I don't fancy our chances if we are separated," said Deena.

"Perhaps, but without knowing what's out there, if it happens, at least we'll each have a survival kit," he stated.

"What about food? Do you want me to put what's left in the backpack?" she asked.

Dan nodded, reminding her of a couple of water bottles to go in. "We can pick up extra bottles on our way through the cellars. Have you got a deep pocket to store one in your rig?" Dan asked her.

"Kind of," she said, ramming a bottle into a pocket. Finally, Deena's eyes scanned the room, ensuring they hadn't forgotten anything. Then, she followed Dan to the cellars.

Dan paused at the corridor running the length of the catacombs. "We're low on salt. We should make up some more pouches before going outside," he whispered.

They turned under the huge centre arch to Dot's storage room. There was salt from what they had taken before, but only enough for around five pouches. Deena scoured the cupboards for more while Dan prepared the paper squares. She was pleased when she found a box half full. There was salt left over with ten pouches made up. Dan put them in the backpack's front pocket and went to leave. He glanced around the cellar as he closed the door behind them. "Wait!" he suddenly whispered, stopping Deena in her tracks. "I just saw it again."

"Saw what?" she asked, confused.

"A light behind there," he replied, pointing at the timbers stacked under the stairwell. Determined to find out what it was, he gave Deena his candle. He moved a couple of lengths of wood, laying them on the floor. Taking the candle back from Deena, she watched as his arm disappeared through the gap.

"Is there a room behind there?" she whispered. Dan shook his head and beckoned her over to see for herself. Deena gasped as she peered through the cavity.

"It's a tunnel!" she exclaimed excitedly. "If these run through the estate, it could be a safer way to get around rather than overground!"

"Not yet. I must get to the gunnery first. I've only one shot left. Something or someone was walking about in there with light. I want to ensure we can defend ourselves if we need to. So, help me block it back up, and we can come back later," he said.

Deena was disappointed, but he was right. It was better to go armed. So, once they had erected the timbers, they walked the catacombs, turning into the long passage at the back of the manor. Dan slowly opened the door to the ground above and motioned Deena to keep her head down while she lit the sage. She signalled a thumbs up; she was ready. Another quick check saw that the coast was clear. They crept along the back wall of the manor.

As they neared the kitchen window where the Ground Crawlers broke in and killed Dot, Deena averted her attention to the gunnery door. Even so, a wave of grief hit her as she passed it. Dan glanced back at Deena. He admired her stoic, fixed stare on where they were heading.

The door to the gunnery wasn't wooden like the rest. Dan suspected it was fortified in World War II when American and British soldiers took residence. Bolts secured the sliding door at the top and base, and a thick, three-inch flat metal bar sat in its housing across the centre. A short, crude, welded handle jutted out. It didn't look like anyone had opened it in many years as the old olive-green paint had mainly flaked away. Dan took hold of the handle, and the metal scraped and squealed as he pulled the bar back. Deena knelt, keeping a guarded watch, and lifted the bolt out of the ground. Dan reached up, releasing the last one. He slid the large door open enough for them to slip in. As soon as Deena squeezed through the gap, Dan quickly shut it. They took stock of everything left to disintegrate over the years. Finally, Dan went to a door on the far side and opened it. "Well, we've found the gunnery rooms for sure," he muttered.

The adjoining room was more extensive, and two large cannons sat to one side. "What are they doing here?" asked Deena

"I don't know. Perhaps they were displayed on the front lawns. Fancy houses and too much money," Dan said. Deena stubbed out the sage, and their methodology for searching kicked in as they departed to either side of the rooms. "There's another stack of ammunition chests here," Dan whispered excitedly, grinning as he was back in the candy store. Of course, Dan wasn't kidding when he said there was a stack of them. "This will take a while, Dee," he said, whistling with admiration at the newfound treasure.

She saw the mischievous look of excitement on his face. Then, looking the stack up and down, she suggested, "Do you mind if I leave you to it? I'm going to carry on poking my nose about." Dan ushered her away, enthusiastically taking down the first layer of chests.

Deena stood in the middle of the room, wondering where to start. She checked her watch; time was ticking. She thought about everyone back at the base. Yes, they needed to be thorough, but they had been there for over a week. What she thought would be a simple in-and-out mission had become so complex. And now, to add to that was an unexpected network of underground tunnels. As she pondered the shelves and empty gun racks across the back wall, she remembered the light Dan saw flickering behind the timber beams under the cellar steps. Her thoughts drifted around as to what or who caused it. Perhaps it was a survivor using the tunnels to move around the estate. There was only one way to find out; exploring it themselves.

She found some old, square tins and gave them a shake. Rubbing her fingers across the faded rusty image on the lid didn't reveal anything. She was disappointed when she pried the top off to find old screws, bolts and washers that had seen better days. The other tins contained much the same.

There were tools in a storage box for mechanical maintenance. So far, she had found nothing of use. Dan sat, his candle beside him, amongst an unruly pile of ammo chests. "I didn't find anything in the other room. Do you want me to help you with the rest of these chests?" asked Deena.

"Sure, I haven't found anything yet either," he said, pointing to a pile behind him. "I've done those." Deena pulled a chest from the unsearched pile. There was still a lot to go through. Deena opened the crate and chatted as they searched. "I'm still hoping we'll find some thirty-eight calibre shells," he said.

"We need to get a move on with this mission. I worked it out earlier; we've been here for over a week, and we still have so much ground to cover. I'm scared that we'll be too late for the team by the time we get back to the base," said Deena sadly.

"I hear you," Dan sighed. "All we can do is be as thorough as we can as fast as possible. Skipping out on areas isn't an option. We have no idea where this skull is hidden."

"I have an excellent feeling about the tunnels. It seems logical they would have hidden it underground," said Deena.

"Yes, I agree, and we'll go there next, I promise," Dan said, taking another chest down.

"We've encountered dark, evil stuff we had no idea about before exploring the manor. But regardless of whether we're underground or overground, we still don't know what we are up against until we meet it head-on," said Deena despondently.

Dan managed a smile, but he, too, felt a sense of helplessness deep down. With everything they had endured, keeping a positive mindset was tough. But they knew that to fail in their mission would mean the end of the world for human habitation. Deena got up to stretch her legs, and as she walked around the room, she spotted an old bunk in the corner. Next to it, spanning the rest of the wall space, were three tall metal cabinets, each with double doors. The wall facing opposite had metal shelving racks that had once housed large artillery shells. "Hey, Dan, have you looked at this end of the room yet?" she asked.

"No, sorry. I got distracted by the ammo chests. I wanted to finish them before searching that end," said Dan.

"Do you mind if I do it?" she asked.

"Sure, go for it," he said while digging around a crate.

Deena tried the doors of the tall metal cabinets. They were locked. So, she asked Dan for the penknife. He took it from his rig and offered to open it, but she shooed him away. "Go, go on. Go and do the crates. I can manage this by myself," laughed Deena.

Dan left her to it, smiling as he went. Deena pulled the smaller blades out of the penknife and chose one that would be the best fit to jimmy the locks. A couple of minutes of intense jiggling and manipulating opened the lock on the first set of doors. She opened them to reveal a framework of angle iron shelving stacked with old radio equipment. "Dan, come and look at this," said Deena.

Dan jumped up, grabbed his candle, and went over to her. It was dusty, and the wiring had degraded, but he was astonished to see it was untouched since the day they had shut the doors on it.

"It's a self-contained mobile radio communications station. The Wireless Set 10," Dan said, fascinated. "This would have given them a direct and secure link to London."

"Why would they leave it here? This stuff should be in a museum," said Deena.

"I suppose when the war ended, there was no need for it. Perhaps the soldiers shut up shop and went home to their families," he said, shrugging his shoulders. "This station would've been crewed twenty-four hours a day, hence the bunk."

"Cool, well, history lesson over with, thanks," she said, cutting him short. Dan laughed, returning to his crates as Deena searched in and around the shelving units. Finally, with an unsuccessful rummage, she continued to the next pair of doors. Then, with the penknife in hand, Deena opened them up. "Jeepers, look at all this equipment," she gasped.

Dan again abandoned his crates and rushed to see why she was fussing. But, he was shocked at what was behind the doors. His eyes danced around the array of switches and buttons that sat on the shelving inside. Finally, he traced his finger across a name on one of the machines, TYPEX. "This is incredible. I've never seen a British enigma machine," he muttered.

"A what?" asked Deena.

"It's an encryption, interception, and spy radio. It played a huge part in winning World War Two by spying and intercepting German messages and, at the same time, deciphering its code. Both sides used them in fixed locations," said Dan excitedly. Deena pulled one of several small cases off the shelf and undid the clips. Lifting the hinged lids revealed portable radios inside. "This is a complete World War Two communications station. It's got everything they would've needed," he said in amazement.

Deena left him to satisfy his curious archaeological persona and began checking behind and between the units where possible. Deena slipped her arm into small gaps, her fingers exploring blindly. Then, she felt a familiar disc shape amongst the thick dust and cobwebs. Stretching a little further, Deena grasped it between her fingers and eased it out of the tight gap. She brushed off the dirt and showed it to Dan.

"Another rune," he said, taking it from her eagerly. "It's Mannaz."

"So, what does it mean?" asked Deena. She thought back to what happened with the rune, Algiz, when she called upon Heimdall while Dan's mind flitted through his knowledge, trying to recall what he knew.

"I'm sure Mannaz is the symbol for humankind. It represents our place in the universe and opens communication for honest and unbiased advice from others. A sort of societal rune that cuts out ulterior motives between people," he said.

"So, like a truth rune?" she surmised.

"Well, yes, I suppose so," he said.

"With the other rune, the deity, Heimdall, was connected to it. Is there a god for this one as well?" she asked.

Dan nodded. "Yes, and it's the same god, making it nice and easy to remember."

Deena's fingertips tingled with the combined energy they possessed as she slipped it into her jeans pocket. She continued, but her height hindered the last of her search on the top shelves, so she asked Dan for an ammo chest to stand on, giving rise to a snigger from him. She gave him a curt look as he placed it in front of the cabinets for her. Dan shook his head at her stubborn independence as he walked away. He resumed going through the ammo chests and smiled as he glanced back at her, standing on tiptoes atop the trunk.

Within minutes, Deena sprung off the crate and rushed over to him. "Are these the right ones?" she asked excitedly, handing him three cartridges. Dan couldn't believe she'd found them in the back of the communications cabinet of all places. He inspected them and gave her a broad grin. "Is that a yes?" she said, clasping her hands together excitedly.

Dan nodded and opened the revolver chamber, sliding each shell into its slot. Then, he snapped it shut with satisfaction and secured it back in his rig. "That gives us four shots," he said. "I feel better about going in the tunnels now."

"Great," she said. "When I've finished over there, I can help you with this lot." With the workload shared, it didn't take long to get through the last of the chests. Finally, they had a quick look around the areas that were left. Then, satisfied they had done enough, they decided to move on and explore the tunnels.

Creeping along the back of the house, Dan stopped to look inside the outbuilding above the wine cellar. It contained a couple of sinks, gardening tools, and utility meters for the estate. As they turned to leave, he spotted a pair of wellington boots caked in dried mud standing neatly against the wall inside the door. The muddy boots and random rakes and spades made him think of Jack. He recalled how fondly Dot had spoken about him. Was it possible he was still alive? They returned to the cellars, and it was a relief to shut the door behind them. Dan relit the candles and, on their way through, collected water bottles for their next excursion. Under the stairwell, Dan moved the timber aside.

"Wait!" said Deena, suddenly.

"What's wrong?" he asked.

"Something is in this tunnel, right? What if it's not friendly? What do we do?" she questioned.

"Are you having second thoughts about going in? Then, if we need to, we just run in the opposite direction until we know we're safe. I don't know what else to suggest." He sighed, taking his candle from her. "Please don't bottle out on me."

"I'm not bottling out!" said Deena, feeling peeved.

Dan grinned at her. "Come on then, what are you waiting for, an invitation?" he asked as he disappeared behind the timber.

Deena followed him in. Dan held his candle up to try and see a little further ahead. Earthen walls ran on either side of them with intermittent timber struts aligned with support beams above their heads. The deeper into the tunnel they went, the colder it got. Deena turned the collar up on her jacket and zipped it up. "No sign of that light you saw yet," she remarked.

"I'm not sure I want to see it, if I'm honest," he replied.

"It looks like we're nearly at the end. I'm sure there is a wall ahead,"

Deena said, squinting into the darkness.

It wasn't the end of the tunnel but a junction, so Dan asked, "Left or right?"

"Does it matter?" she said, shrugging her shoulders.

"I suppose not," he said. "You know that aerial picture we saw in the gallery? Can you remember what's on either side of the manor?" he quizzed.

"Some of it, why?" she asked.

"I'm trying to plan where we're likely to end up," he supposed.

Deena closed her eyes and tried to visualise the map. She pointed to her left and rattled off a list of what she could remember. "The stables, maze, lake, oh and the boathouse... cottages... there's something else, but I can't think what it is," she pointed right, "... the orangery, gardens... a church and an abbey. Sorry, but that's all I can recall," she said, opening her eyes.

"The maze; the white lady pointed to it. Do you mind if we go that way?" he asked excitedly.

They stopped as they neared another junction, and Dan said, "Another left. It must go back to the house. Do you want to explore it, or are you happy to carry on?"

Deena didn't answer. She tugged at his jacket and pointed down the tunnel where they were heading. A yellow glow of light was coming their way. Dan grabbed Deena and ran up the junction leading back under the house, extinguishing the candles. They flattened themselves against the wall, hoping that whatever, or whoever, wouldn't see them. As it neared the passage where they were hiding, Deena prayed it wouldn't turn towards them. The glow got brighter, and it was almost upon the entrance. Dan hoped they were back far enough that the incoming light source wouldn't give them away.

An extended human arm holding a lit staff torch appeared. They both felt relief until it came entirely into their view. Deena and Dan both gasped at a creature that wasn't human. Suddenly, the beast's attention drew toward them. It thrust its lit staff into the darkness of the tunnel. It stood there, listening and grunting.

CHAPTER ELEVEN

Neither dared to move a muscle. This creature belonged in a mythological story, not walking about life's realities. Large goat horns curled about its skinless skull, and its bloodshot eyes bulged in their sockets from the lack of flesh. The cold air snorted from its nasal cavities. The neck and torso were that of a man, with bicep and abdominal muscles to put any bodybuilder to shame; it looked formidable. Yet, as the creature lowered its staff torch, they could see from the waist down. It was that of a long-haired goat, even down to the cloven hooves. As it grunted and turned to leave, the cold vapour from its breath trailed behind it in the disappearing glow. Dan slowly turned towards Deena, whispering, "What the fucking hell is that!"

"How should I know? I've never seen anything like it," she muttered.

Dan lit their candles and said, "We need to move before that thing comes back."

As Deena led the way to the main tunnel, they walked silently, trying to understand what they had witnessed. Eventually, Dan spoke. "I've heard tales of Goat Men. There are eyewitness accounts across America, but I never believed them. So, if that Goat Man had seen us, what do you think it could do to us?"

"I've heard of sightings too, but I put it down to fertile imaginations. Guess we're both wrong on that score," said Deena, "and I don't want to think about what it could do to us."

"Do you think that's the only one? Or is there a possibility there could be more?" asked Dan.

"I don't know!" she said, exasperated. "I don't know any more about this creature than you!" she asserted.

The tunnel opened into a cellar. Thick stone walls supported an arched passage that turned at a right angle. Nestled back under the arches were small rooms. "Where do you think we are?" asked Deena.

"At a guess, somewhere under the stable blocks," said Dan. Then, around the corner, he spotted a narrow door at the furthest end of the cellar.

139

He peeked around it, whispering, "The tunnel goes this way."

Deena didn't hear him as she was busy nosing in various rooms. Wooden chests and barrels were sporadically scattered. The cellar turned at a right angle. A tiny triangular room sat in the corner, not much bigger than four feet across. Deena stood in the odd-shaped space. It reminded her of the towers when she spotted the tiny, recessed shelves built into the walls and thought, 'This has got to be worth a look.' She began a fingertip search starting from the ground up, but the lower shelves proved empty. Unfortunately, the higher cubby holes were out of her reach, so she found a small chest she could stand on. It wasn't until she stepped on it that she noticed Dan leaning against the wall with his arms folded, with a grin across his face. Deena wagged her finger at him and muttered, "Not one word from you!"

Dan looked away, trying not to laugh. But instead, he couldn't help but whisper, "You're such a short arse."

"I heard that!" she said, fumbling on a shelf. "Hey, Dan! I've found a lantern, but it's wedged." Dan took her candle, and Deena pulled it free with encouragement. It was a simple miner's lamp, a square, metal frame with glass sides and an air-vented top with a hook attached. Deena opened the small latch on one side. "This is ideal for outside!" she said. "The moonlight is bright enough for the open ground, but I don't fancy the woodlands without light."

"We'll have to be ready to blow it out quickly if that Goat Man reappears. Speaking of which, we should get a move on," said Dan.

Deena set a candle into the lantern's well and closed it. "That's brighter already. I have a few more shelves to do. It won't take long," she said, placing the lantern at her feet.

Dan kept guard, watching either end of the cellar for the glow of the Goat Man's staff. Finally, Deena found several more items and hurriedly said, "I've finished here."

Hastily they headed south, away from the manor and deeper into the tunnels. Deena passed the lantern to Dan so that she could examine her finds. There was a scroll, but the carved sand timer grabbed Deena's imagination. The base had an inscription in runes, but unfortunately, she couldn't decipher them. That was Dan's job. Five beautifully sculpted animals formed each of the four columns, holding the hourglass. One blended into the next. A dragon sat at the base of each pillar; its wings wound around meeting the next, forming a beautiful, edged design. Then, a snake spouted from the mouth of the dragon and a butterfly from its forked tongue. The butterfly's antennae formed into the barbs of a fishtail. The fish's mouth gaped, and the barbels transitioned into a flow of tail feathers, creating a raven. The raven's wings met the next around the top, as the dragons did below. She tilted it back and forth, allowing the sand grains to flow from one side to the other. Then, Deena turned her attention to the scroll. She untied the familiar white ribbon and unrolled it. Dan stopped and turned towards her so that Deena could see better. But it wasn't quite what she expected. "A pentacle?" questioned Deena.

"That's not one of the elements," said Dan.

Deena shook her head, "No, but the elements sit at the pentacle's five points when you cast a spell in Wiccan magic."

"Do you think this is part of a spell?" he said, smirking.

"Whoa, now, we have had to believe in things we can't understand, see, or touch, so why should this be any different? But, Goat Man, need I say more?" said Deena.

Dan gave Deena an apologetic look and said, "I imagine witchcraft as mumbo jumbo. You know, older women sitting around a cauldron with herbs and animal bones, claiming to make hexes or cast spells for cures, love, and all that nonsense. So, why do you call it a pentacle? I know it as a pentagram."

"It's usually called a pentagram when inverted, denoting the dark side. This one is upright, indicating the light side. Think about it, what's our goal in this mission?" asked Deena.

"So, do you know what to do with it?" asked Dan.

"No, not yet," sighed Deena, rolling the scroll back up and putting it in the backpack with the sand timer. They continued their journey through the tunnel. The wooden struts and beams looked strained under the weight of the ground above. Occasionally, dirt and shale shifted to the terra firma, startling them. Deena was getting nervous.

"These tunnels have been here longer than we've been around. So, don't worry, I'm sure it's safe," said Dan. But Deena wasn't so sure. Ragnarök had left its scars deep in the landscape; the world was over as they knew it. In her mind, she knew nothing was safe, and nothing was as it seemed.

"There's another tunnel further down this one," Dan said. As they got to it, it veered back on them. "Want to take a quick look?" he asked.

This tunnel was narrower than the others, and it wasn't far before they found themselves at a dead end. "Hey, look," he whispered, "there's a way up." He hooked the lantern to his chest rig and dug the toe of his boot into the earth above a wooden brace between the struts. "The braces act as a ladder. Stay there. I'll see if I can get up first." And with that said, he dug his fingers into the earthen clay above the next brace and began climbing. A stone slab sat above his head.

Clinging to the last brace with one hand, he felt around the edge of the slab until he found a grip. Then, he shifted it across far enough to wriggle through. Deena nervously paced below, watching for the staff torch's glow. "Psst, Dee, you'll never guess where it leads to. Come up."

Deena didn't need any encouragement. The climb narrowed the higher she got. Finally, Dan helped her squeeze past the stone slab and onto dry turf. As she sat on the edge, her feet dangling below, she brushed her hand across the dry grass. Without sunlight, everything was dying. It was another sharp reminder of the time they didn't have within the inhibiting darkness.

They were standing in the centre of the maze. The pagoda surrounded them in a stunning filigree web, all but for the archway. Deena traced her hands around the decorative ironwork and whispered, "Right where the white lady wanted us. I don't know what we're supposed to find. Do you think this was her favourite place when she was alive?"

"Maybe, but it was the way she looked at me when she pointed to it, as though I needed to know it was imperative to come here," said Dan.

"Well, let's get searching," suggested Deena. Dan volunteered to search the outskirts of the maze. Inside the pagoda were three long stone seats intersecting with the outer edge. The stone slab they moved to get out of the tunnel was in the centre. A couple of Grecian statues stood between the benches, and two more stood at the entrance to the pagoda. Deena glanced at each figure, deciding where to start. Then, lighting a candle, she knelt at the first statue. He was a handsome, male Grecian figure dressed in nothing more than a fig leaf. She made eye contact with him and quietly said, "Nothing personal, sir, but I will have to frisk you." Carefully she ran her hands over the statue, and when she had finished, she stood up and said, "Thank you, sir, for your cooperation." Amused, Deena was thankful that, despite everything, she still had her sense of humour. The next statue was a couple of cherubs sitting at the feet of an elegant, young Grecian woman. Deena deemed her toga ill-fitting due to the left breast being so wilfully exposed. Having found nothing, she moved to the next. Another Grecian beauty held her hand out to Deena, but it seemed the sculpted figures held no secrets.

Confused, Deena thought maybe there was something in the design of the lattice. She carefully scanned the patterns in the ironwork, but there was nothing. Deena picked up the backpack at a loss and sat on the middle bench. While waiting for Dan, she thought about the tunnels being the safest way to get around, aside from the Goat Man. Given a choice between it and the Ground Crawlers, she decided to take her chances with the Goat Man.

Dan had been gone for some time, and she was nervous sitting alone. She checked her watch. Six a.m., May the fifteenth. 'The team must be so anxious,' she thought. They knew nothing of what they were up against in the mission. But, despite all they had encountered, they were alive and progressing. Thoughts of her family filtered around her. Deena shook them off as she felt tears well up inside her.

She abruptly stood up and looked about for Dan. There was no sign of the lantern's glow. Worried, she placed her knee on the bench to gain height. Her fingers found grooves in the lichen-ridden stone as her hands palmed the surface. Curious, she looked closer. She traced more indentations but needed to scrape the lichen away to expose the carvings to make sense of it. Ideally, she required the penknife, but Dan had it. She stood on the bench and called for Dan as loudly as she dared. The lantern popped up a couple of hedgerows away. "I think I've found something, but I need the penknife," Deena said excitedly.

It didn't take Dan long to find his way back to Deena. Eagerly, she showed him the carvings on the bench. Then, using the penknife, he began carefully scraping the surface. Next, Deena inspected the other seats to see if they had carvings or inscriptions, but they were bare. "Do you think this is what the white lady wanted us to find?" asked Deena.

"It's interesting, but until I can clear this stuff off it, it's hard to tell what the carvings are," he muttered.

Deena searched for a sharp-edged stone and helped him scrape off the lichen. When they had finished, Dan stood back to look at the carvings.

Rune words were around the edges. In the centre was what appeared to be a full-sized spear. "Can you decipher it?" asked Deena.

"Yes, but there's a lot to translate," he replied. Dan knelt and began with the inscription above the spear, "So, this first bit at the top reads, 'Altar of Gungnir.' Odin's spear, I knew it! Incredible," said Dan, turning his attention to the following line of the inscription. "Blades... and shaft... bind... to... err... together!" muttered Dan. "Okay, the next line is 'upon this altar in threads of grey... blue.' Threads of grey-blue, what? It's not making sense."

"Try the next line," Deena urged. "Perhaps it'll make more sense when you've deciphered it all."

"'Odin's power... shall live for... live... forever.' So, the spear must contain Odin's power somehow. Let me get this last bit, and then we can work out what it means," said Dan, pleased with his progress. "'In the... heart... of one... who is... true.' Let me read it all together," said Dan excitedly.

"'Altar of Gungnir; Blades and shaft bind together, upon this altar in threads of grey-blue. Odin's power shall live forever, in the heart of one who is true.'"

"It's a riddle," remarked Deena.

Dan studied the spear's carving, noting the blade's shape. "I think we are already halfway to understanding it," he said. "We have the shaft and the tip of the blade. Once we have all the pieces, we need to come here to 'bind' it together," said Dan, searching his rig. Finally, he pulled out the blade tip, placing it in the groove. It glimmered as though laced with a thousand tiny stars as it lay in its rightful place. Deena was mesmerised. "We have to find the rest of it," muttered Dan.

"That's amazing. It looks alive with power. I can't wait to see what happens when we put all the pieces there," gasped Deena.

"The carving gives a clue about what we need to look for," said Dan. "See? Four small blades go around the shaft below the main blade at the top. A piece is missing from the tip, and there should be a tomahawk blade at the end of the spear. It's an exceptional weapon."

"We could certainly use it. I don't like being out in the open," remarked Deena. "We should get going. We've found what we were looking for." Dan agreed and picked up the blade, backpack, and lantern, ushering Deena towards the stone slab.

Deena descended first. Dan dropped the backpack to her as she jumped to the tunnel floor. Then, climbing down, he braced himself below the shaft opening to close the slab, leaving a gap for a fingertip grip if they needed to use it again. The thought of Ground Crawlers, let alone the Goat Man within the confines of the tunnels, was a scary prospect. Nevertheless, he made his way to Deena. He took the backpack from her and slung it over his shoulder, grinning broadly. "What are you so happy about?" she asked him.

"The spear!" he said with delight. "I hope we can find all the pieces. Can you imagine the difference that would make for us in this mission? "'Odin's power shall live forever!'" he recalled. "That's what it said."

"Do you think it has godly powers?" she asked him.

"Yes, I do. Specifically, Odin's power! You saw how it glistened when I put the spear's tip in its place on the altar," he said. "Never in my dreams, as an archaeologist, did I ever even remotely think I would come across an artefact such as this," he said, dancing around her.

"Never in my dreams, as a parapsychologist, did I think I'd be sharing a mission with an over-excited idiot to save the world from the evils of darkness! If you don't calm down, you will attract the attention of something awful. So chill, will you?" she said, exasperated. "Have you given any thought to the rest of the riddle? The second line said, 'upon this altar in threads of grey-blue.' What does that mean?" Deena enquired.

"Yeah, I haven't worked that out yet," replied Dan. The deeper they went into the tunnel, the wetter it got. Intermittent puddles had turned to ankle-deep water.

"Where's all this water coming from?" asked Deena. "It's getting deeper. Do you think it's safe to keep going?" she cautioned.

"It's fine. But make sure you keep the matches and candles above water if it gets too deep. Which will obviously happen to you first," smirked Dan.

"Quit with the short-arse jokes, will you?" she said, giving him a playful shove.

Dan stopped at an entrance to another tunnel off to their right. "Do you want to try this route? It might be dryer, or we can stick to this one?" he asked her.

"I've already got wet feet. So, we may as well keep the way we're heading. That one would take us over the other side of the estate," said

Deena, lifting a waterlogged boot. "All the tunnels need to be explored. But I'd prefer to stay this side, or we could go round in circles, which wastes valuable time."

"I know, time that we haven't the luxury of," he said. They continued a few hundred metres, and the water level in the tunnel was now at waist height. Deena struggled to keep her rig dry as she lunged forward with every step through the stagnant water. Dan took her rig, looping it over his shoulder to keep it dry. Soggy matches were useless to them. He knew they would need to find somewhere safe to light a fire out of this tunnel. Hypothermia was a killer too, and as much of a threat to their lives as anything they had encountered.

The water was getting deeper. Deena held the backpack above her head to keep the food dry. "If this gets much deeper, we may have to turn back," said Dan.

"No way! We've come this far. So, let's keep going," she said through gritted teeth. The cold was starting to get to her. Dan noticed she was shivering, and her lips had a bluish hue. She desperately needed to get out of the water. The water began to lap below his chest, so he lifted the rigs above his head. Then, finally, the water started to recede.

"Dee, there's another tunnel. Look," he said, pointing to their right. "I think we should take it to get above ground and find somewhere to dry off." Deena merely nodded. She was freezing, and the shivers were constant. Her chest felt tight, and it was a concerted effort to catch every breath. Deena tried to wring out the cold water from her jacket, but it was hopeless. They desperately needed a fire to dry out. There was no chance of that within the earthen tunnels. The new route further south meant they were at least moving away from the lake. The cold water had exhausted them both. They needed to rest, and soon.

"When we first walked up the driveway, weren't there cottages on this side of the estate?" asked Dan.

"Y… yes, there is… th… three," stammered Deena.

"We urgently need to get to them, or we will be in serious trouble," said Dan.

The ground beneath their feet was now dry. So, Dan stopped and put everything down. Deena's shivers were worsening to the point of convulsions. He put his arms around her and rubbed his hands rapidly up and down her back. Deena was in no fit state to protest as he repeated his actions on her arms and legs, trying to warm her up. He took off his jacket, wrapped it around her, and pulled her into him. His body core temperature hadn't fallen as low as hers, and Dan pleaded that it would be enough in his mind. He looked down at the lantern and picked it up, giving it to her under his jacket. Every bit of warmth was a help. It took a while before the convulsions began to subside.

"I'm sorry," whispered Deena under his jacket. Dan's eyes pricked with tears. He took a deep breath, relieved that the shaking had finally stopped. Deena's head emerged from under his swaddling, and she gave him his jacket back with a weak smile. "I'm feeling much better. Thanks for, you know, warming me up," Deena muttered awkwardly. Hugging the lantern as they walked, she savoured the little heat it gave off.

They had walked quite a way down this tunnel section, and Deena wondered if it would ever end. The cold made her feel disorientated. Suddenly, Dan turned around and stared into the darkness behind them. He waited a moment but heard nothing. Then, a yellow glow appeared around the tunnel bend. "Dee, we need to run!" he said, grabbing and propelling her forward. She turned to look back, and her eyes widened, panicked at the brightening flame of the Goat Man's staff torch. "Run!" Dan shouted. They took off as fast as they could. Deena's joints felt stiff and painful with every stride. Fear and adrenalin took over as she ignored the weakness in her body. Finally, they neared the end of the tunnel, approaching a wall of earth.

"Please don't be a dead end," she whispered breathlessly. Dan grabbed the shoulder of her jacket, pulling her into another tunnel straight into the path of another Goat Man.

"Shit!" exclaimed Dan as he tried to skid to a stop. Deena's knees buckled underneath her as she desperately tried to turn back; she plunged to the ground on her hands and knees. Then, she looked up and struggled to her feet, seeing its approach. As they passed the entrance to the tunnel they had left, the other Goat Man stood waiting, snorting into the air. It stomped its cloven hoof on the ground as they ran past it. Then, a second thump on the floor and a third. The earth beneath them rippled with force. Dan glanced back, but the Goat Men weren't following.

Confused, he stopped running. He wondered if they were a threat at all

147

for a split second. Then, deep below the ground, Dan and Deena could hear a rumbling sound. They began running again, and whatever it was, they weren't going to hang around to be buried alive. Suddenly, there was an explosion of rock and earth behind them. The force projected them through the air as something huge rose from the floor. Terrified, they scrambled along the tunnel's ground. The flying dust and debris marred their vision of the unknown creature. The next moment, Deena screamed as a giant fireball hurtled down the tunnel towards them.

CHAPTER TWELVE

The fireball seared through the air, and flames streamed behind the ball of intense heat, lighting the tunnel. Adrenaline pumped through Dan and Deena's exhausted bodies as they tried to outrun the impending danger. Then, as they neared a bend, another fireball impacted, creating a violent tremor that hurled them forward, extinguishing the candle. If they were going to live, they had to escape whatever was launching the deadly attack. No sooner had they regained their footing than another fireball and another. Their bodies were still ice cold from the flooded tunnel, and the intense heat from the fiery projectiles pained every aching joint. The next one hit close to their heels. Seconds later, the next flew past their heads. Deena's jeans burned against her skin. Frantically, she rolled along the ground putting the burning embers out. Dan grabbed her, dragging her with him. "Keep running!" he screamed.

Deena, stumbling as she ran, looked back over her shoulder. Yet another burning missile was winging its way towards them. Whatever was behind them was incredibly strong and extremely big. The attack was relentless, and the tunnel felt endless. Deena's legs felt like lead. She spurred forward, pulling on every ounce of energy she had as the ground shook violently with another hit. The fireballs kept coming as they neared an entrance to their right. Dan pointed to it as he ran into it. "I don't know how much longer I can keep going!" Deena cried in weak gasps.

Dan turned and looked back; two more fireballs passed the entrance. They kept running as the tremors pulsated up their legs. "It's not giving up!" shouted Dan, frustrated. He, too, was on the point of collapse. He slowed a little as they rounded a bend out of sight. All was quiet for a moment. 'Was it over?' he thought. The heavy hooves echoed in the tunnels and then stopped abruptly. Then, bellowing and snorting sounded as it stomped through the tunnel away from them. "I think it's gone," whispered Dan.

"I need a minute. I'm exhausted," murmured Deena between breaths. Dan was also glad of the breather.

They hadn't been resting long before the stomping returned. Deena gave Dan a horrified look. "It's coming back to find us. It isn't going to give up until it kills us!" said Deena, panicking as she got to her feet.

As they prepared to run, the creature came into view. It was a giant Minotaur on its hind legs. Its horns glinted in the flickering flames that lapped his torso. It didn't run towards them but progressed one heavy step at a time. Its sights were fixed on the two of them as it raised its arm with a fireball. "Run, and don't stop until we're out of these tunnels!" shouted Dan. As they took off, every joint and muscle in their bodies relived the excruciating torture despite the brief rest. Hit after hit caused the ground to shake beneath them. Finally, they came to a dead end. Dan looked around in desperation. "Climb up! Like the one to the maze," he urged her. "Hurry!" he pressed.

Deena fumbled with a heavy wooden trap door. "Start climbing. I've almost got it," said Deena. Pushing it up enough to gain height, she gave it one last shove, flinging it open. Dan was already halfway up the shaft. The creature was too close for comfort. As he neared the trap door, he almost lost his grip as a fireball exploded beneath him. Flames shot up the shaft. Deena leaned into the vertical passage as far as she could, grabbed the shoulder straps to his chest rig, and pulled with all her might. As soon as he was out, Deena slammed it shut. Dan momentarily lay still on the ground. "Are you okay?" she asked quietly. "Do you have any idea where we might be?" she continued.

Dan sat up, looking around. In front and on either side of them was dense woodland. Behind them was an old building. Dan got to his feet and peered through a window. It was in complete darkness. "Let's see if we can get in. We need to sort ourselves out and rest before going further," suggested Dan. Tentatively, they edged their way along the walls, briefly glancing through windows.

Finally, they neared the front corner of the building, and Dan watched before stepping out onto an open grassy area. The lake was in front of them, no less than two hundred feet away. The moon's silver light shimmered along the old wooden pier and danced across the surface of the gently lapping water.

Deena pointed to their left at another building, divided by a woodland trail. "Let's focus on getting in this one," Dan whispered. He crouched and went along the front of the building. On the other side of the woodpile was a door. So, Dan knelt, whispering to Deena, "Wait here." It was locked, so he reached for the penknife and slid the blade between the frame and the door. Dan felt the latch. He eased the spring catch back, and with a bit of pressure against the door with his shoulder, he was in the lodge. Deena didn't waste any time following him in. Dan shone the lantern around the room. It was nicely furnished, with wellington boots neatly paired on a mat beside the door.

"Do you think anyone lives here?" asked Deena.

"I didn't see movement through the windows. Perhaps it's only used for ground staff working on the estate," Dan muttered, pointing at the boots.

Deena walked over to the fireplace and asked, "Can we light a fire? I need to warm up properly."

"I don't see why not," he said. "I'll bring in some wood. See if you can find paper or kindling to get it going," he said, setting the lantern down on a coffee table beside a comfortable armchair.

Deena spotted a dustpan and brush near the hearth and swept up the old ash, disposing of it out of the door. Dan picked a selection of dry wood. As Deena walked back through the room, she picked up an old book for kindling. She couldn't wait to feel the warmth of the fire. Dan returned with logs, putting them on either side of the hearth. Deena retrieved her matches and struck the first one, and the red sulphur tip disintegrated.

"Here, try mine," suggested Dan. Once again, the match head crumbled. "Somebody has lit a fire here before us. I'll go and look for some matches." As Dan got up, he heard a door latch on the other side of the room. Before he could turn around, the unmistakable sound of a gun cocking made them freeze. A gruff voice came from the darkness at the back of the lodge.

"Don't you fucking move!" said the growling voice. "I will shoot you! You're trespassing!" the voice warned. Dan slowly turned to see who was behind the gun. "I said, don't fucking move!" he said, stepping forward and waving a double-barrelled shotgun at them.

Dan abruptly turned around, facing the fireplace. He slowly raised his hands over his head. Deena followed suit. Dan caught Deena's attention and whispered, "Let me handle this."

"Shut up! Who the fuck are you?" he demanded.

"I'm Dan, and this is Deena," he said, with his hands still poised above his head. "The United States Government authorises us to be here on…" he

151

began.

The man laughed haughtily, interrupting him. "The United States Government! Do you honestly think I'm gonna let you come in 'ere and loot my place? What do you take me for, idiot! You'd better start telling me the goddamn truth, or I'm gonna shoot you!" he raged.

"It's true! It's true what Dan said. We were sent here by the United States Government. We work for the Office of Nuclear Energy, Science and Technology," said Deena.

"Well, you do 'av American accents," he growled. "Give me one good reason I shouldn't blow you away!" he said unperturbed.

Dan's mind was racing. Then, finally, it dawned on him as he glanced at the boots neatly inside the door; it had to be worth a try. "Jack? You are Jack, aren't you? Put the gun down, please? Dot wouldn't want you to do this," pleaded Dan.

The gruff man lowered the double-barrelled shotgun. "Dot? Is, is she all right?" he asked softly. Then, he drew the gun back menacingly and said, "You better not 'av 'urt 'er!"

"She was kind. She helped us. Please, put the gun down," Deena blurted out.

"My wife's kind to everyone! Now, I'll ask one more time. Did. You. 'Urt 'er?" he demanded.

Dan slowly lowered his hands and turned to face the man, and with tears in his eyes, he said, "We didn't hurt Dot, but something else did. I'm so sorry, Jack."

Jack released the cock on the shotgun and dropped to his knees. He let out a cry of despair. "No, you're wrong! Not my Dot. She, she can't be dead!" he said bitterly as his voice trailed off, and tears flowed.

Dan looked him in the eye, and Jack knew he was telling the truth. Deena got up and went to Jack's side. She eased the gun from his shaking hands, gently helped him to the chair by the fireside and said, "Dan, could you get this fire lit? Then, I'll see if I can find some blankets."

Jack tapped Deena's hand and pointed to the dark doorway where he first stood. His jaw locked in grief as he choked back his tears and said, "The blankets are in the bedroom."

It was heartbreaking listening to Jack coming to terms with the loss of Dot. They sat in silence in the warmth of the fire. Then, finally, Jack asked what had happened. Without the gory details, Deena and Dan tactfully explained about the Ground Crawlers breaching the main house.

"I've seen those things," he said, his face contorting with the pain of knowing her fate. Eventually, Jack rose to his feet, pulled the blanket around his shoulders, and shuffled across the room. "I need to be alone. You can stay 'ere for a while," said Jack as he disappeared into the bedroom, shutting the door behind him.

Deena and Dan sat, gently stoking the flames. The warmth felt so good after what they had been through, and neither said a word. Instead, they stared into the orange blaze as the cries of a broken man filtered through the lodge. "Poor man," said Dan. "I didn't realise Dot was his wife."

"How could we? You did the right thing. I would want to know if it were me," said Deena.

"Did you look at what the hell was throwing fireballs at us?" Dan asked her.

"Kind of," she replied. "It was a massive bull-like creature. But I can't get my head around the flames that poured out of its body; it was impervious to them, as though they were a part of it."

"Like some sort of Fire Demon?" Dan questioned, astounded.

"If you want to call it a Fire Demon, yes. It certainly wasn't human," she said, staring into the flames.

"We now know there is more than the one Goat Man. Did you see what it did when it saw me?" he asked her.

Deena turned to Dan, nodded, and said, "I felt it. But, when that Fire Demon came out of the ground, it was like an earthquake. Do you think that's what the Goat Man was doing? Calling it up?"

"Maybe," Dan muttered.

Deena's gaze wandered back to the fire, deep in thought. The flames danced and licked the charred wood as she tried to rationalise what had happened in the tunnels. "I think the skull is underground," she stated.

"What makes you so sure?" Dan asked curiously.

Someone or something has gone to great lengths to protect those tunnels, and I reckon there are many more of those Goat Men down there. They weren't armed and showed no aggression other than stomping their hoof. The Goat Men didn't pursue us. They called up something else to do that," she said.

153

"So, you're saying that they are keepers of the tunnels, and if they see anyone, they call up the big fiery dude?" asked Dan.

Deena gave him a hapless expression and said, "We have to go back down the tunnels, but I don't know how to protect ourselves from them."

"There is one way," he muttered. "Don't get seen!" he said bluntly.

Deena smiled at the simplicity of his statement, but he was right. "If you've managed to dry out, can we get some sleep?" she asked him. Dan nodded, and together, they settled to get some proper rest.

Jack's gruff tones rudely woke them. "Wakey, wakey, you sleepy 'eads! We've gotta talk."

Deena stirred, lifted her head, and twisted around to see Jack standing over them, arms folded. "Are you all right, Jack?" she asked.

"I want some answers to what's goin' on around 'ere. I 'eard you two talking about the tunnels. I think I deserve to know," said Jack firmly.

"Fair enough. Can you give us a few minutes to get up?" asked Deena.

Jack grunted and made for the kitchen. Deena sat up, giving Dan a nudge. She nestled a couple of logs into the embers, encouraging the fire back to life.

"What did Jack want?" asked Dan.

"Answers apparently," Deena whispered.

"I may be old, Missy, but I ain't deaf!" Jack grumbled from the kitchen. Dan laughed and asked Jack if he could help him with anything. Jack handed him a saucepan of water. "You can put that on the fire," he said as he got three cups out, putting a spoon of instant coffee in each. "I ain't got milk. You want sugar?" he asked.

"Two for me, please, and one for Dee," he said. Jack made no eye contact with him.

"I'll, um, go and put this pan on," Jack grunted as Dan left the kitchen.

"I don't think he's dealing with his loss very well. He won't even look at me," Dan whispered lowly.

"What's the pan of water for?" she asked.

"Black coffee," said Dan, pleased at Jack's hosting skills.

"Nice one, Jack," she said, poking the fire to increase its burn at the prospect of a hot, sweet coffee.

Deena checked her watch; it was ten days into their mission. The pan of water was simmering on the fire, so Deena took it to the kitchen. Jack stood leaning against the countertop with his arms folded and head down, staring at the floor. "Jack? Are you okay?" she asked. "I can make the coffee for you if you want to go and sit down."

"No worries, Missy, I'll do it," he said, turning his back to her and pouring the hot water into the cups. Deena and Dan sat patiently, listening to the metal spoon clinking around the cups as he slowly stirred the coffee.

The silence was awkward as they sat together on the sofa, clutching and sipping their cups. Jack sat, absorbed by his thoughts. Then, finally, Dan broke the silence and said, "I take it you're not from around here. Your accent is different to what I've heard."

"I'm from East London originally. Came down in the summer of '76 to work in the steelworks 'ere. That's when I met my Dot. We've bin' together for forty years," he said. His voice quivered as he continued, "She worked 'ere as a live-in maid. Then, I 'ad an accident on-site, and I couldn't work there anymore, so she got me a job as 'ead gardener and groundsman. When we married, the family let us live in the lodge. We weren't blessed with children, but as long as I 'ad 'er by my side, it didn't matter." Tears trickled down his cheeks as he composed himself. "So, you know my story; 'ow about you tell me yours?"

Deena was only too happy to let Dan begin the story from within the facility when Ragnarök hit. He spoke of the team and the General, how they flew to Britain from America, and finally, how the world's fate was waiting for them to complete their mission successfully.

Jack listened in awe. Not only the decimation of the world but everything that has transpired since. "I figure maybe you could use some 'elp then. So, tell me what you need, and I'll see if I can sort summing out for you," said Jack.

"Dot was a lucky lady to have had you in her life. Thank you, Jack," said Deena.

"But you ain't 'aving my gun. Not with them things out there," Jack muttered as he got up and returned to the kitchen. Deena reached for the backpack and her chest rig and began emptying everything, neatly placing it out so the warmth of the fire could do its work. Dan had managed to keep them out of the water, so hopefully, it would be okay, although there was a cold, damp feel to everything.

Jack returned, giving them a plate each with a thick slice of dark currant loaf with butter. "'Av some of this, it's a proper Welsh recipe. It was my Dot's speciality. 'Bara Brith,' she calls it," he said, settling into his armchair. Deena tucked into the speckled loaf. It was rich, sweet, and sticky, with a handsome portion of currants and sultanas. "If you like it, I'll wrap you one up to take with you. Now, what do you need?" asked Jack. His eyes rested on Dan's rig, adding, "I see you got yourself a revolver there, Dan."

"Yes, we found it in the cellars, but we've had a job finding ammunition. So, I've only four shots," said Dan.

Jack stretched his hand out to Dan to look at the revolver. He opened the chamber and grunted. Then, without a word, he returned it and disappeared into his bedroom. A few minutes later, Jack returned and sat in his armchair. He held a closed fist out to Dan. "'Ere, try these," he said, dropping three casings into Dan's hand.

Dan inspected the bullets closely. They had the thirty-eight-calibre stamp on the base, but these were silver, unlike the brass ones. "Are you expecting werewolves, Jack?" laughed Dan.

"Nah, I found them in one of the old cottages years ago. I stuck them in a drawer; they ain't no good to me," Jack said with a gruff chuckle.

"Well, they're the right calibre for this gun. Thanks," said Dan.

"If you poke your nose about, you may find more," suggested Jack. "'Av you bin' to the boathouse yet?"

"Boathouse?" asked Deena. "Is that the building on the other side of the woodland trail?" she considered.

Jack nodded and remarked, "It's full of stuff. Rubbish, I'd call it, but you might find something useful. Also, if you consider going out on the lake, there's a rowing boat. I'll look and see what I can spare for your travels." Deena and Dan began repacking their supplies and sat beside the fire while listening to Jack rummaging and scuffling from room to room.

Finally, Jack sat with them and handed them a spare lantern, two boxes of matches, six candles and two vials of Dot's elixir. "I figure you're gonna need them more than me," he said, handing the vials to Deena. "Better I stay put with those things out there. 'Ow, long do you reckon it'll take you to find this skull?"

"I can't even hazard a guess, but we can't take too long. The team urgently need us back," said Dan.

"Well, I wish you luck. 'Ere I promised you this," said Jack, passing Deena a parcel. "Bara Brith." Deena and Dan headed to the door to leave. Then, putting their jackets on, they thanked Jack for his generosity.

Closing the lodge door, Deena and Dan walked towards the boathouse. The danger within the darkness was aforethought, and as they neared the forest trail, Deena's heart began to race as she stared down the overgrown footpath. Quickly, they crept past the tree line, ignoring the occasional twigs breaking and shadows that fuelled their fears. They spotted a door as they rounded the edge of the L-shaped building. Inside it smelt damp. Dan held up his lantern and slowly made his way to steps that led below ground.

"More cellars, Dee," he said as he hung his lantern on a nail protruding from a wooden beam. "Light your lantern as well." Dan began exploring and pulled back a blue tarpaulin revealing a small rowing boat. It was rough and ready, but inside it, a couple of battered oars lay neatly, side by side. "Help me find some rope," said Dan. Deena found a length of rope slung over an old chest and gave it to him. Dan tied one end to the boat and said, "There's a pier opposite at the lake's edge. We should try to get over to the islands and look around them later. Could you help me take the boat out ready?"

Deena folded the tarp as best she could and placed it on the bottom of the boat. Dan looked at her, confused, to which Deena defensively said, "If it rains, we can keep dry under it. Have you seen those clouds out there? I've only just dried out!" Amused, Dan picked up his end of the boat, carrying it to the pier between them. Placing it at the water's edge, Dan tied the rope around one of the pillars.

Back in the boathouse, they routinely began their search. Eventually, Dan found a collection of old fishing rods stacked upright in a corner and on the floor beside them were tackle boxes. He went through them only to find various flies and weights, line spools and reel parts. "Someone loved fishing this lake," said Dan.

"Jack, maybe?" replied Deena. Dan smiled as he thought about Jack in the rowing boat, laid back in the sunshine with his rod cast. The image instilled the sense of a once much happier world. Yet, their mission was so much more than the two of them. Knowing there were pockets of survivors was enough to compound the importance of saving Earth.

"You look deep in thought. Do you want a hand with these boxes?" asked Deena.

"That'd be great, thanks," he said, pushing a box to her. So, Deena knelt and opened it. The top layer contained cotton reels, feathers, and various luminous threads. Then, taking the first tray out, she found two small hessian pouches. Curiously, she released the drawstring on one and opened it. Inside was a bundle of cotton wool. She put the pouches to one side, sifting through the bottom of the box. She couldn't fathom what it was about the cotton wool that compelled her to take it. Deena asked Dan, still unable to decide whether it was worth taking.

"Do you think we'll have a use for it?" he asked her.

"I don't know, I can't think of a specific use, but I feel I should take it," she said. So, she stuffed one in her jacket pocket. Why she took one, she had no idea, just a gut feeling. Something she had learnt better than to ignore of late. Dan moved on to some shelving across the back wall. A variety of ropes, neatly noosed, hung on hooks secured from the underside of the shelves. "Considering this is a storage building, it's impeccable," said Deena, swinging one of the ropes back and forth.

"I reckon this is Jack's hideaway, a man cave," said Dan. A sense of male pride emanated from the essence of the building. Various tins, boxes and tubs containing odds and ends were categorised mindfully. It seemed Jack was an organised man. He would've been able to put his hand on anything. It certainly made it an easy task to search. Dan worked his way through the assortment of boxes and tubs until he found something that didn't belong. "Guess what I found, Dee?" he said.

Deena turned and looked at the palm of his hand holding a silver bullet and exclaimed, "Another one!"

"Jack said we may find more," he said, elated that they now had four of the unusual silver bullets. "We still have the cellar to explore."

Each with a lantern in hand, they descended the steps. The light gently penetrated the darkness until they reached the cellar floor. As they held their lanterns aloft, thick stone walls met a rough flagstone floor. The cellar was one whopping space. Then, Dan noticed a door to his right. "This is the back wall, so I'm guessing that..." Dan paused, pulling the door open as silvery strands from decades of spiderwebs pulled apart, revealing an entrance leading into the underground network, "… it's another tunnel," he said. "We may as well go back up. We're wasting our time down here."

Before leaving the boathouse, Dan wanted to have a last look. He was moving things about to look behind and underneath, which served him well. There, in a dusty corner, he found old glass bottles. There was something inside one. He shook the bottle, trying to scrutinise its contents through the dirty glass. "It looks like it could be one of those scrolls. I don't think it will come out easily," he said, poking his finger into the flange around the bottleneck. "I can't get hold of it."

"I can sort that out," she said, taking the bottle from a surprised Dan. Then, she swung it against the shelf swiftly, shattering the glass. "Problem solved," she said, casually picking up the scroll.

Eagerly, Dan asked, "What symbol is on it?"

"Water, ironically," she said.

Dan laughed and asked, "Have you figured out what we are supposed to do with these?"

"Nope, still not a clue," she sighed.

Dan put it in the backpack. He didn't know why they found them, but they had to be significant. Dan scraped the glass across the floor out of their way. "Are you still up for going across the islands?" he asked Deena.

"Sure, as long as it doesn't entail me getting wet," she replied.

"We have a boat. So, you won't even get your feet damp," Dan promised.

CHAPTER THIRTEEN

Deena jolted back to the here and now and tried to wake Dan. But another hour had passed before he showed signs of movement. Finally, groaning in pain, he struggled to open his eyes as Deena hugged him and sighed, "Thank god, you're okay."

"What the hell happened? I feel like I've done ten rounds in a boxing ring," he moaned, clutching his sides.

"Don't you remember? The Banshee, she attacked you," Deena replied.

"What the hell are you talking about, what Banshee?" he muttered, struggling to sit up.

Deena quickly pushed him back down. "Ouch, that hurt!" he yelped.

"Don't get up. They'll see us," Deena whispered fearfully. "Don't you remember anything?" she asked.

He paused in his confused state and asked, "Who'll see us?"

"You've been out for hours. I managed to get you back to the boat, but these creatures were waiting for us when I got close to the shore. I couldn't wake you, and I didn't know what to do," her voice trembled.

Dan held his head and squeezed his eyes shut with pain. "I've got a bitch of a headache!" he said.

"I'm not surprised. Stay low in the boat, and I'll explain everything," whispered Deena.

Dan lay silent as Deena recalled the events. He couldn't remember anything. All he knew was that one minute he was fine, then everything went blank, and the next, he collapsed to the floor completely paralysed, and even that much was hazy.

"What are these creatures you're going on about?" he asked. Deena grimaced and described them in as much detail as she could. "They're not Ground Crawlers? Perhaps they could be a subspecies?" he deliberated.

Deena shook her head in profound disagreement and said, "These things howl like wolves but are four times the size."

Dan sighed, "So, we have three choices. Either we go back to the pier, and I can see these creatures for myself and devise a plan to tackle them head-on. Or we go to the other side of the lake to avoid them and make our way up to the manor," he replied.

"You said three options. What's the third?" asked Deena.

"We stay in the boat until we starve to death!" he smirked.

"Very funny, that's not an option!" she sighed. "The creatures saw me, but they were waiting for the boat to get close enough, so I don't think they will jump in the water."

"I want to see them for myself," said Dan extending his limbs as far as the boat would allow. Then, wincing in pain, he said, "Feels like everything's still in working order. I'll be fine."

Deena sat up and gently dipped the oars. Twenty feet from the water's edge, she stopped rowing and turned to watch the pier with Dan. "I don't see them," he said.

"Give it a few minutes. They may be hiding, watching us," whispered Deena.

"Try rowing across to the other side of the pier," suggested Dan.

Deena steadily steered the boat around the lake's edge, stopping intermittently to watch and listen. Nothing stirred. There was no sound of twigs breaking, no shadows nor growls, but they remained patiently in the boat, ensuring they were gone.

"Do you want to go back to the boathouse and then make our way to the cottages?" whispered Deena.

"That's a good idea as the cottages are the only buildings left this side, south of the estate," replied Dan.

Slowly, Deena rowed towards the pier. Both were on edge. Without knowing what these creatures were, or their capabilities, being caught by them would be catastrophic. Deena nestled the boat against the pier, and Dan secured the rope. Then, they stood in the shadows, watching and waiting. Finally, Dan walked the narrow path skirting the lake's edge. He prayed the creatures couldn't smell fear as adrenaline and terror drenched him. "There's no point in returning to the boathouse," he whispered to Deena. Deena nodded, keeping close to him. Dan signalled her to watch the trees while he kept an eye on the lakeside. Eventually, the tree line broke to open ground. Only neatly spaced trees edged the pathway to the main

161

driveway. Dan knelt behind shrubs as he scanned the landscape.

"That's a long way out in the open," whispered Deena. "We could've used the tunnels; there is access from the cellar in the boathouse." With the memory of the Fire Demon still a little too fresh, he raised an eyebrow at her suggestion. Deena sighed and firmly whispered, "Look, it doesn't matter if we are underground or not. Everything is out to fucking kill us anyway! So, I don't see what your problem is."

"Point taken, but this is a direct route," he muttered, getting to his feet. Along the edge of the woods, the grass was longer, and in its withered, dried state, it had drooped, forming raised clumps making it more difficult to walk across. They still had twice the distance they had already walked to get to the cottages. Deena retook the lead, keeping an eye on the woods and the open ground. Her heart pounded as she thought of the possibility of a double attack, both by Ground Crawlers and these wolf creatures. Her thoughts were abruptly interrupted by the sound of twigs breaking.

Deena's attention whisked around to the woods. It was so dark in there; she couldn't see anything. Deena backed away from the trees. Dan screamed at her, "Run! Get to the cottages!" Deena turned to see one of the creatures stalking them from behind, and Dan wasn't going to hang around to see where the rest of them were. Instead, he bolted past Deena praying the cottages weren't locked.

As he ran, Dan fumbled in his rig for the penknife. Deena picked up her speed and caught a glimpse of two more running down the forest's edge. It was a well-planned ambush. Had Dan not seen the one behind them, it would have been well executed on their part. 'Pack hunters, just like wolves,' thought Deena. As they sprinted for the cottages, the creatures came out from the trees and split up.

Three gave chase to Dan and Deena, and two others bolted towards the back of the buildings. Dan slammed his body weight against the first cottage door. It wouldn't open. He desperately kicked at the door as hard as he could. "Dan!" screamed Deena as she flew around the corner, pointing beyond him. Dan's eyes widened with fear as he spotted another of the creatures at the far end of the cottages. It was already lying-in wait, as though they knew where they were heading. It flattened its ears and let out a deep, menacing growl in a half-crouched position. In their panic, they pounded on the door with their boots.

162

The wolf creature slowly moved towards them one deliberate step at a time, its eyes fixed on its prey. Two more appeared from behind the cottages. Deena looked frantically around them. All six creatures had them surrounded, and there was no escape. Dan kept up his physical assault on the cottage door as they approached from all sides. Their growls grew more intense the closer they got. Dan shouldered the door with as much force as he could, and as it burst open, he fell through it. Deena ran inside, slamming it shut behind them. As she did, the creatures pounced forward. She pressed herself hard against the door as the beasts hurled themselves at it one by one, trying to get to them.

Finally, Dan jumped to his feet and looked for something heavy they could use. There wasn't much of anything in the cottage. He found a few barrels of grass seed and rolled them on their base edge to Deena. They were heavy enough to bolster the door. The creature's assault continued until, eventually, it went quiet.

"Shush," said Dan. "I'm going to take a look." He crept low and peered out of a dirty windowpane. He couldn't see them. Feeling brave, Dan moved to the next window. His eyes met with one of the formidable creatures staring at him as he looked out. Dan froze as it drew its muzzle back in a ferocious snarl. Its canines were massive. Dan gulped hard, trying not to think of those teeth ripping into either of them. Slowly he sank to the floor, out of its sight. Crawling over to Deena, he whispered, "Clever doggies!"

"Now do you believe me?" she whispered.

Dan looked at her in despair and said, "Those things are enormous and extremely vicious. They look like something dragged out of hell!"

"Hell Hounds? Maybe, I don't know if they are flesh and blood or entity, and I'm not sure I want to chance whether they can inflict damage," she whispered.

"We have to come up with a plan. These creatures are not going to go away. Any ideas?" asked Dan.

"Nope, but I reckon they were watching and waiting for us when we left the lake, deliberately stalking us," she said.

"But why do that? They could've easily killed us before we got down here," said Dan.

Deena shrugged her shoulders, "I don't know, maybe they like the chase. Perhaps the hunt itself is all part of the fun for them. Like a cat will play with its catch, they're toying with their prey."

"Bloody great. So, how the fuck do we get out of this one?" sighed Dan.

Deena pulled out the tri-field meter from her rig and said, "It won't pick anything up through the walls. They're too thick, but maybe by the door or a window. I hope they are entities as I don't fancy our chances if they are a sub-species of the Ground Crawlers like you suggested."

"Now that I've seen them, I don't think they are," said Dan.

Deena switched the meter on and placed it by the door. Then she whispered, "Now we wait for one to pass close enough." Dan moved to the window and watched two roaming about, but they weren't close enough to set off the meter. Then, a thought unnerved him, 'Where are the other four? Are they around the back, ready to ambush us if we try to escape?'

Suddenly, Deena scrambled back from the door as the LEDs shot from green to red. The vicious snarls and scratching at the door scared her witless. Dan was right. There was no way these Hell Hounds would give up until they had what they wanted. Dan watched the meter flashing wildly. "That clarifies one thing," muttered Deena, "they're not flesh and blood. So, now we must figure out how to defend ourselves against them."

"While we figure it out, we should barricade ourselves into another room where they can't see us through a window," said Dan. "If they get into the cottage, we'll be sitting ducks if we stay here." Dan crept to the back of the cottage and found a narrow wooden staircase against the sidewall. He nipped back, and grabbing the backpack, he whispered, "Come on, keep low." The stairs creaked under their weight as they crept up each step. There was a small bedroom and bathroom at the back. The largest bedroom was at the front of the cottage.

"We'll use this one," said Dan. "It's got stuff in here that we can use to barricade the doorway, and there are two windows that we can watch from. So, it gives us an advantage."

Deena looked out of the window. Below, she could see two Hell Hounds at one end, and a third was disappearing towards the back of the cottage. As Dan began to push the bed across the room, Deena hurried out to the back bedroom. She watched with dismay at the four of them, parading and pouncing on each other playfully like puppies. "Damn things!" Deena muttered to herself. Returning to Dan, she helped him pile up what they could against the door. "Do you think that'll keep them out?" she questioned.

Dan stared at the furniture piled up and said, "If I'm honest, no, but it may buy us a bit of time." He sat against the wall with the backpack and beckoned Deena to join him as he pulled out the Bara Brith. Deena ignored him and stood back from the window, staring outside.

"We need to think of a way to combat these things," she muttered, "not sit and have our last meal!"

"I can't concentrate when I'm hungry. Are you sure you don't want some?" asked Dan.

"No thanks," she sighed. "I hope Jack's safe in the lodge."

"From what he said, I don't think he intends to gallivant about the estate," said Dan.

"At least with the Ground Crawlers, we can shoot them," she said, crossing the room to sit by Dan.

Dan's eyes widened as if he'd had an epiphany. "Werewolves!" he exclaimed.

"What are you on about?" she asked, confused.

"When Jack gave me the silver bullets, I asked him if he was expecting werewolves!" he exclaimed excitedly. "The Hell Hounds look like mythical werewolves. Do you see where I'm going with this?" he said.

"So, you think it will work on the Hell Hounds because silver bullets kill werewolves in the movies? You'll be hanging garlic around my neck next," she said sarcastically.

"Stop being pessimistic," he said. "I'm serious. The Goat Men are mythological, the… big fiery dude, the Norse gods, all mythological!" he asserted.

"Okay, how do we test your theory without getting eaten?" asked Deena.

"I could fire a shot from up here," he suggested, getting the revolver out of his rig.

"If it doesn't work, you're going to piss them off, and we could be in big trouble," she stressed.

"Dee, they're not going to go away! They know they have us trapped. We have to take the chance," he said firmly.

"You're right. I'd rather you take a potshot out of the window," she sighed. "There's no way the sage is going to be enough, we haven't enough salt to throw at six of them, and by the way, you only have four of those bullets, and there are six of them."

"Better hope I don't miss then," he said with a wink as he loaded the revolver.

He knelt beside the sill and slid the sash window open. He paused, watching their movements as he aimed the gun at them, waiting for the perfect shot. One of the hounds came into range, staring right at him. Dan aimed the barrel, ensuring he had his target before squeezing the trigger. The revolver kicked back, and the shot rang out. Deena watched as it seared through the chest of the Hell Hound. It let out an excruciating howl, alerting the others. The pack raced towards the injured hound as it writhed on the ground. Deena didn't take her eyes off the black mass as it twisted and squirmed. Each of the five began to howl and bay at the loss of their pack member. Then, the five fled across the open ground towards the orangery as the carcass disintegrated. The remnants of the congealed remains bubbled and festered until forming a dark mist that was gently blown away by the breeze. "You vaporised it!" said Deena. "It's gone."

Dan turned with a look of satisfaction and, returning the revolver to its holster, said, "Yes, I did. One down, five to go." He stood up and shut the window. "Werewolves. See, I was right."

"I want to make sure they have gone," she said, dismantling the barricade. Deena ran to the cottage's rear to look out the window. She couldn't see them. Perhaps losing one of their kind scared them off, at least for now.

"We need to find more of those silver bullets. I reckon they'll be back as soon as they feel brave enough. Predators like that don't give up easily," muttered Dan.

"I still can't believe the silver bullets worked," Deena said uncannily.

"Let's search these cottages while we have a reprieve," he said, ruffling her hair as he passed her on the landing.

The cottage was small. Dan went downstairs to look around the kitchen and lounge. Deena began her exploration in the bathroom. It was fundamental but functional, and thick dust lay in the old, enamel bathtub. She tried to turn the tarnished brass taps to no avail. A cabinet stood beside a dated, chipped sink, which proved empty. Next, she went into the bedroom. That, too, yielded only dust and cobwebs. She strolled back to the front bedroom, searching for the Hell Hound's return at the windows. It looked calm with no signs of the marauding pack. So, Deena took a few moments to check the cupboards. Disappointed, she went in search of Dan. She found him in the kitchen. "Those Hell Hounds seem to have been scared off for now. Have you got much more to do?" she asked.

"Nearly done," he said. "Did you find anything upstairs?"

"No, have you?" she asked, watching him open and close rickety cupboards.

"Yes, I've left them by the backpack for you," said Dan, pleased. Curious, Deena left him to his search and went to have a look. She knelt and picked up two crystals. The blue sapphires were stunning. Holding them to her lantern, she studied their shape and cut. They were the same as the others. She sat holding them so deep in thought she hadn't noticed Dan beside her. "So, do you want to get to the next cottage while it's safe?" he asked. Deena nodded, opened the backpack, put the crystals and tri-field meter in, and was ready to go.

Dan moved the barrels aside enough to slip through the door. The next cottage wasn't very far, but they would be in trouble if the Hell Hounds or Ground Crawlers showed up. So, Dan told Deena to keep a lookout until he was sure he could get into the next cottage. "I'll signal you when I'm in," he whispered. Deena watched as he deftly made his way to the next building. His eyes darted about before trying to get in. It wasn't locked. 'I wish I'd known that when the Hell Hounds were on our heels,' he thought as he signalled Deena. Hesitantly, she crept towards him until close enough to dart inside.

The cottage had shallow beamed ceilings. There was a distinct smell of dampness, and the musty air made it hard to breathe. Deena ventured down the narrow hallway. The stairs didn't look safe to climb as several steps had rotted. On either side of the passage was a door. She wandered into the centre of what was once a living area and lifted her lantern to get a better look. It seemed this cottage was a dumping ground for anything and everything. "The roof has been leaking for a long time, judging by the damp," muttered Dan. "I'm going to look at the other side of the cottage. You do this side. Please wait for me before going upstairs. The staircase looks dangerous."

Dan left her to it and crossed the hallway into the kitchen. It was more generous than the other cottage but was in dreadful condition. The ceiling had partially collapsed in one corner, and rainwater nestled in the crevices between floor tiles. A few dilapidated cupboards and a broken sink had remained fixed to the walls. At the back, he found a walk-in pantry with a deep enamelled laundry sink at one end and shelving around the remaining walls. He chose to go through the kitchen first. It didn't take him long, so he returned to Deena, disappointed at having nothing to show for his efforts.

Deena was moving things as she worked her way through the room. "I'm done in there. Where do you want me to start?" asked Dan.

Deena pointed to the far end and said, "If you start over there and work towards me, that'd be great." When done, Deena wiped her hands on the remnants of a curtain. Everything, it seemed, was coated in a dank, vile-smelling green slime. Finally, she asked Dan, "Are you sure you want to risk going up those stairs?"

"We should at least try. If we are careful, we should be fine. Stay to the side, as the centre of the step will be the weakest part," advised Dan.

She placed the backpack at the foot of the stairs and said, "The less weight we carry up, the better. I'll go first as I'm lighter than you."

With both hands behind her on the bannister, Dan waited while Deena tested each step before progressing to the next. Once she reached the top, Dan started his way up. He could feel the sponginess of the waterlogged wood beneath his feet. "It's bad up here. Parts of the roof have collapsed," said Deena.

"I figured it wouldn't be too clever up here," said Dan, assessing its state. Dan poked his head around each door. "I don't know if it's worth the risk."

"Let me try. I'm smaller and lighter," said Deena. "The floor in the front bedroom doesn't look too bad, but the corner has collapsed on the far side."

"There is stuff on the window ledge, I can't see what, but there's no way we can get to it," he sighed.

Deena edged her way into the room as far as she dared. Then, holding her lantern out, she tried to shed some light on the objects. She thought about getting a pole to knock them off, but if they fell and lodged between the remnants of the floorboards, they would be impossible to retrieve. "How about finding something long enough to breach the collapse and rest it on the windowsill? I might be able to get across," she suggested.

"I'm not happy about it. Let's forget it," sighed Dan.

"No, I can do this!" she exclaimed. "Please let me try?" she pleaded.

"Okay, but if I think it's getting too dangerous, you stop. Understood?" stated Dan. Deena broke into a broad grin and asked him to help her get something from downstairs. He had reservations about her plan, but he knew the only other option was to leave the stuff behind.

Downstairs, Dan found an old door. He tested it, applying pressure to ensure it wasn't rotten. Deena falling through the floor and injuring herself was not an option. "I reckon this door is your best bet," said Dan. "The width will allow you to spread your weight. I'll carry it up." He slid the door up the staircase on its edge, careful to stay close to the wall. Next, he lined the door up to the ledge, lowering it onto the sill in the bedroom.

Deena poised herself on one knee and placed her hands reasonably apart. Then, slowly, she crawled towards the windowsill. Finally, the sill was wide enough for Deena to turn herself around to sit on it carefully.

"Whatever is there, slide them down the door to me," he said. "We can look when you're safely back this side." So, Deena emptied the ledge of its hoard and reversed her way back to Dan.

Dan filled his pockets with the items, grinned at Deena and said, "I'm glad you had the guts to do that." Then, he turned to leave the room. Deena tugged his jacket playfully, asking what he had. He laughed and said, "It's all good, really good." She stepped in front of him excitedly, and without thinking, she walked backwards, taking the first couple of steps downstairs. But unfortunately, her boot slipped on the damp plinth below her. As Deena fell backwards, she scrambled to grasp the handrail, but it happened so fast. She landed on her back, crying in pain as the stairs collapsed beneath her.

He froze, stunned at what happened. Fear swept over him at the silence that followed. "Dee? Dee, can you hear me? Answer me!" he called. There was no reply, not a murmur, and that scared him. The centre section of the staircase was gone. He hugged the wall as far as possible and peered into the dark hole below. He could see her beneath the remnants of the stairs. He called her again, but there was still no response. She lay there lifeless, and Dan began to panic. He needed to get to her, but it was an eight-foot drop, and Deena was directly below. If he jumped down, he risked landing on her, injuring her further.

Dan stretched his leg across the width of the stairwell, touching the wall opposite with his boot. "Spiderman it is then," he sighed, securing the lantern to his belt. Holding the flashlight between his teeth, he placed his heels firmly against the wall, and with arms stretched, he allowed himself to fall forward. Suspended between the two walls, he inched his way over the collapse to the bottom of the stairs. Dan grumbled, annoyed that Spiderman made this stuff look so easy.

He relentlessly smashed through the plinths from the bottom of the staircase to get to Deena. Finally, Dan could see her. He cleared away as much debris as he could. Then, Dan gently lifted her head, stroking her cheeks. He noticed blood on his fingers as he brushed her hair away from her face. She had hit the back of her head, giving her a nasty wound. He leant forward and held her mouth close to his face. Her breaths were shallow as he felt her gentle exhale on his skin. Dan cradled her close to him, scared. 'What if she doesn't wake up?' he thought. Dan grabbed his water bottle and splashed a little over her face to bring her around. He tapped her cheeks and sprinkled more water on her forehead. To Dan's relief, Deena murmured and tried to open her eyes. He persisted in his efforts, begging her to wake up. As Deena tried to move, Dan told her to stay still, tilted her head forward and offered her a sip of water. "What happened?" she whispered hazily.

Dan asked her, "Is it just your head, or are you hurt anywhere else?"

Deena winced, gritting her teeth as she struggled to move, muttering, "Where's the railroad?"

"What are you on about?" asked Dan, confused.

"I feel like I've been hit by one," she said, holding her head.

Dan laughed, "Still got your sense of humour then. I'm not sure if that's a good or a bad thing. You've been unconscious for at least a half-hour."

"That long?" she said in disbelief. "Where are we anyway?" she mumbled.

"We're under the stairs, well, what's left of them," he said.

Deena looked around in confusion. "I did all this damage?"

"Not quite. Most of it was me getting to you," said Dan. "You missed my epic Spiderman routine."

"I'm not even going to ask. My head hurts enough as it is," said Deena.

"You've cut the back of your head open. Do you mind if I rinse some water over it? I think Dot's elixir is in order," he said firmly.

Dan ignored her protests and the loud ouches as he dabbed on the elixir. "What did we get from the bedroom windowsill?" she asked him. Dan took off his jacket, laying it on the floor. He unzipped the bulging pockets and took out the items, spacing them out. At first, it looked like a mixed bag of rubbish.

Nevertheless, she sifted through it carefully, picking up the small vial of elixir first. "We're going to need that if I keep up my idiot antics," she muttered. Next, she held up a tiny glass pot with a rusty lid. Dan took it from her and forced the cap open, emptying the contents into the palm of his hand. "Hairpins?" questioned Deena. Then, Deena's eyes caught sight of a familiar disc.

"It's the rune, Isa. It represents a delay or to stand still," said Dan. "The divinity to this rune is Verdandi. She is the second of the three Norns who weaves the present."

"Did you hit your head as well because you are not making any sense?" asked Deena, confused. "Who are the Norns?" she questioned.

Dan laughed, explaining, "They weave the fate of all living beings. They live at the well in Asgard but spend most of their time deciding everyone's fate by weaving it into the roots of the tree of Yggdrasil. Firstly, there is Urd. She represents 'all that was,' meaning the past. Then, Verdandi weaves 'what is coming into being,' meaning the present, and Skuld, who decides 'what will be,' meaning the future. So, they are the goddesses of fate."

"I've heard of the wheels of fate, but I never thought in a million years I would have to take this seriously," said Deena, picking up one of the crystals.

"How many pairs of these do we have now?" she asked.

"Four: black onyx, amber, sapphire, and these," he replied.

"So, what are these cut from, Mr Archaeologist?" she asked Dan.

"It's a tumbled cluster, and judging by its honey amber colour, it's possibly aragonite, a calcium carbonate. It promotes a deep connection with the Earth and its resources. So, these crystals must have important properties to what is happening with Ragnarök to restore our world."

Deena winced in pain as she craned forward to see what else was on Dan's jacket. She threw a couple of tiny broken seashells aside, picked up a box of matches, and gave them to Dan. "Well worth the rigmarole of getting to the windowsill," she said happily.

"How's your back and head now?" asked Dan tentatively.

"Very sore. I need to sit down for a bit. I can't leave like this," replied Deena, groaning in pain. "If those Hell Hounds show up, I'd be a sure-fire meal for them."

Dan checked her head, it was a nasty wound, but it had stopped bleeding. Then, he went to the window, staring outside deep in thought. He vowed to be more vigilant, look out for her, and be more protective. Dan smiled, knowing it would annoy the heck out of her, but so what? He turned his head towards the sound of Deena's voice. "What's the score outside? Let's get to the last cottage if it's quiet. The longer we leave it, the more likely the Hell Hounds will regroup."

"Could you run if they turned up?" he asked her. Deena didn't answer him. Instead, she stood up and struggled towards the cottage door. "Whoa! Where do you think you're going?" he asked as he sped to the door.

"Don't forget the backpack," she said firmly. "We have to get moving."

Dan grabbed the backpack, grumbling, "You're so bloody stubborn. You have to do it your way. If we get eaten, it's your fault!"

Deena couldn't help but smile at the thought of his temper fraying as he swiftly followed her out of the cottage. She took the lead and stopped at the corner, double-checking around them before crossing over to the next place. As Deena ran, she regretted leaving so soon. Pain seared her spine like a hot knife, and her head pounded with every footstep. Dan was close behind her as she slumped against the door in distress. He could see the pain in her eyes as much as she tried to put on a brave face. Finally, a few shoves with his shoulder opened the door to the last of the cottages. Dan ushered her inside, closing the door behind them quietly. "Shush, and don't move," he whispered.

"Are the Hell Hounds back?" she whispered.

Dan shook his head, "Ground Crawlers," he whispered, pointing to the bottom of the estate. "A large horde."

"How large?" Deena asked fearfully.

"Eight, maybe ten, too many. I'm hoping the horde hasn't picked up on us."

"Shit! That's the biggest yet," exclaimed Deena.

"We must secure the cottage and bunk down until they move away. Besides, you need the rest. I know you're hurting," Dan told her.

Dan jammed what he could against the door and found some old cushions to lay on the floor for Deena to rest. The pillows smelt mildewy, but it was all he could find to hand. "Thanks, Dan. I'm sorry for being an idiot," apologised Deena.

"I'm just glad you're okay. Sit here while I check out the rest of this place," whispered Dan.

Deena eased herself onto the cushions. As damp and smelly as they were, she didn't care. They served well for her bruises. Dan wasn't gone long when he silently slipped back into the room to join her. "Is there much to look through?" she asked.

"A fair bit, but we should wait out the Ground Crawlers first. I've been watching them from upstairs. It looks like two hordes come together. Hopefully, they'll leave if they think there's nothing for them."

Deena felt guilty. It wasn't the first time she'd put herself in harm's way. She cast her mind back to the facility when she fell to her knees and almost jeopardised the mission before they started. Dan could see Deena was deep in thought, questioning herself. The furrowed brow and brief shakes of her head as she reprimanded herself gave her away. Dan intermittently went to the windows during the following hours, checking how many Ground Crawlers were still in their proximity.

At last, as he watched from upstairs, they finally began to disperse, and the coast was clear. Deena got up and dusted herself off as Dan returned. The smile on his face said it all. The Ground Crawlers had gone. "Do you feel all right? You're not dizzy or anything?" Dan asked her.

Deena shook her head. "I'm fine, a headache and a little stiff," she replied.

"I bet you've got some peachy bruises, in any case. Do you want me to check them out for you?" asked Dan, smirking with a twinkle in his eyes. The glare Deena gave him was enough to say no chance. He let out a schoolboy giggle, pointed towards the ceiling, and muttered, "I'll go upstairs then."

The layout of the cottage was identical to the first. Dan started in the main bedroom. There was only an iron bed which was missing its mattress, a couple of cabinets and a single wardrobe. The curtains hung limply, mouldy from years of condensation. He pulled them back and checked the sills. The cabinets proved empty other than the odd spider. Broken coat hangers lay in the base of the wardrobe while a few more swung idly on the rail. Dan crossed the landing to the bathroom. The porcelain set was in pretty good condition considering its disuse. He tried the tap, and it turned, but that's all it did. He stared into his reflection in the broken mirror of the bathroom cabinet, sighing as he casually opened it.

Tiredness kicked in, and he knew they would need to rest soon. Deena was quiet, so Dan went down the stairs. He envisioned her collapsed on the floor, out cold. He quickened his pace, and as he swung around the door frame, he was faced with her as she sat crossed-legged on the floor at the far end of the room, grinning broadly.

"Look at these," she said excitedly. "I found them in a wall cubby."

Dan took the larger of the curved-shaped blades from her. "And these were in the cubby?" he asked in disbelief as he examined it.

Deena nodded, "There's two of them, oh, and this," she said, handing him an odd-shaped piece of wood. "I reckon they could be part of the spear."

Dan sat on the floor opposite her with the lantern between them. He placed the larger blade on the floor and picked up the curved double-edged piece. It was ten inches long, with a metal shaft jutting off the base a couple of inches from one end. "This must sit in a housing or mount of some kind," he speculated. "Pass me that wooden bit." In the candlelight, he twisted them about, trying to fit them together. Then, after a couple of minutes, he proudly held it up to Deena. "The forging of the metals is the same as the tip. This bigger one is a tomahawk blade. We need to return to the manor and keep them with the shaft until we've found all the pieces," Dan suggested.

Deena got up and carefully placed the blades in the backpack. "Are you done upstairs?" she asked.

"Not quite," he said, getting to his feet. Deena could hear Dan moving above her as she diligently went through the rickety kitchen cupboards. After such an exciting find earlier, it didn't matter that she left empty-handed. At the foot of the stairs, she waited for Dan. His smug smile told her he had found something. He reached into his jacket pocket as he came downstairs and held it up. "Is that a pocket watch?" she asked.

"Nope, it's way better than that," said Dan grinning. He placed the round, ornately engraved metal case in the palm of his hand. "Wait for it…" he said as he pushed in the hinge pin. The front of the metal case sprung open to reveal a delicately detailed compass.

"Oh wow, that's handy!" she said, surprised.

"Especially if we lose our bearings in the tunnels," he said, snapping it shut and tucking it back into his pocket.

Before leaving the cottage, they sat discussing their plans to get back to the manor. Deena didn't relish the thought of going back the way they came. It was too open, too exposed. Moreover, there was the risk of the Hell Hounds, not to mention the massive horde of Ground Crawlers they had seen at the south end of the estate. "We should look around the cottages outside. There may be a tunnel somewhere. If we can't find one, we'll have to go back to the boathouse or the lodge to access the tunnels. So, if you're ready, we'll look around the back," suggested Dan.

Dan loaded the revolver. The first three chambers he loaded with silver bullets and the latter with brass. It was better safe than sorry without knowing which, what or whom they'd encounter. Nervously, they ventured outside. Their eyes darted as far as they could see as they crept around the back of the cottage. The tree line of the woodlands was sinister, knowing what could lie within. Pensively, they watched for any movement before creeping along the cottage walls. Dan paused as he reached the first corner and studied the shadows. Nothing stirred, nothing moved. Then, relieved, he whispered to Deena to stay there while checking for entrances between the cottages. Deena watched as he traced the walls quickly. "Nothing," he whispered. So, they moved towards the middle house, and again, Dan checked between the buildings. "Fingers crossed for the last one," he whispered, "or we'll be heading to the boathouse instead."

Deena followed Dan closely. They had barely passed the bottom of the last cottage when Dan spotted a split-second glint of eyes. He spun around, facing the woodlands, arms stretched out, pointing the gun's barrel into the darkness. Then, blindly, Dan slowly swung the revolver from left to right, looking for the next flash of eyes from any menacing glances. His forefinger was around the trigger; he was ready for them. "What did you see?" Deena muttered quietly.

Dan could hear the panic in her voice, but he didn't dare to take his eyes off the tree line. "I'm sure I saw eyes, probably Hell Hounds, possibly Shadow Men, or something we've not had the displeasure of meeting yet," he whispered. "I'll keep watch; look for a way down."

Deena hesitated, "Are you sure? I can wait it out with you."

He urgently nodded towards the end of the last cottage and said, "Go!"

Deena stepped back until she was firmly against the wall. Dan remained steadfast in his readied state of heightened awareness. With each side-step she took away from him, the pit of her stomach churned a little more. Deena had an awful feeling about the whole situation. It was quiet and far too peaceful. She tried to ignore the dread that was filling her body. The lantern on the ground between Dan's feet highlighted his silhouette. Deena was only ten feet from the end of the cottage. She took a moment to watch the corner of the building as she made another side-step. 'That doesn't feel right,' thought Deena, looking down. Kneeling, she felt the ground. There was grass, but it was patchy. She pulled up a clump and discovered a wooden door. Excited that she had found a trapdoor to the tunnels, Deena frantically began ripping handfuls of grass away until she had exposed all the edges. On opposite sides were bolts that slotted into the frame. They were rusted and wouldn't slide open. So, Deena began checking through her rig to find anything that could help her loosen them. As she pulled the penknife out, she smiled, flicked the most prominent blade from its housing, and began to scrape the rust away.

Dan's attention immediately turned towards the sound of Deena vigilantly working at the bolts. Thankful to see that she had possibly found an entrance, he slowly backed towards the cottage wall. Making his way to Deena, he kept his eyes fixed on the sight at the end of the gun's barrel. Deena managed to loosen the bolts. Dan turned to her as he heard the clunk as they slid back, hitting the back of their metal casing. He watched as she got up, leaning forward to lift the hatch. Suddenly, Dan screamed at her, "Dee! Behind you! Move! Move!"

CHAPTER FOURTEEN

Dan's frantic shouting briefly immobilised Deena with sheer terror. She slowly turned to face two Hell Hounds fewer than thirty feet away. Stumbling backwards, she lost her footing. Twisting around, she tried to scrabble to her feet. The Hell Hounds took a couple of paces towards her. One saw its chance and seized it, leaping forward, landing astride her. Its jowls curled back, revealing savage teeth that lunged at her face.

Instinctively, she raised a fist, landing a punch to the side of its muzzle. Angry growls filled the air. Dan prayed Deena wouldn't get in the way as he fired a shot. The bullet plunged into the beast's neck. The other hound backed off as the first roared, howling with pain. Its weight collapsed on her, and the air began to fill with the putrid odour of sulphur. Deena pushed herself backwards, wriggling from under the hound. Dan rushed to help her. "Its claws caught my leg," she said, crying in agony. Black smoke lingered from the dissipating carcass making the stench worse. Dan winced at the sight of her leg. Several lacerations had torn through her jeans and into the flesh of her thigh. "Let's get in the tunnel, and then I can take a closer look," he said.

Dan reached for the hatch, and before putting the revolver in his rig, he looked around. He hadn't seen where the other Hell Hound went or where the others were. But Dan knew they'd be watching, waiting for their next chance. Then, shining his lantern into the depths below revealed steep steps descending into the tunnel. Deena went first, and Dan followed, ensuring he pulled the hatch shut. They wouldn't survive an attack if the remaining four Hell Hounds got into the tunnels with only two bullets left.

"I need to do something about my leg," she said, clutching her thigh.

"Keep an eye behind me for the Goat Men," he whispered, putting down his lantern. One laceration was particularly deep, and he needed to stop the bleeding. He took his water bottle, pouring some on the wound to clean it. Deena focused her stare over Dan's shoulder with gritted teeth into the tunnel ahead. With no first aid kit, he had to improvise. He inspected his shirt and ripped a strip off the bottom. "I need to bandage it. This will have to do for now," said Dan. Drop by drop, he doused the laceration with elixir, quickly bandaging it, keeping as much inside the wound as he could. "Hopefully, it will stop any infection and help it heal faster," he said.

"Talk about being in the wars lately," remarked Deena. She picked up her lantern while Dan grabbed their gear, offering an arm for support. Slowly, they walked towards the manor. As they neared the first exit to the north, Dan realised that if they kept northeast, it would bring them out at the boathouse or further up at the lodge, but that meant going overground to the manor. Going north was ideal for staying underground, but that was the flooded tunnel. He sighed, remembering how cold Deena got last time.

"Okay, what's wrong?" asked Deena.

Dan nodded north and said, "Floods, or overground from the boathouse."

Deena groaned, "I don't want to risk being in the open with an injury. We'll get targeted."

"I guess we're going swimming then," said Dan.

The water began lapping at their ankles closer to the lake. Dan took Deena's rig in readiness for the rising waters. They emptied their pockets, putting everything in the backpack. Deena took the lead, holding her lantern high as they waded deeper. The water was ice cold, and shivers began to set in.

Deena felt relieved when the water level fell. The mud beneath their feet stuck to their boots in heavy clumps, weighing them down. It was exhausting. Deena desperately tried to stop shaking as they continued north. Passing the exits to the west, the end of the tunnel was in sight, and they would soon be below the manor.

It was a gruelling trek, and Deena's leg throbbed relentlessly. She linked arms with Dan for support as she limped towards the cellar below the stables. Then, with the door shut behind them, she rested against it and said, "My leg doesn't feel right."

"The stagnant water we waded through hasn't helped. Can you make it to the main cellars? Then, I'll build a fire, and I can treat it properly," he said.

They hobbled through the catacombs to Dot's kitchen cellar. Dan told Deena to rest while he fetched their bedding to keep her warm. He returned, wrapping Deena up tightly. Her shudders lessened as she waited for Dan to build a fire. He chose the artillery cellar, close to the door leading to the front of the manor, hoping the smoke would filter through the gap at the bottom of the ill-fitting door.

When Dan had sat her beside the fire, he insisted on cleaning the lacerations, carefully flushing the wounds before applying more elixir and binding her thigh with clean cloths. Together they sat huddled beneath the blankets in silence, regaining their strength as they dried out. Deena savoured the last warmth from the fire before Dan dampened it out. Then, wrapping a blanket around her shoulders, she asked, "Can we go and get something to eat?"

The mere food suggestion caused Dan's stomach to make an exorbitant rumble. "Yeah, we can leave our stuff here," he said, laughing at the low-level grumblings in his belly.

Deena was still limping as they turned towards the cold meat storage room. They discussed their next move as they ate. Dan was adamant about getting into Megan's room. "I know she's hiding something. Your leg is the perfect way to get her to go to the cellars to help you," he said, pleading with her.

"She's dangerous. Besides, she will ask where you are," replied Deena.

"Well, tell her we split up, and you desperately need her help. Then, I'll nip into her room once she's out of the way. Come on, please, it may be the only chance we get," he said, giving her his best puppy dog eyes. Deena sighed, annoyed at agreeing, even though it was against her better judgment.

"Great," he said. "I'll hide in the drawing room. I'll be able to see you both leave from there."

"Fine, but make sure we've got sage to hand. We don't know how the Twins will react if Megan refuses to help me," said Deena.

"Don't worry; I only need five, ten minutes max," said Dan reassuringly.

"We'll go from the base room. It's the easiest access to the staircase and drawing room," said Deena.

With their plan prepared, Dan stepped through the panel door. Tiptoeing to the drawing room, he shrunk into the shadows. At the top of the stairs, Deena nervously glanced toward Dan before knocking on Megan's door.

179

There was no answer. Deena listened before trying again. Still, there was no response.

She returned to the stairs, signalling to Dan that there was no answer. Dan ushered her back to knock again. Deena rested briefly against the balcony before stepping forward to endeavour a third time. Then, something dripped from above, landing on her jacket sleeve. She touched it with her fingertips; it felt slimy. Another globule hit. With that, Deena looked up in horror. Poised on the balcony above was a Ground Crawler, sniffing the air as the smell of blood from her wound filled its senses, salivating with the expectancy of a meal. More Ground Crawlers scurried down the walls in the beams of moonlight streaming through the glass dome high above her.

Deena looked up, slowly turning her head, watching the balconies. There were at least four that she could see. Deena glanced at her leg, and panic set in as blood seeped through the bandage. Feeling in her pocket for the bushel, she dared not move for fear of the Ground Crawlers pinpointing where she stood. Right now, the Twins were the least of her worries. First, she had to disguise the smell of blood. The Ground Crawlers had begun their descent, stopping to sniff the air every few seconds. Her hands shook as she placed the match head firmly on the striking strip. To her relief, it ignited, and holding the flame to the sage, she gently blew, making it smoulder.

Then, she looked over the bannister towards the drawing room, hoping that Dan could see her and instinctively know something was wrong. But it was too dark. She repeatedly wafted the sage around her, then held it close to her wound, hoping it would disguise the metallic smell of blood, trusting it would fool them. A Ground Crawler was now only a stone's throw away. Crouched on all fours, it expanded its chest and stretched out its neck. Its low guttural clicks instilled a terror that she had begun to feel only too often. She kept her stance. To move even an inch would be detrimental. It came towards her menacingly.

Deena couldn't be sure it didn't know she was there. Although blind, it seemed to look right at her. Then, despair set in as she felt resigned to her fate. Her belly knotted, and she felt sick with anguish as it stood only two feet away. The creature craned forward, sniffing and oozing saliva from its vicious mouth. She knew it was close enough to smell the blood, and no amount of sage would save her. So, with nothing to lose, she stepped forward, thrusting the sage bushel into the Ground Crawler's face. The embers burned its skin, and smoke shot up its nose as it inhaled sharply. The Ground Crawler gave out a horrific scream that echoed around her, making each creature suddenly halt. Hurriedly it stepped back, sneezing and rubbing its burnt nose against its front legs.

Dan rushed out of the drawing room at the horrific sounds from the balcony. Halfway up the stairs, he suddenly stopped. Helplessly, Dan watched as Deena stood her ground, waving the sage in the Ground Crawler's direction. As he fumbled for the gun, it suddenly leapt onto the balcony's edge above her, pivoting and bounding upwards. It scrambled towards the glass dome, and Deena's thoughts immediately turned to Bronwyn. Dan raced up the staircase to Deena. He placed his arm around her shoulders and whispered gently, urging her back to the base room. Safely behind the panel door, Deena sank to the floor, bursting into tears. Dan turned a blind eye; she was in shock.

"We must stop your leg bleeding before continuing," he muttered. "What made them take off like that?"

"I stubbed its face with the sage, and it burnt its nose, breathing in the embers and smoke. I didn't know what else to do," she replied.

"It worked, and you are still here. Did you see how many there were?" asked Dan.

"I counted four, maybe more," she answered.

"I'm going to check that the kitchens are still secure. Perhaps they got in that way," he said. "Stay here."

Dan returned ten minutes later, shaking his head in confusion. "The back kitchen is still secure. I'll check behind the staircase," whispered Dan. Within minutes he was back, looking even more confused. "It's all as we left it," he said.

"I'm scared for Bronwyn. They scattered towards the dome. Maybe they got in up there somehow," she suggested.

"I know I shut that tower, and we put the wardrobe across the hatch in the wall," he said.

"I know, but I've got a bad feeling. I need to go and make sure Bronwyn is okay and get her down here. It would be safer. She's too isolated at the top of the building," urged Deena.

"Not until sorting you out first," said Dan. "Here, let me help you." Dan took over applying pressure to her wound until it stopped bleeding. Then, he poured on more elixir and tore strips from a pillowcase for a bandage. Finally, Dan insisted she sit down and not reopen the wounds. Deena sighed. Of course, he was right, and she could only hope Bronwyn was safe in her tower.

Dan thought, 'If they fled to the top of the building, it would stand to reason that's where they got in.' He knew they secured it, and the only weakness they found was the crumbled tower. "Do you think someone let them in deliberately?" muttered Dan.

Deena looked at him baffled and said, "Don't be stupid. No one would voluntarily let those damned things in."

"At the lake, we got attacked by the Twins. Megan stood at the bank, perhaps she left the manor doors open, and that's how they got in," suggested Dan.

"Maybe," agreed Deena.

"I'll get more water bottles and food from the cellar," said Dan, peering at her leg. "Good, the bleeding is slowing down. I won't take long."

"I've got four water bottles, ham and some cheese, and a couple of packs of cookies," said Dan on his return. He hovered at her side, pensively clutching a small cloth wallet.

"And what's that?" she asked, pointing to his hand.

"It's, um, it's a sewing kit. I found it in Dot's kitchen cellar. I've got an idea, but I'm not sure you'll run with it," he said, grimacing.

"Oh no, no way, Dan," she said, looking at her leg. "It's fine. It's stopped bleeding, honestly!" she insisted.

"See, I knew you'd be like this," he sighed. "If I stitch it, it'll stop it from opening back up, and you won't have massive scars." Dan undid his leather belt and offered it to her. Deena reluctantly took it from him. "What colour thread do you want? I've got black, white, or a lovely shade of sky blue," he said, grinning.

"I don't care," she snapped, covering herself with a sheet as she wriggled out her jeans. She sat against the wall and doubled the belt in readiness while Dan threaded a needle with black cotton.

"Please don't scream," he whispered.

Deena rolled her eyes at him as she placed the belt between her teeth. "Just do it!" she mumbled incoherently. Dan began suturing the biggest of the lacerations first. It took nearly an hour to close the wounds. Deena gave him back his belt with the addition of teeth marks and thanked him. Then, she picked up her jeans and gave them to him. "Here you go. You can do those as well," said Deena, still gritting her teeth. "They're a little draughty since the Hell Hounds got hold of me." Dan placed the lantern between them as he turned her jeans inside out and began stitching. "My leg is still weeping," she said, inspecting her wounds.

"They will, for a bit. I'll bandage it for you in a second. There, that's the best I can do," said Dan, handing over her jeans. "Hopefully, it'll hold."

"Thanks," she said, inspecting his work. "Great job!" she praised.

"No problem. The best way to get to Bronwyn is via the back kitchen and use the servant's stairs," he suggested.

"We need to go with every possible defence. Gun, sage, Gaussmeter..." began Deena.

"Gaussmeter?" questioned Dan.

"Have you forgotten the Twins? You can't tell me they don't know we are here after the horrendous screeches that Ground Crawler made. It was enough to wake the dead."

Dan laughed at the irony of her comment as he tucked in the ends of the makeshift bandage. "Right, you are all done," he said.

Dan checked the revolver, and not wanting to make the mistake of firing the wrong shot, he removed the silver bullets and put them in his rig. Then, finally, he glanced over at Deena, tidying the bedding. "I don't think Bronwyn will care about a bit of mess. Are you ready?" he asked her.

Deena followed him down the cold, stone steps into the cellars. As they passed through to the servant's stairs, Dan double-checked that it was still secure. 'They had to have come in from above,' he thought. Deena and Dan were careful to be quiet as the stairs encompassed Megan's room. Finally, they got to the servant's quarters without a problem. They waited, watching for movement for a few minutes. The Ground Crawlers seemed to have fled the building. "Keep your lantern lit. The Shadow Men are waiting for us," he whispered as he watched flashes of red eyes. They crept side by side, keeping as much light around them as possible. Deena pointed toward the room to the hidden tower. Then, Dan gasped as he entered. Someone had moved the wardrobe away from the wall. The Ground Crawlers chiselled deep claw marks into the stonework upon entry. "Someone opened this up, deliberately letting them in," whispered Dan angrily.

"No way this was Bronwyn! She couldn't have done this," murmured Deena.

"I wasn't thinking of Bronwyn," said Dan, as he shut the hatch back up and manoeuvred the wardrobe against it. Deena kept a watch through the doorway at the balcony rails. A part of her was expecting a Ground Crawler to appear over the edge, but she only saw flashes of red eyes as the Shadow Men shifted between the pillars, waiting for them to make a mistake.

Dan shut the door behind them, using the torch to push back the Shadow Men as they edged towards Bronwyn's room. Deena tried to open the tower door, but it wouldn't budge. It wouldn't even rattle in its frame. So finally, Deena stepped back for Dan to try. He looked at Deena, confused. "This wasn't locked when we left here, was it?" he asked her.

Deena shook her head. "Shush, listen," she whispered.

A tiny voice whispered from behind the thick wooden door. "Deena... Deena, is that you?" she spoke.

"Bronwyn, what's going on? Can you let us in?" urged Deena.

"Wait, it's heavy, hang on," Bronwyn whispered back.

Deena kept her ear pressed to the door listening to Bronwyn huffing and puffing as she struggled to move something heavy. Suddenly there was a squeal and then a loud heavy thud. Deena quickly pushed the door open to be presented with Bronwyn flat on her back with her feet in the air, laughing. "Are you all right?" gasped Deena.

"Yeah, sorry about that," giggled Bronwyn. "That's really, really heavy!" she remarked.

"What's been going on for you to barricade yourself like that?" asked Dan.

Bronwyn shut the door to the tower and beckoned them into her room. She sat on her bed, sighed, and said, "I was on my way back from the bathroom when I heard someone coming up the stairs. I waited to see who it was. I mean, seriously, I couldn't believe what I was seeing," said Bronwyn, pausing wide-eyed. "It was Megan. I stayed well back so she couldn't see me, but she wasn't alone. So, the three of them went into that bedroom, the one you argued in, you know, with the hatch to the hidden tower? I'm not sure I can even explain what I saw them doing. It's not even possible. The two girls were playing with the Shadow Men at first. Then they floated off the ground! They were hovering and, without even touching the wardrobe, it began to move from the wall. Honest, it was well-weird! I'd seen enough, so I came back to my room. Then I remembered you talking about those Ground Crawler things in that tower. So, I thought the safest thing to do was to put something heavy against the tower door, you know, just in case," said Bronwyn, glancing at her sore hands and rubbing them together.

"You did the right thing," said Deena. "As solid as those little girls look, they are spirits. They can move things with the power of their minds. They are dangerous."

"The Ground Crawlers did get in. Deena had a run-in with them at the top of the main staircase. So, get your stuff together. We're taking you to the cellars," said Dan.

Bronwyn looked sad and said, "I'm fine here."

"I know, but you'll be safer, and it's easier for you to get water and food supplies from the cellars," said Dan.

"Are you sure it's safe downstairs?" Bronwyn asked Deena.

Deena nodded, "Yes, but we need to be quiet. We don't want Megan to hear us."

Bronwyn looked around at what had been her haven for the last few weeks. Dan noticed her staring wistfully at her bed. "We'll sort a bed out for you," he said.

"Oh, it's not that. When you first found me, I remember I was a snivelling wreck," said Bronwyn. "Knowing you two will put everything right makes me feel so much better."

Dan and Deena exchanged an anxious look. If Bronwyn knew what they were up against, her confidence in them might not be so high. Dan took Bronwyn's bag, ensuring he shut the tower's door behind them.

Dan, Deena, and Bronwyn got safely to the base room with sighs of relief. Bronwyn's eyes searched around the room and finally rested on the bundle of bedding. "Is this where I'm staying?" she asked. Bronwyn looked at Deena and muttered, "But this is your room. You need this space."

"We don't mind you being here as well. It's safe, I promise, and besides, we come and go, so you'll have it pretty much to yourself," said

185

Deena.

"Nah, I wouldn't want to intrude, if you know what I mean. Besides, I know a much better place I can stay," said Bronwyn as she took Deena's lantern and confidently made her way down to the cellars. As they got to the bottom of the steps, Deena whispered to Bronwyn, "Where are you going?"

Without breaking her stride, Bronwyn skipped around to face Deena. Then, continuing to walk backwards, she said, "You'll see." They walked the entire length of the catacombs, stopping at the very end. Bronwyn folded her arms smugly.

"So, are you planning on staying in the catacombs? It's a bit open, isn't it?" asked Deena.

"Well, not as you would think," said Bronwyn, grinning as she turned towards the short adjacent wall along the passage to the wine cellar. Then, slipping her hand into a crevice in the corner of the walls, she lifted a latch and pushed her body weight against the stonework. Dan rushed to help her and was astonished when he stumbled into an enclosed room.

"But, how did you know this was here? You said you hadn't been working here long," muttered Dan.

"Megan told me to find Dot on my first day to help her in the kitchens. This room is Dot's 'rainy-day pantry.' No one is allowed in here but her," said Bronwyn. "This place is full of secrets."

Deena squeezed in behind them. Then, looking around in amazement, she gasped, "One hell of a pantry."

The room was more significant than the individual catacombs. Shelves were stacked high with tinned and dried foods. There were numerous wooden barrels on either side and at the far end where space allowed. Behind the door was an organised array of cardboard boxes, with their contents neatly handwritten in black marker pen. "There are quite a few butane gas cooker rings, like the ones you use for camping, they're here somewhere if you need them, and there are quite a few gas bottles to go with them," chirped Bronwyn.

"It's freezing in the cellars, so you can keep them to keep warm or heat water, but please don't cook food on them. That was Dot's mistake. Those Ground Crawlers have a very acute sense of smell," said Dan.

"Okay, if you are sure you don't want to take one," said Bronwyn.

"Carrying any unnecessary weight would slow us down. But coffee would be nice when we can pop back and see you. If you don't mind?" asked Deena.

"No problem," said Bronwyn, beaming. "Now, I have to sort out a bed, and I can try and make this place a little homelier."

"You still need to protect yourself from the Shadow Men. Dot said she'd seen them down here also," Dan advised her.

Bronwyn smiled and muttered, "Don't worry, I'm used to watching out for them."

"We'll help you sort out a bed, and then I think we all need some rest," said Deena.

Exhausted, Deena and Dan collapsed on their bedding back in the base room. Neither knew how much time had elapsed since they left Jack at his lodge. With one episode after another and their injuries, it felt like days since they last rested. They looked at each other through blurry dog-tired eyes. "Salt, we need to do the salt thing," Dan muttered as he rubbed his face, keeping his senses.

"Oh? So, you're not up for it tonight?" giggled Deena.

"So not funny, Dee!" sighed Dan. Deena stepped over him, found what salt they had left, and performed the protection circle. Then, stepping inside it, she lay beside him and lit her watch. She stared at the luminous digits, switching between date and time until Dan asked her what she was doing.

"I'm trying to work out how long we've been here. But I'm so tired I can't think straight."

Dan turned on his side and took hold of her wrist, "Well, it was the sixth of May when we got here. It's now the eighteenth, so that's twelve days. Please, can we sleep now?" he asked, yawning. Deena curled herself around him to keep warm. It was so bitterly cold. Earth was cooling rapidly without the sun in its orbit. Dan pulled the blankets over their heads to keep in what warmth their bodies could generate as they drifted off to sleep.

As Dan woke, he opened his eyes to the familiar darkness. He felt rough, but the sleep was uninterrupted. Dan listened to Deena's gentle breaths as he thought about how to tackle the estate's west side. There were still the stables and coach houses to check out as well. His mind scoured the pros and cons of using the tunnels against the risks of going overground. Ground Crawlers and Hell Hounds or face the Goat Men and the 'big fiery dude.'

187

Dan shook his head at the dilemma the dangers posed as Deena began to stir. "Why didn't you wake me?" she asked him.

"I haven't been up long," he said, fumbling to light the lantern. "We've got a long day… night; whichever, ahead of us. How do you feel? Rested enough?" he asked.

"Yeah, I think so. A bit stiff from the cold, but I'm okay," said Deena as the glow from the lantern lit up her smile.

Deena pushed off the blankets and lit the digital face of her watch. "Shit! Nearly nine hours!" she exclaimed. "Damn it!" she cried.

"Dee, stop panicking. We needed to recuperate properly," reasoned Dan. "So, how about we focus on getting organised." Deena agreed and lit her lantern to gain more light. Then, she went through the backpack and her rig. Dan laid out all the items they had found in front of him. He collectively put them together: crystals, scrolls, spear pieces, etc. Then, sitting cross-legged on the floor, he looked at them one by one, pondering their purpose concerning their mission.

"We need candles, sage, matches and more salt before heading out," said Deena. Then, she looked across at Dan. "Are you going to give me a hand or sit there doing nothing," she asked irately.

"I'm not doing 'nothing.' I'm thinking," said Dan, furrowing his brow. "What do you make of this lot?" he asked, sweeping his hand through the air.

"I don't know any more than you do, Dan," said Deena, exasperated.

"What about this? You must have felt it was important to pick it up," he asked, pointing to the sand timer. "I didn't look at it when you found it." Dan held it to the lantern and studied the intricate carvings on each stem. "Fascinating," he ruminated. "Each column is identical, with animals entwined up them. A dragon, snake, butterfly, fish, and a crow."

"It's a raven, not a crow," said Deena. "The raven has myths attached to it."

"Now I'm interested," he chipped in. So, Deena knelt beside him and, taking the sand timer, she thought for a moment.

"In Greek mythology," she said, "the raven is considered a bad omen. According to some stories, Apollo sent a white raven to spy on his lover, Coronis. They are also said to be the gods' messengers in the mortal world. There's also a…"

Dan cut her short. "Now we are talking! Okay, so this could be massively important! It could hold some sort of message or—I don't know—a clue," he said excitedly.

"If you let me finish, there is more," muttered Deena. "I was going to say, in shamanic traditions, the raven is a spirit animal used by people who want to control the universe. In most ancient cultures, crows and ravens were considered harbingers to guide human souls to the afterlife. In the paranormal field, they open the channels between the dead and the living, allowing us to hear messages from the spirit realm."

"So, say the raven on this sand timer is significant. It would represent the spirit. What about the other animals?" asked Dan, taking it back from her.

"The dragon at the bottom, what does it represent to you?" she asked knowingly.

"You've already worked this out, haven't you," he said curiously.

"I have a good idea," she said, "but I want to know your thoughts before saying anything."

Dan shrugged his shoulders and scrunched his brow in thought, not wanting to come out with some stupid notion utterly irrelevant. "Okay, wings, scales... mythical creature... breathes fire... if they did exist, they would probably eat humans," he laughed.

Deena smiled, "What about the snake?"

"Right, quit playing with me. You've worked it out, so tell me!" said Dan, frustrated.

"I reckon it's to do with the elements on the scrolls—well actually, I'm almost sure of it. Think about it. The five points on the pentagram also relate to the five elements," said Deena.

"... and each of these animals signifies an element too? So, the dragon would be fire," he said thoughtfully.

"Yes, and as for the snake, they slither over the ground, feeling every vibration of Mother Earth," she said.

"That's spirit, earth and fire," he muttered, "then we've got a butterfly and a fish. That's easy. The fish has got to be water..."

"And the butterfly is air," Deena said, finishing his sentence.

"That works for me, but why connect the sand timer and the scrolls? What are we supposed to do with them?" he asked, pinching the bridge of his nose in mind-boggling exasperation.

"I haven't thought that far yet. It has something to do with time, but that's as much as I've got, sorry. Perhaps it's to do with… I know it sounds weird, don't laugh at me when I say this, but witchcraft."

"Like voodoo?" he suggested raising his eyebrow at her.

"No idiot. Not voodoo, Wiccan. They work closely with Mother Earth and the elements when casting magic spells," she said.

"Are you a witch?" he giggled.

"No, I'm not, cheeky!" retorted Deena. Dan couldn't help but laugh. She was cute when she was angry.

"In parapsychology, we studied different types of witchcraft, cultures, and beliefs. So, that's how I know," said Deena firmly, feeling the need to redeem herself.

Her reaction amused Dan even more. "I'm kidding, Dee. I've studied stuff like that in archaeology," he said. "Witchcraft is something practised for thousands of years throughout the world. Although, I don't know much about casting spells."

"Me neither," sighed Deena.

"We've got the sand timer, pentagram, and the three element scrolls. So, if we can find the other two, we may be able to work it out. Or even better, something profound happening that will tell us," said Dan.

"What else haven't we given much thought to?" asked Deena, glancing over their treasures.

"The crystals, the blades for the spear and the rune riddle. We haven't worked out what the riddle means," listed Dan.

"There's a lot we haven't worked out. But, right now, I think we should get going. We still need to stock up before leaving for the west side," said Deena.

"No need," chirped a voice from below the cellar steps. They looked to see Bronwyn coming up, clutching an armful of stuff while struggling to keep hold of her candle. "I've been awake for hours, and I thought, if you don't let me go out with you, I can help you another way," she said, grinning broadly. "I didn't want to go outside to get stuff, but I know you need these," said Bronwyn, lowering the last armful to the floor.

"Thank you so much," gasped Deena at the number of candles rolling across the stone tiles.

"Hang on, and I'll be back in a sec.," she said, disappearing down the cellar and re-emerging with a cardboard box. "There's bottled water and something to eat," she said, pleased with her efforts.

"That's amazing. Thanks, Bronwyn. You've saved us so much time," said Deena hugging her.

"The only thing we need now is sage and matches," said Dan.

"Oh wait, sorry, I forgot I'd put them… in my …," said Bronwyn sticking her hands in her pockets. She pulled out two full boxes. "I haven't any sage, but I know where you might find some. Do you know where the orangery is? If you go around the back, there's a fruit orchard and kitchen gardens where Jack has herb beds. Unfortunately, I'm not sure which bed the sage is in, but it's worth looking."

"Thanks, we'll make that our first port of call. We have some, but nowhere near enough to last us if we run into trouble," said Dan. The three of them ate together before preparing their rigs. Bronwyn was fascinated with the equipment they had. "I'm not sure when we'll be back, so Bronwyn, please, keep yourself safe," said Dan.

They rounded the end of the catacombs and made their way to the timber pile that hid the tunnel entrance. "This is where we leave you, Bronwyn," said Deena.

Dan began moving the upright timbers out of the way. Bronwyn looked confused, not understanding where they thought they were going considering they were under the stairs. Her eyes nearly popped out of her skull when she saw the opening. "I didn't know about this secret!" she said as she rushed forward, sticking her head into the tunnel, only to be promptly pulled back by Dan.

"Oh no, you don't, young lady! It's far too dangerous in there," he said.

"You can't go with us," said Deena. "There are dangerous creatures in the tunnels. You must promise me you won't attempt to follow us."

"I'm not afraid of a few bugs and critters!" protested Bronwyn.

"We're not talking about bugs and critters; more like monsters and demons," muttered Dan.

"Fine!" she huffed, folding her arms. "I only wanted to have a quick look."

"We'll be back as soon as possible, I promise, and thank you for everything," said Deena. Bronwyn watched from the mouth of the tunnel as they disappeared into the darkness. As she lost sight of them, Dan's words of monsters and demons echoed in her head, and with that, she grappled with the long timbers to block the tunnel back up as best as she could. Bronwyn made her way back to her room with a lump in her throat and tears in her eyes. She badly wanted to go with them.

Dan and Deena reached the end of the first section of the tunnel. He peered around the corner, hoping no torch flames were looming. The coast was unencumbered as they travelled westward around the tunnel's curve and down the long straight passage. Deena drew her breath as she watched an orange glow coming toward them. "Where do we go?" she whispered frantically.

Dan muttered, "Stay here." Then, before Deena could think of protesting, he gave her his lantern and flattened himself against the tunnel wall. The torch flame steadily progressed towards them. Deena was scared they wouldn't have time to escape. Dan went a short way and then raced back to her. "Come on!" he urged as he grabbed his lantern and sped towards the Goat Man. He stopped abruptly and blew out his lantern. "Keep yours alight. Quick, you go up first," he whispered.

CHAPTER FIFTEEN

He pointed to a precarious ladder leading to a narrow opening above. The Goat Man was getting close. Dan hurriedly removed his rig and shot up the ladder. The figure of the Goat Man was a mere twenty feet away. The frustrated enemy's grunts below were disturbing, but thankfully, the cloven hoof didn't call its master. The torch flame passed below them as it continued its patrol. Deena shone her lantern around them. "What is this place?" she whispered.

Dan got to his feet and said, "A tower of some sort. Weirdly, there is no way out other than down."

"Another secret place? Bronwyn said the estate is full of them," said Deena, straining her eyes.

Above them, suspended within the walls, were sections of wooden platforms at varying heights, spiralling the curvature of the tower. "This has got to be worth a look," said Dan grinning. He found a ladder lying against the wall. Setting it upright, he butted it up alongside the first platform. Deena waited for him to get onto the first ledge before venturing up.

"I don't get why they would put these ledges up unless it were to hide stuff. So, hopefully, we'll find something useful," said Dan. Set in the wall were recesses. Dan enthusiastically rummaged about and found nothing but dust and rusty nails. So, he pulled the ladder up and bridged the gap to the next ledge. He held it steady for Deena. Should the ladder shift, there was nothing they could do to stop it from slipping and crashing to the floor along with either one of them.

Safely across, he glanced over the edge. They were about fifteen feet up the tower. There were only a few recesses, which yielded nothing. Deena knelt and searched the ashes of a used fireplace on the next platform while Dan checked the cubbies. "Look at this," she said, brushing off the grime. "I've found an axe."

"That's a machete," he explained.

"It's a bit elaborate for chopping firewood. That's strange; it's buried in the ashes," said Deena, handing it to him. Dan saw writing engraved on the wooden handle, but the ash obscured the inscription. He sat beside Deena and cleaned it up, expecting a maker's mark or name, but a rune inscription emerged as he cleaned the grooves. Dan fell silent, tracing each rune with his finger, deep in thought. Finally, he anxiously drew a sharp breath. "What's wrong? What does it say?" she asked.

"Revelation of Loki," he whispered. "Elements in time."

"What's scary about that? Who is Loki anyway?" asked Deena.

"Loki is a Norse god. Technically, he's a giant, not a god, and Odin's adopted brother. So, should we come up against him, we probably won't live through it," he replied solemnly. He twirled the machete around in his hand, inspecting it more closely. "It doesn't look or feel special like Odin's spear. The blade isn't the same metal either," he muttered.

"Perhaps, but the runes make it special," stated Deena. "Elements in time, you said. So does that mean it's only a matter of time before Loki is here?" she questioned.

"Maybe," said Dan thoughtfully.

"What's so bad about him? I need to know what we're up against if he is coming," said Deena.

"Loki is the trickster god. He's originally from the land of the giants but has no loyalty to any gods. He is the father to Jormundgand, the giant serpent that encompasses our world; he is the father to Hel, the queen of the underworld in Niflheim. He is also the father to Fenrir, the giant wolf that kills Odin during Ragnarök. But get this; he is the mother to Odin's eight-legged steed, Sleipnir."

"What? How is that possible?" asked Deena in disbelief.

"That's just it. With Loki, you don't know what you're going to encounter. He can disguise himself, even change his sex and turn himself into anything he wants. As a result, he causes trouble and a lot of it, usually to get what he wants. He caused so many problems in the gods' worlds that they had him chained to a rock using the entrails of his son, which they forged into a vast chain, and to cut a long story short, he breaks free when Ragnarök happens and takes the side of the underworld against the gods.

"Shit! He's fighting alongside the underworld, and there is a possibility that this giant, unidentifiable god could get to our Earth. I don't fancy our chances either," she groaned.

"Yeah, now you understand why I'm worried. As the story goes, at the time of Ragnarök, Loki gets locked into battle with Heimdall at the Bifröst

Bridge. Remember, I told you about connecting the gods' worlds to ours. Loki and Heimdall are supposedly mortally wounded, but if Loki has somehow managed to survive, he could get to our world, especially if Heimdall couldn't stop him. I can't think of any other reason why his name should turn up unless Odin needed us to know that there could be a real possibility he could get here. But, why on a machete?" he questioned.

"Well, Heimdall can't be dead because I called upon him with the rune, and he answered me," said Deena.

"Point taken; but, in the battle and confusion of Ragnarök, Loki could also have survived and got to Earth," he said.

"Perhaps, if Loki could get to our world, we need to be prepared and assume that he is here, somewhere," said Deena trying to be brave. "Can I ask, how do we know we haven't already come up against him? If he can disguise himself, he could have taken any form he wants."

"We don't, and if we have, he's toying with us," he said, putting the machete in the backpack. He picked up the ladder and bridged the gap. The next level was fruitless. They hoped that the highest point would prove to be better. Deep in thought, neither spoke as they raised the ladder to the final floor. The floor spanned the turret's front, and a narrow ledge ran either side to the corner. Deena began her search in the cubby holes while Dan looked at the ledge above him. Dan climbed the ladder to eye level with the eaves. He held up his lantern, scrutinising the space. Something caught his attention on the far side. Swiftly climbing down, he moved the ladder around and climbed back up. "Dee, I've found crystals. There's something else, it looks like a scroll, but it's wedged," muttered Dan. He took his time, easing it out. As he climbed down, he gave it to Deena. Carefully, she unrolled it.

"It's the symbol for air. We've only got earth to find now," she said eagerly.

"Can I have a look at the crystals?" he asked. "I'm trying to figure out what we should do with them. Perhaps, it's to do with their energies. These are red jasper."

"Do you know its properties?" she asked him. Dan sighed, and with a look of hopelessness, he shook his head. "Me neither. We need to get to the orangery," said Deena.

Dan poked his head into the ground below to check it was safe before dropping back into the tunnel. Next, he got the compass to check their direction. "We'll have to go west. Maybe a connecting tunnel will take us south," whispered Dan.

The tunnel seemed never-ending. Suddenly, Deena stopped, and as Dan turned to her, she said, "How come you get to carry all the cool stuff?"

"Cool stuff? What's that supposed to mean?" he asked, confused.

"You know, the cool stuff. You've got the blades to the spear, the penknife, the machete, and the gun!" said Deena.

"And..." he queried.

"Well, if we get attacked by Ground Crawlers or whatever, you've got all the weapons. I haven't anything to defend myself except digital equipment or sage," she said indignantly.

"Are you serious, Dee? You know I've got your back," he said.

"I know you have, but I want the machete, please? I would feel a lot better knowing I had it if need be," she said, smiling sweetly and holding her hand out.

Dan sighed, pulled it out of the backpack, gave it to her and asked, "Are you happy now, or is there anything else you want?"

Deena secured it to her chest rig and said, "Nope, I'm happy now. Thanks." Eventually, they came to a tunnel heading northwest. "There must be one that heads south soon, surely," muttered Deena dragging her feet. "These tunnels are getting monotonous."

It was a couple of hundred feet before they came across another tunnel linking from the other side. At last, they were heading south. Unfortunately, the lantern's glow cast light only a short way, leaving them with little sense of direction but for the compass. Without it, the network of tunnels would be impossible. Twenty-five minutes later, they found themselves at a junction leading northeast. "This must go back towards the manor on the east side of the estate," said Dan.

Deena wandered a few feet into it. "I feel very uneasy," she said. "Something bad is down there. I can feel it," she said, shuddering.

"This tunnel is different, narrower, and solid stone, unlike the others. Do you fancy taking a quick look?" asked Dan.

Deena was reluctant to go any further, but Dan's adventurer's eyes widened pleadingly, and she gave in. "Fine, only a short way. We've got other stuff to do," she sighed.

"Great!" exclaimed Dan, striding away from her. Deena couldn't shake the feeling of dread, so she hung back. Dan was a good twenty feet in front when she heard him call her. "Hey Dee!" he said. "There's a stone wall with carvings and holes. Come and look."

"You mean it's a dead-end," she shouted, making her way to him. Two-thirds of the way up, a circular stone sat within the wall. Four identical slots formed a square within it, with a more significant niche in the middle. Inside the circle were individual rune markings crudely carved into the rock, and rune inscriptions covered the rest of the wall. "Can you decipher it?" she asked.

"Yes, but it will take time. I'll need a pen and paper. There's too much to remember," said Dan.

"We'll come back to it," muttered Deena, scrutinising the slots. "Is that a seam or crack down the centre above and below the circular stone?" She reached forward, tracing her fingers over the hairline cracks. "It's not only down the centre. There's a horizontal crack on each side," she said.

Dan set his lantern down, taking out the candle. He turned to Deena, smirking as the flame danced erratically, and said, "I do love an adventure! We must get this open!"

With the candle back in the lantern, Dan ushered her back. Then, placing his feet slightly apart, he put both palms in the middle of the stone circle, pushing as hard as possible.

"All the pushing and grunting in the world isn't going to open it," chuckled Deena.

"Have you got a better idea!" snapped Dan.

"Oooo tetchy," she laughed. "It may help to decipher the inscriptions first; it looks like it could be a puzzle lock."

Dan hung his head and said, "I don't get it. Why make it so damn difficult for us?"

"To make sure the wrong people don't get their hands on the skull," said Deena. "We've got this far, and apparently, there is no giving up, and what's left of this world depends on us, remember?" she affirmed. Dan grunted at hearing his own words thrown back at him. "We need to go," said Deena.

They turned into the south tunnel; it was several miles before coming across another junction leading east. "That must go to either the maze or the cottages," said Dan.

"I'll be glad to get above ground," sighed Deena. "I'm starting to hate these tunnels." Dan felt much the same way. The never-ending walls were enough to send anyone mad. Suddenly, Deena quickened her pace. "I see steps," she said excitedly.

"Wait!" Dan called out. "We need to be prepared before we go up. We don't know where we'll come out."

They split what little sage they had, along with matches and salt. Dan insisted on putting new candles in the lanterns as the absence of light could be detrimental, if not fatal, for them.

The steps led to the rear of the orangery. They crept halfway down the building with their backs hugged against the wall. Dan pointed to various vegetable beds. Silently, they shone the lantern over withered plants until they found the sage shrubs in a self-contained bed. It was good that they were so dried and wilted. They would burn better. They stuffed as much as they could into the backpack.

"Let's look for a way into the building. It would be safer to sort it out inside," said Deena, casually turning the fancy pewter handle and pulling one of the enormous doors open.

They stood in a large foyer, facing another set of tall doors. The décor was very Victorian, with filigree plasterwork and scrolled pillars. Deena opened the doors and walked into the massive space. Dan marvelled at the building, but the trees were dying, and their fruits had fallen without sunlight. "We need twine to make the bushels," said Deena.

Dan put his gear down, took out the sage and put it in a neat pile. They found a metal cabinet, and upon opening it, there was an array of gardening hand tools scattered on the shelves. Amongst them was a ball of gardening twine. He gave it to Deena. "There's not much, but…" he said.

"It'll have to do?" she finished.

They sat on the floor and began cutting the sage into lengths, fashioning it together. They made seven decent-sized bushels before running out of twine. "We've still got sage left," said Dan.

"We've made enough for now. We can leave the rest here and come back for it if we find more twine," suggested Deena. "So, where to now?" she asked.

"That aerial map showed a few places this side of the manor. I know there is a church and an old abbey. Let's make for the nearest buildings and work our way across," suggested Dan.

"Fine by me," she replied. "Not the tunnels. I'm sick of tunnels."

"No problem, overground it is then," laughed Dan. Then, with the backpack sorted and sage ready, they stood before the doors to leave. "Ground Crawlers and Hell Hounds, here we come!" whispered Dan with renewed determination as they stepped out into the open. Adrenalin pumped through their bodies as they began the next phase of their mission.

Dan and Deena chose to keep only one lantern alight as the less they drew attention to themselves, the better. The orchard at the rear of the orangery was huge, and the smell of rotting fruit was pungent. Nervously, they walked around the edge of the orchard. The open ground lay to their right, and they chose to cut across towards some buildings. Within the darkness, everything seemed still, quiet, and unassuming. Dan blew out the lantern and took the torch, gripping it tightly. "The Shadow Men can't cross open ground as they can only move between shadows," he whispered to her. Deena nodded in response. Lantern aglow would mean that anyone or anything would see them coming, making them a great target. They cringed as their boots crunched the gravel underfoot, crossing a driveway. To the northeast, the manor house was visible from the road. A copse of trees lay to their right. Dan flicked the torch on for a couple of seconds to get their bearings.

"Is this the church?" she whispered, relighting her lantern. "It's huge. A lot has collapsed." There was no way she was going into the ruins without light. Dan put the flashlight in his rig before they made their way to the closest crumbling wall.

"It's the old abbey. The row of arches should lead to a chapter house," said Dan. The building had been slowly disintegrating over the centuries. The stonework was scattered across the ground, making it impossible to keep a straight line. Finally, they reached the corridor of the archways.

Keeping a watchful eye, they entered the chapter house. In the centre of the polygon stood a giant pillar. Deena's eyes followed it up only to see the night sky. The roof had long since gone. She circled the column and looked through each tall arched window, which had lost its stained glass. Instead, grass and weeds had carpeted the floor beneath their feet. Ivy decorated the walls, and vines hung like drapes around the windows. "We need to keep moving, Dee," said Dan. Deena caught up with him as he veered into a further arched passage. Looking back over her shoulder, she suddenly stopped. She spun around to see a dark, cloaked figure passing between arches at the other end. "What's wrong?" he asked.

"I don't know if my imagination is getting the better of me, but I swear I saw someone," said Deena. "Don't laugh, but it looked like a monk with a hood!" Dan couldn't help himself and let out a snorted giggle. "I saw... Stop laughing!" she said.

"Sorry, Dee, but really? A hooded monk? Well, I suppose we're in the right place for it," he chuckled.

Deena ignored him and walked towards the archways where the mysterious figure had disappeared. Dan gave chase, and at the very end, Deena watched cautiously. Then, not seeing anyone, she stepped out. "He's gone," whispered Deena.

"There's a church further up. So, maybe he's headed that way," said Dan.

"That would make sense, I suppose. Although, he didn't seem concerned about how dangerous it is out here," said Deena.

"Let's go. We've got enough to do without running after people daft enough to be outside," said Dan. "We need to finish searching the abbey."

They snuck around the ruins, starting in the east wing. Some areas were more intact than others. They wandered in and out of collapsed doorways and open-air rooms, searching for any nook and cranny holding a hidden treasure. A double-arched entranceway led northeast. From here, they could see the chapter house to the northwest. Again, there was open ground ahead of them. Northeast, a large copse laced a road leading back to the manor. Deena pointed to the chapter house and drew a circle in the air, indicating to walk the outer walls. Dan nodded and led the way around the dilapidated structure. They discovered steps leading underground in the corner where the arches met the chapter house. "More tunnels?" questioned Dan as he disappeared down the steps. At the bottom, he whispered to Deena, "Definitely a tunnel." He took out the compass, checking its direction, and said, "This must meet up with the one we took from the manor. We'll explore it later."

They crossed between the steps and the chapter house and followed its outer wall, and where the passage wall met the circular structure was another recess. Large sections of the wall above had collapsed, and the scattered stones made it challenging to get around the rest of the border. "I reckon we'll have to skip this bit," said Dan.

"Wait, I can see steps under the rubble," said Deena. "Give me a hand." Dan helped her remove the loose stone, revealing more stairs under the ruins. Finally, he made it to the bottom. Its direction didn't run under the chapter house, so they presumed it must lead to the church. Deena and Dan finished searching the abbey's main building, so they crossed to a small copse, partially hiding the remnants of a corner of an outbuilding. Dan moved loose rocks casually with his boot when something clinked. It sounded metallic. So, he knelt, holding the lantern close to the ground. He moved stones aside and spotted a shard of metal.

"This looks like the other part of the blade. It's the same type of metal!" said Dan excitedly. He got the smaller blade from his rig. It married up perfectly.

"Does it complete the spearhead?" asked Deena.

"Yes," he said, feeling a surge of energy vibrating through the blade. "Although, I'm not sure it is fixable," he said, putting the pieces into the backpack. "Let's go back to the tunnel leading to the church."

Retracing their steps, they got as far as the arches when they heard low guttural clicks. Deena and Dan briefly exchanged a panicked look as they stood rooted to the spot. They were close. Dan pulled out the revolver, lining up the brass bullets in the chamber. Then, he cautiously panned it around, ready to shoot at anything that moved. "Where are they?" asked Deena.

"They must have felt the stones landing when we cleared the tunnel," whispered Dan. "They know we are here."

"Up there!" Deena said, pointing to the roof of the abbey passages. Dan aimed the gun at three Ground Crawlers, poised and ready to sense any vibrations or movement below.

"Don't move!" urged Dan. "Can you see more of them?" he pressed.

"No, I don't think so," replied Deena.

"I need you to be sure because we will have to run if they pinpoint…" he began. Dan fell silent as a vicious snarl emerged from behind them. "Oh, you're fucking kidding me!" he said, slowly turning to look over his shoulder. To their rear were four Hell Hounds relishing their hunt, slowly stalking them. Deena rammed her hand into her jacket and pulled out a sage bushel. Her hands shook as she fumbled with the matches trying to light them. "We haven't got time for that! They'll be on us before it gets going," he said in desperation.

"What else can we do?" she said, reaching for the machete. "We're in real fucking trouble here!"

"I've only got two silver bullets. It's not enough to take them all out!" snapped Dan urgently.

CHAPTER SIXTEEN

The Ground Crawlers seemed less of a threat than the impending danger of the approaching Hell Hounds. "The runes!" Dan exclaimed. "Use Isa! Hurry up, ask Verdandi for help! Ask her to change our fate because it's not looking too good right now!" he shouted.

Deena gripped Isa between her palms. The rune began to tingle, and electrical charges surged up her arms into her body as she begged Verdandi for help. Suddenly, the air pressure dramatically changed. It became dense and heavy. Deena opened her eyes and looked at Dan, trying to understand what was happening. Instead, Dan pointed to the Hell Hounds. She turned to face them. To her amazement, their movements were in slow motion. She looked over to the Ground Crawlers. They, too, were barely moving. Incredibly, one had leapt off the roof of the arches and was hanging in mid-air. "Dee, come on! We don't know how long this will last!" shouted Dan. "Get in the tunnel!" he urged.

Running through the thick atmosphere proved difficult, like running in water. It was hard to draw breath and was exhausting to move faster than their assailants, but they were gaining distance. Deena struggled down the steps into the tunnel below. "Keep going!" shouted Dan. "Don't stop for anything!" he continued. They had only gained a few hundred feet when the atmospheric pressure suddenly released them. They knew it wouldn't be long before either of the creatures would be racing down after them.

Terrified, they began running. The only sound was the pounding of their hearts. The tunnel curved north, and as they rounded it, the glow of a Goat Man's torch came towards them. However, vicious teeth were advancing from behind. Then, as Deena and Dan tried to escape, the Goat Man raised his cloven hoof and heavily stomped three times, and the earth began to tremble. The watchers had summoned their master. Bellowing as it rose out of the ground, the colossal Fire Demon was now between them and their hunters. The first fireball hit the ground, and then another. Neither knew if the Fire Demon was going after them or their assailants.

Deena scrambled up the tunnel, daring to look behind her. She couldn't see anything in the darkness, but the ear-piercing shrieks of their aggressor's deathly screams filled the tunnel. It was only a matter of time before the Fire Demon turned its wrath on them. Dan picked up the pace as they continued racing through the tunnel but were repeatedly thrown off their feet as fireballs blasted behind them. This time, there were no screeches, which to Dan and Deena only meant one thing. The tunnel lit up behind them, and blasts of heat momentarily seared their skin. Dan grabbed Deena, dragging her with him, not knowing how much further they must run. He flicked the flashlight on, pointing it ahead. "Not far, Dee!" he shouted.

Dan grasped the latch, almost crashing into the door, flinging it open. Deena sped through and stopped, gasping for breath as Dan slammed it shut. They were in yet another tunnel. "Don't stop!" he shouted. "We have to get out of here." Deena looked desperate; she wasn't sure how much further she could run. "Left or right?" he asked urgently.

"Left!" she shouted breathlessly. "We should come out near the church. The other way may take us towards the manor. It's too far." Dan turned on his heels, and once more, they began running. Then, further ahead, another door. He quickly opened it, and with their backs against it, they took a minute to catch their breath and listen. Then, finally, it was silent, with no screeches and no more fireballs. Deena's shoulders dropped with relief.

Dan walked a short way down the walled passage while Deena got herself together. Then, returning to her, he asked, "Are you okay to carry on?"

Deena muttered, "The darkness is continuing to empower the entities. We have to find the crystal skull and soon."

"I know," he replied solemnly.

"The longer the darkness continues, the more strength they gain. We were lucky to get out of that alive," said Deena, opening her clenched fist and revealing the rune, Isa. "It's only thanks to Verdandi that we are still here." She tucked the rune in her pocket, and together they walked under an arch leading them into a cellar.

Dan lit their lanterns and muttered, "We're definitely under the church." Then, holding up an old chalice cup and a robe, he added, "If this is sanctified ground, surely evil wouldn't be able to enter here?"

"I wouldn't bet on it," said Deena. "Christianity has no place in

Ragnarök."

"I guess so. We should be looking to the Norse gods," said Dan.

"Is that what you believe?" said a voice.

Dan and Deena stared at each other before Deena called, "Hello? Who's down here?"

From a darkened doorway stood a figure dressed in black. It wasn't until he moved into the candlelight that his white collar stood out. "I am Father Rhys, the priest here," he said. "Is there something I can do for you?" he questioned. Deena stared for a moment, trying to figure out whether he was living. "Has the cat got your tongue, young lady?" he asked, smiling.

"No, I just... Sorry, I wasn't expecting anyone to be here," she said sheepishly.

Deena felt she was trespassing, and that they shouldn't be there. Dan stepped forward and shook the priest's hand. "I'm Dan, and this is Deena," he said, introducing themselves.

"I'm pleased to meet you," he replied. "May I ask, what are you doing in my cellars? Pillaging the church is highly frowned upon, you know."

"Oh, we weren't..." stammered Deena.

Father Rhys laughed, and as he turned to leave, he said, "I'm pulling your leg, lady. Follow me." They followed him up a flight of stairs and into his living quarters. He offered them a seat at a small dining table in the kitchen.

"Is it only you here, Father, or is anyone else here with you?" asked Dan.

"Just me now," he replied. "Have you seen anyone in the manor? Is everyone okay?" he asked.

"We've come across a few survivors," said Deena. The priest put biscuits on a plate, placed them in the centre of the table, and sat with them. He listened with intent as Deena told him of whom they'd encountered. His face dropped when he heard what had happened to Dot.

"Brother Thomas said there were ungodly creatures out there," said Father Rhys.

"I thought you said you were alone," said Dan.

"Brother Thomas is no longer with us," he sighed.

"What happened? Did the Ground Crawlers kill him too?" asked Deena shocked.

"In a way, I suppose they did," he said. "We had that terrible comet storm and then nothing but darkness. Brother Thomas tried to get to the manor to see if everyone was safe. He wasn't gone long when he came back babbling about these creatures out there, said it wasn't the work of God, and before I could stop him, he knelt before the pulpit and plunged a knife into his chest."

"That's so sad," said Deena.

Father Rhys lowered his eyes, shook his head slowly, and said, "He lost his faith. He was rambling about it not being an Armageddon of biblical proportions but destruction by the devil himself. I tried to reason with him, but he kept saying, 'It was all lies.' He had a knife hidden in the sleeve of his robe. I didn't know; otherwise, I would have stopped him. I thought he was kneeling to pray, but he…"

"It's okay, Father, you don't need to say anymore," interrupted Dan.

"But, if you are the only person here, whom did I see in the abbey ruins?" asked Deena.

"I don't know," said Father Rhys. "I haven't left the church since Brother Thomas told me about those creatures. A coward in God's eyes."

"Father, God's work or otherwise, you are not a coward. On the contrary, you have every right to fear what is out there," said Deena. But, not wanting to chance him losing his faith as Brother Thomas did, she refrained from speaking of the Norse gods and how it was central to what was going on.

"Father, we aren't here by chance," said Dan. "We were sent here by our government to retrieve something specific. Maybe you could help us?" he entreated.

"We are running out of time, and we need all the help we can get," pleaded Deena. "To save our world, we must find what we are looking for."

"I don't see that I have anything else to do with my time. So, what are you looking for?" asked Father Rhys. Deena paused, unsure of how Father Rhys would react. She couldn't ask him about the skull, the crystals, or the runes without divulging that Ragnarök was real. Dan put the kibosh on any diplomatic approach on her part.

"An extraordinary crystal skull," Dan blurted out.

"Dare I ask the significance of this crystal skull?" Father Rhys asks, sitting forward with interest.

Deena groaned at Dan. "What, Dee? We need whatever help we can get! We haven't got time for pussyfooting around!" stated Dan.

"Fine!" said Deena, "Then, you tell him that Ragnarök has destroyed our Earth. "You… destroy his faith as well."

"Lady, it's fine. I know what is going on is far from normal. I'm an old man. I've been around a long time, so nothing you say can shock me or move my faith," said Father Rhys calmly. Dan placed his elbows on the table, leaned forward and began telling him everything to date.

Father Rhys remained silent when Dan finished explaining, staring at the table. They sat and waited patiently. Finally, he raised his head, looked at them, and asked, "Do you truly believe in what you have told me?" asked Father Rhys.

"Yes, of course we do," said Dan.

"There are many beliefs in this world, mine being one of them. However, I think that all beliefs should be respected. It does not matter if it is different from mine. I didn't get this long in the tooth not hearing of such things as Norse mythology," said Father Rhys. "I don't know the whereabouts of this crystal skull, but if it is that important, I will help you. Where do you want to start?" he asked, getting up.

"We need to search everywhere. We don't know the importance of some things until we come across them, and believe me, we've found objects in the most obscure places like these," said Deena, fishing out the red jasper crystals.

Father Rhys took them from her and inspected them a little closer. "I'm sure there are some of these in the vestry and the church. I never worked out what they were. I thought maybe from a statue long gone. I can show you where, but Brother Thomas's body still lies in front of the pulpit. I wanted to bury him…" he said, trailing off in sadness.

"It's fine, Father. I'm sure we can find our way," said Deena kindly.

Deena and Dan left Father Rhys in his chambers and went to the vestry. On one side was a clothing rail where robes hung, ready for service. Deena spotted ledgers neatly stacked on a desk. She opened the top register, scanning the entries. "Father Rhys is close to the community. He has carried out all the entries for marriages, christenings, and burials for the last thirty years," muttered Deena. She searched the desk drawers, rummaged amongst old invoices, and found empty pocketbooks and ballpoint pens, so she tucked one in her pocket with a pen. Then, Deena turned her attention to the other side of the desk. In the bottom drawer, she found the crystals that Father Rhys had mentioned. "Dan, I've found two pairs of crystals. Have you had any luck?" she asked.

"No, nothing yet," he mumbled. "This monk's bench is cool, though."

Deena watched him lift the hinged bench, revealing a storage compartment. She went and knelt beside him. "It's packed with stuff, said Deena. They pulled out bibles, hymn books and old sermons. Underneath was a mishmash of things. They took out old decorations that had seen better days and sifted through the remnants in the bottom. "Hey, Dan, another rune!" she said, handing it to him.

"It's the rune, Raidho. It signifies movement, travel, or a journey. Its deity is Freyr. He is the ruler of peace, fertility, rain, and sunshine. His Father is Njord, the sea god," said Dan.

"How do we use it?" asked Deena.

"I guess we'll find out when we need his help," said Dan. Deena tucked it in her pocket with the others and asked him to look at the crystals she had found. He picked up the first pair, holding them close to the lantern. "These look like sunstone," he said, passing them to Deena, "and these look like blue lace agate."

Deena placed them in the backpack. "I'm not looking forward to going to the main part of the church. If Brother Thomas died when Ragnarök happened, his corpse will not be pleasant," she said, squirming. "Do you think we should move his remains for Father Rhys?" she asked.

"Good idea. We'll go and ask Father Rhys after we have searched here," suggested Dan.

So, they walked the length of the nave. Wooden pews lined either side of the aisle. In front of the pulpit, Brother Thomas's robe outlined his emaciated corpse.

"The easiest way to move him is to wrap him in cloth and carry him out," said Dan.

Deena pointed to a table behind the pulpit and suggested using the tablecloth. She stepped around Brother Thomas, grimacing at the rotting odour emanating from him. Clearing the table of its contents, she removed the tablecloth. They took an end each, laying it out beside Brother Thomas. Tentatively, they rolled him onto it. Deena began to gag as they pulled the cloth over him. She sat back, resisting the urge to vomit. She looked at where Brother Thomas's body had lain for the last few weeks as she composed herself. As he decayed, body fluids stained the stone floor beneath him. She noticed a small wooden cross and picked it up. Brother Thomas had cut the cross from around his neck. "I think we should give this to Father Rhys," said Deena. They finished cocooning Brother Thomas's body with enough length to knot each end.

"That's secure enough. We'll search the rest of the church before moving him. There are rooms on either side of the aisles, and I want to check out the pulpit as well," said Dan.

Deena spotted a font at the west end of the church. Thoughts of Lily and Ben flooded to mind. She shook herself out of it and realised she still had Brother Thomas's cross in her hand. She walked to the font, took out her water bottle and washed it.

Dan stood in the pulpit, staring at Father Rhys's sermon. The base of the podium had a built-in cabinet. So, he squatted and opened the doors. On the top shelf sat Father Rhys's bible. Neatly placed to one side were two more crystals. Dan took them out, gazing at them in awe. Then, he went over to Deena. "Out of all the crystals, these are the most valuable, and their colour is incredible," said Dan passing them to her.

"Dan, these are emeralds! No wonder Father Rhys kept them in the pulpit!" she exclaimed.

"Although, lately, the world's economy has collapsed somewhat," he chuckled, "the only value they have now is to our mission. Let's get these rooms done, and then we'll see Father Rhys."

Together they entered a room on the east side of the church. A small table and chair were at one end. Cupboards lined the outer wall with colourful biblical storybooks. Finally, in the centre were wooden chairs that only a child could sit on. They left empty-handed and crossed the nave's west. The church predominantly used it for storage. Leaning in one corner was a large synthetic Christmas tree with boxes stacked beside it. Deena opened the boxes to find fabulous giant frosted baubles of all colours. As Dan searched the cupboards at the other end, Deena leaned against the wall, staring out a leaded window into the graveyard beyond. She smiled at a weeping angel kneeling over a tombstone when movement caught her eye.

Cupping her hand to the glass, she squinted into the darkness, and for a moment, she thought she must have imagined it until a familiar cloaked figure passed between two monuments. "Dan! Come here, quick!" she urged. Dan rushed to the window bobbing his head about, trying to see what she had seen. "If you stay still and watch, you'll see him," she whispered.

"Who?" asked Dan, confused.

"The cloaked man, the one I saw at the abbey. He's out there," she said. Dan watched, pressing his forehead against the glass. "There!" said Deena, "moving towards the back of the church."

Dan caught a fleeting glimpse of the figure as it disappeared. "That is definitely not Father Rhys," said Dan.

"I know, but Father Rhys said there was only him and..." She trailed off.

"Brother Thomas?" said Dan incredulously.

"It has to be. Father Rhys wouldn't lie," said Deena.

"Whoever it is, they're gone now," said Dan, turning his attention to the cupboards. The only thing he found of use was a box of candles. So, he suggested taking some to Father Rhys and keeping some for themselves.

Deena knocked gently on Father Rhys's door. He welcomed them with a heart-warming smile, asking how they got on. "Great, we found the crystals, and we brought these up for you," said Deena, handing him the box of candles. "I hope you don't mind, but we kept some."

"Thank you. Do you need more? Candles are the one thing the church always has plenty of," said Father Rhys.

"We've enough but thank you. Father, we saw the hooded figure again. He was in the graveyard behind the church. Are you sure there is only you here?" asked Deena.

"I'm sure, lady. I wish Brother Thomas were still here. It would be nice to have the company," sighed Father Rhys.

"We've prepared Brother Thomas's body to move him so you can use the church. Is there anywhere in particular you would like us to take him?" asked Deena

"I suppose the mausoleum would be the best place. It's the family's burial chamber, but I don't suppose that is of consequence now," said Father Rhys.

"Oh, I almost forgot," said Deena, pulling the wooden cross out of the backpack. "I found it under his body. I've washed it, and I thought you may want it, or should we put it with him?" she asked.

Father Rhys took the wooden cross from her, looking at it thoughtfully. Then, taking his aspergillum from his pocket, he opened it, and dabbing a little holy water on his finger, he traced it over the cross, muttering a blessing. Then, graciously, he gave it back to Deena.

"I would like you to have it, lady. Brother Thomas doesn't need it now. You have a dangerous job ahead of you. It may not be your belief, but it is mine. May it keep you safe," said Father Rhys.

"What's the best way to get to the mausoleum, Father?" asked Dan.

"Go back to the tunnel you used to enter the church cellars and follow it north. It runs under the graveyard. It'll take you directly into the lower level of the mausoleum," said Father Rhys.

Deena and Dan stood on either side of Brother Thomas's swaddled remains. Exchanged grimaces told of the unpleasant task of moving him. Dan strapped the backpack on securely, leaving his hands free. They carried him through the nave and into the cellar using the flashlight. "Wait, I want to see if I can get to the graveyard from here," said Deena.

"What for?" asked Dan.

"I need to know who that cloaked figure is," she muttered, taking the flashlight from Dan. She went to a door on the far side, opened it and peered up a flight of steps, whispering, "Are you coming with me?" Dan stepped over Brother Thomas, following her outside. Deena panned the flashlight into the graveyard as far as the beam could reach. "I didn't realise it was so big," she whispered.

She and Dan made their way to the nearest gravestone offering concealment in a half-crouch. They looked for movement within the shadows. Bravely, they continued through the headstones, briefly dobbing down behind them, checking for the cloaked figure. "There he is," whispered Deena. "He's at the bottom of the cemetery."

They were cautious, following the ominous figure at a safe distance, or so they thought. The figure stopped abruptly and turned to face Dan and Deena. He stood motionless but for his long robe swaying in the breeze. He had caught them off guard between headstones. Dan backed up to the closest monument, watching Deena stand her ground. "Brother Thomas?" she called out. "Brother Thomas, is that you?" she repeated. There was no reply, so Deena took a shaky step toward him. "Please answer me; are you Brother Thomas? Father Rhys told us what happened. I have your cross if you want it."

"I serve another god now," rumbled a voice beneath the robe.

The hooded monk slowly raised his arms from his sides, his palms facing downwards. Then, his fingers stiffened and elongated. As he raised his arms higher, he turned his palms skyward. Deena turned to run, but something knocked her to the ground. White mists and orbs rose from the ground as she struggled to get up. She watched in horror, realising the hooded monk was calling the spirits from their graves. Brother Thomas drove the spirits toward Deena, throwing his arms out in front of him. Contorted faces of the dead passed through her body. It left her feeling weaker with every hit. Finally, finding courage, Dan ran to her, pulling her to her feet, shouting, "We need to get out of here, Dee!"

CHAPTER SEVENTEEN

A ferocious wind whisked up and leaves spun in the air around them. The force of the squall made their eyes water, making it difficult to see. The howling wind got louder as the monk continued driving spirits from all directions, and there was nowhere to hide from them. Deena yanked on the backpack strapped to Dan. "I need his cross!" she shouted. "Can you distract him while I get close enough to give him this back? Then, if he realises what he's doing is wrong, it may be enough to stop him."

Dan struggled to his feet and ran across the graveyard, away from her. Deena waited, and once the hooded figure fixated on Dan, she sidled around the back of a headstone. She cringed as Dan took the hits. The atmosphere filled with the energy and cries of tormented souls the monk was controlling; he had to be Brother Thomas. She passed him on the far side, creeping up behind him. Sensing her, he turned abruptly, and Deena thrust the cross at him. "Take it! It's yours, take it!" she screamed at him.

As quickly as it all started, it stopped. Brother Thomas disappeared before her, the wind dropped, and the spirits returned to their resting places. It was as if nothing had happened. Deena looked at the cross in her hand and thought, 'Brother Thomas certainly didn't want this back.' Dan was still stumbling about in the shadows beyond. Finally, Deena caught up with him, and they sat against the weeping angel to catch their breath, trying to make sense of what had happened. "What the fuck was that about?" asked Dan.

"I don't know. But when I tried to give Brother Thomas his cross back, he disappeared. He said something that has worried me, though," she said quietly. "He said he serves another god now."

"What did he mean by that?" muttered Dan.

"I don't know. Anyway, I reckon we should keep this cross handy. He didn't like me offering it back," she said.

Dan got to his feet, brushed himself down and slung the backpack over his shoulder, muttering, "Let's get inside before he comes back." Deena got up. Both were wincing in pain from the relentless attack Brother Thomas had served on them. Then, Deena noticed something caught on a headstone, flapping in the breeze. Dan waited while she went to get it. Finally, she wrapped it around her neck. "Nice scarf," laughed Dan.

"Never look a gift horse in the mouth," said Deena. "It's getting colder."

They collected Brother Thomas's remains back in the cellar, carrying him to the tunnel. "After what he did to us, I'd be happy to sling him in a corner somewhere!" said Dan.

"I know, but we promised Father Rhys," said Deena.

They followed the tunnel north. The deadweight of Brother Thomas's remains was getting weightier with every step. Finally, great heavy doors sealed the crypt. Pulling them open, they stood in amazement at its enormity. They lowered Brother Thomas to the floor and walked in. On either side were alcoves stacked two high, housing stone tombs. "Do we search it? Or is that considered desecrating the resting place of the dead?" whispered Deena.

"I don't think we should open any tombs. Brother Thomas gave us enough of a hard time without inviting more restless souls to his cause," said Dan.

"I'll second that," she muttered.

"Why did he command the spirits against us, and how did he acquire that power so quickly? Surely, that's more than a disgruntled monk," said Dan.

"I don't know. I have never come across entities with this power and energy before," said Deena. "It's worrying, and I'm scared they will get too strong for us to fight against."

"We should bring Brother Thomas in and get those doors shut. We don't want anything following us in," said Dan.

"Where do we put him?" asked Deena.

"There are empty spaces further down. One of those will do," said Dan, picking up one end of the swaddle.

They lit their lanterns and quickly searched before moving to the next floor. Finally, a single, thick wooden door opened into the upper chambers. "This is incredible," said Deena. "It's more of a shrine to the ancestry than a burial place."

"This has got to be worth searching," said Dan. Staff torches sat in metal brackets on the pillars between the elaborate chambers. Dan took his candle and lit each one in turn. When they were all alight, they stood in the centre, stunned at the magnitude of the treasure within the walls. Marble statues and winged angels stood at the foot of each tomb, protecting the dead within the sarcophaguses. Paintings of ancestors hung from the walls in tribute. Between statues sat large wooden chests, padlocked through a hasp. "We need to find the keys. I don't want to break them open. It would feel disrespectful," said Dan. "But, at the same time, we need to get into them." There didn't seem to be anywhere obvious where the keys would be. So, they searched to no avail.

"Okay, I give up," said Deena. "I don't think they would leave them here anyway."

"Neither of us is happy to break them open, but we could pick the locks," suggested Dan reaching into his jacket pocket. Dan gave her a couple of hairpins. So, she sat beside the first chest and tried the delicate process of picking the lock. Dan couldn't help but smirk at her frustrated grunts and sighs as she attempted to open it. "Done!" he exclaimed, waving the padlock.

"How the hell did you do that!" she groaned.

"Use two hairpins simultaneously and wriggle them until you feel it click," he suggested.

"Wriggle it, okay, whatever you say," said Deena.

Dan opened the chest, pulling out a dusty top hat and walking cane. Deena looked across and laughed at him, walking like a penguin and twirling the wane in the air like an old Hollywood movie star.

"You are an idiot," said Deena giggling.

"So, you keep telling me," Dan said, winking.

Deena carried on with the padlock, not wanting to admit defeat. Dan discovered it was primarily traditional clothing a person would have favoured in life in the chest. He shut the lid and hung the padlock through the hasp. As Dan opened the next trunk, Deena got up, went over to him, sighed, and said, "I give up."

Dan showed her how to pick the lock. "You never know when you'll need a skill like this," he said as the padlock popped open.

"Thanks, I can take it from here," she said, lifting the chest lid. Inside, she shuffled retro clothing aside to find only a pair of men's leather shoes

215

in the bottom. She closed it with disappointment. They opened the chests until they reached a larger recess, housing two children's coffins with winged cherubs.

"They must be Emily and Charlotte's tombs," said Dan.

"It's sad, even though they nearly ended our mission early on the lake. The thought of children laying in there, it's not right," said Deena, as she walked between the stone coffins. A painting of the Twins hung above, their arms linked, poised on a chaise longue. Victorian images, it seems, do not allow for a smile, only an enigmatic, slightly stoic, blank stare. Megan had a lot to answer for, as Dan and Deena couldn't help but think she was behind the children's evil behaviour.

"I still want to get in Megan's room," muttered Dan.

"Perhaps we can figure out a way when we get back to the manor," suggested Deena.

They both stared uncomfortably at the pair of small identical chests. "One each?" said Dan. "It feels wrong, but..." Dan trailed off as he knelt unwillingly at the other trunk. Dan unlocked his first, and upon opening it, he found a long white Victorian dress with a blue sash and matching hair ribbons. To one side was a pair of buttoned ankle boots. Reluctantly disturbing the contents, he glanced at Deena and asked how she was getting on. "Still wriggling it," she muttered. He returned to the chest and took out the carefully folded dress. He was surprised to find a single crystal at the bottom. He took it out and showed it to Deena. "There's only one. The other must be in there," he said, pointing to Deena's chest, who was still struggling with it.

Deena let Dan take over the padlock. Then, she unlatched the hasp and opened it. Inside, the contents were identical. Deena slid her hand under the folded clothing and found the other crystal. "Rose quartz," she said sadly. "Unconditional love. It also helps a person to sleep. Should we be taking these from the girls?"

"They're part of a much bigger picture. So, I say, yes," said Dan.

"Let's hope the Twins don't realise. They've already got it in for us on a grand scale," she whispered secretively as if they might be listening from inside their sarcophagi. They continued to open and search every trunk in the upper chamber until they stood at the wooden doors at the far end.

"These doors must open to ground level," said Deena. "Do you want to go back through the tunnels or risk outdoors?" she asked.

"It would be a lot quicker outside than doubling back. Not unless we missed something in the lower chamber. Did you see anything that could open into a tunnel?" he asked her.

"No, but it's worth a second look," she said. They extinguished the torches in their brackets and headed to the lower chamber. "Perhaps, there could be an entrance in an alcove," suggested Deena.

"You may be on to something," said Dan shining his lantern around the crypt.

"The stone coffins will be too heavy to move," said Deena.

"We'll have to settle on looking in the empty ones," he said.

Deena began poking her head into the recesses. Dan joined her, pushing on the back walls. Four from the stairway proved successful as Dan called to Deena to give him a hand. They managed to slide a stone slab a few inches, but the alcove was confined. So, Dan took his boot to it, forcing it open. Unfortunately, the tunnel was shallow, only allowing one person at a time on hands and knees. "I'll go first," he said, waving the compass at her. "I need to check our direction." Dan pulled the backpack along with him, alternating it with the lantern as he crawled. It was hard going, but the tunnel finally opened, and they could walk side by side.

"Any idea where we are?" asked Deena.

"The compass is indicating southeast. So, I guess we keep going until we can head north," said Dan.

Eventually, as they came to a junction, Dan suddenly exclaimed, "I know where we are! Southwest takes us to the abbey. This way," he said, pointing northeast, "is where we found that hidden tower without a door."

"We're not far from the manor then," said Deena thankfully.

They entered the cellars under the stairs leading to the base room. Deena wanted to go and see Bronwyn first, and as they walked the catacombs, Bronwyn ran excitedly toward them. "There's been awful screeches and wails outside. I've been so worried about you," said Bronwyn, flinging her arms around Deena.

"We had a few close calls," said Deena, "but we're fine."

"Do you want that coffee?" asked Bronwyn.

"You know what, that sounds like the best thing ever," sighed Deena.

Bronwyn lit the camp stove and put on a small saucepan of water.

Deena looked around her room. "Bronwyn, have you been creeping around the house and bringing stuff down here?" asked Deena, amused at her added comforts.

"Maybe," she said coyly. "Don't worry, I was careful. So, where are you off to next?" she probed.

"We need to get to the stable block and the bedrooms on the south-facing middle floor," said Deena.

"Don't forget, I want to get in Megan's room," said Dan.

"Good luck with that one," said Bronwyn. "She never lets anyone in there."

"We need a plan to get her out of there long enough so I can search it," said Dan.

"And as much as I don't want to, we need to check the woodland trails," said Deena.

"There's the motorbike in the gunnery cellar. Maybe we can use that if we can get it started," suggested Dan.

"Or you can saddle up, Maestro," suggested Bronwyn.

"Maestro? Who's Maestro?" queried Dan cagily.

"I've been trying to take care of him since I've been down here, but getting to the stables is hard. He's beautiful and fast, being a thoroughbred," said Bronwyn.

"Perhaps we could use both," suggested Deena.

"Dee, you can ride Maestro. Horses and I don't get on," said Dan quickly. Deena smirked. The fear on his face at the thought of being up close and personal with a horse was priceless. "So, how can we get Megan out of her room? Any ideas, ladies?" asked Dan, changing the subject. They all looked at each other, waiting for a strategy to come to mind as they finished their coffees.

Deena stared into the dregs of her coffee cup with nothing to offer and sighed, "Perhaps we should sleep on it. I'm all out of ideas and energy for the moment."

"Good thinking," said Dan. "Thanks for the coffee, Bronwyn."

Wearily, Deena and Dan went back to their base room. As Deena stood at the top of the stairs, she couldn't help but laugh. Bronwyn had been busy making a bed with more pillows and an extra thick quilt for them. Deena sunk into the well-cushioned bed and muttered, "Oh, that feels so good."

Dan searched the backpack for the salt as they prepared for well-earned rest.

After four hours of sleep, Dan began to stir. He sat up, lit the lantern, and pulled the quilt back over him, savouring its little warmth. "It's so bloody cold," whispered Dan to himself.

"I'll second that," said Deena waking up. "I'll nip and ask Bronwyn for one of those gas rings. I'm freezing."

"I'll go," offered Dan. He slid out of the covers and lit the other lantern, taking it with him. Deena was sitting with the quilt wrapped tightly around her when he returned. Bronwyn followed him in, carrying a couple of gas canisters. Dan set up the stove, lit the rings and turned them up. The three of them sat huddled around the naked flames.

"While we warm up, has anyone thought about getting Megan away from her room?" asked Dan. Deena shook her head slowly and shrugged her shoulders. Bronwyn stared at the flames on the burner, her mind working overtime.

"I've got an idea!" Bronwyn suddenly exclaimed. "How about you hide upstairs? I'll knock on her door and tell her I'm worried about her because it's getting so cold. If she wants it, I'll say there's a cooker ring with a gas bottle, but I need her help to get it."

"That could work!" said Deena. "But we'd have to put it somewhere other than your room, Bronwyn. I don't want Megan to know where you are staying."

"The only option is the cellars," said Dan. "Perhaps we can put it in a cupboard but pile stuff around it, so it'll take time to retrieve it."

"Now that's a plan!" said Bronwyn. "If I keep her talking and interrupting her, I may be able to buy you more time. Or take her to a different cupboard first and say I got confused about which one it's in."

"Are you sure you are up for this? You know how horrible she is," said Deena.

"Don't worry, I can hold my own when I need to," said Bronwyn.

"Great, if you've both warmed up, let's put our plan into action," said Dan.

Dan, Deena, and Bronwyn went to the cellars. First, they planted the cooker ring and gas bottle in the laundry room, the furthest point from Megan's

219

room. Then, having put an old table against the cupboard, they piled what was to hand.

"There, that should do it. If we choose another cupboard elsewhere, we can do the same thing," said Dan.

"There's plenty of choice in the catacombs," suggested Deena. Having found somewhere suitable, they put furniture around and in front of it. "Remember to bring her here first," said Deena.

"Don't worry, I know what to do," said Bronwyn.

"We'll use the servant's stairs. Deena and I will wait in the bedroom on the other side of the main staircase. Megan is bound to use the quickest route down. We'll go in as soon as we know the coast is clear," said Dan.

"Okay, let's do this," said Bronwyn, leading the way.

Bronwyn waited for them to hide before knocking on Megan's door. The first few knocks fell on deaf ears. Then, with no response, Bronwyn began her heavy persuasion. "I know you are in there, Megan. Please, answer the door," said Bronwyn, frantically knocking. "Please, it's freezing. I need your help," Bronwyn begged. "There's a gas cooker ring in the cellars. I know you must be cold too. Please, Megan, please help me."

"Oh, she's good," whispered Dan to Deena.

Bronwyn's efforts paid off, and Megan eventually opened her door and stood with her usual arrogant stance, with a blanket around her shoulders. "Quit blubbering," she said sharply, looking down her nose at Bronwyn. "What cooker ring?" she said, unable to help herself.

"I remember Dot having one. Please could you help me find it?" asked Bronwyn. Megan shut her door and strode to the servant's stairs, with Bronwyn following behind. As Megan disappeared around the door, Bronwyn gave Dan a quick thumbs up. Then, without wasting a moment, Deena and Dan crept to Megan's room.

Dan closed the door quietly behind him and flicked on the flashlight. "Where do you want to start?" asked Deena.

Dan's flashlight rested at the door on the other side of the room and said, "In there. We don't want Megan to know we've been in here, so put everything back exactly the way it is. She'll know straight away if something's moved." Dan cautiously opened the door. His instincts were right; there was a nursery. He panned the flashlight around the room. An old-fashioned crib stood next to a Victorian rocking horse with a toy chest in one corner. Dan's mind began to run away with him. 'If that starts rocking, I'm out of here,' he thought. Around the room were various cupboards, a rocking chair, and a changing table. A big thick rug lay in the centre of the floor. A floorboard moved beneath his foot as he walked across it. He stopped and tested it again. It was loose. He pulled the rug back, pressing his hand on either end of the sawn piece of timber. 'It could be a replacement, but then again, maybe,' he thought, prying the plank out of the floor, 'It could be a hidey-hole!'

Then, with smug satisfaction, he knelt to get a better look. He shone the flashlight into the recess and reached in. 'I knew she was hiding something, but how did she know to hide these? Or maybe someone told her to hide them, but who?' thought Dan. He put the timber back in its place and straightened the rug. "Have you found anything yet?" he whispered to Deena.

"Underwear and tights," she giggled, holding up a pair of rather large knickers. Dan couldn't help it. He spurted a loud laugh. Then, still laughing, Deena neatly folded them, placing them back in the drawer. "That smirk tells me you have found something," she whispered.

"Yes," he said, sitting on the edge of Megan's bed. "Look at these."

"What rune is that?" asked Deena.

"It's Perthro. The goddess of this rune is Frigg," he said excitedly. "Odin's wife!" he exalted.

"What does it mean?" asked Deena.

"That is the best part. It means the 'beginning and end are already established,' and what we do between will not be in vain. It also represents hidden things," said Dan. "But I can't work out how Megan knew to hide it. So, there is this as well."

"It's the last scroll of the elements, earth!" she exclaimed. "We can work out what to do with them now."

"Do you think Megan is working with the entities to stop us? I mean more than the Twins," asked Dan.

"It's the only explanation. How else would Megan know to hide them?" said Deena.

"I don't know, but we've been here too long. We need to go," whispered Dan.

He shone the light around the room, ensuring it was in order, before

221

quietly opening Megan's door onto the balcony. The last thing they needed was to get caught. As they dived back into the first bedroom, the entrance to the servant's stairs flung open, and Megan strode onto the balcony, followed by Bronwyn. "It's not fair. You promised you'd share it!" shouted Bronwyn, tugging the blanket around Megan's shoulder.

Megan swung around to face Bronwyn with the cooker and gas bottle clutched to her chest. "Shut up, snivelling brat! You lose!" she snarled as she backhanded Bronwyn with the gas canister, knocking her to the floor. Bronwyn watched as Megan slammed her bedroom door behind her.

Deena rushed to help Bronwyn up. "I'm fine," whispered Bronwyn. "Did I give you enough time?" she asked hopefully.

"Come on, we have to go," Dan whispered urgently. All three ran up the cellar steps into the base room, laughing at their adventure.

"It worked!" exclaimed Bronwyn.

"She clouted you hard with that gas bottle, Bronwyn. Are you sure you are okay?" asked Deena.

"I will probably have a bruise, but it was worth it. Did you find anything?" asked Bronwyn.

"Yes, we did," said Dan excitedly. He grabbed the backpack, put the six scrolls in front of him, sat back, and waited for something profound to happen.

"Well? Any ideas at this point would be helpful," he muttered, frustrated.

Deena leaned forward, placed the pentagram in the middle, and put each element scroll clockwise in the correct order for the five points. Spirit, water, fire, earth, and air. They studied the positioning but still had no idea.

"Maybe something is missing," pondered Deena. "Crystals? No, there are too many to be related to this. Oh, wait, the sand timer! The columns have the animals representing the elements."

Dan pulled it from the backpack and looked at it carefully. However, it wasn't until he turned it upside down that he saw the markings. "Dee, there's an inscription on it," said Dan.

"I forgot to tell you, with so much going on," said Deena, handing him the notepad and pen from her jacket. Holding the sand timer close to the lantern, Dan tried to work out the symbols, but they were too small.

"Pass me a candle. I've got an idea," said Bronwyn. She carefully dripped hot wax onto the inscription and then blew on it to cool it, asking,

"Have you got something I can use to scrape away the excess wax?" Dan gave her the penknife from his rig. With the wax set, Bronwyn shaved it off in thin layers. As she got to the surface of the sand timer, she took care not to pull the wax out of the grooves. When she had finished, she handed it back to Dan.

"Fantastic. That makes it so much easier to see," said Dan.

Dan copied the rune symbols onto the paper and then translated them. "I'm not sure what it means. It doesn't make sense," said Dan, handing Deena the notebook.

"Use elements and time to slow him down. Beyond a thousand steps, reverse the sands when true form commands," muttered Deena. "Beyond a thousand steps? That's a long way up or down."

"I take it we use the sand timer and the scrolls to slow time down. But slow who down?" said Dan worried.

"Guess we'll find out when we get beyond a thousand steps," sighed Deena.

Dan put everything in the backpack and said, "We should make our way to the stables next. Bronwyn, please keep safe while we're gone and don't worry about feeding Maestro. Deena will check on him," said Dan.

"You are terrified of horses, aren't you," giggled Deena.

"No, I just... I prefer to keep my distance, that's all," Dan muttered.

With their chest rigs checked and strapped, Dan said, "We'll use the tunnel behind Dot's kitchen cellar and head east. It will lead us under the stables. Perhaps there may be a tunnel up to the courtyard. I'd rather try that than creep around outside." They said goodbye to Bronwyn as they moved the timbers. As they walked the tunnel, there was no sign of a staff torch's glow.

Finally, they reached the stone walls of the L-shaped cellar. It didn't take Deena long to find a narrow passage behind the triangular space leading to a stairway. Judging by the wear in the centre of each step, it was in regular use. A wooden bannister had a saddle astride above their heads as they entered a tack room. An array of tack was hanging on wall-mounted hooks and racks. Dan picked up a harness and, looking at it quizzically, asked, "How the hell do you know which strap goes where?" Deena laughed as he hung it back on its hook. On the floor, beneath the saddle racks were carrying trays filled with grooming equipment. Shelves housed saddle soap, hoof oil, and leg bandages. Below, there were rails with neatly hung rugs.

Deena admired how organised the tack room was. Dan rounded the corner, through a corridor and into the feed store. Deena followed him in. Against the walls were fodder bins with clean, black plastic buckets stacked in readiness for the stable hand to prepare the horse's feeds.

"Tell you what," said Deena, "the horses here didn't want for anything." She went to the food bins and lifted the lids to find oats, barley, beet pulp and horse nuts. Gallon molasses and cod liver oil containers stood in a corner next to red salt blocks. Dan opened the barn door to see they were outside the courtyard, and there were another two adjoining barns to his right. "We'll have to go outside," he said, stepping back in. "There are two more barns this end, and we have to go under the arch to get to the coach houses in the courtyard."

"At least we can dart from one to the other in relative safety," said Deena.

Deena followed him into the next building. Then, quietly shutting the barn door, they turned to see bales of straw stacked almost to the ceiling and at least ten deep at the farthest end. "Bedding for the horses," muttered Deena.

"Nothing here worth searching," said Dan. "Let's get to the last barn."

Dan went in first, closing the door behind them. Hay nets hung on the wall with buckets beneath, and horse rugs caked in dried mud draped over a freestanding wooden saddle rack. Deena went over to the hay nets. The smell of horses and saddlery made her think of home. She could see Martin riding across the ranch paddocks on horseback, smiling and waving to her as he herded young steers into the corral. She squeezed her eyes shut, trying to rid the images from her mind. There was no time to feel sorry for what once was. "If Maestro is as fast as Bronwyn says, then it makes sense for you to get the motorbike started, and I can ride Maestro through the trails. We can cover twice as much ground," she said. "But, first, I need to check if he is shod or not."

"What difference does that make?" asked Dan.

"If he's shod, the iron shoes will cause more vibrations on the ground, alerting the Ground Crawlers. I can use bandages over his hooves to muffle the impact. We have to get the estate covered," said Deena firmly.

"I suppose it's no different to the vibration the bike will cause, but I can't say that I'm not worried about it, though."

"We need to stay in proximity to each other. Then, if we run into Ground Crawlers, we can split and confuse them. You've still got shots left, haven't you?" asked Deena.

"Only a couple," he replied, returning to his search.

Dan opened a drawer in an old cupboard. It contained tack hammers, hole punches, and hand tools for leatherworking. In amongst it, he found a blade. "Dee!" he called out. "Isn't this the same as the other one we found?" Deena went over to him and dug about in the backpack.

"Yes, it is!" she said, holding up the other blade. "What about the mount? Is it with it?" she asked.

"I haven't found it yet. But I'll keep looking," said Dan.

"Are you okay to carry on here?" she asked him. "I need to nip back and make an oat mix for Maestro. He'll need the energy before I ride him. I reckon it'll take us an hour to search the courtyard. That should give him enough time for his belly to settle. Don't worry. I'll be careful."

Dan smiled and nodded, "I'll come and find you when I've finished here."

Hurriedly, she grabbed a bucket in the feed store and scooped a selection of horse nuts and grains. She found the water tap and mixed it. She eyed up the molasses, pouring in a little. Now, she needed to find Maestro's loosebox. She tentatively walked under the archway into the courtyard. The stables all had double-hung doors. She quietly slid the top bolts one by one and peered in until she found him. He raised his head, giving a whinny. She slid the bolt to open the lower half of the door. She gently patted his flank and put the bucket down for him. His muzzle eagerly dove into the food. Deena stood back and looked at him. He was magnificent at seventeen hands high. Then, she stroked his black withers, ran her hand down his sleek leg, and checked his hooves. 'Good, he's not shod,' she thought. She gave him a last pat and left the stable.

As she turned to bolt the stable door, she froze. She looked over her shoulder, frantically searching the shadows. She was sure she had heard something. 'Maybe it was Dan,' she thought, sliding the bolt across. Her eyes darted about, searching for movement. She heard something but couldn't pinpoint it. Dan stood motionless between the barns and her as she reached the arch. Her heart began pounding. She knew what this meant, but where were they? Dan pointed towards the coach house. Deena looked to the roof. Her blood ran cold as two stood perched, ready to pounce. She looked back at Dan. He had the gun drawn and aimed at the roof above her. Horrified, Deena turned and watched as two more scurried towards her across the stable's roof.

CHAPTER EIGHTEEN

Deena's first thought was Maestro. She needed to prevent the Ground Crawlers from sensing him in the stable. Praying his muzzle was still in the bucket, she looked across at Dan, the revolver still trained on the roof of the stable block. Deena lit a sage bushel and threw it towards Maestro's stable door once it was smoking. It landed a couple of feet away, creating a smokescreen. With any luck, it would at least serve as a deterrent. Now, they needed a distraction. She looked for a stone or anything she could throw to send them in another direction, but there was nothing. So, waving her hands to get Dan's attention, she mimicked throwing an invisible object. He picked up the backpack shaking his head. She was going to have to forfeit a piece of equipment. Pulling the Gaussmeter out of her rig, she looked at it with regret, almost apologising at the prospect of wilfully throwing it away. The Gaussmeter didn't have much weight, and Deena felt disheartened that it didn't make much of a thud as it hit the ground. She watched for the Ground Crawlers to make chase. Their heads turned, but none leapt to the Gaussmeter's resting place. Deena looked across at Dan, frustrated. No way was she parting with any more equipment.

There was nothing else for it. Deena held her breath and took slow, steady steps backwards to the tack room. When close enough, she slipped inside, looking for something weightier to throw. So, Deena raided the saddlery for stirrup irons and snaffle bits. Then, quietly, she stepped outside, took a snaffle in hand, and flung it as far as she could. It landed further than the Gaussmeter and gave a heavier thump to the ground. She watched the Ground Crawlers for a reaction and quickly threw a stirrup iron to the same area, hoping they would go after it. Finally, the two on the stable roof started the chase, leaping to the ground close to them. It took all their courage to hold steadfast. Within seconds the two on the coach house spun around, following them.

Dan tiptoed over to Deena and held his hand out for a couple of stirrup irons, flinging them further afield. "Quick, get to the coach house," whispered Dan. Deena didn't hesitate in being as light-footed as possible across the courtyard. Dan shut the door behind them, muttering, "I hate those damn things!"

"We need to stay quiet until they've gone. Because, if the Ground Crawlers know we are in here, it won't take much effort on their part to get in," whispered Deena.

They stood motionless against the double wooden doors, adrenaline still pumping through their bodies and their hearts pounding with fear as they waited and listened. Then, finally, Deena opened the door a crack and looked out. "I can't see them," she said under her breath. Feeling brave, she checked the courtyard. Nothing stirred. Satisfied, she shut the door and surveyed the coach house. There were four horse stalls on the far side. They were disused but leather horse collars and harnesses were stored within.

Deena went to a horse-drawn buggy and a wagon at the rear, placing her lantern on the cart's bed. It was ancient with its wooden spokes and rusted bands that had sprung open, losing their tension. The buggy, it seemed, was still in use. The leather seat was polished, and the canopy was pushed back. "There's a loft at the other end. Are you coming?" asked Dan.

Deena picked up her lantern from the wagon's bed and followed him. Large wooden pillars acted as stilts to the loft above. However, Deena had reservations about the built-in ladder, casually nailed to the loft floor. "Do you think it's safe to go up?" she asked Dan.

"I'll go first," he said, "and if I end up in a crumpled heap, then no, I don't suggest climbing them."

The hayloft was a fair size. Deena walked towards the end wall, kicking small piles of hay as she went with the toe of her boot. Then, at the sound of something scraping across the wooden floor, she knelt, sifting through the hay carefully, and with a broad grin, she passed a blade to Dan. "Fantastic!" he exclaimed. "Is the mount with it?" he said.

"No, I'll keep looking. Did you find the other mount?" asked Deena.

"No, I didn't. I don't get it," said Dan.

"What do you mean, you don't get it?" asked Deena.

"I know these are the shattered parts of Odin's spear. Especially with finding the Altar of Gungnir. If Odin threw his spear to our world to help us during Ragnarök, why are most of the pieces hidden? Norse mythology states Odin dies in battle, so the pieces should be out in the open, but they aren't. We wouldn't be finding the pieces in drawers or amongst towels if the pieces were scattered. Somehow, even the shaft had disguised itself as a brush handle," he said.

"Point taken. So, you're saying someone has deliberately hidden pieces to stop us from finding the complete spear," said Deena.

"You can't tell me they've fallen and miraculously hidden themselves," said Dan. "I don't understand it. It's bizarre."

"Well, the mount isn't amongst the hay, but I'll keep looking," sighed Deena.

Dan walked along the eaves, running his hands across the top of the walls. The mounts could be anywhere. Nothing more was found in the loft, so they climbed down and split up, taking one side of the coach house each. Deena started with some ancient farm machinery indicative of a bygone age. The old horse plough was proof of that. A world away from modern-day farming. 'When we restore the light, we will have to go back to basics, and maybe this will have a use once again,' she thought, tracing her hand over the brace.

The estate was still very much in its past, and things were stored with the thought that they might have a use one day. Dan left nothing unturned, knowing the mounts could be overlooked as pieces of junk. The wagon had miscellaneous boxes stored on it. So, he climbed up and sat on the wagon's edge, his feet dangling down, casually picking out various wood-crafting tools. Despondently, he put everything back, jumped down, and looked at the buggy. He pulled the canopy out and stepped up into it. He sighed, jumped down and looked back at the carriage as he walked towards Deena, spotting a mounted trunk at the rear. He immediately went back to take a closer look.

He pulled the canopy back, and the material folds covered the chest. 'That explains why I didn't spot it earlier,' he thought. He unbuckled the leather straps and lifted the lid. Holding the lantern up, he peered inside. 'Very clever!' he thought, smiling to himself, 'but not quite clever enough.' He reached in and pulled out two mounts. He crept up on Deena, busy with crates on the floor. She jumped, making him laugh when he put his hand on her shoulder. "How many times do I have to tell you not to do that!" she yelled.

"I found the two brackets!" he exclaimed excitedly. "Are you nearly done?" he pressed eagerly.

"Yeah. Do you reckon it's safe to go to the other coach house yet?" she asked.

"Only one way to find out," he said, grinning.

They watched the rooftops across the way as they opened the doors. Deena looked at Maestro's stable and was relieved to see it intact. Then, pointing to the roof above the coach houses, Dan raised his eyes and listened. It seemed quiet, so they moved to the next coach house. The hinges squealed as Dan opened a door wide enough to squeeze inside. He held his lantern up, pausing to take in their surroundings. There was less in this than in the last, and to the far side were vehicles covered with tarpaulin, so Dan made a beeline for them. Deena left him to it and strolled around the huge barn. There was no loft in this one, and odd boxes were stacked here and there, so she searched them first. She had just begun when Dan called her over. "Come and take a look at this," exclaimed Dan.

Deena sighed, accommodated Dan's excitable boyish charm, and asked him, "What has got you all pumped up this time?"

"Look, it's a Willys-Overland!" he exclaimed. Dan jumped into the driver's seat of the Second World War vehicle, admiring the simplicity of the four-by-four all-terrain jeep. The gun mount was still there between the front seats. "Shame it's missing the Browning thirty millilitre machine gun. We could sure as hell use it," ruminated Dan. He looked behind at the tattered seats, and jumping into the back, he undid the popper studs and enthusiastically said, "Even the radio still has its cover on it!" Deena sighed as her attention span waned for Dan's newfound treasure. She turned to go back to the box she'd begun. "Wait, I haven't shown you this yet!" he called after her.

Deena groaned and turned to face him as Dan leapt down and pulled back a second tarp revealing a tractor. She sighed, went back to him, and said, "Are you going to look for stuff or play with big boy toys?"

A deflated Dan leaned against the jeep, scuffing his boot on the floor in thought. He spotted a metal jerry can strapped to the side of the vehicle. Dan lifted it out, hoping for extra fuel for the motorbike. He gave it a shake hoping that even a drop would help. But instead, something rattled inside it. Dan released the hinged top and turned it upside down, shaking it until its contents spilt out. Then, he stooped down in disbelief at what he had found. Grinning, Dan grasped them in his fist in triumph. "I've got a great find!" he called out, running over to Deena and placing two silver bullets in her hand.

"You know what this means, don't you? We have enough to kill off the Hell Hounds," said Deena. Dan grinned and put the bullets in his chest rig. Deena wasn't hoping to find anything as the few boxes she'd gone through had yielded nothing. When Dan finished searching, he went to help Deena.

"Almost done," she said, sifting through a box of spanners and sockets.

"Do you want to sort our transport for the woodlands now? Or finish the second floor of the manor first?" he asked.

"I'd rather get the woodlands done first; get it out of the way. We've searched the outbuildings. Then, we'll have done outside altogether," said Deena.

"Great, so do you want to get Maestro ready while I nip to the cellars to get the bike?" he asked.

"Excellent, I'll meet you back at Maestro's stable. It's the fourth loosebox from the arch. If you can't get the bike started, you're on the back of Maestro with me," she said with a mischievous grin.

"Um, no. I'll get the bike started if it kills me," grunted Dan.

Dan stood at the wooden stair leading from the tack room to the tunnels, reassuring Deena he'd be fine. She watched as he disappeared down the steps and then gathered the tack for Maestro. Then, remembering seeing leg bandages, she went to get them. A part of her was excited to ride such a beautiful horse, but the other part was terrified. There was the prospect of muffling his hooves, lessening the chances of Ground Crawlers detecting him. Outpacing them would be difficult, and she knew they would have to outwit them, splitting up to confuse them. Deena knew it would take a while before Dan returned, so she took the time to think before saddling Maestro. She tried to envisage every possible scenario with the Ground Crawlers and the best course of action. However, she was pleased that Dan had enough silver bullets to permanently deal with the rest of the Hell Hounds, making her feel better about the whole thing.

Dan reached the artillery room and pulled the cover off the motorbike. He stood astride it, pulling it off its stand and flipping out the kickstart. He tried to start it, stepping down hard. But it didn't fire. Dan groaned and tried again, opening the throttle. But again, it failed to start. So, he pulled the cap off the sparkplug and tried unscrewing it from its housing, but it was too tight. 'I need a man drawer,' thought Dan. Then, it suddenly occurred to him, 'How am I going to get back to Dee with it.' He couldn't take it back the way he came as the stairs were too narrow and steep. He walked over to the far side and opened the door to see the steps leading to the manor's front. It would be a struggle, but there were only half a dozen steps. He closed the door in deep thought.

"I thought I heard someone down here," said Bronwyn.

Startled, Dan spun around to face her and said, "Stop creeping around! You're as bad as me." Bronwyn grinned and asked where Deena was. "She's with Maestro. I'm trying to get this damn bike started," replied Dan. "I need pliers or spanners. I've seen some, but I can't remember where."

"There must be something in the cellars. Jack was always doing maintenance down here, especially with the washing machines. They were always breaking down," said Bronwyn. "Bloody nightmare when you are halfway through a load."

"That's it! Thank you, Bronwyn," exclaimed Dan. He grabbed his lantern and rushed off to the laundry room. Ten minutes later, Dan was back, triumphantly sporting a pair of mole grips. The spark plug was grubby, and the contacts a little rusty, so he cleaned them up. When Dan was satisfied with a clean connection, he screwed the spark plug back in and readied himself for a kickstart. "Fingers crossed," said Dan as he tried again. "Almost…" he began.

The last thing he wanted to do was flood the engine. So, he gave one last-ditch attempt. Dan was elated as it finally fired. He gave a gentle rev on the throttle before turning it off and restarting it. Then, satisfied he had fixed its troubles, he turned the engine off. "Are you riding or pushing it?" asked Bronwyn.

"The Ground Crawlers have been hanging around the stables, so I'm pushing it. It will be safer, and we need to save fuel," said Dan.

He knew the Ground Crawlers were bound to pick up on them between the motorbike and Maestro, but they hadn't seen them in the woodlands. Instead, the Hell Hounds seemed to frequent the woods, and the Ground Crawlers favoured the manor. Dan wheeled the motorbike towards the cellar door. Bronwyn waited until he was up the steps, then gave him a wave, closing the door behind him.

Dan kept the bike on the grass verges where possible. No sense in attracting attention. He knocked softly on the stable door upon reaching the courtyard, not wanting to startle Maestro. Deena swung open the top flap to see Dan grinning and pointing to the motorbike.

"Brilliant, you got it started," she whispered. "I'm nearly ready. I need to tighten the girth," said Deena.

A couple of minutes later, Deena led Maestro out, soothing him as she pushed the door shut. Dan stepped back. "He's huge!" he said.

Deena smiled and whispered, "I've bound his hooves to muffle them the best I can."

"Where do you want to start?" asked Dan.

"Let's start east. Save the worst areas until last. Can you give me a hitch-up on this big guy?" she asked. "I can't carry my lantern and control Maestro, so I've left it in the tack room. I'll ride by moonlight," she said.

Dan gave her the flashlight. Deena tucked it in her jacket and offered her heel to mount up. They headed to the furthest trail northeast and followed it until coming to a connecting south trail. "These trails must all meet up. If you go south, I'll carry on with this one. We should run into each other further down," suggested Dan.

Deena turned Maestro onto the south trail, taking a steady pace as she heard the bike's engine roar away. She watched the trees on either side as she went. Then, partway down the track, she pressed him into a gentle canter until she could see the trail's end, where Dan was waiting for her.

"There are wildlife trails between the trees," said Deena. "Should we follow them in, or..." she paused.

"Only if a trail is wide enough. I don't want trouble if we can't manoeuvre quickly. Also, we should double back on a trail at the top of the lake. This is heading west, so it will only bring us further down where we started," said Dan, putting the bike into gear and following her pace.

"I don't think my butt likes this English saddle," she said, cringing with discomfort. Dan couldn't help but laugh, although the seat on the bike was none too comfortable either. They passed the junction that Dan came down and headed for the far side of the lake. Both were watchful in the hope of

233

not seeing eyes following them. Deena had the height advantage on Maestro, and Dan had the ground visually covered on the motorbike. It was working out better than they first thought. They rounded the top of the lake and followed it towards the back of Jack's lodge. "Can we swing by and see Jack?" asked Deena.

"Yes, but we can't stop because we can't leave Maestro unattended," said Dan.

"I need him to know we are okay and still looking for the crystal skull as I don't want him to lose heart. He's already lost enough," said Deena.

The trail began to lead away from the lake. The trees were getting denser, and the path narrowed. They could hear screeches in the distance, so they stopped and turned their attention skyward, trying to determine whether it was owls or the Banshee was back on the warpath. They continued south until they came to another track. Dan stopped the bike and checked the compass. "We can keep south, or this goes southwest. Your choice," he said.

"Southwest should take us towards Jack's, shouldn't it?" she asked. Dan nodded and turned onto the new trail. The clouds parted, and beams of moonlight shone down, making the dirt track a little lighter.

"Are you all right to up the pace?" asked Dan. Deena looked down at Maestro's hooves. The bandages were holding. So, she took the lead at a gentle canter until coming to a fork in the trail. Dan got out the compass and said, "Yeah, this way is northwest. I reckon it will come out between the boathouse and Jack's lodge."

Deena looked deep in thought, so Dan asked her if she was all right. "Yeah, I'm fine. Do you think about how survivors will cope once we figure everything out?" she asked.

"I guess it'll be like going back in time before technology. Humans are the most adaptable species on this planet. It will be hard work, but if you've managed to survive Ragnarök, everything after that will be a doddle."

"I suppose," she said. "Have you thought about what you're doing when this is all over?" she asked.

"I haven't thought that far ahead. I'm concentrating on getting through this mission alive," said Dan. Then a thought occurred to him. He sniggered and added, "Find a mate and repopulate the world."

Deena rolled her eyes at him and thought, 'Typical!' Then, finally, they could see a break in the trees at the trail's end. The moonlight swayed on the ripples of the lake in the distance beyond. They paused at the top of the track to take stock of their position. The lake was to their front, and a narrow footpath followed its edge. "We must be further up from Jack's lodge," said Deena. "We need to go to the left."

"It's very narrow, Dee. I'm not sure if we can get through this way," said Dan.

"I don't want to backtrack. We'll manage if we stay in a single file. Then, if need be, we can merge into the trees if it gets too tight until we get back on the path," said Deena.

"Okay, do you want me to lead?" asked Dan with a sigh. Deena backed up Maestro, gesturing for Dan to go ahead. The first hundred feet weren't too bad, but it got treacherous. Dan had to get off the motorbike, struggling over fallen trees strewn along the bank's edges; it was exhausting with rocks and brush. "You and your bloody bright ideas," he muttered at Deena.

"We shouldn't have far to go now," she said. "This is the last tricky bit from what I can see."

"Thank fuck for that!" grunted Dan as he pushed the front wheel over another tree trunk. Then, finally, the trail widened enough for them to make good the rest. Deena could see a dim light in the window of Jack's lodge further down.

"Looks like Jack's still up," said Deena.

Suddenly, without warning, Maestro reared, striking his forelegs out in front of him. Deena tightened her grip as she pulled him back down. But he rapidly backed up. Deena desperately tried to control Maestro as Dan looked on, horrified. "Calm him down!" he urged. "There are Ground Crawlers at the bottom of the lake! Keep him still!" he said anxiously. But Maestro was having none of it. He danced around in circles, whinnying and tossing his head in fear.

Dan quickly got off the motorbike, grabbing the bridle's noseband. "Shush... Shush," he repeated, whispering. The whites of Maestro's eyes showed as his nostrils flared, taking in the scent terrifying him. Then, pawing the air with his foreleg, Maestro stomped his hoof to the ground. "Take him back up the trail. Hopefully, you'll be too far for the Ground Crawlers to detect you," whispered Dan.

Deena did an about-turn, urging Maestro back up the trail. Dan hid in the tree line, keeping the Ground Crawlers in his view. Thankfully, there was no approach on their part. He reached for his gun and checked the chamber, lining up the brass shells just in case. Dan waited for an age before they moved away from the lake, disappearing into the darkness. He thought twice about getting back on the bike. So, instead, he walked back up the trail to find Deena.

Dan walked ahead with the flashlight back to the motorbike. "You gave Maestro some love," giggled Deena.

Dan turned and scowled, pausing long enough to say, "Only because I didn't want to get eaten!"

Outside Jack's lodge, Dan softly knocked on the door. A moment later, it opened a sliver to reveal a smiling Jack. "Well, I'll be blown. If it ain't my American adventure friends," he said. "What can I do for you this time?" he wondered.

"Nothing, Jack, we wanted to check in with you," said Dan.

"I've got coffee left if you want some," offered Jack.

"Thanks, but Deena's riding Maestro, and we don't want to leave him unattended," said Dan, standing aside for Jack to wave to her.

"I see you got that old thing running," smiled Jack, pointing to the motorbike. "I'll 'av a use for that when you two 'av all this darkness problem sorted out."

"Have you been making plans, Jack?" asked Dan.

"I've decided I'm going to bring survivors here and 'av a… what do you call it… like, a commune. It's not like we 'aven't got the room 'ere. Get everyone working together. My Dot's gone now. It'll be a good thing for the people."

"That's a charming idea, Jack," said Deena.

"Tell you what, Jack, before we go, I promise I'll drop it off to you," said Dan as he sat back on the bike. "I saw Ground Crawlers at the bottom of the lake. I watched until they moved off, so please be careful."

"Thanks for tellin' me," said Jack, reaching behind the front door and pulling out his double-barrelled shotgun. "I've got Betsy to 'and." Dan smiled and shook his head in amusement at the nickname.

"Oh, before we go, we came across Father Rhys in the church. I'm sure he'll be happy to help you with your plans," said Deena giving him a wave as she turned Maestro towards the boathouse.

They were particularly vigilant as they approached the boathouse trail, unsure of the Ground Crawler's direction. But Deena knew that should anything be lurking, Maestro would sense it and react before she or Dan had any idea that something was amiss. 'Even though it is a huge risk riding him,' she thought, 'it has its benefits too.' Finally, they stopped at the mouth of the trail. "What about checking around the back of the boathouse?" asked Deena quietly.

"I won't get the bike through the trees, but I'll go on foot, stay here," said Dan, cutting the engine. Dan went around the back of the boathouse, eventually re-emerging, picking twigs out of his hair. "It's overgrown, I couldn't get all the way around, but from what I could see, there's nothing but brambles and trees," he said, giving his hair a final tousle.

They set off once again. The track was wide enough to ride side by side, so Deena pushed Maestro into a gentle canter. Once again, he matched her speed to the end of the trail. Dan stopped, trying to figure out where they were. "If we go left, I think it brings us to the other trail, taking us full circle," he said.

"We need to follow it past that," she said. "There's a trail southwest parallel to this one. It should take us to the bottom end of the estate."

"You're right," he said, pulling out his compass, "we should come out near the cottages."

"It's good that Jack has positive plans to move forward," said Deena. "The first thing I'm doing when this is over is to look for Martin, Lily and Ben."

"I don't have anybody to look for, but I'll help you find them," said Dan.

Deena felt bad he didn't have anyone back home, but he was here, fighting for the world, which meant everything to her. So, they started back up the track until they met with the southwest trail. Deena rode alongside Dan at a gentle canter. They had gotten about a mile when Deena pulled Maestro to a halt. "There was a narrow trail to our right," she said. "I'm sure there's something down there. It looks more than an animal trail. Do you want to go and look?" she asked.

"Sure, that's if I can get the bike down there," said Dan, turning around. Tree roots had grown across the path, making a bumpy ride for Dan, but he stuck with it. A quarter of a mile found them at old ruins. "I don't remember seeing this on the aerial map in the gallery," he said.

"No, I don't either. Perhaps the photograph was taken long after this had overgrown. Hidden by the trees," said Deena.

"Are you going to dismount and help me?" asked Dan.

"Sure," said Deena, swinging her leg over the saddle and sliding to the ground. She lifted Maestro's reins over his head and tied them loosely to a low bough, prompting Dan to ask, "Will he be okay like that?"

"He'll be fine, and if he gets startled, the reins will slip free. I don't want him hurting himself in a panic," Deena replied. "We won't be far as the ruins are not scattered." Maestro had already hung his head and took the weight off his hindquarters. Then, satisfied that he was relaxed, Dan and Deena walked into the mysterious vestiges.

"What do you think this place is?" asked Deena.

"I'm not sure. It may be a folly," mused Dan. He flicked the flashlight up and down the medieval walls housing glassless windows. The ivy was thick, taking hold of the stonework. Finally, they stepped over fallen masonry and went inside a single tower. "It doesn't look very safe," said Dan.

"Nothing we have done since we got here has been safe," she muttered, gazing up a spiral stone staircase. Dan reluctantly followed her up. The steps were steep and narrow. At the top was a small room with a window. "Your right. It is a folly. Utterly pointless," said Deena as she looked around the space.

Dan looked out the window only to see the treetops that hid the folly so well. Disappointed, he said, "I'll have a quick look around the rest of the ruins, but you should get back to Maestro." They parted ways, and Dan disappeared around a decrepit wall. Meanwhile, Deena stroked Maestro's muzzle and spoke gently to him, to which he gave snorts of contentment. Dan emerged a while later with a big smile.

"I know that grin," said Deena.

"It's like you know," he said, handing her another blade gleefully.

"Brilliant, that's the fourth side blade. Did you find the mount?" asked Deena.

He shook his head and said, "I had a good look in the surrounding undergrowth, but I couldn't find it."

"But we will need that bit," she said. "It must be complete."

"We may still find it yet," he said, putting it in the backpack.

They were coming towards the end of the main trail, and the rear of the cottages was visible when Maestro suddenly stopped. He threw his head in the air, flaring his nostrils and snorting. Maestro whinnied in terror, and his eyes displayed a fear that alarmed Deena. Then, without warning, he reared, striking his front hooves hard on the ground and backing up. Deena struggled to stop him from bolting. Dan quickly killed the engine on the bike and tried to grab the reins, but Maestro pulled away from him. "He's petrified!" shouted Deena, still trying to get him under control.

"Can you manage while I take a look?" he asked. Deena frantically nodded as he ran to the end of the track. They were coming fast across the open ground towards them. "Ground Crawlers!" screamed Dan as he ran up the trail to Deena.

CHAPTER NINETEEN

Panic set in, and Deena didn't know what to do, so she circled Maestro, trying to think. She couldn't gallop away. They would undoubtedly catch up with them. Dan raced up the track, fumbling with the gun when he tripped and fell. Deena could see them coming as Dan lay motionless amongst the scrub and pine needles. Maestro reared and twisted in the air to flee the approaching danger. Deena was flung from his back as Maestro raised again, pivoting and bolting up the trail. Dan cringed as flashes of bluish-white muscular monsters chewed up the ground, scattering debris over him. He watched, horrified, as five Ground Crawlers raced after Maestro. Neither he nor Deena dared move. They could only hope that Maestro could outrun them. They listened with despair at the thundering hooves moving further away from them. Then it happened; the terrified shrill squeals of Maestro filled the air. Both felt sick at the knowledge of his fate.

Deena looked down the trail at Dan, still lying there. Deena trembled with the reality of what had happened. Finally, Dan got up and brushed himself off. Deena sobbed as she limped toward him. He put his arms around her as tears streamed down her face. As her sobs lessened, she blamed herself.

"It's not your fault," he whispered as he wiped away her tears. "He saved us. We could not have survived an attack by that many." Dan led her to the motorbike, got astride and told her to get on behind him. Deena gripped him tightly as he sped into the open. Opening the throttle, he hurried between the cottages towards the manor. Deena jumped off and raced down the steps, opening the artillery cellar's door. When Dan had pushed the motorbike inside, she quickly shut it. Dan lit his lantern and gave Deena a wistful look.

"I need to see Bronwyn. She will be devastated by what's happened," said Deena, distraught.

"I'll come with you. But, Dee, it isn't your fault," he emphasised.

"I know you are right, he saved us, but it shouldn't have meant losing his life," she said.

Dan didn't know what more he could say. But to him, it was better that Maestro took the hit than them. Of course, the Ground Crawlers were hungry, and it didn't matter to them if it was a horse or human, but that didn't remove the guilt of survival at the expense of an innocent creature.

Deena opened Bronwyn's door and stepped inside her room. The look on Deena's face immediately told Bronwyn something awful had happened. So, she cast off her blankets and hugged Deena, asking, "What happened?" Tears streamed down Deena's face as she told Bronwyn what happened on the trail.

"Those things are dangerous, but you are okay. Maestro isn't the one who can save this world. You are. Sometimes sacrifices must be made for the good. Think of it this way, he died a hero," said Bronwyn.

"I thought you'd be mad at me," said Deena.

"Of course, I'm upset about Maestro, but you both need to focus on a much bigger picture from what you've told me. Everything depends on you," said Bronwyn. "Right, I will make coffee while you decide what you're doing next."

With the welcome coffee drunk, they talked about where they still needed to look for the crystal skull. "We've only the woodlands on the west side and the south-facing second floor in the manor," explained Dan.

"You've forgotten about the narrow tunnel with the weird door. You need to decipher the inscriptions," said Deena.

Bronwyn looked confused, so Dan described it to her. "Sounds like something in a fantasy movie," she giggled before falling silent.

"What's wrong, Bronwyn? You've gone quiet," asked Dan.

"I want to go back with you to America. I don't want to stay here," she announced.

"I'm not sure we can. It's touch and go with the fuel to fly back; the extra weight..." he said softly.

Deena scowled at him, stopping him from finishing what he was going to say. "Of course you can, Bronwyn," said Deena quickly.

"But Dee!" he said curtly. "We can't risk it."

"Yes, we can. We are not leaving Bronwyn behind," said Deena sharply.

"Fine, but when the plane starts spluttering, and the engines cut out, don't say I didn't warn you," he said.

"Please, Dan, I won't bring anything else, only myself," begged Bronwyn. Dan shook his head, looking at the girl's pleading faces, and against his better judgment, he gave in and agreed.

"We have to go. Thanks for the coffee," said Dan, leaving her room.

Bronwyn grabbed Deena's arm as Deena went to follow Dan. "You won't leave me behind, will you?" asked Bronwyn.

"No," said Deena, "I promise we'll take you."

Deena found Dan back in the artillery cellar, rocking the motorbike, sloshing the petrol tank back and forth. Deena stood in front of him with her arms folded and an accusing look. Finally, Dan stopped what he was doing and sighed, "What now?"

"How could you be so mean to Bronwyn?" she said sternly. "She's a seventeen-year-old girl who is scared. No one else needs to know we are taking her with us. Besides, you've already said yes," said Deena.

"Not that I was put under pressure by the two of you, though, was it?" said Dan sarcastically.

Deena retaliated. "This is my mission. I say she comes back with us. End of conversation!" she said firmly.

"Great! Pulling rank on me now. Okay, have it your way, but no one else," he grumbled and asked, "Manor or west side?"

"West first. Let's get the woodlands done and dusted," she replied.

She understood why Dan was being short. It was the first time she'd argued with him. Well, other than when he tried to kiss her. However, Deena couldn't help but smile at that situation, and her demeanour softened. "I'm sorry, I shouldn't have spoken to you like that," she said.

"It's fine. But you need to understand that it's my responsibility to get us back in one piece," Dan replied.

"Let's leave what we don't need in the base room. Then we can head out to the back of the manor," suggested Deena. They returned to the base room to find Bronwyn had tidied up again. "I forgot, I've left my lantern in the tack room," groaned Deena.

"Stay here. I'll get it," offered Dan. He lit a couple of candles, leaving her in the comfort of the base room. She dozed off as she closed her eyes deep in thought, listening to his footsteps fade out of earshot.

Dan gave Deena a nudge as he put down her lantern. She lit it, and they returned to the cellar to get the motorbike. Dan pushed it along the passage at the back of the manor. Then, parking it outside the wine cellar, they went to the cold room. Having filled their stomachs, they returned to the door leading to the back of the manor. Quietly, Deena opened it, checking the area beyond, before getting the bike up the steps. It was nerve-wracking being back out in the open.

As soon as Dan started the motorbike, she jumped on, and they sped across the lawns towards the woods. Dan stopped briefly to point to the only trail he could see. Raised tree roots and rotten branches hampered the track. He meandered around them where he could. A fast getaway would be impossible, but they persevered until they reached a clearing.

"The church is over there," he said, pointing. "The mausoleum is behind the trees further back. Do I follow the tree line around to it?" he suggested.

"Yes, but not too fast," replied Deena. Dan kept close to the trees as they headed to the mausoleum, watching the open ground and the dense woods. Passing behind the building, Deena tapped Dan, pointing to a narrow path, so he turned into it. Branches hung low, causing them to duck. It was so overgrown that Deena used the machete to clear some parts.

They reached a fork in the track, riding the upper trail first, assuming it would likely be a loop. "The lower track should take us near the back of the graveyard," said Deena. Dan gave her a thumbs-up, picking up speed as the trail widened. This track was more straightforward than the last, and it wasn't long before they were back at the fork. Again, Dan checked the compass, ensuring his bearings. "This goes south," he said, "It will take us to the far end of the estate."

He gently accelerated down the track. It was tranquil, other than the motorbike. Not a creature stirred, and that suited them fine. A small trail led to their left, so Dan turned into it. It came out at a clearing opposite the church. As he turned to go back onto the trail, Deena asked him to stop. "I think we should walk the church and graveyard walls before leaving this area. It saves time coming back," she said.

"On the bike or foot?" he asked her.

"On foot would be better. Park the bike near the church," she said.

"Okay, you're the boss!" he said reservedly. So naturally, Dan wasn't enthusiastic about it. But instead, he appeased Deena's meticulous methods.

"How are we for fuel?" she asked.

"Enough to get back to the manor with a bit to spare," he said. "Have you got that cross? Brother Thomas lurks around here, and its walls aren't very high. I don't want a repeat performance from him." Deena pulled it out of her jacket, holding it up at Dan. "Keep it handy," he murmured.

They began the long walk down the side of the church wall. Within minutes, Dan started sighing loudly and said, "I'm going back for the bike, even if I have to push it. If something happens, at least we can get the hell away quickly. Here, you keep the flashlight."

Deena was resigned that Dan wouldn't listen to her, and minutes later, he reappeared with the bike and said, "You look, I'll push." Deena panned the flashlight along the ground and the church wall towards the graveyard. Unfortunately, the surrounding walls were only five feet high. Not so bad for Deena, but Dan couldn't help feeling somewhat exposed. "I feel I should crouch," whispered Dan, stooping level with the fuel tank. Deena glanced back at him and couldn't help but giggle. "Yeah, well, it's all right for you short-arse," he muttered.

"I heard that!" said Deena. "This wall goes on forever."

"Do you think we are safe from Brother Thomas on this side of the wall?" whispered Dan.

"No, I don't. We saw Brother Thomas in the abbey ruins. I don't know if he has the power to call up spirits from outside the walls and to be honest, I don't want to find out," she said.

Dan dobbed down as far as he could, even though it hurt his back. But he thought better than to say anything. So, he struggled until they reached the end of the graveyard. Deena peered over the wall into the grounds between tombstones. She shuddered at the eeriness before slumping against the wall. "Are we all good?" he whispered.

Deena nodded, whispering, "I need to catch my breath for a minute."

Dan was glad to rest as his back was breaking. 'Perhaps,' he thought, 'it would've been easier to do this her way.'

After a brief rest, they continued across the back of the graveyard. Again, screeches travelled through the ether, adding to the sinister atmosphere. Deena continued to search with the flashlight. She thought it was a waste of time until she saw a glint of an old green bottle partially buried in the ground. Deena dug it out with her fingers. Dan leaned the motorbike against the wall, peering over her shoulder with interest as she diligently wiped off the mud, revealing another crystal. She passed it to Dan and knelt, searching for the other one.

"There has to be two; there's always two," she muttered, parting the grass in a fingertip search.

"This is made of jade. There are no two identical pairs so far. Let me look," he said, taking the flashlight from her. "I'm sure it can't be far away."

Deena kept a lookout as Dan slowly and methodically searched. "Dan, it could be on the other side, in the graveyard," whispered Deena.

Unfortunately, ten minutes of searching proved fruitless, and Dan bent to Deena's idea of jumping over the wall. "I'll keep watch from here. I've got your back," Deena said with a wink as she waved Brother Thomas's cross.

He painstakingly searched within the first six feet of the graveyard. He didn't want to go further without Deena. So, he urgently whispered, "Dee! Jump over!"

Deena scrambled over the wall. "Have you found it?" she blurted.

Dan shook his head and asked, "Do you want a better look here? We didn't have much of a chance last time."

"We didn't have any chance last time," she stated. "If Brother Thomas shows up, at least we know how to get rid of him."

They stuck together, ducking and diving around headstones, searching for the missing jade crystal. Then, they decided to go deeper into the graveyard with no sign of Brother Thomas. They followed the footpaths leading between hundreds of graves, trying to keep out of sight. Finally, they got close to the church, and Dan paused beside a tomb. "We should check the church's outside walls," he whispered.

With the lack of Brother Thomas's appearance, bravery was on their side, and Deena made a break for the church. Dan ran after her, pressed his back against the church wall, gave her a frantic look and asked, "What's the rush?"

"I don't want to be here any longer than I have to. I can't help feeling that we are pushing our luck. What if Brother Thomas is lulling us into a false sense of security, and then when we least expect it, and probably vulnerable, bam! He's there," she whispered.

"You fret too much," said Dan, grinning. Deena gave him a nonchalant stare. She knew he was winding her up. He was as scared at what was within the darkness as she.

They approached the far corner at the rear of the church, and Deena stopped and whispered, "Dan, it may be in a completely different area. We didn't find that mount at the folly either."

"As much as I want to finish this mission, I know that if we don't check it out and don't find it anywhere else, you'll insist on coming back," he said.

"I don't like splitting up, but we need to search it quickly. Which do you want? The walls or the gravestones?" she asked.

"Are you serious? After what Brother Thomas did last time!" said Dan, surprised at her suggestion.

"I'm deadly serious. We're taking too long on this mission. The team doesn't know if we are dead or alive, and supplies will be thin on the ground for them, let alone if the generators are still holding up," Deena said, frustrated. "Now, grow some balls! Which do you want?" she repeated.

After a moment's thought, reluctantly, he said, "I'll do the gravestones if you want, but we're no good to anyone dead. Can I have that Gauss thingy, please?"

"I threw it at the Ground Crawlers at the coach house, but you might find these helpful," she said, unravelling her makeshift scarf and giving him the night vision goggles.

"These are great, thanks," he said as he crouched and made for the nearest headstone. Deena continued along the wall towards the bottom, flitting her attention every few minutes to Dan. He wasn't hanging about as he zigzagged the graveyard, only briefly glancing through the night vision. When she looked at Dan again, Deena was nearing the end of the stretch she was searching. He hurriedly made his way to her, desperately waving his arms. Something was wrong, so she ran towards him, but couldn't see anything amiss. Then, finally, Dan grabbed her, pulling her behind a headstone. "Shush!" he exclaimed.

"What's going on?" she whispered.

"See the rise over there?" he said, pointing. "I could almost see the tree line over the wall, and I'm sure I saw that bloody Megan and the Twins."

"What? Really?" she asked.

"I don't know what, but they're up to something!" he said. "We must get out of here and into the church cellars." So, stealthily, they used the headstones to hide. Dan stopped a hundred yards from the back wall and looked through the night vision. He suddenly dropped to the ground and exclaimed, "We are in a shit load of trouble!"

"Why? What have they done?" she gulped.

"Not so much what, but it's who is with them. Don't move! I need a moment to think," he whispered.

"It would help if you told me what the fuck is going on!" she urged. "Give me the night vision!" she demanded.

Dan passed them to her with a look of defeat and said, "I don't know how we will get out of this one."

Deena felt her heartbeat quickening. It wasn't like Dan to say something like that. Her hands trembled as she panned the ground space over the wall. "Oh fuck! How the hell have they lured them over here? Megan isn't even concerned if they will attack her either," she said in disbelief. Then, Deena glanced toward the church. She grabbed Dan's arm, pointing behind them.

Dan turned his head slowly and drew breath; Brother Thomas was standing at the top of the cemetery. He gave a riotous laugh that was all-encompassing. Deena turned her attention back to Megan and her two little helpers, and something else caught her awareness. Deena groaned, "We're in bigger trouble than you think! I can see glints of eyes to their right."

"We have to get out of here! Any suggestions, and quickly would be great!" said Dan.

"Getting the motorbike is too dangerous. So, our best bet is to get past Brother Thomas and into the church," she said, holding the cross up.

"It's too far to get to the church. If the Ground Crawlers come over the wall and…" he broke off. Dan didn't have a chance to finish his sentence. Deena took off towards Brother Thomas. He scrambled to his feet and ran after her. "What the hell are you doing?" he called out.

"Getting to the church before the Ground Crawlers are aware of us," she shouted.

Then, Brother Thomas lifted his arms, raising the spirits. They braced themselves for the hits and tried to dodge the oncoming forces. They weren't going to get out of this lightly. Every time Deena got close to Brother Thomas, he moved from side to side. Dan hid behind a gravestone and drew his gun. Deena tried relentlessly to get near the robed

247

malevolence, but it was like chasing a carrot on the end of a stick. Dan checked the gun chamber. He only had a couple of bullets for the Ground Crawlers, so he put the two brass shots in first and then the four silver ones.

As Dan got up, a spirit burst through his torso, sending him reeling. He looked up to see Brother Thomas grinning from under his hooded cloak, enjoying the power he was conjuring. Dan held his chest as he tried to get back up. Deena had gained some ground, but she, too, was taking hit after hit, practically crawling on hands and knees. He looked through the night vision goggles behind them. The Twins and Megan were inside the walls, hurling rocks using telekinesis, luring the Ground Crawlers ever towards them. Dan's pain was excruciating, but what was coming was far worse.

Finally, he reached Deena, pulling her back to her feet. They leaned against each other for a moment. Then, Dan pointed at Megan, and an expression of desperate fear befell their faces. The approaching horde was within the confines of the graveyard. Panic set in as they struggled against Brother Thomas's onslaught. Then, the winds picked up, howling around them like a vortex.

CHAPTER TWENTY

Brother Thomas's evil laughter embodied them as he turned his attention to the west of the graveyard, beckoning the Hell Hounds, "Come, come, my friends. Come join me!" he said with vulgarity.

"Oh shit!" cried Deena. "What do we do?" she urged.

"Only the gods can save us now!" said Dan, stressing his voice above the winds.

Deena dug her hand into her jeans pocket, pulling out the four runes. "Which one? I don't know which one to use!" she cried out in despair as Hell Hounds and Ground Crawlers approached from all sides.

"The one with the letter R on it. Raidho! Pray to Freyr, and for fucks sake, hurry up!" he shouted.

"But what does it do?" she asked.

"Just ask for help! I'll take the hits until it does its thing, but you must keep hold of me!" he shouted. "Now, Dee!" he commanded.

Deena picked out the rune, Raidho, firmly grasping it in one hand and stuffing the others back in her pocket. She grabbed Dan's jacket while she closed her eyes and begged Freyr for help. Deena felt Dan fall to the ground and went down with him. She thought perhaps her pleas would be too late. Deena didn't dare to look. She didn't want to see them, any of them. Finally, she called out as loud as possible in desperation, "Help us!"

With that, a strange sensation came over her. It was as if she was out of her body and rising skywards. She felt weightless and opened her eyes only to see the densest black. She tried to touch her face, but there was nothing. Suddenly, Deena plummeted at lightning speed but could see no ground below. Then, there was the thud, knocking the wind out of her. Opening her eyes was a monumental struggle. She put her hands to her face; she could feel it.

Dan lay out cold, not far from her. She crawled to him, shaking him as hard as she could. "Dan! Wake up!" she cried.

Dan stirred, holding his head. "What the hell happened? It felt like my body was stretched out like a piece of gum," he groaned.

"Tell me about it. How we got here, wherever we are, is beyond me," said Deena.

Dan looked confused, drew his knees up, and said, "Well, we're definitely in the woods somewhere. Give me a minute." Deena sat beside him. She, too, felt like she had been strapped to a medieval torture rack. Then, as the sensation subsided and her limbs returned to normal, she wondered what part of the woods Freyr had dumped them in. Dan shook himself, got up, and said, "At least we are out of that situation. There is no way we could have dealt with that lot! Now, where the hell are we?" he quizzed.

Deena shrugged and said, "I guess we start walking until we recognise something familiar." Eventually, they came across an animal trail, and Dan suggested following it. Deena groaned when the forgotten folly came into view. "We're right at the bottom of the estate."

"As far away as possible from that lot!" muttered Dan. "Perhaps the gods are trying to tell us we've missed something?" he contemplated.

"Maybe," she said, flicking on the flashlight. "There is no harm in taking another look."

Finally, Dan commented at the tower's base, "I can't help feeling we are wasting our time here."

"Perhaps we could rest in the tower first. My legs feel like lead," said Deena.

Dan smiled, okaying her request. He, too, was feeling out of sorts after their ordeal. Then, as they turned to enter the tower, a deafening scream filled the air. They put their hands over their ears to block it. Dan looked skywards. "The Banshee!" shouted Dan.

They averted their eyes. Deena felt for the cotton wool in her pocket. Then, panicking as she stuffed her ears, she gave some to Dan, shouting, "We haven't got any salt!" Dan fell to his knees; the shrieks resonated as they did before. Deena crouched beside him. She shook him, shouting above the Banshee's inordinate screeching. "Dan! Get into the folly's tower!" she exclaimed. "Get up!" she ordered.

Dan struggled to his feet, not daring to open his eyes. He couldn't understand why the Banshee affected him so powerfully, not Deena. His legs felt weird enough before she showed up, but now he found standing impossible. Deena desperately tried to help him to the steps. Unfortunately, the Banshee wasn't letting up. So, Deena took Dan's face in her hands, getting his attention, shouting at him, but her words were lost within the intensity of the formidable screeches. She desperately pulled at his jacket. Dan struggled to get up, so, on hands and knees, he crawled towards the steps of the folly. As the screeches hit them, the sound waves made them reel. It was far worse than the first attack. Dan kept his eyes fixed firmly on the first step. He shuffled onto it while protecting his ears from the Banshee's assault. He kept his eyes shut tight for fear of looking at her emaciated rag-clad form, which would undoubtedly spell his end. It was gruelling getting up each step.

Deena could still hear Banshee's screams, but the resonance couldn't penetrate the thick walls. So, she ran down to Dan, grabbed him, and practically dragged him up the spiral staircase. As he recovered, he looked up at Deena, muttering a thank you. Together they sat with their hands over their ears, waiting for the Banshee to give up on her ruthless attack as an abysmal job.

As the Banshee circled the tower with her prey inside, she sensed her efforts were in vain. She would wait for another opportunity where they couldn't escape her so easily. Deena and Dan sat silently, listening, making sure the Banshee had left. Finally, Deena tapped him on the shoulder, whispering, "I think we're safe, for now at least."

"I wouldn't trust that theory. We've got to get back to the manor somehow, and the motorbike is still at the graveyard," whispered Dan.

"I know, it's dangerous. But we must venture back out," muttered Deena.

"I'm not risking going out yet," he said, struggling to stand up. He squeezed past Deena and made his way to the top floor. Leaning on the deep recess of the window, he looked out through treetops into the darkness. Deena followed him into the tower's only room. Dan's back was to her, and she waited momentarily before quietly asking him if he was all right. "Yeah, I'm fine," he said, turning to face her. "I'm thinking, that's all."

"Care to share?" she asked.

He smiled at her as he took in the vision of her anticipation. She was cute, quirky, and courageous, if a little short. For him, it all added to her charm. But then, he shook himself, knowing it would never happen. "What do you suggest we do?" Dan asked her. "I'm worried; the attacks are getting more frequent, and how the hell did Brother Thomas manage to round up troops against us? I mean, Hell Hounds and Megan with the Twins decoying the Ground Crawlers towards us, and on top of that, he set the spirits of the graveyard onto us as well!" he exclaimed in disbelief.

"I know, the attacks are getting worse. But I don't think this is only about the strength the entities gain from the darkness. I think there is a much higher power at work," said Deena.

"And what do we do? We go out with little protection, and we've lost our transport. So, tell me, how the fuck are we supposed to get back to the manor alive?" said Dan angrily.

"I know it's frustrating, but it's not my fault either!" exclaimed Deena.

"I'm not blaming you. I just don't know how we can get through this mission in one piece," Dan said apologetically.

"You and me both. But it does tell me one thing," said Deena.

"What? What does it tell you? Because I am at a total loss," snapped Dan.

"We are getting close to finding the crystal skull. Why else would they be organising multiple attacks like that?" she stated.

"That's a fair point," he muttered. "So, how do you suggest we get out of here? I'm sorry, but I'm exhausted and out of ideas."

Deena walked across to him, put a gentle hand on his arm, and said, "Let's rest and gather our thoughts. We need to think."

Dan gave a long sigh and sat against the tower's wall. Deena sat beside him and asked, "Is there anything to eat in the backpack?"

Dan leaned forward, pulling the backpack closer. He undid the zipper, peered inside, and pulled everything out. "I don't think the cheese fared well in our escape," said Dan. "It's in bits in the bottom of the bag."

"If it's edible, I'll eat it," said Deena. "I'm starving."

"Here," he said, passing her the backpack, "go for it." She offered some to Dan, and he waved his hand at the prospect of trying it. "It's all yours. I'll wait until we get back to the manor," said Dan, with a twisted look of distaste. "When you are ready, we need to discuss our options."

"We don't have any, as far as I can tell. So, either we try and make it overground, or we head for the closest tunnel, which is at the cottages, and we take our chances with the Goat Men and the big fiery dude," she said.

"What about getting the bike from the graveyard?" asked Dan.

"If we can get back to the manor, we don't need it," she said.

"No, I promised Jack I would leave it outside the lodge for him," he insisted.

"I think finding the crystal skull is far more important. There isn't much more to explore. We are so close now," she urged.

"Fine, but I'm keeping my promise to Jack," he said. "Can we make it to the cottages from here?" he asked.

"We haven't got much to defend ourselves with, so we must be careful," she replied.

Dan patted the gun, still safely strapped in his rig. He gave the night vision binoculars to Deena and sighed, "What if the Banshee is waiting for us when we leave?"

Deena shrugged her shoulders, and as she got to her feet, she said, "Let's hope she's not."

"What kind of an answer is that?" he said with disdain.

"The kind of answer that says don't overthink everything. Otherwise, we won't ever leave this tower for fear of what's out there. Are you ready?" asked Deena. Dan hurriedly shoved everything in the backpack, throwing it over his shoulder. Then, at the top of the tower's spiral staircase, Deena hesitated, whispering, "Shush, as quietly as possible."

Dan followed Deena closely as they walked to the narrow trail. Deena saw Maestro's hoof prints in the dirt and felt a deep pang of regret. Shaking it off, she carried on. As they neared the main trail, Deena crouched and used the night vision to survey the track as far as possible, whispering, "I think it's safe. Stay close to the trees." A relieved Dan followed her towards the cottages. Yet, his mind cast back to the last time they were at this trail and the chaos that ensued as the Ground Crawlers took up their pursuit after Maestro. Dan may not be a fan of horses, but Maestro's demise was undeserved.

They took every precaution not to be detected. It was slow going but better than being picked up by whatever may be lurking. Crouching within the trees at the trail's end, the open ground between them and the cottages seemed vast in the moonlight. Again, Deena used the night vision, taking her time to scrutinise as far as possible, when she whispered to Dan, "Have you got your gun handy?"

"Yes, why?" he asked, pulling it from his rig.

"We've got a reception party waiting for us," she said, handing him the binoculars.

"I don't think they know we are here yet. Here, take another look," whispered Dan.

"We could be clever about this. I've got an idea. If you can accurately line up the Hell Hounds so that you have quick successive shots, we can eliminate all four of them," she whispered excitedly.

"Excuse me for wanting to be sure but tell me your plan first. It doesn't involve either of us being a decoy, does it?" sighed Dan.

"Nope! No decoys are necessary. How are you for climbing trees?" she asked. Dan's eyes widened at her ingeniously simple plan. "Come on! Let's find a good tree to climb," urged Deena.

Dan panned the night vision for a suitable tree that would give him the best line of sight and the widest open ground angle. He beckoned Deena to follow him a short way southward. He stopped beside an ancient yew tree. Its impressive boughs grew to a great expanse all around its trunk. Some limbs were low enough for them to climb with relative ease. "I'll go up first. Then, climb up behind me to a safe height," whispered Dan.

He left the backpack at the tree base and chose the best way up. Deena waited, then finally, she sat astride a bough far enough from the ground. Then, as loud as she dared, she called up to Dan, "Are they still there?"

Dan didn't talk back. He simply put his hand out, waving it at her to be quiet. That was enough said. Dan checked the gun chamber and aligned the four silver bullets in readiness for the Hell Hound's well-earned departure. Determined not to miss, Dan got comfortable with his back against the tree's trunk, his right foot firmly on a neighbouring branch, giving him better balance when firing. Dan raised the night vision and took a long look, observing them until they were all in his sight. Then, he squeezed off the first shot, and without hesitating, he quickly swung the gun's barrel to his next target before any Hell Hounds could react. Dan fired a second and a third. He raised the binoculars but couldn't see the last one. Dan's focus on each target was so diligent that he didn't spot where the fourth one disappeared. "Where are you, you bastard," he muttered. "I can't see the last one," Dan called down to Deena.

Deena resisted the urge to go up and look for herself. Instead, she glanced at her watch. It was 10.30 p.m. After an eternity clinging to the tree trunk, she looked at her watch again. Finally, at 10.47 p.m., she groaned,

"I'm coming up!"

"Don't bother," he said, "it won't show itself. It's intelligent enough to know that it will end up the same way as the others. So, we may as well climb down." Dan looked regretful at the tree's base, apologising that he didn't get all of them. "That last one will be more dangerous to us than the pack," said Dan, grabbing the backpack. "The band was easy to spot. This one, however, is hunting alone and will be more vigilant. Hopefully, it will stay away for now. Let's get to the tunnel quickly."

Dan opened the hatch, allowing Deena into the tunnel first. They knew to watch for the Goat Men and their betraying glow. The quicker they could get back to the cellars under the manor, the better. "Do we go to Jack's, the boathouse or the flooded tunnel?" asked Deena.

"Only one of those options keeps us underground, which means getting wet. You nearly ended up hypothermic last time. So, maybe we should head for Jack's," he said, concerned.

"Please, I don't want to go to the manor overground. We don't have the defences to protect ourselves. We've got gas stoves to warm up and blankets back at the base room," Deena said, pleading.

"You don't want to go above ground, do you?" he laughed. "Fine, if you're sure, we need to take the first turn north."

Bronwyn met them as they pushed the wooden timbers aside. She looked them up and down and exclaimed, "Shit! What the hell happened to you two?"

Deena gave her a sorrowful look, shivering. The cold was so harsh that she could barely put one foot in front of the other. Then, through chattering teeth, Dan said, "We desperately need to warm up."

Bronwyn ran to the base room and lit candles and the gas stove. Then, squeezing past them on the cellar steps, she returned, clutching her stove with spare gas bottles.

Deena and Dan huddled around the warmth. "I'll be back in a minute," said Bronwyn disappearing back to the cellars. She was gone for only five minutes when she tried to drag something up the steps. "Dan! Can you take this from me, please?" she shouted up the stairwell.

Dan struggled to his feet to see Bronwyn with a large board. He took the one end and dragged it into the room. "What's this for?" he asked.

Bronwyn manoeuvred it at the top of the steps and covered the entrance to the cellar stairs. "There!" she exclaimed. "That should keep some of the heat in the room."

The three sat in silence as the room slowly warmed. Deena shrugged off her blankets, allowing her clothes to dry. As they crowded the gas stoves, Bronwyn was the first to speak. "What's been going on out there? You two are in less than fine form. I'm sorry, but I must ask, do you think you can find this crystal skull? You've been here for weeks, and every time you leave, you come back in one hell of a state," she said. "I don't want to speak out of turn, but putting the world right is impossible. Do you know how the skull will bring the sun back?" she queried. Deena slowly raised her head, looked at Bronwyn and said nothing. Bronwyn shook her head, thinking, 'I shouldn't have opened my bloody mouth. I hope they don't change their mind about taking me.' "I'm sorry, I get frustrated here on my own, not knowing what's going on. I shouldn't doubt you," said Bronwyn apologetically.

For a couple of minutes, neither Deena nor Dan answered her apology. Eventually, Deena gave a long, tired sigh, stood up and said, "You have every right to question our ability. We aren't experts. All I can say to reassure you is that we won't give up looking."

"It's fine, and I'm sure we would be thinking the same in your position. After I've dried out, the first thing I'm doing is to go and see that bitch, Megan," said Dan, through gritted teeth.

"Oh wow, she must have done something horrific to upset you like this," said Bronwyn.

"Yep, she nearly got us killed. There is something more going on with her than meets the eye, and I intend to find out!" he said with distaste.

"Dan is right. We need to find out what she is up to," said Deena.

"How are you going to do that? She's not going to tell you," said Bronwyn.

"I don't know, but we have to try. Megan was out there leading the Ground Crawlers towards us at the graveyard. She used the Twins to help her," replied Deena. "There must be a reason for her not to be afraid."

"Wait, that's it, Dee; what did we do? We used the runes to get us out of trouble!" exclaimed Dan.

"How is Raidho going to help us with Megan? You said it's the rune of travel," said Deena.

"Okay, you two have got me completely lost now," said Bronwyn.

"Not that rune. What other ones have you got?" asked Dan.

Deena fumbled in her pocket and opened her palm, revealing the five runes. Dan took them from her and studied each one, recalling their meanings. "This one," he said thoughtfully. "Mannaz is the rune of humankind."

"That's great, but how will it get the truth out of Megan?" asked Deena.

"It's what it signifies, and it may work," he said. "It doesn't only signify humankind, but also social order, friends and enemies, and attitudes. So, we can use it to ask for help with cooperation from Megan."

Deena took the rune from him, looking at it with hope and scepticism and asked, "Which of the gods do we call upon?"

"Mannaz is the connection rune between our world and the gods' worlds, and Heimdall stands between at the Bifröst Bridge. So, it makes sense to call upon him," said Dan.

Deena nodded and clasped the rune in her hand. Dan put his hand on hers and quickly said, "Not yet. We must be face to face with her."

She gave back the Mannaz rune. "I think you should do this one anyway. Megan has really got under your skin, and I think you will get better results than I," said Deena, smirking.

"You're right. Megan has pissed me off big time," laughed Dan.

Their mood lifted. It was getting pleasantly warm when the gas ring burned out. So, Bronwyn replaced the bottle. "I'm not looking forward to going back into the cold," said Dan. "It's getting cosy in here."

"I can tell you are not used to it," laughed Bronwyn. "It's always cold and damp here in Wales. You get kind of used to it. A day of sunshine is a bonus to us, Welsh people."

Deena smiled at their banter. Hearts lifted, and the conversation turned to what had transpired since they last saw Bronwyn. She sat, listening intently, and in disbelief, she said, "So, you've collected stuff not knowing what it's for because your gut tells you?"

"Nothing is as it seems. There are strong ties here to Norse mythology. We are finding rune inscriptions everywhere," said Deena.

"That reminds me! The wall that could be some sort of door; we must get back to that too," said Dan.

"I had a dreadful feeling as we approached it. There is something extremely weird about it," said Deena.

"I haven't seen any of these rune markings here before," said Bronwyn.

"Perhaps a person wouldn't notice them unless you knew of the runes. Some may have occurred during or after the event of Ragnarök," said Deena.

"I need to see Megan before anything else," said Dan.

"Can I come with you? I'm sure there is something I can do to help," pleaded Bronwyn.

Dan shook his head at her, which was met with disappointment. "It's too dangerous. More for you than us as we must leave you by yourself. We don't want to make you a target," said Deena.

"It's okay, I get it," said Bronwyn. "Can I at least look through some of the stuff to see if I can make any sense?" she pleaded.

"Sure, I haven't got a problem with that," said Dan. "A fresh pair of eyes might be what we need."

Warm and dry, Deena and Dan got ready to tackle Megan. "Any idea how to get her out of her room? If she's there and not on a malevolent jaunt with the Twins," asked Deena.

"Ah yes, the Twins. Have you got sage to hand if we need it?" he asked.

"Yes, but you haven't got a plan to get her out of there," stressed Deena.

"I don't need one because I'm going to threaten to smash her door down if she doesn't come out, and if that's what I have to do, then so be it," he said with determination.

"Fair enough," said Deena, checking for matches. "I'll be ready when it goes tits up."

Dan gave her a sarcastic smirk and said, "O ye of little faith, bring the lantern with you."

He pushed open the panel and stepped out. They took a moment in final readiness at the base of the staircase. The stairs looked even more formidable with the knowledge that Megan was playing a part in what was happening. However, challenging her could prove to be a big mistake. "Are you sure we need to confront her?" whispered Deena.

"I want the truth!" he whispered firmly.

"Fine, then let's do this!" she said. She moved around Dan and boldly took to the first flight of the staircase. Dan hurried behind her, clutching the one rune he believed would get his badly wanted answers. They took a moment to watch the balconies surrounding them as they got to the middle tier. "I'm going to light the sage ready. I don't trust Megan not to set the Twins on us before we get to the top of the stairs," whispered Deena. Dan nodded and clutched the rune, Mannaz, even tighter. Then, as the sage smouldered, they climbed the next tier of steps to the balcony.

"Are you sure about this? We both know she isn't trustworthy. Is the truth that important?" she whispered. Dan shook his head in dismay and gave her a stern look. "Okay!" Deena exclaimed under her breath. "I don't think this is the best idea you've had, by the way. But hey, if you insist, then…" she stopped. She didn't bother to finish her sentence as she knew it would fall on deaf ears. And so, outside Megan's door, Deena stood back and motioned for him to knock. "This is your show," she whispered.

Dan took a firm stance and knocked on Megan's door with grit. They waited for a minute with no response. He tried again, knocking louder and longer, but still nothing. Finally, he looked at Deena, who shrugged and said, "Perhaps she's gone walkabout with the Twins."

"Nah, she's in there," he said as he confidently rattled the doorknob. "Megan!" he shouted, "Open up. I know you're in there! We need to talk to you!" He pounded the door, yelling, "We need to talk to you! Now please, Open. This. Door!" Dan let out a long, frustrated sigh ending with a grunt as he put his forehead against the door in defeat, resolute that his plan wasn't going to work. Suddenly, he sprang backwards, surprised as the first bolts slid back. Dan looked at Deena with a big grin. "I knew it!" he said, giving Deena a cheeky wink.

Deena wafted the sage about them, anticipating Megan sending the Twins out first. But, instead, the doorknob twisted, and Megan flung the door open. She stood imposingly with her arms folded. "I'm sick and tired of you two. Now, what do you want!" said Megan curtly. She looked sternly at Dan, then Deena. "And what have I told you about burning that stuff up here? It stinks!" she said, wrinkling her nose.

"We have good reason to be burning sage, Megan, as you know!" retorted Deena.

"I haven't the time for your imbecility!" she said with contempt, returning to her room.

"Wait!" said Dan quickly. "We do need to speak with you."

Deena began rambling at Megan as Dan glanced at the Mannaz rune in his palm. He tightened his hand into a fist and closed his eyes. The rune began to tingle, spreading up his arms and through his torso. Dan tried to ignore the electrical energy filling his whole being. He could barely hear what Deena was saying. Focusing hard, he kept calling. Finally, Dan dared to open his eyes. Deena shouted at Megan, "Tell me what you know, Megan! Who are you helping?" she demanded.

"I can't tell... I can't! You don't understand," she whimpered, "my soul belongs to..."

CHAPTER TWENTY-ONE

Megan squirmed as she resisted telling the truth. "Stop it…" she begged, "please… My soul is his…"

"Whose? Tell me who!" demanded Dan.

Without warning, Dan and Deena were floored from behind. As they looked up, they witnessed Megan whisked off her feet by a dense black mist that had some form. They watched helplessly as it spiralled past the balconies towards the glass dome. Dan shouted, "Cover your eyes!" Shards of glass rained down. As the last glass fell, Dan looked to the night sky. There was no sign of Megan. "What the fuck was that?" asked Dan.

"I have no idea," muttered Deena.

Dan stood up, carefully picking off glass fragments. Then, helping Deena to her feet, he asked, "Megan said her soul belongs to him. Who is she talking about?"

"Whoever 'he' is, he has complete control over her," said Deena.

"Megan comes across as someone who can hold her own, but she may have her work cut out with this one," mused Dan.

"Brother Thomas also said he serves another," said Deena.

"We are no further forward in knowing what she's up to," sighed Dan.

"Well, we know she's working for someone powerful that doesn't want us to succeed," said Deena.

Dan looked at Deena and said, "While Megan is busy elsewhere, we can finish searching the rest of this floor."

"Good idea. We know Megan has hidden stuff, so perhaps another search of her room is in order," suggested Deena.

"I'll do it," said Dan.

Deena gave him the sage. "You had better have this. We don't know where the Twins are," she said.

"With Megan out of the picture, maybe the Twins won't be a threat. Because, if you've noticed, it's always Megan directing them," said Dan.

"Maybe so, but there's the Shadow Men too," reminded Deena as Dan headed into Megan's room.

Dan looked around the neatly organised bedroom. The gas stove was alight beside her bed. So, he walked over to feel its warmth. He wondered if Megan was horrible or if whoever she was working for had made her this way. The more he thought about it, the more he figured she already had a mean streak, fuelled by the situation Ragnarök had put them in. Dan didn't feel the slightest twinge of guilt for ransacking her room with this thought in mind. So, he emptied the chests of drawers, putting the contents into a pile in the middle of the room. Glancing at the mound, Dan moved to the double wardrobes. As he stripped clothes off hangers and checked pockets, he wondered how Deena was getting on.

There were six bedrooms on the south-facing balcony. Deena began with the first bedroom they had started searching before they were interrupted by the Twins. Deena made quick progress and thought about Dan finding the blade's tip hidden in the towels. The next room was adjoining. She paused at the doorway, half expecting the Twins to be waiting to sing their sick nursery rhymes. However, there was no sign of them. 'Maybe they are not evil in Megan's absence,' she thought, stepping into the room.

Dan finished going through Megan's clothing, dumping the hangers at the bottom of the wardrobe. Then, he turned his attention to her bed. It was an old metal bed frame with a solid head and footboards. So, he pulled the bedspread back and knelt to look. There were a couple of suitcases. He reached under, pulling out the larger of the two. He unzipped it and threw it open; it was empty. He shoved it out of the way and reached for the other case. This one had some weight to it. It was full of old needlepoint tablecloths. It wasn't until he pulled them out individually that two more crystals were nestled in the middle.

'You sneaky bitch,' he thought, examining them. He grabbed his flashlight and muttered, "Selenite." He put them on top of the bed. 'Megan is determined to hide things from us, but why?' he thought. 'Why would anyone want this world to die if there was a way to bring back the light?' he reasoned.

He determined he had searched everything and stood up and picked up the crystals, slipping them into his jacket. As he did, a thought occurred to him. He began stripping the bed, and in a flurry, he strewed bed linen across the room. Dan wasn't concerned about the mess as he pulled the mattress off the bed. He pulled at the seams to find Megan had carefully unpicked a slit big enough for a hand to fit inside. He tore it open, feeling amongst the springs and padding for anything that didn't belong. There was something in fingertip reach. He pushed the wadding aside and pulled it out. Excited, he rushed to find Deena, almost tripping up the steps in haste. He called out to her, "Dee, where are you? Look at this!"

"I'm in here!" she shouted back.

Dan made his way to the fourth bedroom. "Look! It's the last piece! It's the final mount for the spear. I thought we'd never find it," he rambled excitedly.

Surprised, Deena took the mount from him and smiled. "That's brilliant. Where was it?" she asked.

"Where would you hide something valuable? Think cliché," he said.

"Well, that's easy, under the mattress," she replied.

"Kind of, not under but in it. But I did find these under it," he chuckled, showing her the selenite crystals. "Um, I've left Megan's room in a mess. Please, tell me you're not going to make me tidy it up?" he said painfully.

"No, she's not given us a thought since we got here other than to cause us problems," said Deena reassuring him. So, Dan asked if she wanted some help. "That'd be great if you've finished ransacking Megan's room," she giggled.

"There's been no sign of the Twins. Where do you think they are?" asked Dan.

"I don't know. The Twins have allegiance with Megan, so perhaps they are obliged to follow her, wherever that is," suggested Deena.

Dan began by pulling bedding out of a cupboard and shaking out the sheets and blankets. Deena couldn't help but notice that Dan had a skip in his manner as he went around the room.

"Right, stop. What are you excited about?" Deena asked him.

"We've have all the pieces to the spear," he said, grinning insanely. "You know what that means? We must go to the maze's centre when we've finished here. I want to lay the pieces on the altar and see what happens," said Dan in a slightly higher pitch than usual, barely containing his excitement.

"I'm not sure what you think will happen, Dan. You will only be able to fix it if we can find strong glue and duct tape," she laughed.

In his heart, Dan knew there was something extraordinary about the spear. 'Why have an altar with the pieces carved into it if there was no reason for it?' he questioned. Since they arrived at the estate, Deena hadn't seen him search with such enthusiasm. There was nothing in the fourth bedroom, so they quietly shut the door and went to the corridor leading to the two sequential rooms.

Dan took a moment to look out the window at the pagoda in the moonlight. A deep well of excitement bubbled inside him. He turned his attention to searching. The bedrooms on this side of the manor were nicely furnished but unused, and they found nothing of consequence. They slipped into the next bedroom, which was in disarray. "This is going to take ages," groaned Dan. Deena understood his frustration, but they needed to be thorough. This room seemed to be a dumping ground for better furniture. In one corner was a four-poster bed laden with bedding and pillows. On hands and knees, she checked underneath it. There were two drawers on wheels.

"Dan, can you clear enough space to pull these out? They are full of stuff," she asked him. Dan dutifully indulged her request.

"Wow, you weren't wrong. I'll give you a hand," said Dan.

They began delving, pulling things out. Then, simultaneously, they each put their hands on a crystal. "More!" said Deena excitedly, holding it to the lantern.

Dan smiled, watching the yellow and orange colours dance in the candlelight. "It's citrine quartz," he said confidently. "It's good for keeping the mind clear and rejuvenating. Citrine carries the power of the sun."

"Well, if it carries the sun's power, they have a purpose to our mission," said Deena.

"I'm glad that thing took Megan. We wouldn't have found them otherwise. She would have made sure of that," said Dan.

"I know you are right, but god knows what has happened to her," said Deena, concerned. "I wonder if Bronwyn has made any sense of our finds?" she wondered.

"It'll be interesting to see what she thinks, considering she doesn't know about Norse mythology, the runes or anything much really," said Dan critically.

"I know she's young, but she may see something different to us," said

Deena.

Dan grunted in response to Deena's defence of Bronwyn, delving back into the drawer. Then, pulling out the second drawer with nothing found, they proceeded to the last room. Deena stuck her head around the door and groaned, "Ugh, no way. It's full of clutter."

"Yes, but it is one of the last places to be searched. The only other place is that strange door. I'm looking forward to opening it," said Dan with a boyish grin.

Deena sighed and, working opposite Dan, sifted through what she deemed as tat. Her hands felt sore with the dust and grime taking a toll. Hope dared to rise in her being as she found a travel trunk. But once again, it was full of rubbish. Handkerchiefs caught on old candle snuffers and broken oil lamps. Lace cloths filled the bottom of the trunk. Then, moving them aside, she found more crystals. "Dan!" she exclaimed. "Look, another two!" she grinned.

Dan rushed over, taking them from her. "Serpentine," he said. "I know a little about it. Its name is derived from Greek. Serpens means snake. I know from my excursions that the Aztec's prized green stones and serpentine was greatly valued. They say it is Mother Earth's true stone and life force. It's a healing stone for our Earth," he muttered.

"Every time we find crystals, their values and meanings have a bearing on our mission," Deena said, deep in thought. The crystals certainly raised many questions. What part they play, she still didn't know for sure. She had her ideas but couldn't put them into a theory that worked. "We still haven't found the other jade crystal! Deena suddenly exclaimed. "We can't go without it. We have to find it."

"If it isn't in this room, we will have to think back to where we may have missed," said Dan. Then, with a sudden realisation, he added, "The nursery! We rushed it before. It may be there. I only ransacked Megan's room."

"We can go back to the nursery," Deena said, dumping the junk into the travel trunk. Then, she looked around the room, thinking about the best hiding places. Dan laughed, watching her screw her face up in thought as she panned the room. Deena ignored him and went to the window, looking out over the majestic steps to the manor. She surveyed the grounds beyond, then turned and leaned against the windowsill. On either side of her, curtain drapes swagged back. She unhooked the tieback on one side, let the curtain fall straight, and pulled it across. Then, she did the same to the other curtain when she heard something drop. Deena got on her knees, sweeping the floor with her hands under it until she found it.

"I've found another rune!" she exclaimed.

Dan took it from her and inspected it. "It's the rune, Uruz. It represents the auroch, a wild ox. It signifies natural physical strength and speed. The deity connected is Thor, the most masculine of all the gods," he said, giving it back to Deena to put in her pocket. Pleased with their find, they finished their search.

Silently they made their way across the balcony towards Megan's room. Deena took a sharp breath, making Dan spin around to ask what was wrong. "Shit! You weren't kidding when you said you had made a little bit of a mess! Damn, she has got her work cut out. You know she will be furious at us when she sees this," whispered Deena.

Dan chuckled. "It will keep her busy and out of our way."

Deena shook her head, amused. She hadn't had the chance to see the nursery and took a moment to admire it. It was quaint. She gently rocked the crib and thought of Lily and Ben. Then, she closed her eyes, shook herself, took a deep breath, and turned her back to the crib to join Dan, looking through a toy chest.

"Shall I start over here?" she asked. Dan nodded and continued with what he was doing. The toy box yielded nothing. So, he turned his attention to Deena and asked her how she got on. "Nothing yet. If we can't find the jade crystal here, I don't know where else to look," she said, "and we haven't got the time to double back over the entire estate."

"I know. I'm trying to think if there is anywhere that we may have overlooked," said Dan.

"The crib!" exclaimed Deena suddenly. "Strip the bedding! No one would think to look in there!" she cried.

Dan quickly pulled off the little blankets and removed the frilly padding. Then, finally, he lifted the mattress and grabbed the jade crystal. "Brilliant! Let's get out of here before Megan gets back," said Deena, elated.

On the balcony, Deena looked behind them at the mess they'd made. She winced at the thought of a furious Megan on the warpath with them in her sights; it wasn't going to be pretty.

Dan closed the panel to the base room behind them, filled with excitement. They sat on their bedding, laughing at all the shenanigans in Megan's room. "You can deal with her if she catches up with us," giggled Deena.

"Thanks a bunch," said Dan, grinning. "I think we should lay out everything we have and try to make sense of it."

"I'll go and get Bronwyn," said Deena.

As Deena disappeared into the cellars, Dan paired up the jade crystals with a smug sense of satisfaction.

Dan could hear the girls chatting as they approached the cellar steps. Deena's head popped up first, followed by Bronwyn. "Bronwyn, did you have a look through the stuff? I'm wondering if you've had any ideas?" asked Dan.

Deena raised an eyebrow at Dan, catching his eye to suggest that sarcasm was not happening unless he wanted her to shoot him down in flames. "Well, I did get to thinking about the crystals you've found," replied Bronwyn.

"Do you have a theory?" asked Deena.

"I don't think it's any coincidence they are in pairs," she said, picking up the jade crystals. Then, with one in each hand, she sat between them. "Each is shaped the same. Faceted on the one side, but if you turn them over..." she said, putting them alongside each other, "See?"

"See what?" asked Dan.

"The crystals are deeper on this side and then get shallower. If I put them together with the deeper oval to the inside, what does it remind you of?" she asked. She picked them up before either could suggest and placed them over her eyes.

"That's brilliant!" exclaimed Deena.

"How many pairs do we have?" asked Dan as he quickly began pairing them. He counted them. "Thirteen pairs! And the clear quartz."

"They must fit into the eye sockets of the crystal skulls!" said Deena eagerly.

"But, what about the clear quartz?" asked Dan.

"Do you remember, when we found it, I counted thirteen facets!" said Deena enthusiastically. "Thirteen crystal skulls, thirteen pairs of eyes and a quartz crystal with thirteen facets!" she exclaimed.

"The only thing is, we don't know which crystals go into which skulls, if they have a specific order, or how it all fits with the quartz," said Dan.

"I think that's one for the team," said Deena, giving Bronwyn the biggest hug.

"Guess what, Bronwyn? We've found all the pieces of the spear of Gungnir. So that's our next port of call," said Dan.

"But it's broken. I don't know why you've bothered finding all the pieces," said Bronwyn.

"Yes, it's broken, but you don't understand; it's the spear of Gungnir!" snapped Dan.

"Hey, that's not fair! It's not her fault she doesn't know," said Deena sharply. "Bronwyn, we don't know if we can fix it. But we know we are supposed to find it. There's an altar in the pagoda we must take it to. We have no idea why, or what could happen, or if anything when we do, but it's worth a try."

"We need to get ready to go," said Dan.

"What? Are you going now? But you've only just got back," said Bronwyn.

"I promise we won't take long as we need to rest before going elsewhere. Are we going via the tunnels?" Deena asked Dan.

"I think that would be safer. Have you got everything you need?" asked Dan, emptying the backpack and putting in the blades and mounts. Deena nodded, and the three descended into the cellars.

Dan handed the spear shaft to Deena and took down the timbers to open the tunnel. They quickly slipped through the narrow gap. As they secured the final lumber, Bronwyn whispered goodbye before returning to her cosy room, watching the shadows as she went. She sat on her makeshift bed and pulled a blanket around her. Bronwyn knew Deena and Dan must be close to completing their mission. She felt a sparkle of excitement. Nevertheless, she was apprehensive about what lay ahead in the States as she had no idea what to expect. But she knew she didn't want to be left here alone.

They paused to check for Goat Men before heading east under the stable block at the end of the first tunnel section. Then, they turned south. 'So far, so good,' thought Deena. But they still had some distance before reaching the shaft of the pagoda. Dan looked up at the slab above and said, "I'll go up first." He propped the spearshaft against the tunnel wall, putting his lantern and backpack beside it. Dan found the first rung, digging his fingers into the soft clay-like soil. Then, as Dan worked the slab open, she turned her attention behind them and was horrified to see a yellow glow stretching up the tunnel.

"Dan!" she said urgently, "Goat Man coming!"

"Shit!" he exclaimed. "Get your arse up here!" Dan commanded. Deena blew the lanterns out in seconds and frantically climbed up. Her heart was racing. Dan pulled her onto firm ground. He stuck his head into the tunnel and watched as the glow got brighter with its approach. Sitting up quickly, Dan put his finger to his lips. Then, peering down from above as far as he dared, he could see the backpack, cringing as the Goat Man kicked it with his cloven hoof. It gave a loud snort, kicking it again. Finally, its putrid breath rose towards Dan and Deena, escaping into the open air. They gagged at the stench. As soon as the coast was clear, Dan muttered, "That thing needs mouthwash!" Deena couldn't help but giggle as Dan climbed down to get their things.

Dan set his lantern down on the altar, carefully taking out the blades and mounts and placing them into the corresponding grooves on the altar. Finally, he stood with the spearshaft in his hand and turned to Deena. "Are you ready for this?" he said.

"Wait, the grey-blue threads, we still haven't worked out what it means," whispered Deena.

"I'm going to lay the shaft and see what happens. We know to work it out if nothing happens before trying again," said Dan.

"What do you think will happen?" asked Deena.

"I don't know, but when I put the shaft in place, take a couple of steps back, just in case," he suggested. As Dan laid the shaft down, Deena took a wide birth. Then, as he stood by Deena's side, they waited in anticipation. For a few moments, there was nothing. Dan looked at Deena with disappointment. Then, she suddenly nudged him, pointing to the altar. Dan watched, amazed, as tiny sparks began to fire from the blades.

Within seconds, the intensity increased tenfold until the pagoda filled with the bright light from the magnitude of flying hot metal. The pieces of the spear rose into the air and began forging together. Dan couldn't take his eyes off it. Then, Deena started to have a choking fit. "What's wrong?" he asked, panicking. Deena couldn't speak as she grasped at her scarf. Her eyes began to water as it wrapped tightly around her neck. Flustered, Dan tried desperately to unravel it. As it loosened, it took to the air as if it had a mind of its own. Deena watched in disbelief whilst still gasping for breath. Her scarf bound itself around the middle of the shaft. The fiery sparks turned from white to blue and the blades heated to such an extreme temperature that they shied away from it. Then, the sparks stopped as quickly as it all began, and the spear fell to the ground. Tentatively, Dan knelt beside it, put his hand a few inches from the tomahawk blade, turned to Deena with amazement, and said, "It's stone cold! How is that possible?"

"I'll tell you what else is impossible; is that it rose into the air and fixed itself!" she remarked.

Dan looked at the altar. Burn marks were visible around the grooves where he had laid the pieces. "Incredible," muttered Dan. He held the lantern closer to Deena's scarf wrapped around the shaft. "Threads of grey-blue. Dee! It was your scarf!" Then, a thought occurred to him. "There is only one explanation for this. It must be from Odin's cloak!" he marvelled.

"So, we had the answer to the riddle without even knowing it," she said, surprised.

"This spear is incredible!" he exclaimed. "The Ground Crawlers will have their work cut out now."

Deena asked to look closer, so he handed over the spear. It was perfectly balanced. Taking a few paces back, she made impressive sweeping and cutting motions through the air as if practising a battle against multiple Ground Crawlers. "It's so light," she said, giving it back to him.

Dan stood, his mouth gaping. "How the hell do you know how to do that stuff?" he asked her.

"I don't. It seemed to flow naturally. Here, you try it," Deena suggested.

Dan raised an eyebrow. "Right, this is the bit where I make a complete idiot of myself," he laughed.

"No, please, give it a go," she pleaded.

Assigned to looking like a complete amateur in comparison to Deena's display, he tentatively took a bold stance, raising the lance aloft. It was as if the spear was leading him, telling him exactly what to do. Grinning, he asked her, "How did I do?"

"As awesome as me," she replied. "It seems the spear makes a warrior out of whoever uses it."

"The riddle said, 'Odin's power shall live forever in the heart of one who is true.' So, it must work for us as we have a pure heart restoring our world," said Dan.

"Does that mean it wouldn't work if someone with bad intentions got hold of it?" asked Deena.

"I guess so," said Dan, "but there is no way I'll let anyone near this spear unless I'm inflicting it on them."

Deena laughed and suggested getting back to Bronwyn. "I can't wait to tell her about this."

Bronwyn greeted them as they came up the steps into the base room. "Seriously?" she questioned when she caught sight of the spear. "How? How is that even possible?" she quizzed. Deena proceeded to tell her every detail that happened at the altar. "That's incredible," she exclaimed. "I thought you were wasting your time. I know you will put our world right. So, where do you go from here? You still need to find that skull."

"There is the strange door in the tunnels. We need to decipher it. Then maybe we can work out how it opens. The skull must be behind it as there is nowhere else to search," said Deena.

"If that's the only place it can be, it's bound to be dangerous," said Bronwyn.

"I know. Someone has gone to great lengths to stop us from finding it. I don't think Eisenhower would have made it so difficult. Well hidden, yes, guarded, yes, but not like this," said Deena.

"I agree," said Dan. "Whomever it is trying to stop us doesn't want our world restored."

"Something or someone powerful is beyond the door," said Deena. "We need to think hard about what we take with us."

"Where's the notepad? I need to decipher its inscriptions first. It may give us a better idea of what we need and what we are up against," said Dan.

"So, we are coming back before opening it?" asked Deena.

"I think that's best. Leave everything here except what we need to defend ourselves in the tunnels," suggested Dan waving the notepad at her before putting it in his pocket. He picked up the spear. "Ready?" he asked Deena.

Deena double-checked her rig. Then, she bid Bronwyn goodbye with a brief hug. To Bronwyn, they were already heroes.

They stopped at the entrance to the tunnel leading to the mysterious stone door. Dan gave Deena the spear and asked her to keep watch. Deena remembered the dreadful feeling she had when they first found it. She could still feel it. The hairs on her arms stood on end. Deena sensed a tingling like a low voltage passing through her. It was unnerving waiting for Dan, and she was relieved when he eventually made his way back, showing her the notepad. "That's a lot to translate," she whispered. "Do you want to do it here or return to the base room?" Deena offered.

"I'd rather do it here," whispered Dan as he sunk to the ground. He leaned against the wall, focusing on the translation. Deena kept a tight grip on the spear, thankful she had the ultimate weapon at her disposal.

Deena became impatient. She watched him sitting there, staring at the notepad. "Dan," she whispered, "have you done it yet?"

Dan broke away from the notepad giving a disconcerted look. Then finally, he muttered, "The skull is definitely behind this door if we can get it open."

"That's good, isn't it? It's what we are here for," said Deena.

Dan showed her the notepad. Deena studied the outlay of the door and the rune inscriptions. "Look at the next page," he said.

Deena looked cautiously at Dan as she turned the page. She read his translation, "Gods of runes protect this gate, call their names for Midgard's fate. Twist the spear six-quarter turns, one thousand steps into the dern."

"What's a dern?" she asked Dan.

"It's a hidden or secret place," replied Dan. "But it can also be a gateway or darkness."

"A thousand steps. Why is that ringing a bell?" she pondered.

"It's on the sand timer," said Dan.

"'Battle your demons and face your fears, face a god, and rest your spear. In true form, timing is key. Strike him down three, three, three. Leave with that for which you came, for re-entry cannot be regained.' Seriously, Dan? I don't like this," said Deena giving him the notepad. "Whatever is beyond this door is scaring me."

"Yes, me too. I'm not sure what to expect either," Dan muttered, re-

reading the riddle. "How many runes have you got?" he asked. Deena reached into her pocket, counted six and gave them to Dan. "These are the same as the ones around the circle, except we are missing one, the rune, Ingwaz," he said.

"What does Ingwaz mean?" she asked.

"It signifies completion and new beginnings. The deity is Freyr. Ingwaz sits alone on the door, so perhaps it is beyond the thousand steps."

"This riddle is confusing the shit out of me," sighed Deena. "Once we open that door, we can't leave until we've found the skull."

"Which means we must ensure we have everything for every conceivable eventuality before opening it," said Dan.

"What does it mean to battle your demons and face your fears?" asked Deena.

"Whatever is down there will challenge our fears, I suppose," replied Dan.

"What about facing a god and resting your spear?" asked Deena.

"Dee, I don't know! Perhaps it's because it is a god's spear, as in Odin's," he said irritably.

"I'm sorry, but we're so close, and we need to understand as much as possible before going further. The last thing I want is to go down one thousand steps to be picked off at the last one," said Deena.

Dan could hear she was upset and said, "We're tired. Perhaps we should go back and get some rest."

"Shame they didn't give us a straightforward key to open it," muttered Deena as she turned back towards the manor. "Whoever has made everything about this mission so bloody difficult for us," she said despairingly.

"Wait, what did you just say?" asked Dan.

"This mission has been made so bloody difficult?" she queried.

"No, about a key? Twist the spear! Quick, pass it here a sec.," he said, almost snatching it from her. Before Deena could protest, Dan was running towards the door. A second later, metal against granite filled the tunnel, followed by a loud clunk.

"Dee, get down here!" shouted Dan. Then, as Deena ran down the tunnel towards him, he looked at her excitedly, exclaiming, "The spear is the key to this doorway!"

"Dan, what have you done? We're not ready yet! You bloody idiot! If

273

we take the spear out, we may be unable to open it! You didn't think about that, did you?" she shouted. "You may have jeopardised the whole mission!" Deena complained.

"It's fine. It said six-quarter turns to open it. So, all I've done is slot it in," said Dan.

"We can't leave the spear in the door. So, if it doesn't work when we come back, the demise of our world is entirely on you!" retorted Deena.

Dan sighed, pulling the spear out as Deena strode back up the tunnel. He picked up his lantern and went after her. "Dee, will you slow down, please? I'm sorry, okay? I didn't think," he said.

Deena took the spear from him with a look of distrust. "That's exactly your problem. First, you get an idea into your head and then do it without talking to me. Then, finally, when I pull you up on it, you behave like a petulant schoolboy!" she said sharply.

Dan didn't bother to answer back. As hurtful as her comment was, he knew there was an element of truth.

CHAPTER TWENTY-TWO

Dan pushed aside the timbers, offering Deena to go through first. Still angry, she marched ahead of him towards the base room. Bronwyn was so pleased to see them. "Hiya," she chirped as Deena's head appeared above the cellar steps. Deena managed a strained smile as she wearily sat down. Bronwyn watched as Dan cautiously entered the room, saying nothing.

"Okay, what's wrong?" asked Bronwyn.

Dan muttered, "Nothing."

"Don't give me that!" said Bronwyn. "I know you both well enough to recognise something is amiss."

"Ask the idiot over there. He's jeopardised the mission!" said Deena furiously.

"What, how?" asked Bronwyn, looking at Dan.

Before Dan could defend himself, Deena snapped, "Someone put the spear into the door's locking mechanism, and now we might not be able to open it!"

"What mechanism?" asked Bronwyn.

Deena stretched out her hand for the notepad, to which Dan sighed, handing it over. She showed Bronwyn the drawing of the doorway, explaining it to her. "We couldn't leave the spear in it, so we had to pull it out. But it says we cannot re-enter."

"Did you turn it, Dan?" Bronwyn asked him.

"No, I didn't!" exclaimed Dan. "Deena's being melodramatic!" he asserted.

Deena got up and challenged him. With one hand on her hip and the other pointing an accusing finger at him, she argumentatively said, "Melodramatic, am I? At least I'm not a childish, impulsive idiot like you!"

"Whoa, both of you!" said Bronwyn, stepping between them. "I think you both need to chill out!" she attempted.

Deena spun around and sat down with her back to Dan.

"Now, who's the one being childish!" snapped Dan.

"Enough!" Bronwyn shouted at them. "You are behaving like a

275

married couple having a domestic! You're supposed to be a team. What else do you understand from the inscriptions?" asked Bronwyn, trying to steer them away from arguing. Dan held his hand out for the notepad. Deena gave a look of distaste at him before handing it over.

"The translation is on the next page," said Dan to Bronwyn.

As Bronwyn read it, she flicked back and forth between the rune inscriptions and the translation, trying to understand it. "So, what are these rune markings?" she asked, pointing to the seven around the centre.

"We have been finding runes inscribed into discs. Dee, show Bronwyn the ones we've got," Dan requested. Deena gave them to Bronwyn. They sat down together, laying them out as they were on the notepad.

"You're missing one, said Bronwyn.

"That one means new beginnings," said Dan, "I don't think we're to find it until we have the skull."

"I don't understand this riddle. A thousand steps, that's a long way down. That can't be under this estate, surely," said Bronwyn.

"We haven't worked it out yet," said Dan. "Maybe we won't until we get the doorway open."

"If we get it open!" said Deena sarcastically.

Dan glared at Deena and muttered, "Perhaps we should get some sleep."

"That's my cue," said Bronwyn getting up. She gave the notepad and runes to Deena. "Please don't go without seeing me?" she begged.

"We won't," said Deena reassuringly, "I promise."

When Bronwyn was safely out of earshot, Deena turned to Dan and said, "You are still a childish, impulsive idiot!"

Dan sighed in agreement to keep the peace. He knew he had been impetuous, and no one was harder on him than himself. Deena reminded him to do the salt ritual, and it wasn't long before she fell asleep. Dan pondered how he could get out of telling the truth about the riddle. He felt perhaps she wouldn't venture beyond the door if she knew what was waiting for them. But, Dan surmised, would it be fair for her not to know? His mind went around in circles. Finally, after laying there for what seemed too long, he focused on getting some sleep.

Deena was awake before him, and she slipped away with her lantern to see Bronwyn. Dan awoke to an empty room. He looked around in the candlelight, a little confused. 'She'll be back when she is ready,' thought Dan, folding the bedding. With this done, he took out the notepad, sat down and solemnly stared at the translation. He knew what awaited them was a formidable battle. How it would transpire, he didn't know; that was the scary part.

Nevertheless, he decided to be honest with Deena. How she would react was anyone's guess. He looked through what they had collected and how they may figure beyond the doorway. Finally, he decided all the crystals should remain in the base room. If they were part of the bigger picture, he didn't want them falling into enemy hands. However, the inscription on the sand timer is directly related to the doorway. 'Beyond a thousand steps, reverse the sands when true form commands,' he reiterated in his head. 'That's worrying. What other forms could He have if whoever has a true form?' he wondered. Dan shook his head, dispelling his fears and put the sand timer, pentagram and element scrolls in a 'to take' pile. Consciously, he knew who He was, but to say it, was too much. So instead, Dan turned his attention to the spear, laying it beside the sand timer and the scrolls. "Everything for every conceivable eventuality," he said out loud. "How am I supposed to know that?" he protested.

"You've started without me then?" a voice from the cellar steps said. As Deena entered the base room with Bronwyn, Dan's first thought was, 'Here we go, ganging up on me again!'

"I went to see Bronwyn because I know you're hiding something. So, are you going to tell me?" asked Deena firmly.

Dan smirked at her with her hands on her hips and quickly replied, "I promise I will tell you everything in a minute. I'm trying to organise what we need first."

"If I don't know what we're getting into, I can't contribute to what we need, can I?" said Deena.

"She's right," said Bronwyn. "It isn't fair to keep her in the dark; no pun intended."

Dan sighed, responding to Deena's impatience. "Fine, we'll have food, then discuss it."

"Great, we'll get the food, and meanwhile, you can sort your head out," said Deena.

Dan was dreading telling her his suspicions, and when he heard them returning, his stomach somersaulted. He ruffled his hair in anticipation as Deena sat with water bottles and Bronwyn nestled between them with a hoard of ham and cheese. "Right, now I want the truth," said Deena.

"Okay, fine, but before I say anything, we are in this together, and there is no turning back from this," said Dan.

"Ooh, that sounds serious," said Bronwyn, to which Dan and Deena glared at her.

"Sorry, I'll be quiet," she said sheepishly.

Dan began to explain his fears about what was beyond the doorway. Neither Deena nor Bronwyn said a word all the way through. "So, that's the score as far as I can figure it out," said Dan gravely. Silence prevailed. Deena didn't know what to say, and Bronwyn struggled to understand Dan's unveiling of the danger they would both be in beyond the thousand steps.

Eventually, Deena said, "Then we had better get ready."

"What happens if you don't do this?" asked Bronwyn quietly.

"Then the world dies, and we die with it," said Dan.

Bronwyn sat quietly while Dan and Deena began going through what they had and needed to get. She was stunned by the concept of what lay ahead. Only now had the enormity of their task dawned on her. The world's existence was indeed on their shoulders, and they were the only ones who could save It and themselves. "Bronwyn... Bronwyn!" said Deena. Bronwyn snapped out of her sense of helplessness.

"I'm sorry, what?" she asked.

"Are you okay?" asked Deena.

"Yeah, I'm fine, just scared for you both. Can you do this?" asked Bronwyn.

"I know it sounds daunting, but there is no failing this mission. So, we must ensure we have everything we need before we go. Could you help us?" asked Deena.

Bronwyn asked, "What can I do?"

"We need things from the cellars. Could you get them for me if I give you a list?" asked Deena. Bronwyn nodded, and Deena wrote everything down. Then, Deena offered her lantern and said, "You'll find it easier with this, and thank you, I know how difficult this is."

"It's fine. I survived so far, and I'm not ready to die yet," muttered

Bronwyn.

"No one wants to die," said Deena. "We will get through this, I promise."

Bronwyn gave an appreciative smile, and as she left for the cellars, Dan said sharply, "You shouldn't have promised her that."

"I know, but she needs reassurance. I can't leave here with her terrified that we're not coming back."

Dan shook his head and picked up the spear. "At least we have this," he muttered.

"I hate to tell you this, but I don't think we do," said Deena. "We need to leave it in the doorway once is unlocked. It's the key; that's if we can still open it. If we remove it, the door may close, and we won't be able to get out."

"Your sarcasm is noted. Thanks for that," Dan grumbled.

"What are we going to do about sage bushels?" asked Deena. "We left the surplus in the orangery."

"Then we'll have to go and get it. There must be some string somewhere in the manor. Ask Bronwyn when she gets back," suggested Dan.

Deena picked up the machete, placing it with the scrolls and sand timer. The puzzle pieces were coming together and weren't painting a pretty picture. Bronwyn returned and said, "I couldn't find much salt, but I've got brown paper squares and more candles."

Deena could see she had been crying but chose not to say anything. Nevertheless, it was apparent she was frightened and not without reason. "That's great, thanks. Did you come across any twine or string? We need to make sage bushels," asked Deena.

"I don't remember seeing any, but I can go and look," said Bronwyn.

"Go with her, Dee, while I go to the orangery. It'll save time," suggested Dan.

At the bottom of the steps, Bronwyn suggested looking through the boxes in her room, as Dot had listed everything. So, Deena shut the door behind them and set the lantern down on a barrel. "You know, it's okay to be scared," said Deena.

The tears began to flow. Bronwyn sat on the edge of her bed with her face buried in her hands. Deena sat quietly beside her and hugged her. "You

279

heard what Dan said. I'm not an idiot. I don't know how you're going to survive it. I'm crying, and I'm not the one that must go down there," blubbered Bronwyn.

"Dan and I have each other's backs. I'm positive the two of us will manage. We've got this far, haven't we?" said Deena gently.

"I don't know how you've coped so far, and now you must tackle those steps and beyond," said Bronwyn between sniffles.

"I'm trying not to think about it. Because, if I did, I would probably chicken out," said Deena laughing.

Bronwyn managed a smile, pointing to the boxes. "Shall we start?" she suggested.

Deena got up, pulled a few boxes out, and read their contents. "Miscellaneous," she muttered. "Guess I'll have to open this one."

"There's a few like that. Shall I open those as well?" asked Bronwyn.

"Be my guest," said Deena. Bronwyn's sobs calmed as she busied herself.

"Are butcher's twining any good?" asked Bronwyn. "There are a couple of spools."

Deena took them from her. "Perfect! The two should be more than enough," said Deena. Unfortunately, Dan wasn't back from the orangery when Deena and Bronwyn returned to the base room. So, Deena placed the twine aside with everything else they needed to take.

"I know this sounds selfish, but what should I do if you and Dan don't return?" asked Bronwyn.

"We will return, but if you need a backup plan, I suggest you find either Jack or Father Rhys. Stick with them and survive the best you can. I don't know what else to suggest," said Deena. Bronwyn said nothing, only nodding solemnly.

A good hour went by before Dan returned. "How come you were so long?" asked Deena.

"Fucking Goat Men!" he muttered. "I had to double back twice!" He slung the backpack on the floor and sat down.

"We found twine," said Bronwyn.

"Great," he replied. "You two can make bushels while I take five to get my breath back."

Bronwyn took the sage out of the backpack and asked Deena what to

280

do. She watched, fascinated, as Deena made the first bushel. "How do you know how to do this stuff?" she asked.

"I studied parapsychology as part of my degree. I used to go regularly on investigations," replied Deena. "Ghost hunting, but on a technical level. That's why the Government picked me to do this mission. Lucky me!" said Deena with disdain.

"I'm glad they picked you," said Bronwyn smiling. "You always know what to do."

There was enough to make eight bushels. Deena put them in a pile and said, "The next thing we need to do is make salt pouches." Unfortunately, there was only enough sea salt to make four. Deena knew it was nowhere near enough. She thought hard. Then suddenly remembered the jar of bath salts they found in one of the bedrooms. "I'm sure I took them," she said, standing up and looking around her. "They must be here somewhere." Deena began moving the bedding around, searching. Eventually, she found them under a pile of pillows, relieved they could make more.

Deena and Dan began filling the backpack thoughtfully. "Right, is there anything else?" asked Dan.

"I'm not taking my equipment," said Deena. "It won't be any use beyond the door."

"I have put new batteries in the flashlight," said Dan.

"Good thinking. We don't want to be without a light source. We'll eat before we go, but Bronwyn, would you ensure there is food when we get back?" she asked.

Bronwyn smiled at her request, knowing it was her way of giving her something else to think about other than worrying about them.

"Right, no point in putting it off. Everything is ready. Let's eat and get moving," said Dan.

They paused at the tunnel's entrance in the cellars and exchanged glances of trepidation upon knowing what they were about to embark on. Dan removed the timbers, and with the tunnel exposed, they said their goodbyes to Bronwyn. She watched them disappear into the darkness once again. But, this time, it was with the knowledge that this might be the last time she saw them. Bronwyn returned the timbers with a heavy heart and went back to her room.

Deena and Dan turned west towards the abbey ruins. They stopped briefly at the ladder leading up to the hidden tower, ensuring the Goat Men were not around. It was a long stretch to the ruins from here. Eventually, they came to the southeast junction. Dan peered around the entrance, confronted with an oncoming Goat Man. He was some way off, but they needed to get away. Dan whispered to Deena, "Head for the ruins!"

Deena didn't hesitate and began running. Dan followed suit, not stopping until they came out at the chapter house. Above ground, they sat catching their breath. "How long do we wait?" asked Deena.

"I'll be able to see the Goat Man pass from the bottom of the steps. You stay here and keep an eye," whispered Dan, leaving his lantern with Deena. He stayed silent in the darkness until he saw the staff torch head northeast towards the manor. "Okay, it's safe," he whispered up the steps to Deena.

They made their way to the narrow tunnel with heavy hearts, knowing what they were getting into beyond was weighing heavily on them. Finally, at the tunnel entrance, Deena asked, "How will we do this? Do you want me to stay here while you go and try to open it?"

"Yes, keep watch. I'll shout if I need you," whispered Dan.

Dan walked the tunnel to the doorway. He inspected it, tracing his hands over the rune markings, reminding himself of the translations. "Gods of runes protect this gate, call their names for Midgard's fate," he muttered. 'Damn it!' he thought. As Deena glanced down the tunnel at him, he whispered to her, "I need the runes." Deena dug into her jeans pocket, giving them to him. "I need them to call upon the gods before turning the spear," he said with excitement and reservation. The schoolboy adventurer had kicked in. Dan faced the doorway, studying the order of the runes encompassing the inner circle. 'The missing rune is Ingwaz. So, Raidho must be the first. Travel or movement,' he thought. 'I need to call upon Freyr.' He called upon him three times, but nothing happened. "Dee! I'm not sure I'm doing this right. Nothing is happening," he said, confused.

"Try calling on all of the rune's gods. See what happens then," she suggested.

Dan thought about it for a moment. 'Maybe she's right, but then we aren't asking for help. It's their protection for Midgard's fate.' He opened his hand, put the rune Raidho in his pocket, and turned to face the door. 'The next rune is Isa, which implements a delay. So, I need to call upon Verdandi,' he thought. 'Okay, here goes.' Dan called upon her three times, but again, nothing happened. Determined not to be phased, he picked out Algiz. 'Algiz,' he thought. 'The rune of protection. We're going to need this one. Right, Heimdall's turn.' So, Dan called upon him three times. Then Uruz, the rune of strength. Again, he called upon its deity, Thor. The next was Mannaz. Its deity is also Heimdall, the rune of humankind and social order. Finally, he reached for the last rune, Perthro; its deity is Frigg, Odin's wife. The meaning is for hidden things or secrets. Dan wondered why this rune would be the last before Ingwaz. Then it dawned on him. A dern was a hidden place, or perhaps it would reveal where the crystal skull was. Taking a deep breath, he called to Frigg. Still, nothing happened. Confused, he asked Deena to come to the door. She turned to him and asked, "Now, what's wrong?"

"I've called to all of the gods, but nothing has happened," he said.

"I don't know. Maybe we need to complete the sequence," whispered Deena.

"Sequence?" he asked.

Deena grabbed the spear, plunging it into the slots. "How many turns?" she asked.

"Six-quarter turns," he replied.

Deena started to turn the spear, and the centre circle moved. It was heavy, so she asked Dan to help. He grasped the spear shaft, twisting it as hard as possible. The four outer sections began to separate with each quarter turn, opening the doorway. A rush of dense negative ions escaped from behind, making it hard to breathe. Weirdly, the centre circle was unsupported but remained in situ. They held fast the spear, not wanting it to close back up. The last two-quarter turns were a real struggle. Then, at last, it clunked into place. "Do we let go?" whispered Deena.

"You let go first. Then, if I feel resistance, we've not done it right," whispered Dan.

Deena tentatively stepped back and asked, "Well?"

"It seems okay," he said, letting go slowly.

Behind the doorway, the air was as dense with negative ions as the sudden rush when the door began to open. She peered into the dark, but the only visible thing was the steps. Her eyes followed them downwards; there seemed no end. "It's hard to breathe. If we get into trouble, how are we supposed to fight or run?" asked Deena, worried.

"I don't know, but we have to do this," he said. Dan shone the flashlight to the side of the steps; he could see no floor below. There was nothing above, under or anywhere, only the stairway. "Be very careful," he said. "It's a huge void. But, on the other hand, I reckon it could be a bridge between our world and god knows where."

"Are you serious?" whispered Deena.

"Deadly serious. We can't make any mistakes, and you are right. We should leave the spear in the centre circle. The doorway will close if we take it out. Then we will be fucked!" said Dan.

CHAPTER TWENTY-THREE

Dan strapped the backpack securely to him and picked up his lantern, and Deena adjusted her rig to be comfortable. One thousand steps were a long way down, and losing her balance was not an option. Dan stepped through the doorway first. Then, Deena took the first couple of steps and looked around her. They hung in mid-air in a vast black void of nothingness. Deena knew there was no going back until they had found what they were looking for; the thirteenth crystal skull. How, when, and where was yet to be discovered. She carefully followed Dan downwards to what seemed a stairway to nowhere. The endless steps took a toll on both. He questioned whether this was all part of the plan, to exhaust them before getting started. After a brief rest, they tackled the remaining steps. "Hey Dee!" shouted Dan, "I can see a doorway at the bottom."

"Thank god for that," said Deena. "But I'm not looking forward to climbing back up them."

Dan laughed, agreeing it would be a nightmare. He waited for Deena before going through the doorway to who knows what or where. At the bottom, they waited, regulating their breathing in the mass of negative ions. "You are right. I don't think we are in our world," said Deena quietly. "The air here is so different."

"I know. I've thought that too. We don't know where we are; if we are anywhere," said Dan. "Are you ready to go through this doorway?" he asked.

"There's no turning back," whispered Deena, taking in their surroundings. She felt around the side of the doorway; she could feel nothing, see nothing. It was weird. This portal was sitting in this void, waiting for them to enter. They stepped through to meet walls that went as far as the eye could see. Then, the shadows above disappeared into the black.

"Which way?" asked Dan.

"I don't know," whispered Deena. Dan got out his compass. He knew they'd entered the steps from the west. But the needle was going haywire.

It spun around looking for north, but it couldn't find it. Dan gave it a shake, but still, it wouldn't work. "What's wrong," asked Deena.

"I don't know. It's not working!" said Dan, frustrated.

"It can't be," she said. "Unless there is a magnetic force above or below us."

"Surely that's not possible," said Dan, confused. Deena took the compass and tilted it downwards. Immediately the compass needle stopped spinning, detecting north below their feet.

"It's not possible to be in a big black void either," she said.

Dan sighed, putting the compass back in his pocket. "Guess that's useless then," he muttered. To their left was an entrance. Dan went past it, walking to the end. It veered, twisting left and right. After a few minutes, he came back to Deena. "I'm not sure it makes any difference which way we go," he said.

"Let's take the first turning and see where we end up," suggested Deena.

"We could go around in circles without the compass," whispered Dan.

"That's a chance we'll have to take," she said. Taking the lead, she bore left and right, then back on themselves. Deena gave a quizzical look, to which Dan shrugged his shoulders. It didn't make sense. "What do you reckon this place is?" asked Deena.

"It's some gigantic maze, a labyrinth," Dan answered.

"Then we must find its centre," she whispered. "Do you think the crystal skull is here?" she questioned.

"It has to be. It's what is guarding it that worries me," replied Dan.

Deena didn't answer. She knew that what was waiting for them wouldn't give it up lightly. Putting it to the back of her mind, they kept turning this and that way. They doubled back for long stretches away from the direction they needed at some points. Deena was confused about where they were, and they had no idea how vast the labyrinth was. Finally, they hit a long straight, and to their left was a recess. They went to look. "What do you make of this?" she asked quietly.

"It's similar to the door we came in, but it's bricked up," he whispered. Deena shook her head about why a purpose-built labyrinth would have an inaccessible doorway. Nevertheless, she stopped dead as she turned, spotting a familiar glow.

Panicking, she whispered loudly, "Goat Man!"

"You are fucking kidding me! Down here?" he asked. But then, he saw it steadily approaching. He grabbed Deena, pulling her up a path opposite the sealed door. Dan stopped and told her to stay put. Then, stealthily, he made his way back. Dan realised they were in a loop. They could outwit it if they were careful. He watched to see which way it would go. It turned towards Deena, so he ran back, grabbed his lantern, and told her to follow him quietly. They moved swiftly to the bottom of the pathway and across, hiding around the corner where they had first run. They waited, relieved as it turned the way from which they came. Cautiously they continued back on their path. "I didn't expect them down here," said Dan.

"Me neither," said Deena, "But then, I suppose we should have. They are not of our world."

"I'm not looking forward to outrunning the big fiery dude down here," said Dan. "There aren't enough hiding places."

Deena frowned at the prospect as they made their way around the maze of corridors. Eventually, Deena asked, "Are we heading back the way we came?"

Dan stopped and shone the flashlight down the stone-walled corridor. "I'm not sure if we are back where we saw that blocked doorway," said Dan, squinting into the shadows. He strode forward until he reached a similar section. Walking around a huge pillar, he looked for the doorway, but there wasn't one. "Everything looks the same. Its design is to confuse us," said Deena.

"It's doing a good job," said Dan, annoyed. They rounded the pillar and kept walking.

"I'm sure we are going in circles. We don't know if this comes out anywhere," groaned Deena. "What if we end up hopelessly lost and there is no way back to the steps?" she worried.

Dan stopped, faced her, gave a hapless look, and said, "It's too late to think like that. We must trust that we will eventually come out somewhere. The crystal skull has to be hidden somewhere in this labyrinth." With that, Deena groaned and put a sloppy step forward. The passageways were laborious and disconcerting. They walked the symmetry of the walls; left, right, east, south, west, and north. It appears they had been walking for hours.

Eventually, Deena looked at her wristwatch and lit up the backlight to check the time. Unfortunately, the digital numbers were flashing wildly.

Not even her watch, it seems, worked in this godforsaken place. Deena sighed and said, "My watch isn't working."

"Maybe time doesn't exist in this place," he said quietly, "much like my compass. Our direction doesn't exist either. We are in a void where nothing exists. Yet, here we are, in this labyrinth, wondering about trying to find something that we know has to exist."

"Dan, shut up. You are not helping our cause. I'm confused enough," said Deena.

"Well, I've given up trying to keep our direction. But this must eventually come out somewhere, at some point. So, we need to keep going," urged Dan.

Finally, they reached a dead end. Dan put down his lantern, took out the flashlight, and pushed against another sealed door. Suddenly, he turned to Deena wide-eyed and said, "I've had a thought. This is the third sealed doorway we've come across, isn't it? We came in on the west, so the second would be the south. So, we must be on the east side. It stands to reason that it would be north if we find another one."

"Yes, but we will end up right back where we started with that theory," said Deena.

"Good point, so if we find the north doorway, we have gone too far. So, we know to double back and find another way," said Dan.

Deena groaned loudly. It was getting hard work, and between gritted teeth, she said, "This is one massive, head fuck!"

"At least our breathing has regulated to the atmosphere down here," said Dan switching off the flashlight.

Deena returned to the pathway they were on and pointed to the north. "This way?" she asked. Dan nodded and caught up with her. It was only a short distance before they hit a junction. "Left or right?" she asked.

"If I had a coin, I'd toss for it. Stay to the right?" suggested Dan. Deena shrugged her shoulders to say, 'Fine, whatever.' Either way could take them to the maze's centre.

As they went the length of a long northbound corridor, Deena asked Dan's thoughts on how a chasm such as this could be devised and put in place in the middle of nothingness. "I can't even hazard a guess. We are not in our world, but maybe in the gods' worlds, or even between," said Dan casually.

"How many are there?" she asked.

"Nine, including our own," he replied.

Deena fell silent. Then she said, "How would we know which one we are in if we are not between worlds."

"I don't know!" said Dan, frustrated. "It's not like I've ever taken regular trips to them, is it? My knowledge only goes so far, Dee. I'm surprised you don't know anything much about it."

"What do you mean by that?" she shot back at him.

"Never mind, it doesn't matter. You'll figure it out sooner or later," Dan muttered.

"It does matter. What did you mean?" asked Deena, skipping ahead and facing him.

Dan stopped in his tracks and thought for a moment before answering. He knew he had to be careful with what he said. "You need to focus more, that's all."

Deena wrinkled her nose and narrowed her eyes at him. Then, finally, she turned and kept walking. Eventually, they came to the end of the corridor and had no choice but to take a sharp left. They traipsed up and down several times before finding the north door. "For fucks sake!" shouted Dan.

"Calm down!" urged Deena, "We don't want to attract attention."

"We'll have to double back," he said, frustrated.

She turned to retrace her steps when she cried out, "We need to run!"

Dan glanced in her direction; the glow of a staff torch was coming towards them. They began running between the walls. "We need to find a place like before!" he shouted. "We need to hide!"

Deena didn't answer and focused on her breathing; it was still an arduous atmosphere to exert in. They hit a long straight before double-backing parallel. Dan prayed they would find somewhere quickly as they wound around the labyrinth. Finally, they reached an L-shaped pathway with an adjacent junction. "This way!" he shouted. He put his back against the wall. Warily, he looked around the corner, dreading the pursuing glow. It was getting closer. Deena grasped his arm, pointing in the opposite direction.

"We need to go, now!" she urged. She and Dan surged past a second Goat Man.

"You know what this means, don't…" he began. Dan didn't get to finish what he was saying when the ground began to rumble. Struggling to

289

keep their feet, they started running again. The Fire Demon arose from the depths below. Adrenaline kicked in as they turned the first junction. It didn't matter where it brought them out if it meant they could outwit the Goat Men and the 'big fiery dude.' They raced down a long corridor when Deena suddenly stopped. "Dan? What's happening?" she shouted.

Keeping themselves upright proved tricky as the ground shifted. "The labyrinth; it's turning!" exclaimed Dan. It moved two quarter turns before reversing three more. "How the hell are we supposed to know where we are now?" he said, bewildered.

"We'll work it out later. Let's get away before it starts throwing fireballs at us," urged Deena. The pounding hooves of the Fire Demon stomped into earshot. Terrified, they instinctively ran. Were they still in the same direction they were initially heading? They had no idea. But, being caught by the Fire Demon was a fate far worse than being lost in this godforsaken labyrinth. They followed the twists and turns until they reached a short wall.

"Down here!" shouted Dan. They braced themselves against the wall in anticipation. Deena pointed to the end wall, giving them a better escape either way. Dan put his finger to his lips as they crept their way down. Deena watched one side while Dan watched the other. The waiting was excruciating.

At last, it came into sight. Its bellowing filled the space as it passed the first corridor. As Deena waited for it to come into view on the other side, her heart sank as it turned towards them. After that, it was like a game of 'hide and seek,' edging their way around until the beast finally disappeared on its original path. "We have no idea where the Goat Men are," whispered Deena.

"And we have no idea what direction we are in now either," stated Dan.

"I tracked the labyrinth as it turned. The north is now the new east," said Deena.

Dan looked at her, surprised and whispered, "Fair play!"

"Well, you said I needed to focus more," she said.

After their escapade, they trudged the corridors until Deena cried, "Look! It's the L-shaped wall we first hid behind. We are on the right track."

"Thank god," said Dan, relieved. "So, smart aleck, what direction are we in now?" he asked.

Deena looked up, searching her mind. Her head bobbed side to side as she mentally worked it out. "If we keep following this around, we will find the east door, which was the north. Keep going until we hit a long straight, turn the corner and then, not very far along, and there should be a junction on our left. That will lead us to the east gate, now the north gate, so we don't want to take that. So, by my reckoning, we need to keep heading south, towards what was the old west. Which, by the way, is the other junction we could've taken."

Dan looked at her blankly, thought for a moment, and chose not to try to fathom out what she had said. Instead, he replied, "Great, so you know where we are." He looked down at his boots, and with a furrowed brow, he exhaled loudly in confusion. Then, as he made off after Deena, his thoughts found him reiterating her earlier words, 'Yep, head fuck!'

They carried on towards the south, as Deena predicted. She counted seven parallels, knowing it was vital if they wanted to find their way back out of the labyrinth. But instead, they found two corridors leading to dead ends. This labyrinth, it seemed, was designed to exhaust and confuse them. "I wonder how much further the centre is?" queried Dan.

"I've no idea. We must be getting close," said Deena.

They walked a long straight before doubling back on a parallel path. Dan asked her what direction they were heading at its end as they turned into another corridor. "East," she said, "which was south." The passages wound back and forth before leading to an extended straight. They could see a flame-lit doorway at the very end as they progressed. "That has to be the centre," whispered Dan excitedly.

With conscientiousness, they slowly approached it. Dan motioned Deena to blow out her lantern. As they got closer, they could hear voices echoing beyond the doorway. Dan braced himself as he took a hesitant glance through the entrance. "What did you see?" whispered Deena.

"It's not good," Dan whispered back. "He is fucking huge!" he cautioned.

"Whom is he bellowing at?" she asked.

"I don't know. I only saw a fleeting glance of a figure. Perhaps we should listen for a minute before going in."

Deena flattened her back against the wall, closing her eyes, concentrating on what the booming voice was saying. "Stupid, stupid mortal! I should never have trusted you to do a god's work! To think I spared you, you pathetic human," the deafening voice spat.

"I did my best! It's not my fault they found their way down here!" she pleaded. "I did everything you told me to do. But, please, let me go!" quivered the voice.

Deena's heart quickened as it dawned on her who it was, and it was enough for Deena to step into the doorway and demand, "Let her go!"

Dan swiftly appeared at her side. "What the fuck are you doing!" he asked in a strained whisper.

"I'm saving Megan. Let her go!" she demanded again.

The giant turned, glaring at her. "Another stupid mortal!" he said vehemently. "I see you've bought a little friend with you. I'm going to enjoy crucifying you, one by one." He turned his attention to Megan and took her off her feet with an enormous swipe. She struggled to free herself from his grip, but it was useless. Her arms and legs flailed mid-air.

"So, you're going to save her?" he said arrogantly. He gave an omnipotent laugh and held Megan up by her arms.

"No, don't!" screamed Deena.

Deena's plea fell on deaf ears as he tore Megan's arms from her torso. She dropped to the ground, writhing in pain and crying as her blood seeped across the floor. As she tried to get to her feet, it spattered around her. The giant looked at Megan in amusement. Sickened, Deena clapped her hand to her mouth in horror as he resumed his torment, picking her up once again. "Please kill me, please, the pain!" pleaded Megan.

"Where's the fun in that?" he laughed, lifting her to his eye level. "I never did see what Odin saw in his little pets," he mused.

Deena couldn't bear to watch, looking away as he slowly ripped off her legs. With each limb severed, the giant gave a satisfied sigh. He enjoyed Megan's screams as much as Deena's reaction. Megan's cries stopped. He wriggled her about in his hand, laughing. There was no more fun to be had now. He looked directly at Dan and Deena, flinging Megan's remains against the inner chamber wall, her body exploding with the impact. Deena felt repulsed by the sounds of body parts hitting the ground. The giant stooped to Deena's level, looked her in the eye, and growled with a menacing grin, "Now, it's your turn!"

Deena took hold of the machete remembering the words inscribed in runes, 'Revelation of Loki, elements in time.' She looked up at him with gritted determination.

Loki pointed at her, laughing, "You don't even know who you are! I'm going to enjoy destroying the last descendant of Jarl."

"Dan, what's he talking about?" she asked, not taking her eyes off Loki.

"You were supposed to have worked it out by now. It's your surname!" urged Dan.

"Kross?" she asked.

"No, your maiden name," he said.

"You mean, Erling?" she asked, "What about it?"

"It means descendant of Jarl. Jarl is the son of the Norse god, Ríg. Heimdall is Ríg. He walked amongst us as a human and had three sons. Jarl is the nobleman. Ríg is the originator of the social classes in our world," said Dan quickly.

"Right, so what does that mean for me?" she asked, confused.

"Oh, this is amusing! It's the most fun I've had since, well, since escaping that infernal rock I was chained to," said Loki scathingly.

"Dee!" Dan shouted, "You are of a god's descent. Please recall your ancestry and figure out what you are supposed to do! This has always been your destiny! The General didn't choose you. The gods did!"

"Well, why didn't you say so!" said Deena as she backed up, grabbing the backpack from his shoulder.

"I suppose you want a sporting chance now?" spat Loki at Deena.

"No need." Deena narrowed her eyes at Loki as she slung the backpack at Dan's feet. "Empty it," she said, clutching the machete tightly.

"What are you going to do?" whispered Dan.

"I'm going into battle!" she said. "Set up the scrolls exactly as I showed you, place the sand timer in the middle and prepare all defences. Remember, Loki's a shapeshifter."

Dan rushed across the chamber, emptying everything from the backpack. Deena circled Loki as she called upon her ancestors to facilitate her fight. Loki's laughter echoed around the astronomical space. "Well, look at you, little warrior, do you think you stand a chance?" he roared.

Deena's ancestors answered her call with a thirst for weaponry, hunting, battle techniques, and the rune's understanding. Her mind exploded with imagery. Then, without warning, Loki lunged at her. So,

293

Deena threw herself out of his way, rolling and getting to her feet. Loki roared and began shapeshifting. His body contorted, becoming a black mist.

A form took shape within seconds; now, Brother Thomas stood before her. Deena shouted to Dan for lit sage and salt pouches. Her hand didn't let go of the machete as she grasped the sage first. Stepping towards Brother Thomas, she swiped at him. He laughed as he moved around her. So, she backed up until the salt was within reach. Brother Thomas raised his arms, and spirits appeared around him. He spurred his arms out, sending souls hurtling towards Deena. Several hits burst through her before getting close enough to throw salt at him. It had an impact, and Brother Thomas recoiled, but it did not eradicate him. He began summoning again. Deena wouldn't give him a chance and plunged the smouldering sage into him. He twisted about himself, roaring as he changed into the black mist. Then, Loki was back in his proper form. Deena instinctively knew what she must do. She shouted to Dan, "Turn the sand timer, now!"

Dan didn't hesitate. He turned it, placing it in the centre of the pentagram. As the sands began to flow, everything but Deena and himself slowed down. He watched, amazed, as Deena climbed Loki's garb. "You haven't got much time left!" shouted Dan.

Deena grasped Loki's cloak collar, hauling herself up. His helmet is adorned with three horns, one on each side and another coming up the back, protruding forwards in the centre. 'Three, three, three,' she reminded herself. Then, taking the machete in both hands, she swung it at the nearest horn. She then climbed down quickly, jumping to the ground. Loki gave out a mighty cry as the sand ran out. Dan watched, astonished, recognising that her ancestral powers were with her. Deena backed away as time normalised. Loki leapt at her. "You little bitch!" he spat.

Shaking his head and regaining his senses, Loki realised that Deena knew how to rid him from the inner chamber. He wouldn't underestimate her again, and he wouldn't take any chances either. He had to kill her, and quickly. So, Loki began to shapeshift again. Dan sat pensively, awaiting her instruction as the black mist formed. Its shape filled her with dread. The last time she was this close to one, she didn't fare too well. The Hell Hound was crouched, ready to pounce. It growled menacingly, making Deena's stomach churn. But there was no running from this one. "Dan!" she shouted, keeping her distance. "This one is for you."

Dan grabbed his gun, but he had only one silver shot. "Get it closer," called Dan.

Deena backed up in Dan's direction as the Hell Hound stalked her. She prayed Loki didn't know about the silver bullets. Suddenly, its attention turned to Dan, snarling at him. Deena waved her arms at the Hell Hound, regaining its focus. Then, she ran towards Dan, and he raised the gun's sight in readiness. "Be ready with the sand timer. I need to try and get a double hit," said Deena.

Dan's concentration didn't waver. Instead, he nodded in acknowledgement as the Hell Hound prowled at a distance. Deena went behind Dan, and as she passed him, she whispered, "Please don't miss. I don't want to die in a world between worlds."

"I've got this," he whispered. Dan bided his time as the Hell Hound wove back and forth, making it challenging to keep it on target. A good tactic on its part. This beast was intelligent, but it wasn't only a Hell Hound; it was Loki. It circled him, keeping its distance. The barrel of the gun followed it.

Then, a shot rang out, filling the vast chamber. The beast writhed, and Loki began to change. Deena shouted, "Be ready!"

Hastily, Dan put his hand on the sand timer. He watched as Deena began ascending his clothing as Loki emerged. Then, she shouted, "Now!"

Dan turned the sand timer. Deena was already astride his neck with the machete outstretched, ready. With two hands, she swung it hard. "Not much time left! Get down!" shouted Dan. Then, she aimed again at the same horn with all her might. Then deftly grabbing Loki's cloak, Deena used it to slide to the floor. Loki's bawls were deafening as he held his head.

"You shouldn't have tried for a second hit," Dan said. "You barely had time to get away. We are too close to take risks."

Deena's eyes fixed on Loki. "I know what I'm doing," she said. Dan shook his head, realising she was brimming with confidence in her ability. Finally, Deena had found her calling.

"You are dead, mortal!" Loki growled at Deena.

"Bring it on, Loki! I'm not afraid of you!" she shouted. Loki rushed at her, but Deena was ready. Diving between his legs smoothly, she slid across the floor, stood, and turned to face him. He lunged again, his huge hand swiping at her. Dan could barely watch as Deena dropped to the ground. "Is that the best you can do, Loki? Or do you want a sporting chance?" laughed Deena.

Loki grunted, and with a sardonic grin, he began shapeshifting. Deena watched as he split his black mist in two, forming into the Twins. The girls giggled at the prospect of completing their nursery rhyme, a chance for them to play their sadistic killing game. "What do you need for the freaks!" shouted Dan.

"Pass me two lit bushels. But be careful," said Deena, "we don't know how powerful they've become with Loki behind them." Then, circling the Twins, she waited for the first line of their sick nursery rhyme. As Dan ran to her, handing her the bushels, she said, "Light one for yourself. They may target us both." Dan darted back to the sand timer, kneeling in readiness. His blood ran cold as Emily teleported towards Deena.

"One, two, we see you," giggled Emily.

As Charlotte teleported towards her, Deena tried to back away and, looking her in the eye, Charlotte sang, "Three, four, don't open the door." Then, Deena swiped the sage through her. She dissipated, but she reappeared.

Suddenly, Emily emerged behind her. Deena spun around as Emily sang, "Five, six, we play tricks."

Deena sank the sage into Emily's face. But, again, it wasn't enough as she reappeared beside Charlotte. The Twins looked at each other, their thoughts shared. Deena was filled with dread as Emily raised her arms, shooting a blast of energy. Deena's feet left the floor, and she was hurled across the chamber. Dan ran to help her. Charlotte noticed him and looked at Emily, another thought shared. Charlotte giggled and waited until Dan was almost within reach of Deena. Then, raising both arms, she flung them towards Dan. He flipped into the air, rocketing back into a pillar. Winded, he lay there catching his breath. The Twin's giggles riled Deena.

"Seven, eight, it's too late," sang Charlotte.

As black cracks appeared up her porcelain face, Deena plunged the sage into her a second time. Charlotte dispersed into a black mist, spinning in the air and absorbing into Emily. An expression of anger befell Emily's face as she teleported towards Deena. Cracks travelled up her tiny face, and her eyes turned black. Horrified, Deena tried to back away, but Emily raised her into the air laughing hysterically, savouring the last line of the nursery rhyme. Deena dropped one of her sage bushels as Emily began to sing, "Nine... ten..."

CHAPTER TWENTY-FOUR

Dan saw his chance. Quickly, he crept up behind Emily, reached out and picked up the sage from the floor. "We kill…" she trailed off.

Dan thrust his and Deena's sage bushels into Emily, cutting her nursery rhyme short. Deena fell to the ground. But Dan kept his hands firmly inside Emily's apparition until she was a black mist. Then, Dan walked backwards, not taking his eyes off the snaking vapour. "The sand timer!" shouted Deena. Dan ran back to the scrolls. Deena regained herself and hurried to him. "Thanks," she whispered.

"No worries. They got a little too close for comfort," muttered Dan.

As Loki returned to his proper form, Deena ran towards him even though she hurt from being dropped from a height. Then, Loki grunted, and as he tried to reach for her, she shouted, "Now!"

Dan turned the sand timer and watched. The ease at which she scaled the giant god was incredible. Loki tried to bring his arm up to push Deena off as she reached his shoulders. Dan shouted, "Watch out!"

Deena had already seen it and grabbed hold of the back of his hair, pulling herself over his shoulders. Then, Dan glanced at the sand timer. "Not much time!" he exclaimed. That simple step of avoiding Loki's attempt to sway her had cost valuable time. So, she quickly swung the machete at the left horn and made her escape, and as Deena got halfway down, Loki took hold of his cloak, flinging her across the inner chamber. She slid across the floor at speed. Instinctively, Dan reached out to catch her, sending them both reeling. The scrolls and sand timer scattered.

"That was too close. Loki could've killed you!" said Dan.

"I misjudged my time," she said, looking at the disarray around them. "The scrolls, quick!" she urged.

"I'll sort them. You keep an eye on Loki," said Dan.

Deena scrambled to her feet, watching Loki holding his helmet while bellowing profanities and death threats at her. Then, finally, Deena laughed and shouted, "Call yourself a god? You couldn't catch a mouse!"

"I'll kill you this time, you bitch! Wait and see!" he snarled as he ran towards her. Midway, he shapeshifted, and Deena took a fighting stance in readiness.

"You are fucking kidding me," she muttered as the black mass formed into a Ground Crawler. "Dan, don't move!" she cried.

Deena had no sage to disguise her scent, and the only weapon she had to defend herself was the machete. Dan was already relighting sage bushels, placing them around himself, hoping Deena could get close enough to grab one. Then, he lined up a brass shell in the gun. With the machete in hand, Deena silently crept backwards. Guttural clicks emanated from the disgusting creature's chest as it tried to locate her. Its head swayed side to side, salivating at the prospect of killing her, a meal worth waiting for. Then finally, it gnashed its razor-sharp teeth together as it locked onto her, and Deena realised she was a marked target.

There was no way she could get to the sage without being detected. It crouched, ready to attack. Deena stood her ground and held the machete to her chest, with the blade facing outwards. Not for a split second did she take her eyes off it. It bounded forward, launching itself at her. Dan raised the gun. Deena knew it was imperative to time this right. As it rose into the air, she dropped to her knees and laid back on her heels, still clutching the machete to her chest. He almost squeezed the trigger when Deena thrust her arms up, allowing the blade to slice its belly open as it crossed over her. She rolled to one side as its entrails slithered to the floor. Dan lowered the gun in disbelief at what he had witnessed. Deena got to her feet and shouted, "Get ready!"

Dan quickly holstered the gun. The Ground Crawler dissipated, and Deena waited for her moment as the black mist writhed in the air. Then, as Loki's proper form returned, he let out an animalistic growl. Deena put herself in a better position to climb his attire. His anger, it seemed, was getting the better of him, but that's what Deena wanted. "Is that all you've got, Loki?" sneered Deena. "You haven't got it in you to kill the last descendant of Jarl!" she taunted. Loki gave out an almighty battle cry. Then, before he could make any headway toward her, she shouted, "Now!"

Again, Dan turned the sand timer, and as he set it down, Deena was already scaling his colossal cloak. She hauled herself onto his shoulders and raised the machete. Then, Deena aimed for the left horn with as much force as possible, using the momentum to hit the centre horn before rapidly getting down. Deena knew Loki would be enraged for severing one of his horns, and she did not care to be within his striking distance. As Deena reached Dan, she turned to see Loki fall to his knees, gripping his helmet and fumbling for his severed horn. Deena laughed as he struggled to his feet. "What's up, Loki? Are you feeling weak?" she ridiculed. In anger, Loki threw the horn at her, causing her to dodge out of its way. "Now, that isn't very nice," she said sarcastically.

"Do you think antagonising him is helpful?" whispered Dan.

"Yes," she said. "I need three more hits."

"I'll be ready," Dan said. "What do you think will happen when he's lost his horns?" he asked.

"I'm hoping he will be so weak he returns to the gods' worlds, giving us time to find the skull," replied Deena.

The black mass swirled in the air, and Deena was ready as Loki formed into the Wailing Banshee. The Banshee, next to the Twins, was Dan's worst nightmare. First, Deena frantically searched her pockets for the cotton wool. Then, she ran to Dan, giving him half. "Remember the rules for this one," she whispered.

Dan nodded, stuffed it in his ears, and said, "I'll aim the salt while you cause a distraction. This bitch has had it in for me. It will be a pleasure to get rid of her."

Deena took a bushel before taking off across the chamber. Dan kept his eyes lowered, focusing on Deena. "Hey, Banshee, I'm over here!" shouted Deena, waving her arms. The Banshee turned, cupping her hands around her mouth, and the wailing commenced. Deena crouched, allowing the Banshee to swoop at her. Dan threw the first salt pouch at the Banshee, which missed, closely followed by a second. It hit, making her reel backwards. Deena took the opportunity to create a smokescreen. The Banshee dive-bombed her, pulling away at the last second, disgusted at the sage's smell. Angered, the Banshee wailed with more force. Deena could see sound waves resonating through the smoke; she crouched, giving Dan another chance to pinpoint her.

Then, Dan hurled two more, one after the other. He didn't miss this time as the salt spread like buckshot in the air. The Banshee screamed and retreated. "Keep it up!" shouted Deena. Again, she used the sage to deter the Banshee from getting too close. But this time, Dan was Banshee's target. Deena raced across the inner chamber towards him. "Crouch and protect your ears!" she shouted. Dan's eyes stayed unblinking, glaring at the floor. Deena got to him and grabbed a pouch of salt with each hand, throwing them in unison at the Banshee. The screeches were excruciating.

She crouched beside Dan when it suddenly stopped. Deena looked, expecting to see Loki changing to his proper form. Then, her eyes rose, to see the Banshee watching from a great height. Deena was sure that should have been enough to rid her, but the driving force was, after all, Loki. Deena got to her feet, taking a salt pouch. She put distance between Dan and herself. Then, Dan picked up another two, loosening the twist of the brown paper enough so it would burst open in the air as before. He waited for his chance. She was too high; he had to wait for her to swoop. Deena was taunting the Banshee, luring her down. Then as the Banshee took the bait, Deena watched from her periphery. Deena held a hand up to Dan to wait.

Deena couldn't afford to miss, and neither could he. As the Banshee cupped her hands, Deena threw the salt. "Do it now, Dan!" she shouted. Dan launched the salt. Dropping to a crouch, they put their hands over their ears as the Banshee's screams filled the entire chamber. Neither moved until the relentless high-pitched cries ceased. Deena looked at Dan as he tentatively uncovered his ears. Then, she glanced up as the Banshee became the swirling black mist. "Be ready," she said, pointing at Loki. "I'm going to try and get all three hits in, but I need to get up as far as possible before turning the sand timer." Deena took off with the machete, running at the black mist as it touched the ground.

Loki had scarcely taken form when Deena grasped his cloak from behind. Loki roared as he grabbed his cape, trying to shake her off. She clung on as he flailed his arms. As Deena progressed to his shoulders, she shouted, "Turn it!" Loki's movements slowed, allowing her to grip his collar and swing nearer his helmet. Deena smashed the machete against the right horn. It began to crack. She wasted no time aiming at the centre horn. 'Only two more,' she thought. She raised the machete above her head, brutally bringing it down.

Loki's cries were deeply satisfying as she again extended the machete. Using as much force as she could muster, the horn fractured. Deena raised her boot, kicking it fiercely. The horn fell, clattering across the floor. Less than ten seconds of sand remained, and Deena knew she had to get down fast. Loki dropped to his knees and cried out, clutching his helmet, feeling for his horns. Only one remained, and that was barely clinging on. Deena ran to Dan.

"What do we do now?" he asked.

"We wait," she replied. Loki crawled across the floor of the inner chamber, looking for his lost horns, groaning with the effort. Finally, Loki's power in Midgard was destroyed. Deena raised her boot, striking the remaining horn, and Loki cried out, collapsing altogether. Deena returned to Dan.

"You were incredible! I mean, awesome, formidable, I don't have the words," he said, giving her a huge hug.

Deena pushed him off, laughing, "We still need to find the rune, Ingwaz."

"Any idea where we should look?" he asked.

"If it is anywhere, he will have it," said Deena, pointing to Loki. Then, she turned to Dan, warning him, "He's still a threat, so be careful."

Dan asked, "I guess we search pockets and such?"

"Anywhere it could be hidden," she said. She grabbed hold of Loki's leather chest plate and pulled herself up. There were numerous leather pouches through his belt, so Deena undid the closest. It was a mammoth task opening a buckle almost the same size as her. She flipped the pocket open; it was empty. Deena climbed to an adjacent pocket, unthreaded the strap, and peered inside. There were items at the bottom. So, she turned to Dan, asking him to keep Loki busy. Dan taunted him, pulling at his helmet, keeping his attention away from Deena. She crawled in as far as she dared, feeling around for the rune. She felt a disc shape, but it felt metal. But something else caught her attention. So, she tucked it into her pocket. She crawled out, slid down and joined Dan, giving him the disc.

"The diamond rune shape is cut out. Strange," said Dan.

"I also found this," said Deena.

Dan's eyes widened at the stunning necklace she held, adorned with amber that danced like fire. "No way! It's Freyja's necklace, Brísingamen," he said, astounded. "The Dark Elves forged it, and it has powers."

"Really?" she mused, holding it up.

"Yes, really. According to Poetic Edda, Loki stole it, but Heimdall fought Loki and returned it to Freyja. So, I can't understand how he would have it back in his possession."

"Perhaps Ragnarök disrupted the gods, and Loki saw a chance to get it back," suggested Deena. She studied the necklace in the light of the flames of the inner chamber's door. "Any objections if I wear it?" she asked.

"Not from me," said Dan, taking Brísingamen and placing it around her neck.

"Give it back! It's mine!" shouted Loki as he crawled towards them.

"Not anymore, Loki!" said Deena scornfully. She turned to Dan, "We need to get out of here. I don't know what will happen if we hang around too long. We need to pack everything up quickly."

Dan rushed across the chamber, hastily stuffing everything inside the backpack. Then, picking up their lanterns, they raced into the labyrinth. Deena pulled him around the corner out of Loki's sight, fumbling in her jacket for matches. Finally, she knelt and lit both lanterns. "The crystal skull could be anywhere in this labyrinth," said Deena.

"What about the rune, Perthro?" Dan suggested. "It's supposed to find hidden things, right?"

"Of course, brilliant idea," exclaimed Deena as Dan gave her the runes. Her excitement was evident. They were so close; they could almost taste victory. "Let's put distance between Loki and us first," said Deena. "A few more turns, and we can call upon Frigga for help."

Dan took the lead as they walked towards the new north. "We should stop here. I don't think the skull would be far from the inner chamber," said Deena. She looked at the rune, Ingwaz, mystified and asked, "Why is this one so different from the others?"

Deena tucked Ingwaz into her jeans pocket. Then holding the rune, Perthro, she focused on calling to Frigga. Although the tingling sensation filled her hand, Frigga was not answering her call. But the rune, Ingwaz, began to warm in her pocket. The heat intensified, and she had to take it out before it burned her. She was surprised to see the edge of the rune shape glowing, so she held it between her finger and thumb. Ingwaz's outline shone on the walls of the labyrinth. As it hit the long straight, Deena felt a strange pulling sensation. "It's showing me the way!" she exclaimed. "Frigga did answer my call!" she exalted.

"That is so cool," said Dan. "Go with it."

The schoolboy adventurer was back. He followed Deena to the end of the corridor. Then, she shone Ingwaz onto the south wall and was drawn to the next turn. Deena was astounded by the will of the rune. They continued through the maze of zigzagged paths before coming to a long corridor. She gasped in awe as the symbol highlighted on the wall ahead reflected towards them on the floor. "This has to be it!" Deena yelled ecstatically. As they ran the corridor length, the pull got more vigorous. Both stared at the wall in amazement as the rune burned its shape into the stone, cutting it deep into the wall. Then to their surprise, the burning light of Ingwaz died out.

"What now?" asked Dan.

"I don't know. Give me a minute to think," said Deena.

"Don't take too long. Remember, there are Goat Men down here," said Dan.

Deena traced her finger over the etched rune, realising that the metal rune was also a key like the spear of Gungnir. She slotted it snugly into the stone, and an Ingwaz diamond-shaped bar shot out. She grasped it and began twisting. The grinding noise of stone moving spurred her on. With each turn, a section of the wall began to open. Finally, the top of the crystal skull came into view, and Deena squealed in excitement. They had found it! After everything they had endured, it was within their grasp. When the vault opened far enough, Deena carefully lifted it out. "It's more stunning than any of the skulls," she said.

Dan took it from her, admiring it as he placed it in the backpack. Suddenly, Deena's attention swung behind them. Loki was on his feet, stumbling towards them. "You thieves! Midgard is mine!" he roared.

"We have to run!" shouted Deena. "Follow me. I remember how to get to the steps!" she insisted.

As Loki staggered, so the labyrinth walls crumbled behind him. Deena took flight towards the north. She turned to take the straight east and abruptly south, shouting, "The west gateway should be on our right, down here." They were nearing the old north door that was now the new west. The steps had to be there. Deena glanced back at Loki, still trying to pursue them. They had made some headway against his giant steps, but would it be enough? They still had a thousand steps to climb. The fear of being buried alive within the labyrinth walls made Deena break into a sprint, almost running past the doorway. Dan found it difficult keeping up with her with the weight of the crystal skull strapped to his back. She waited a few seconds allowing him to see her signal. Then, she began the gruelling climb. It would be a veritable test of her and Dan's stamina.

Dan paused at the doorway, looking up the steps. He could see the distant glow of her lantern frantically swaying in her haste. He took a lungful of air as he prepared himself for the stairway. Focusing on his breathing was difficult as the backpack's weight swayed from side to side. Deena was beginning to struggle. Her leg muscles burned intensely, and with only the sight of endless steep steps ahead, she couldn't help but wonder if she would make it. Dan didn't dare look behind him in case he lost his footing. Throwing his lantern into the abyss of nothingness, he used his arms to propel himself quicker, like climbing a ladder.

Deena could make out the end of the steps, spurring her on. She hurled herself through the doorway, rolling into the tunnel, and then looked back into the black void, searching for Dan. With no sign of his lantern, she began to panic. Thoughts of losing his balance, or Loki catching hold of him, were too much. Then she saw his silhouette against the steps. She screamed at Dan in horror, "Run!" Loki's giant stature wasn't far behind him.

It was hard to tell how many steps were between them, but she could see the stairway disintegrating into the void. Dan heard her, and adrenaline kicked in as he began climbing faster. As he neared the last steps, Loki was almost upon him. Deena lay on the ground, held her arms out and shouted, "Jump!" Dan surged forward, lunging at her arms. The steps fell beneath and Loki with them. The giant god's arms flailed as he fell into the depths of the darkness. Deena gritted her teeth with the effort of holding Dan's weight. No way was she letting go. Dan desperately clung on as Deena slowly wormed her way back until he could pull himself up.

Once he was through the doorway, she stood up and pulled the spear out of the inner circle. The four outer sections slammed shut, sealing the labyrinth. Exhausted, Deena sunk to the ground next to Dan and began laughing.

"Why are you laughing? It's not remotely funny," said Dan, scowling.

"I'm laughing with relief; we have the skull, and I've got this!" said Deena, feeling empowered as she touched Brísingamen.

"I've got to ask; how did you know that stuff to battle Loki?" muttered Dan.

"I called upon my ancestors for knowledge. My mind filled with images and abilities, and I instinctively knew what to do," she replied. "I also have a question for you. Why didn't you tell me of my descent? You knew all about me and never said a word until the last minute?" she asked.

"Yeah, sorry about that. The General told me, but I wasn't allowed to say anything. He said you needed to be close to the crystal skull for your ancestors to answer you," he said.

"I think the General and I need to chat when we get back," said Deena.

"That's the Government for you," he said wistfully. "Are you ready? We should get back."

"Just five more minutes?" requested Deena, shutting her eyes and breathing deeply. Dan smiled and nodded. She had been through an immense trial and had more than earned those extra minutes. He thought back on her battle with Loki. Neither envisaged the enormity of what awaited them beyond the thousand steps. Then he thought about Megan, how evil and cruel a god could be.

Dan moved the timbers, and they slipped into the cellars. As Deena's head rose into view, Dan quickly put his fingers in his ears to lessen the shrill squeals of delight from Bronwyn.

"You're back! Did you get it?" Bronwyn babbled in excitement. "I've been so scared not knowing what was going on."

Deena stood the spear against the wall and wearily sat down. "We have the crystal skull," said Deena, smiling at her enthusiasm.

"Oh, cool, can I see it? Please?" begged Bronwyn.

"Sure, why not," said Dan. He sat beside her, unzipped the backpack, carefully took it out, and showed it to her.

"Oh. My. God! That is, how we say here in Wales, fucking lush!" she exclaimed. "May I hold it?" she asked.

"Of course," said Dan, laughing at her outburst.

"So, this is what will save our world?" uttered Bronwyn. "I'm not surprised it was well hidden."

"It was well guarded, too," said Deena.

"What exactly was down there? Was it as dangerous as Dan said it would be?" asked Bronwyn.

"It was far worse. Firstly, we had to find our way through a labyrinth," said Deena.

"Tell me everything!" asked Bronwyn enthusiastically. Bronwyn sat mesmerised as Deena told her what happened beyond the thousand steps.

"Incredible!" exclaimed Bronwyn. "I guess that means we go to America now?" she asked.

"We have a few things to do first, and we need to rest before flying out," said Dan.

"Is there anything I can do for you? I promised I'd sort food out; would you like that first?" asked Bronwyn.

"Food sounds amazing. I'm famished," said Deena.

"I'll get it. Do you want bottled water as well?" asked Bronwyn.

"Dan, would you go with Bronwyn and give her a hand?" asked Deena. "We could also stash what we need for the flight home."

Bronwyn led the way into the cellars. She had sorted a pile of canned food, and the favourite cheese and ham were stored on her bed. "Is Deena all right?" she asked Dan.

"Deena will be fine when she's had some rest. She downplayed what happened in the inner chamber. I'll be honest; I don't think I could have done what she did. Deena was incredible," said Dan.

Bronwyn could see his admiration for her and recognised the inward smile of a smitten man. "You've fallen in love with her, haven't you?" said Bronwyn giggling.

Dan turned away, embarrassed. He could feel himself blushing. Then, scuttling out of the room, he muttered about getting water bottles. Bronwyn couldn't help but laugh at his reaction. To her, it was apparent from the moment she met them.

In the wine cellar, Dan perused the whisky bottles. Determined to celebrate their return to the States, he picked out an excellent malt whiskey and smiled. "You and I will have a good time when we get back," Dan whispered, pointing to the bottle. Pleased with his new acquirement, he picked up six water bottles and strolled back to Bronwyn.

"Hi," she said, "I figured you may want a change from cheese and ham, so I found some canned fruits, baked beans, and ravioli. It isn't too bad cold. It's protein and good energy food."

"Cheese and ham are always good, but a change will be welcome. Thanks," Dan said. "Have you got something we can put it in?" he asked.

Bronwyn smiled and offered Dan a cardboard box. "No can opener," she said.

"That's fine. I've got a Swiss penknife. Are you ready to get back to Deena?" he asked.

Dan picked up the food box as Bronwyn lit the way with Deena's lantern. As she neared the top of the steps to the base room, she said, "We're..." Then Bronwyn stopped short. Deena was comfortably wrapped up in blankets, fast asleep. She turned to Dan and uttered, "Shush."

Dan put the food box down, whispering to Bronwyn, "Let her sleep. Can we go back to your room to eat?"

Bronwyn nodded and left Deena's lantern at the top of the steps. Dan retrieved some food and water from the box, and they left for the cellars. "Won't Deena be concerned if she wakes up and we're not there?" asked Bronwyn.

"She'll know where to find us. Her instincts intensified as she battled with Loki," said Dan.

"For what it's worth, I admire her too. I've never met anyone like her. Thank you for letting me come back with you. It means a lot. I feel safe around you both," said Bronwyn.

"I wasn't too enthusiastic at first, to be honest, but you've grown on me, and Deena wants you to return with us. I can't go against her wishes," Dan said. "But there is something you could help me with, but it is dangerous."

"Really?" asked Bronwyn surprised. "You would trust me to help you? But, of course, I won't let you down."

In Bronwyn's room, Dan suggested they discuss it over food. He offered a crudely opened can to Bronwyn, which she accepted with a smile.

"I promised Jack I would leave the motorbike outside the lodge for him. I need to retrieve it from the back of the graveyard. I need an extra pair of eyes to watch for danger. Do you think you could do that?" asked Dan.

"I can, but you need to tell me what dangers," said Bronwyn.

"Firstly, I need to know if you can follow my direction and not put us directly in danger," said Dan.

"I promise I'll do everything you say. I know about the Ground Crawlers, but what else?" asked Bronwyn.

307

Dan told her what was out there, from Brother Thomas to the remaining Hell Hound. Bronwyn was silent, deep in thought. "Are the tunnels safer? Can we get close to the bike using them?" she asked Dan.

"We can get as far as the mausoleum, but then we have to break across open ground to the back of the church. So, are you up for it? I can wait for Deena, but I want to get the hell out of this place as fast as possible," said Dan.

"Yes, I'll do it. As I said, I won't let you down," replied Bronwyn with conviction.

"Great, let's eat, then we can go," said Dan.

Dan and Bronwyn made their way to the tunnel entrance with a much-appreciated full belly. "I'm going to check on Dee before we go. Here, have the lantern," he whispered. Dan returned in less than a minute, smiling as he said, "Still fast asleep."

"Good, with any luck, we'll be back before she wakes up," whispered Bronwyn.

Dan moved the timbers and offered Bronwyn ahead first. Then, as she slipped through, he muttered, "Remember what's in the tunnels?"

Bronwyn nodded and said quietly, "The Goat Men. Look for the staff torch."

Dan and Bronwyn turned to the west underneath the secret tower towards the abbey ruins. Even though Bronwyn was scared, she didn't let it show. That was until they were nearing the abbey ruins and saw the dreaded staff torch between the staggered junctions. Dan turned to Bronwyn, "Blow out the lantern," he whispered. "Flatten yourself against the wall. Let's see which way it's heading before carrying on." Bronwyn squeezed her eyes shut, terrified. She had never seen anything like it. Dan watched and waited, exhaling in relief when it turned south towards the orangery. Dan looked at Bronwyn and gave her a nudge. "Are you okay?" he whispered. Bronwyn nodded, still not daring to open her eyes.

"Here," Dan said, rattling a box of matches, "it's safe to go."

"Thank god for that," said Bronwyn.

"There is a tunnel that leads to the church giving us a way directly into the mausoleum. But we need to up the pace," said Dan.

Dan strode up the tunnel, and Bronwyn had to break into a jog. They passed both turnings, carrying on to the end. Before going up the steps, Dan told her they would be crossing the ruins overground and down to a tunnel on the other side of the chapter house. Bronwyn groaned, "I hate the ruins. They're spooky."

Dan laughed and said, "Blow out the lantern at the top of the steps. The last thing we need is to attract Brother Thomas's attention."

"Just in case, where is the entrance to the other tunnel?" asked Bronwyn.

"Go straight across the arches and follow the outer wall around the chapter house. There are steps down into the tunnel in the corner," whispered Dan.

Cautiously, they began their moonlit jaunt towards the arches. Bronwyn's heart was pounding. From what Dan said, Brother Thomas could quickly kill them. They only had to cross the passage and out the other side. No shadows stirred. But then, halfway across, a raucous laugh imparted. Both Dan and Bronwyn stopped in their tracks.

CHAPTER TWENTY-FIVE

Brother Thomas stood in the chapter house doorway, pointing directly at them. "What do we do?" panicked Bronwyn.

"We run! Get to the tunnel and keep running!" pressed Dan.

Bronwyn bolted across. Dan followed, glancing sideways at Brother Thomas, raising his arms. He sped around the arches towards the tunnel steps. The wind began to howl, and leaf debris picked up, swirling around them. "This is really, really bad, isn't it?" shouted Bronwyn.

"Get in the tunnel, hurry!" he shouted back. Bronwyn could barely keep her feet. Dan grabbed her arm, pulling her towards the tunnel, almost pushing her down the steps in haste. Bronwyn stumbled down, and at the bottom, she turned to see where Dan was. "Keep going!" he yelled.

Bronwyn looked up at Brother Thomas, peering down under his hooded robe. He flung out his arms, directing the spirits into the tunnel. Bronwyn gasped in horror, and as she turned to run, an essence slammed through her, sending her reeling. Dan pulled her with him. Bronwyn found her feet and continued running. As Dan sprinted after her, he, too, took a hit. Grappling with the ground on all fours, he wondered how far Brother Thomas could hurl the spirits into the tunnel. The rushing wind was deafening. But the church wasn't far now. If he could get to the cellars, they would be safe. Dan caught up with Bronwyn. Anxiously, she grabbed him. "I don't know which way to go," she said.

"To the church!" he exclaimed, pointing to the left. Dan grasped at the door, flinging it open. Together they went through, slamming it behind them. They leaned against the door as if barricading it. Dan began to laugh. Bronwyn stared at him crossly.

"It's not funny!" said Bronwyn.

"No, but if the spirits can go through our body, they can go through this door," he said, still laughing.

Bronwyn slid to the floor. "Are we safe here?" she asked him curtly.

"I think so. It's sanctified ground," said Dan.

"You think so?" queried Bronwyn.

"It's fine. You can light the lantern now," Dan chuckled. "We can rest here for a bit. Perhaps Brother Thomas will give up on us." So, Bronwyn lit the lantern, and the cellar grew a little brighter.

"I've never been down here. Are we under the church?" she asked Dan.

"There are lots of places you haven't seen. Deena and I discovered them almost by accident," said Dan.

"You two are good together," muttered Bronwyn. "You should tell her how you feel."

"It's complicated. Dee's married," he said with regret.

"Sorry, I didn't know. Deena has never really talked about her personal life. She said the same, that 'it's complicated.' Has she got children?" asked Bronwyn.

"She has two, Ben and Lily," answered Dan.

"Does she know if they are safe?" she asked.

"No, and she won't thank you for asking. She has had to put all of her focus on this mission," said Dan.

"I can understand that. It must be difficult," Bronwyn said sadly.

Having rested, Dan suggested they make their way to the mausoleum. Dan opened the door to the tunnel and peered into the darkness. Brother Thomas, it seemed, had given up for now. Dan led the way, skirting under the graveyard walls. Finally, they stood before the double doors. As Dan pulled one of the doors open, Bronwyn exclaimed, "Shit! This is awesome!"

"Not as awesome as upstairs. Let's move," Dan said. Bronwyn gasped at the buried wealth as they walked the family tombs. "We have to follow it outside around back. Be careful. We are vulnerable out here."

"Wait, are we taking the bike straight to Jack's?" asked Bronwyn.

"Yes, once we've seen Jack, there is a tunnel behind the lodge. So, we'll get back to the manor that way," said Dan. Bronwyn took a large breath of courage. Dan couldn't help but smile. She was trying so hard to be brave. Finally, with their backs to the wall, they got to the rear of the mausoleum. Dan motioned her to stay put while he looked at the open ground. "Stay very still," he whispered.

"Why?" she asked, her voice trembling.

"Ground Crawlers! They are a little way off. We'll have to wait them out," whispered Dan.

"How many?" she asked.

Dan didn't answer. He gave her the lantern and a bushel. "Light it from the lantern. Whatever you do, do not move. You need to blow on the sage to get it to smoke," he whispered, "then waft it around us."

He checked around the building again. He didn't have the heart to tell Bronwyn how close the Ground Crawlers were. Instead, Dan put his arm across Bronwyn in case she took flight as they came into view. He could feel her trembling. So, he got her attention and put his finger to his lips. Bronwyn nodded fervently, squeezing her eyes shut. The Ground Crawlers were mere feet away. Dan was glad she couldn't see as a horde of ten sauntered towards the manor. He waited until they were out of sight before releasing his arm. As he did, Bronwyn slowly opened her eyes. "Are they gone?" she whispered.

"Yes," he said. Again, they paused before moving towards the graveyard. Dan could see the motorbike against the wall in the moonlight as he'd left it. "Crouch and be quiet," he whispered. Dan retrieved the bike and motioned for Bronwyn to get on. He whispered, "We're not stopping for anything. Hold tight." Dan started the motorbike, and Bronwyn wrapped her arms around him as he sat down, clinging to the lantern. He opened the throttle and belted it to Jack's. He put the bike behind the woodpile and knocked on the lodge door.

Jack opened the door a crack, spying out. Then, he opened the door wider and gave a big grin. "Get in 'ere," Jack said. Dan beckoned Bronwyn to come inside. "Well, I'll be damned! Where's Missy? Is she okay?" asked Jack.

"She's fine and resting at the manor. I've brought the bike for you as promised," said Dan.

"Did you find what you were looking for?" asked Jack excitedly.

"We did!" exclaimed Dan.

"Young Bronwyn," he said fondly. "'Ow, are you?"

"Holding up," she replied.

"Do you want a coffee?" asked Jack.

"I'm sorry, but we need to get back to Deena," said Dan.

"Good luck to you," said Jack, shaking Dan's hand.

Jack waved them goodbye. Then, as he bolted the door to his lodge, Jack couldn't help but laugh out loud, elated at the prospect of regaining light to their world. So, there was hope after all.

Dan relit the lantern before going into the tunnel behind the lodge. "These tunnels are eerie," said Bronwyn.

"And wet," said Dan.

"How wet?" asked Bronwyn reservedly.

"Very," said Dan. They passed the turn for the boathouse and headed south before bearing north around the lake.

"You weren't kidding, were you," shuddered Bronwyn as water lapped around her waist. Dan smiled. 'Another short-arse,' he thought.

"How much further?" she asked, shivering.

"Not far. About a fifteen-minute walk," said Dan.

Bronwyn almost fell through the door to her room. So, Dan grabbed her blankets and wrapped them around her. Bronwyn smiled feebly and stammered, "We... we did it."

"You were fearless," said Dan.

They hovered around the stove, absorbing its warmth, when they heard the latch open to a familiar voice. "You went without me!" exclaimed Deena. "I wanted to say goodbye to Jack."

"Sorry, I was trying to save time," Dan said apologetically. "If it means that much to you, we can do a pit stop when we leave."

"You didn't even think to ask me!" retorted Deena.

"I'm sorry, I thought I was doing the right thing," said Dan. "You desperately needed to rest." Deena spun on her heel, marching back to the base room. Dan made his excuses to Bronwyn and went after her, continuing his apologies.

"You risked Bronwyn's life! So, what if something had gone wrong? Could you live with that?" stated Deena.

"I get it. I can't apologise any more than I have. I should've waited, but in my defence, I want to get the fuck out of here and get this damn skull back to the team, who are probably fast running out of supplies! Did you think of that?" ranted Dan.

"Is Jack okay?" Deena asked quietly.

Bronwyn appeared at the top of the cellar steps and said, "He's fine. He asked after you, and I'm sorry. I didn't mean to tread on your toes. Is it okay for me to join you?"

"Totally fine, I'm sorry," said Deena. "Could you help get everything together to leave? I need to eat, so can you and Dan organise it?" she asked. Dan offered the penknife to Deena. She didn't hesitate to work on opening the first tin to hand.

With her appetite satiated, Deena double-checked the equipment. "So, who is taking what?" asked Deena.

"I'll take the skull and the crystals in the backpack," said Dan. "We don't need the scrolls or the sand timer. They've served their purpose. So, Bronwyn, I suggest you organise a small bag to take. Dee, you take the spear, and we will need defences on our way to the plane, so if you fill your rig with whatever we have left from the labyrinth, that would be great."

Bronwyn had already left before Dan had finished speaking. It wasn't long before she returned with a smallish tote bag filled with clothing and personal care.

"If you are ready, let's get out of here!" said Dan grinning. "We'll go to the south gates via the tunnel to the orangery, then overground. Keep your wits about you."

Dan moved the timbers allowing Deena and Bronwyn to slip into the tunnel. The girls led the way with a lantern each. Together, they turned west towards the abbey ruins. Dan dreaded the junctions ahead as the Goat Men always seemed to be there. He wondered if it was wishful thinking that they could get to the plane unchallenged. 'That,' he thought, 'would be too good to be true.' So, they turned south towards the orangery.

Deena linked her arm in Bronwyn's reassuringly as Deena shuddered, nudging Bronwyn as they neared the narrow tunnel. "We entered the labyrinth down there," said Deena.

"I think you can truly call yourself a warrior," said Bronwyn.

"Thanks, but we're not out of the woods yet," she murmured.

"With that spear, that incredible necklace and machete tucked into your rig, you look and are a warrior in every sense of the word," said Bronwyn with deep admiration. Deena gave her a modest smile and hugged her arm a little tighter.

"We're not far now," said Deena.

"Right, you two, before we go up, we need to chat about how we will do this if anything arises," said Dan.

"Firstly," said Deena, "The Ground Crawlers. We should all carry sage."

Dan looked at Bronwyn and said, "Whatever you do, don't run!"

"Secondly, there is still a Hell Hound, and we have no silver bullets. But, Bronwyn, we will deal with it, although I'm not sure how," said Deena.

"Dee, where is the gate's key?" asked Dan.

"In the front pocket of the backpack," she replied. "Turn around, and I'll get it."

"Um, how do I defend myself?" asked Bronwyn.

"Here, you can have this," said Deena, putting the machete firmly in her hand.

"Oh wow, thanks," said Bronwyn. "Are you sure?"

"I'm sure. Are you ready?" Deena asked her. Bronwyn gave a firm nod with an expression of determination.

"We go by moonlight," said Dan.

Extinguishing the lanterns and leaving them at the foot of the steps, they crept along the orangery's rear, passing Jack's herb garden. Finally, Dan whispered, "Cross the footpath one at a time. Meet me in the tree line."

Dan went first. He hated the gravel paths, cringing as his boots crunched beneath him with every step. Dobbing down in the tree line, he signalled them to cross. Deena sent Bronwyn next. Then, the three sat huddled together as Dan instructed them to cross over to the trees lining the imposing drive. "Please don't walk on the driveway. It may be easier, but it's too open and too damn noisy," Dan muttered. Deena and Bronwyn smirked at his distaste for noise underfoot. Dan couldn't wait to return to the plane and put this godforsaken place behind them.

Deena clasped the key firmly in her hand. The gates were a mere ten steps away. "Dee," he whispered, "go and take the padlock and chains off." Deena put the spear down and inched towards the gates. She had only gotten halfway when she froze. A pair of orange eyes glinted on the other side of the drive. Dan put his hand on Bronwyn's shoulder and whispered, "Whatever happens, don't move from here."

Bronwyn wasn't sure what Deena had seen, so she clutched the machete for dear life. Dan pulled out the gun. He wouldn't take any chances, not now that they were so close. As he edged out of the tree line, he could see it. Slowly and purposely, it prowled out of the shadows. Its growls were deep and menacing.

"Dan, pass me the spear!" Deena muttered. Bronwyn edged forward as far as she dared and slid the spear across the ground towards Dan. He, in turn, passed it to Deena as she stepped back from the Hell Hound. "It's been waiting for us," said Deena. She gave the key to Dan, grasped the spear, and said, "Get the gate open! I'll keep it at bay."

Dan watched her slicing through the beast. It was incredible that a creature that appeared to be solid could inflict such severe injuries, but a weapon would pass through it. Was it an entity or something of another world Loki put here? As Dan fumbled with the padlock, she could hear the chains rattling against the iron gates. Bronwyn watched, amazed as Deena skirted the Hell Hound, stabbing and cutting at it. It was working. It was slowing down each time she drove the spear into it. It growled and snarled at her, trying to bite at the spear. Like a tiger cornered and tormented, it was angry and death-defying. She shouted to Dan, "Have you opened it yet?"

"Nearly," he replied, unravelling the chain. Deena wouldn't give the Hell Hound a chance to surge at her or the others. Instead, she raced from left to right, jabbing at it. Hearing the chain drop was music to her ears. Dan pulled one of the gates open and motioned to Bronwyn. "Go!" he shouted. Bronwyn rushed to the gates, slipping through them quickly and hiding behind the gate's pillar. "Dee, come on!" urged Dan. She glanced in Dan's direction. The gates were close enough to dash to them.

"Be ready to close it as soon as I'm through!" she yelled. Deena gave a last stab at the Hell Hound before bolting for the gates. Dan immediately slammed it shut. The Hell Hound pounced at the wrought-iron entrance, and Dan shot back. It stood on its hind legs, snarling and clawing at them.

"Bad doggy!" said Dan, wagging his finger at the Hell Hound.

Dan took the lead along the estate wall. At the far end, he peered around the corner and, looking back at Deena and Bronwyn, whispered, "The plane is as we left it."

They continued to edge forward when, suddenly, Bronwyn cried out.

"Stay still!" stressed Dan.

Ground Crawlers clambered along the wall ahead of them, and two were approaching the plane. First, Deena lit her sage, giving it to Bronwyn. Then, she lit another for Dan. "Do we wait them out?" whispered Deena.

"There are too many. I've only got two shots," Dan whispered back. "If they climb on the plane, they could damage it and then we are stuck here."

"Let's try and get closer, step by step," suggested Deena. "We may be able to get aboard without them detecting us."

"It's risky, but it may be our only chance," he sighed. Dan took the first couple of steps, and Bronwyn and Deena followed. It was excruciatingly slow. Dan counted seven in all. They were dotted around the plane, scurrying on the runway, smelling the air for prey. Finally, he cocked the gun, and Deena readied herself with the spear. They were less than fifty feet from the plane.

"Dan, stay here with Bronwyn. I'll get to the plane's rear and open the door," whispered Deena. "Send Bronwyn next."

Deena began her vigil toward the plane. Twenty careful paces found her with an approaching Ground Crawler. She stood still as it sniffed the air. Bronwyn grabbed Dan's jacket, terrified. "It's okay. Dee knows what she's doing," he whispered reassuringly.

As the Ground Crawler moved around her, she thrust the sage at its face. It spat, shaking its head as the smoke irritated it. Eventually, it moved away. She waited until she could proceed safely. Then, slowly, she reached the plane, opening the door. Dan whispered to Bronwyn to go. She was terrified, shaking her head as tears streamed down her face. Dan sighed but understood her dread, so he whispered, "Match my steps carefully."

He took her hand; it was clammy with fear. Bronwyn set her sights on Deena, not wanting to see the creatures. They were only a few steps from the plane, and Dan gestured for her to get on board. Then, locking the door, he shrugged off the backpack and quickly headed to the cockpit. The engines roared, attracting the Ground Crawlers as vibrations reached across the ground. Dan taxied, picking up speed quickly. Then, they heard a thud on the tail of the aircraft. Ground Crawler's talons screeched across the metal of the carriage as it tried to hang on. The nose of the plane began to rise, and Dan opened the throttle to take off. Bronwyn cried out as the Ground Crawler lost its grip, plummeting onto the runway. She watched through a window as it writhed in pain from its injuries. Bronwyn sat opposite Deena and burst into tears. She had never been so terrified.

"We did it, we actually fucking did it!" exclaimed Dan as the plane ascended into the dark skies.

CHAPTER TWENTY-SIX

Deena slept for the first hours into the flight. Then, she stirred, asking if she had been asleep for long. "A couple of hours," said Bronwyn smiling.

Deena stood up and stretched, stuck her head into the cockpit and, giving Dan the biggest grin, asked him, "Everything okay up front?"

"Of course everything is okay. We're over the Atlantic and on our way home. Tell you what wouldn't go amiss, though, is a hot meal," said Dan.

"Did someone say hot meal?" chirped Bronwyn. "That would be amazing."

"I'm on it," said Deena laughing. She sorted three sachets, gave one to Bronwyn, and joined Dan in the cockpit. "Here, bolognese," she said, handing it to him.

"Could you take the controls while I eat? Do you remember what to do?" he asked Deena.

Deena nodded, but she was terrified of flying the plane, if truth be told. But this mission taught her that fear was to be overcome, and nothing was impossible. Dan took the controls back, and Deena delved into her food, savouring every mouthful.

"How long until we are there?" asked Bronwyn.

Deena replied, "About ten hours."

"Ten hours," groaned Bronwyn, "it's so much colder up here than on the ground."

"There are thermal blankets in the duffle bag," suggested Dan.

"Good idea," said Deena, making her way behind the cockpit. There were only two, so she gave one to Bronwyn and offered the other to Dan, which they shared during the flight. Bronwyn listened as they chatted about the facility and the team until falling asleep. Dan could see the facility below and circled. Finally, he lined the plane to the runway for a landing. Bronwyn awoke to Deena gently shaking her. "Wake up. We are here."

Bronwyn sat up excitedly and said, "Really?" She looked out of the nearest window at the runway below.

"There are a couple of things I need to tell you before getting off the plane," said Deena. "We leave the hanger by a side door. We need to cross a stretch of open ground to a breach. It will take us into the facility. The Ground Crawlers are here, too. We will go first, and Dan will follow."

"Why can't we go together?" asked Bronwyn.

"It's too risky. We'll take the crystal skull with us to ensure handing the skull to the team. Dan will watch our backs until we are safely in the facility," said Deena.

"Dee, get in your seat. We are on our descent," said Dan. "Buckle up."

The landing was rough, but Dan was pleased the General had left the outer hanger open. Dan knew that getting into the airway and shutting the hanger door was imperative. Once inside, he didn't waste time getting to the wheel to secure it, then waved Deena and Bronwyn off the plane.

"We'll walk the airway to the underground hanger," Dan said. "Some of the generators have failed. There's no emergency lighting." So, Dan pulled out the flashlight and lit the way through the tunnels to the small office. Once inside, he strode over, opening the door to the main hanger. "Dee, take the skull and crystals," he said, handing her the backpack. "Make sure it's secure on your back."

Deena strapped it tightly. Then, they crossed the ground floor hangar to the outside side door.

"I'll watch until you have opened the shaft, then I'll make my way over," said Dan, taking out the revolver. He lined up his last two shots and opened the door, tentatively looking for Ground Crawlers. The darkness was still and unassuming.

Deena and Bronwyn linked arms, slowly moving towards the south breach. Deena checked behind them as they neared halfway. Dan stood with his back to the hanger, dutifully watching. She smiled at Bronwyn and whispered, "Are you okay?"

Bronwyn nodded, "Terrified, but okay."

They were only ten paces from the breach when a shot rang out. Deena let go of Bronwyn, turning to where Dan stood. Bronwyn shook Deena's arm, pointing to their right. "Oh shit!" shouted Deena.

Three Ground Crawlers were coming towards them. Dan shouted, "Get to the shaft. Open it now!"

Deena ran to the breach, sliding the door across. "Bronwyn, go down!" she urged. Another shot rang out. Dan hit the Ground Crawler closest to them.

"Go! Go!" Dan shouted. "Get into the facility!" he urged. Deena knew that was the last of the ammunition. She shoved the backpack down the shaft to Bronwyn and ran towards Dan with the spear aloft. He had nothing to defend himself. Dan screamed at her, "Go back, Dee! Go back!"

Deena watched in horror as Dan stomped hard on the ground, shouting, "I'm over here, you fuckers!" The Ground Crawlers changed direction, charging toward him. Deena could see more coming over the roof of the hanger. "Go, Dee, please!" he shouted, still stamping the ground.

Deena turned back to the breach, tears streaming down her face. Gurgling screams filled the air as Dan made the ultimate sacrifice. Deena slipped down the shaft pulling the door across. She sat at the top sobbing. Bronwyn listened to Deena breaking her heart; Dan hadn't made it. Bronwyn, too, cried.

When Deena calmed down, she made her descent. The stench of decaying flesh that filled the facility before she left had all but faded. Only bone and cloth protruded from the debris. Deena gave Bronwyn a mournful look, to which Bronwyn wrapped her arms around her. When composed, Deena picked up the backpack and said they must get to the team. Bronwyn hurriedly grabbed her belongings and followed her.

Finally, they reached the office where she and Dan had left the team. Before opening the door, Deena turned to Bronwyn and whispered, "By the way, the General is an arsehole."

Deena entered the room. It was pitch black. A flashlight beamed straight at her as the General asked, "Is that you, Kross?"

"Yes, it's me. Quit blinding me with that bloody light," said Deena, squinting.

"Did you find it?" he demanded.

"Yes, I've got it," she said, walking into the room, followed by Bronwyn.

"Who the hell is this, and where is Dan?" asked the General.

"This is Bronwyn. Dan didn't make it. The Ground Crawlers attacked as we were crossing from the hangar; there were too many of them," said Deena, desperately fighting back the tears.

"He did what I ordered. He got you back here with the skull," said the General.

Deena didn't say a word as she handed the backpack to Bronwyn. Then, facing the General square-on, anger boiled up inside her. It was too much hearing him being so flippant about Dan. Her fists clenched, and she threw a right hook at the General without warning, sending him reeling across the office.

"It's about time someone stood up to him," said Trevor, clapping Deena. "He has been bloody unbearable since you've been gone. It's good to see you back, and I'm so sorry to hear about Dan."

"It's good to see you too, Trevor. How is everyone?" she asked.

"Holding up, we've been worried about you, though," said Trevor.

The General got to his feet, rubbing his jaw and giving a lame apology. Deena turned her back to him and spoke to George. "How are you, George?" she asked. "You've lost weight, looking good!" she said.

"Yeah, well, I've been on a diet since you left," said George, patting his reduced waistline, chuckling.

Deena introduced Bronwyn to them and asked where Carson and Barker were. "They are with the rest of the survivors. You weren't supposed to bring anyone back with you, Kross!" stated the General.

Deena glared at General Montgomery. "General, in all honesty, I don't give a fuck! It wasn't your call. It was mine," said Deena angrily.

The General adjusted himself, visually reminding everyone he was still in charge. He coughed loudly, getting her attention. "Kross, could I have the crystal skull?" he asked.

Deena took a second before taking the backpack from Bronwyn and thrusting it at the General. "Here, have it! I bet you don't know what to do with it, though, do you!" she snapped.

The General staggered back with force, ignoring Deena's comment and opened the backpack. Kneeling on the floor, the General removed the crystal skull, examining it. Then, delving back in, he pulled out the smaller crystals. Deena stood over the General, amused at his perplexed expression.

"George, Trevor, could you please retrieve the other skulls from the safe? I need your help to figure out how to position the skulls and determine the order of the smaller crystals," said Deena. Then, as George and Trevor left for the laboratory, Deena turned her attention to General Montgomery. "Put them back, General. You are embarrassing yourself," she muttered into his ear. "I have been through far too much to be ordered about by you. Do you understand what I'm saying?" she ventured.

The General looked up at her and asked, "Is this Kross disrespecting me or Erling?"

"You know I am Erling. I always have been," replied Deena.

The General sighed, putting the crystals back in the bag. Then, standing up, he gave her an acquiescent and unchallenging look. Deena took the backpack from him, putting it beside the crystal skull, and then left to help George and Trevor get the other twelve. When they returned with the first six, the General bluntly reminded Deena that all thirteen shouldn't be together as no one knew what would happen. "I know what I am doing, General," said Deena curtly. "I'm following my ancestral instincts. You know, that of Erling?" she declared.

In the office, all thirteen skulls sat alongside each other. To Deena, it was a genuinely mind-blowing moment. Looking at each one, memories of what she and Dan had gone through flashed in her mind. Everything had led them to this—saving Mother Earth. Then, arrived more images, not memories, but those her ancestors needed her to see. The realisation of the importance of the correct alignment was right here in the facility. "What do you need us to do?" Trevor asked, jolting her back to reality.

"We need to take everything to the main lobby," said Deena.

"You're the boss," said George picking up two skulls. Deena, Trevor, and the General followed suit, trekking back and forth.

Deena stood before the American coat of arms, inlaid on the floor. It was dead centre, where the four zones met. "So, what now?" asked the General.

Deena took his flashlight, her mind working overtime. She walked around the coat of arms and proclaimed, "This has to be it. There are thirteen arrows for the original thirteen states, the thirteen British colonies. Thirteen leaves on the olive branch, thirteen olives represent peace and thirteen mullets over the eagle's head. In the eagle's beak is a scroll. 'E Pluribus Unum. Out of many, one.'" Deena rushed to the backpack, emptying the smaller crystals onto the floor. Then, taking the clear quartz, she shone the flashlight on it. Beautiful and without flaws, she placed it directly on the scroll at the eagle's beak.

"Out of many, one," she muttered, deep in thought. "This is the only single crystal. The coat of arms is the exact alignment for the cosmos to realign the sun, bringing it back into our orbit!" she exclaimed. "Thirteen

322

facets, one for each of the crystal skulls."

"Where do all these other crystals go?" asked George.

"They are pairs, each having unique properties. They must go in the right order in the eye sockets," explained Deena. "Could you sort them into their pairs while I go and see Carson and the others? I need to let them know I'm back, and they need to stay where they are. I don't want them to run into danger, not understanding what's happening."

"Deena, what exactly is going to happen?" asked Trevor.

"Ragnarök is the reorder of the cosmos, which pulled our sun out of orbit. So, we must reverse the reorder of the universe and, in turn, pull the sun to its rightful place. We are going to restore light to our world," she replied.

"Okay, now I'm sorry I asked," said Trevor, confused.

Deena laughed, giving him the flashlight, and said, "I won't be long."

Deena took a candle and matches from her rig. Then, carefully, she made her way to Zone D. She knocked softly on the door. "Carson, Barker," she whispered. "It's me, Deena. Open the door."

She heard scuffles behind the barricaded door amongst excited whispers. "Is it really you, Deena?" asked Barker in disbelief.

"Yes, it's really me," said Deena, smiling.

Deena slipped into the office and looked at the huddled figures wrapped in blankets as Barker busied himself barricading the doorway. Then, Carson strode across the room. "Well, saints preserve us! Welcome home, Deena," he said, shaking her hand. "How did it go? Did you manage to find the skull?" he asked.

"Yes, we have it. I can't stay long. How is everyone?" asked Deena.

"Cold, hungry and fed up with being in the dark since the generators went down, but I'm glad to report, no more casualties," said Carson.

"That's good news. Here, I have candles," said Deena. Carson duly lit them, giving them out to the survivors. Then, he returned to Deena, asking how Dan was. Tears pricked her eyes as she shook her head and looked to the floor.

"I'm sorry; he was a good man and a great archaeologist," said Carson.

"I'm preparing to use the crystal skulls as intended. But I can't guarantee what will happen, so could you ensure everyone stays in here? I will come and get you as soon as it's safe," said Deena.

"Sure, no problem. Is there anything I can do to help?" asked Carson.

"Thanks, but I've got it covered," replied Deena.

"Good luck, Deena," chirped Barker, giving her a quick wave. Deena moved the barricade to leave. Barker wasted no less than seconds pushing the barrier back. She smiled as she listened to scuffling on the other side of the door. Unfortunately, Barker's nerves still had the better of him.

In thought, Deena stood in front of the coat of arms in the lobby. Then, she wandered over to Trevor and George and said, "Thanks for pairing them. Can you place the skulls evenly in a circle around the quartz, eyes facing in?"

"Pleasure, although I'm not sure where you are going with this," said Trevor.

"These crystals fit in the eye sockets of the skulls in identical pairs, and we must put them in the correct order. As we are reversing the new order of the cosmos, we need to start with what represents darkness and the sun's crystals in the last skull. Then, we need to work out the order between."

"What if you get the order wrong?" asked George.

"I don't know, so let's ensure we get it right. Does anyone know anything about crystals and their properties?" asked Deena.

Trevor stepped forward and raised a sheepish hand. "I do. It's my hobby. My wife says I'm an anorak. So, I, um… I collect them," he said.

"Brilliant, I need your expertise," said Deena.

"Either selenite or black onyx should be first," said Trevor.

"What are their intentions?" asked Deena.

"For once, I can enjoy being a complete anorak," laughed Trevor. "Black onyx represents the world of dusk into the night skies. Selenite represents the moon and holds Earth's recorded history in its linear markings."

"Wow, hark at you, Trevor!" exclaimed George sarcastically. Trevor was glad it was dark as he blushed. He didn't like being in the limelight.

"I am impressed, Trevor, and take no notice of George," said Deena. "I think we should start with selenite as it combines the night's moon and the Earth's history." Trevor passed them to Deena, which she placed in the first skull. They fitted snugly. "If you were going to solve this yourself, Trevor, what should follow?" she asked.

"Can we put them in order as I go through them before placing them in the skulls? That way, we can discuss the best format for the reversal," he said.

"Go for it. I'll swap the crystals around as you tell me," said Deena.

"Anorak on," said Trevor, grinning. He picked up the sunstone crystals. "These carry the sun's energy and the solar flare's fire, so I am guessing these would be last." Deena put them beside the thirteenth skull while Trevor bit his nails in thought. He couldn't get this wrong. "Would you heal and stabilise the Earth first or protect it from negative energy?" he asked Deena.

"That's a difficult one. What else have you got?" asked Deena.

"Some unquestionably go in the latter skulls. Those representing nature, land and skies would fit in the middle, being the re-creation of our world. Jade signifies purity and creates harmony and balance. So, theoretically, the next one should be either sapphire, aragonite, or jade," said Trevor. Deena thought hard and asked if any were stabilising crystals. "Aragonite," he said, picking them up. "Are you sure?" he checked.

"Yes, heal and stabilise, protect from negative energy, and then purify, creating harmony and balance. This way readies the Earth to re-create nature," said Deena.

"That works for me," said Trevor, helping her put them into order. "The next one must be serpentine. It holds the life force of Mother Nature and embodies the power of creation."

"Perfect!" exclaimed Deena. "That leaves six pairs."

"What a load of mumbo jumbo," muttered George.

"You are in high regard with mathematics and physics, but I'm the expert in energy resources, so shut up!" snapped Trevor. Deena smiled as he shrugged his shoulders resolutely and asked, "Right, so my next question is, do we start from dark to light with creation?"

"That makes sense. You said black onyx represents the world of dusk," said Deena.

"Yes, and the following representation will be blue lace agate. It represents the skies, and it utilises water energy and the energy of life cycles," said Trevor. Deena placed them to follow serpentine. "Red jasper reflects all-natural landscapes worldwide over millennia," said Trevor. "Emerald holds the concept of eternity, reflecting nature, which would complete the cycle of creation."

"Okay, we have three pairs left. What do they signify?" asked Deena.

"Rose quartz has a high spiritual attunement to the Earth, the universe and the divine; amber has an electromagnetic energy which builds an electrical charge," said Trevor. "Which one do you want next to the sunstones in the last skull?" he asked.

"If amber builds an electrical charge, it will power directly into the sunstone," Deena thought aloud. "The rose quartz opens up a channel of high spiritual connection to the universe. That channel would need to be there for the universe first. What about these?" she asked Trevor, holding up the citrine quartz crystals.

"Citrine is a healing crystal, carrying the power of the sun. I reckon it should go between amber and sunstone," said Trevor. Deena placed each pair of crystals behind the skulls, from aragonite to sunstone.

"Talk me through each set, Trevor. I don't want to place them in the skulls until we are categorically sure we have the right order. I haven't got this far to have it blow up in my face."

The look on Trevor's face was priceless as he stammered, "It... it couldn't, could it?"

Deena smiled inwardly at Trevor's reaction, but she didn't know what would happen any more than the others. "Let's hope not, Trevor," she said, patting his shoulder. Trevor took a big breath and walked around the circle of skulls with Deena, identifying each crystal's abilities and intentions in order.

"Thanks, Trevor," she said. "Is everyone in agreement with the order?" she asked.

"There are no complaints from me, Deena. Well done, Trevor, on your expertise," said General Montgomery.

Deena looked in George's direction, waiting for a response. He gave a sideways glance and raised a grunt which Deena took as agreement. So, she positioned herself at the second skull and placed the aragonite into the eye sockets. They, too, fitted snugly. She followed around sapphire, jade, serpentine, black onyx, blue lace agate, red jasper, emerald, rose quartz, amber, and citrine quartz. Finally, she picked up the sunstone crystals and turned to her audience.

"Before I put these into the last skull, I have to say that I'm not sure what will happen. So, perhaps you should keep your distance, take cover, just in case," said Deena. Trevor was the first to leg it down the corridor, closely followed by George. General Montgomery turned on his heel, heading after them. "I'll be right there," she said, crouching beside the last skull. With bated breath, she placed the first crystal, then prepared to sprint as she positioned the final crystal into the thirteenth crystal skull.

Deena huddled with the others in the corridor, peering into the lobby. She crossed her fingers, praying it would work. Everything hinged on this, and Earth's survival depended on it. Then, finally, Trevor nudged Deena's elbow. "It's working!" he exclaimed excitedly. "It's actually. Freaking. Working!" he cried.

They watched in amazement as laser energy beams fired through the crystal to the centre's clear quartz. The crystal skulls omitted a rainbow of colours, jumping from one to another. Each transferred energy to the clear quartz until it began to glow a pure white light. The white light's crackling was extraordinarily loud. Incredulous looks were exchanged between them as the last skull lit up, and its rainbow colours of energy were shared with the others. Finally, the intensity of the white light shot up and bore a hole above and into the night sky. The debris blew out, crashing onto the open ground above. A deep vibration below their feet arose, filling the facility. They listened to rocks grinding above them as the planets began to realign. Still, the brightest light beam crackled, and the cacophonous sounds came and went. "How long will this go on for?" shouted George.

Deena shrugged her shoulders, not taking her eyes off the skulls. Their colours and energies were mesmerising as the energy of the skulls intensified. Then, the beam of white light suddenly dropped into the clear quartz, absorbing all that power. Then silence. No one spoke for a few minutes. Was that it? Was there anything else to happen? Cautiously, Deena walked over to the skulls. The others patiently waited as they watched in disbelief. Was that daylight streaming into the lobby? Deena looked up the shaft, squinting. It had been so long since they had seen the sun. Finally, she shouted to the others, "It's back! The sun is back! It worked. We've reversed Ragnarök!"

The General rushed over to Deena, and with his hand over his brow, he gazed into the sunlight. As he did, a tear rolled down his cheek. "You're emotional! Amazing, I didn't know you had any," said Deena sarcastically. The General wiped away the tear, stating it was because the sun was intense. Then, with a cough to compose himself, he told Deena to get Carson, Barker, and the remaining survivors. Deena chuckled as she walked over to

Trevor and George.

"We owe you everything," said Trevor.

"It was your expertise, too. We all had a part to play," said Deena. "I'm going to get the others. Then, we can discuss getting out of this facility." Trevor and George excitedly rushed to the General to get a peek at the sunlight. Together, they stood bathing in its warmth, soaking up the rays. It had been too long.

Carson and Barker beckoned the survivors into the lobby. Excited chatter filled the air as they gasped in disbelief. "It's true. You have saved our world and us!" remarked Carson. "Now, how can we get out of here?" he wondered.

Deena called to the General, "Do you have a plan? We can't expect everyone to climb up the debris in Zone B."

General Montgomery fumbled in his pocket, pulled out the key he had been hiding from them, and held it up. "I can open the steel doors. I have the key to overriding the system."

"You said the manual override wasn't intact! Again, you lied to us!" exclaimed Deena.

"I had to; my duty is to ensure everyone's safety. I will open the facility, but no one goes outside until we know it is safe. We don't know if the Ground Crawlers are still roaming."

General Montgomery left for the administration block. He entered the communications office, hoping the capacitors had enough power stored in them. 'Only one way to find out,' thought the General. He unlocked the cabinet, flicked the switches, and lit the LEDs. "Thank god," he muttered. He grasped the manual lever and thrust it down. A mechanical hum struck up as the steel doors began to lift. Satisfied, he locked the cabinet, left the key on the desk, and returned to Deena and the survivors.

The General returned to expectant faces surrounding him. "As you can see, the steel doors are open. Stay here while Deena and I check it is safe," he announced. Deena picked up the spear and strode towards the main doors. She pushed the exit panel and stepped outside. The sunlight was dazzling, so Deena squinted until her eyes adjusted. Then, with great satisfaction, she watched a horde of Ground Crawlers writhing in the sunlight. Their skin was incredibly sensitive, and the sun slowly burned them to death. She returned to the General, telling him what she had seen. "Good, we can rest assured that they won't be around for long," he said.

The survivors slowly ventured outside. They said their goodbyes and filtered off to find what was left of their homes and families. Deena went to the car park to see if she could salvage her vehicle. "Wait, where are you going?" asked Bronwyn.

"I'm returning to the ranch to find Martin, Lily, and Ben. Are you coming?" asked Deena.

"Hell yes!" exclaimed Bronwyn, racing to the passenger side.

They were silent as they drove Highway thirty-three. Bronwyn could see she was anxious. It wasn't until they turned onto Highway twenty-eight that Bronwyn spoke. "Are you okay?" she asked.

Deena turned and gave a half-hearted smile and said, "I'll be fine once I know they are safe." Then, she turned right off the highway and headed for Monteview. Deena drew her breath as she got out of the car. Buildings were damaged, fences were down, and there was no sign of any livestock. Deena repeatedly called out their names in turn as loud as she could. "Martin! Lily! Ben!" she called.

Beyond the corral, Bronwyn noticed something unusual. She shook Deena's arm, pointing to a pulsating shard of light. "What's that?" she asked.

"It appeared as a ball of light, then stretched." Deena returned to the car and grabbed the spear before racing towards the corral. "Wait for me!" Bronwyn shouted after her.

"Stay there!" warned Deena. "We don't know what it is!" she insisted.

Bronwyn stayed back as Deena pushed her hand through the white light. Her hand went through it but had disappeared entirely from where Bronwyn was standing. "Deena, I can't see your hand!" she shouted.

Deena stepped aside, shouting to Bronwyn, "It must be some weird energy residue from the skulls. It will probably disappear when it has burnt itself out."

Suddenly, Bronwyn's attention turned to a tiny figure racing towards them from the corral barns. She ran towards the unsteady, stumbling child. He was dirty and dishevelled, like a street urchin. "Mommeee, mommeee!" he squealed excitedly.

It was Ben. He was alive! Somehow, he had survived, albeit scrawny and dirty, and wearing only a tattered tee shirt. Deena heard him shouting out for her, and as she turned her back to the shard, leathery stick-like arms with long gnarly fingers grabbed Deena's legs, pulling her into the sliver of light. Bronwyn heard Deena's cries for help, and as she turned, Deena disappeared. Then, the shard vanished, and Deena was gone. Finally, Ben was within Bronwyn's grasp. She swooped down and picked him up, cradling him tightly as his excited squeals turned to anguished cries for his mother.

"Shush, shush," whispered Bronwyn, rocking him in her arms. "It's okay, Ben. It's okay. I've got you. You're safe now."